I0584264

A Queer Little Book of Tales

H.R. Harrison

A NineStar Press Publication
www.ninestarpress.com

A Queer Little Book of Tales

ISBN: 978-1-64890-216-1
© 2021 H.R. Harrison
Cover Art © 2021 Natasha Snow
Published in March, 2021 by NineStar Press, New Mexico, USA.

This is a work of fiction. Names, characters, places, and incidents are either the product of the author's imagination or are used fictitiously. Any resemblance to actual persons living or dead, business establishments, events, or locales is entirely coincidental.

All rights reserved. No part of this publication may be reproduced in any material form, whether by printing, photocopying, scanning or otherwise without the written permission of the publisher. To request permission and all other inquiries, contact NineStar Press at Contact@ninestarpress.com.

Also available in Print, ISBN: 978-1-64890-216-1

CONTENT WARNING:
This book contains sexually explicit content, which may only be suitable for mature readers. Depictions of homophobia, transphobia, gaslighting, misgendering, mentions of child death, mentions of genocide, past trauma, religious persecution, xenophilia.

To those who have ever felt invisible,
I hope these stories make you feel seen.

A collection of queer fairy tale retellings for the discerning reader. Dive into a world both familiar and strange and meet a colorful cast of characters from all different backgrounds and upbringings, from princes and paupers to aliens and dwarves, from merchant sons to sign language interpreters. And fairies, of course. But it's important to remember… most fairies aren't fairy godmothers.

The White Cat follows the intrepid young prince Yufitri from across the Sea, who meets a mystical talking cat who offers to grant all his desires—even the call for a wife.

The Fairy's Gift tells the tale of a young princess Wynn who was cursed by an evil fairy to… have the body of her dreams? Oh no, whatever shall she do? Save a neighboring kingdom it seems!

In *From Stars They Fell*, when a strange metal ship falls from the sky, an angel with dragonfly wings is left stranded in a strange land, and meets a young man who speaks with his hands.

When the angel takes the job of the young man's interpreter, Oswin, he sets out to find new work. *The Echoes of the Dead* finds him stumbling across mysterious black ruins in the woods, inhabited by a scarred and quiet elf whose kindness hides a depth of despair.

In *A Step Apart and a World Away*, Naomhan, a duke's son, who has always felt apart from the world, rescues a beautiful snake, who turns into a beautiful man promising rewards for Naomhan's kindness. But Naomhan wants only to disappear.

And *In the Shade of the Tree of Life* ends the collection with a tale of anxiety and heartbreak, when a tailor's apprentice of maligned background falls in love with a hermit of a prince.

The White Cat

The old king looked out at the courtyard, watching his three sons going through their sword drills, and was struck by a terrible realization. He had three strong, intelligent, and charismatic sons. And he was only one old man. Should the idea be planted in their heads, whether by chance or by nefarious purpose, he could easily find himself deposed long before his proper time.

So, he returned to his wing of the castle, and he began to plot.

That night at the evening feast, the king made his announcement. "My dear sons, I have grown old, and too soon the time will come for one of you to take my place. However, as you are all suitable candidates for the throne, I have a proposition for you. You shall all undertake three quests, and whosoever is the most successful shall win my crown."

The eldest frowned, but his brothers rejoiced. The second brother because he wanted the throne for himself, but the youngest cheered for a different reason. Always he had been the baby of the brothers, always sheltered, always forbidden from anything even slightly dangerous. But this, this was a call to adventure!

"For one year, I want you three to seek out the finest little dogs to be a companion to me in my old age. Whosoever brings me the sweetest, prettiest dog shall be declared the victor."

As the brothers left to their quarters to prepare for their journeys, the youngest, whose name was Yufitri, was busy deciding where he would go. Instead of going to his wing, he went out into the town and found the merchants' tents.

"Where should I travel to find the little dog my father seeks?" he asked them.

He received many answers, but a sallow-skinned man with dark, clever eyes smiled and said with an accented tongue, "I know many breeders of companion dogs in the north, across the sea. I would be happy to take you there, my prince. For a price, of course."

After haggling over the cost, Yufitri agreed to meet the merchant at the docks come week's end and returned to his home. He packed swiftly and lightly, making sure to bring his heavy wool coat to ward off the biting chill he could only imagine the sea and northern lands would have.

His brothers had decided to travel east and south, so Yufitri was happy with his decision. At the end of the week, the three brothers agreed to meet at the river's mouth in one year's time, so they could return to their father together. They embraced and wished each other well. The two elders saw the younger to the docks where they waved at the departing ship until it was fully out of sight.

Yufitri was ecstatic during the journey, asking the merchant many questions about the ship, the sea, their destination— anything he could think of. By the time the ship landed, just over a week later, the merchant was quite happy to be rid of him. He agreed to meet the prince in eleven months' time, took his money, and went into the city to peddle his wares.

Yufitri, meanwhile, in halting, uncertain speech, asked where he could find a pretty little dog. His royalty was kept secret to avoid purse snatchers and scoundrels who would seek to take advantage. The merchants kept sending him farther and farther north, but none of the dogs he found were to his satisfaction. He was certain his brothers had found ones far prettier at better known markets. In addition, the climate of this strange new land was surprisingly like the one he knew if not wetter. His coat stayed folded and tucked into his bag. Yufitri was getting rather irritated with the entire venture. Finally, an old seller told him of an eccentric breeder of tiny dogs who lived in the northern mountains.

And as Yufitri gazed at the snow-capped mountains, so far away as to appear blue and purple against the sky, his lust for adventure blossomed once more in his chest. He hired a guide, and they were soon off. The guide was a small man with pale skin, red ears, and pale-yellow hair so thin it floated above his head.

Yufitri was fascinated by this pallid man with such strange features and enjoyed watching him in the driver's seat of the cart of goods he was bringing north, the secret prince nestled among them. The sun turned the guide's cheeks and neck the same red as his ears. The man grumbled in his foreign tongue while he rubbed at the irritated skin with some sort of pleasant-smelling ointment.

As the mountains grew larger on the horizon, the air got colder, and Yufitri's coat got used after all. His guide also gave him a pair of socks to wear as they began to climb.

Yes, this was what he had been expecting on his journey north. His breath escaped in puffs of smoke, and his teeth chattered even as he burrowed closer into his coat. But they chattered below a grin, and when his guide arrived in the village he'd been traveling to, he gave Yufitri directions to the breeder, pointing up toward the cloudy peaks. The locals, looking as pale-skinned and red-eared as the guide, stared at Yufitri's strange clothes and his sandy skin.

A local innkeeper gave him vague directions, and once he had bought supplies in the small marketplace, Yufitri set off on the next leg of his journey. The woods bordering the town were dark and deep, and the trees were strange to him, tall and tapering with coils of spines instead of leaves. The path through, narrow and overgrown, was soon lost to him. He wandered in vain until the sun set, throwing all into darkness.

Filled with despair, Yufitri continued to wander, praying he would find any sort of exit. However, just as he was about give up, he spotted the twinkle of firelight in the distance. Ignoring the roots that sought to ensnare him, he stumbled toward it and soon found himself before a large castle. There were no guards on the ramparts or manning the gate. In fact, it appeared deserted but for the light spilling out from the windows.

Hoping whoever was inside was at least friendly, Yufitri walked up to the main door and banged on it as loudly as he could. It opened more abruptly than he expected, catching him midbang, and his momentum carried him forward into the entrance hall. He looked around but saw no one.

There was a tug on his coat. He whirled around to find a pair of pale floating hands, palms out in a gesture of surrender. Yufitri was torn between fear and rabid curiosity.

The fear would have won out if there hadn't been the sound of scratching down a hallway and an approaching light.

Held by another pair of floating hands was a lantern, whose light revealed a small white cat. It walked with a dignity and purpose that Yufitri had never seen on a cat before, and its silver collar was studded with precious gems.

When the cat reached him, it sat, peering up at him with gleaming green eyes. "Hello, king's son. You have come far to find this place."

Dumbfounded, he looked around for a person or perhaps a floating mouth, but no, it had definitely been the cat speaking.

Wait. He'd had no difficulty understanding the cat's words. "You speak my language?"

The cat nodded its head. "In a fashion. Spells of understanding and communicating are fairly simple. I hear myself in my tongue, but you hear yours. I can remove it if you wish."

"No, I appreciate it. It feels as if it's been years since I could speak plainly."

The cat seemed to smile. "Come," it said, standing and half turning toward the corridor it had come from. "Warm yourself by the fire, king's son. I am sure you are unused to this chill."

This time Yufitri did not object to the hands taking his coat, and he followed the cat and the lantern deeper into the castle. They passed beautiful tapestries and opulent decorations as they walked.

"Oh," he said. "I didn't introduce myself. My name is—"

"Do not tell me."

"What?"

The cat stopped and turned, looking him straight in the face. "Names hold tremendous power, especially here. Do not tell me your name, and I will not tell you mine. That way, there is balance."

"But you know who I am. What difference would my name make?"

The cat shook its head and continued forward. "It makes every difference. I know *what* you are. I know you are a king's son from a distant land. But knowing your name gives me power over your soul, your essence. I do not want that power over you."

Yufitri frowned. "I don't understand."

"The magic of this land is strange to you. But I assure you, I do this for your benefit." They came to a room. The stone floor was draped in a rich, soft rug, and the couches set up near the fireplace looked soft and comfortable.

The cat dismissed the lantern with a flick of its tail and padded over to a soft chair into which it leaped and curled up. "Sit," it told him.

He sank down into the couch with a sigh of contentment. The cat closed its eyes, purring quietly.

"Are you truly a cat?" Yufitri blurted out.

It opened one eye and regarded him in the firelight. "At the moment, yes," it answered. "I can tell you nothing more."

"Did you want to be a cat?"

"I can tell you nothing, king's son."

"Is that a part of the spell?"

The cat said nothing, so Yufitri assumed the answer was yes and lay down across the couch, his vertebrae cracking as he did.

The heat and softness threatened to make him fall asleep. The fire crackled, the cat purred, and the couch seemed to get softer with every passing moment. His eyes slid shut, but before sleep came to him in earnest, a gentle touch on his shoulder caught his attention. Another pair of floating hands urged him to wake and follow.

He looked at the cat still curled up on the chair. "Follow them," it said. "They'll take you to a proper bedchamber. Did you truly think in a castle as grand as this that a host would have you sleep on a sofa?"

So up he got and followed the hands down a different hallway, but not before bidding the cat a good night and pleasant dreams.

The next day, Yufitri woke to gentle hands shaking his shoulder and pointing toward a set of unfamiliar clothing folded atop the chest at the foot of the bed. Two pairs of hands helped him undress, then put on the foreign clothes. A short shirt with tight sleeves and short pants came first, and then a longer shirt that ended at his knees and buckled at the waist. It had tight sleeves only to the elbow and then fell open, dangling strangely around the long sleeves of the first shirt. And to finish, soft deerskin shoes.

He felt like his top half had been overstuffed, leaving legs oddly bare, but he found, as he acclimated to the unfamiliar clothing, he was much warmer. A long cloak was draped over his shoulders and fastened with a pin.

Now that he was fully dressed, the hands gave him a gentle push toward the door and led him down to the dining hall. The white cat sat at the head of the long table, sitting primly on a velvet cushion so it could look over the empty dishes. The rest of the table, save for one seat, was filled with other cats of varying size and color. Their eyes, jewel-bright and glittering, watched him as he entered. He was a bit intimidated but took the empty chair beside the white cat and sat to its right.

Green eyes gleamed at him, and the cat inclined its head politely. "I am glad the clothes suit you, king's son. Don't worry; you can have yours back when you leave. I am having them washed."

"Did they offend?" Yufitri couldn't help a smirk.

The cat seemed to smile, its eyes narrowing softly. "A little. Cats have delicate noses." The rest of the table started to purr, presumably in amusement. The food emerged from the kitchen, carried by the floating hands. He was surprised how quickly he was getting used to them.

However, he was not excited to see the plates contained an opening course of roasted mouse. The cat saw his face and called a pair of hands over with a paw. "Make sure our guest gets his proper meal," it said. "I will not be the sort of host who serves food unfit for human consumption."

The hands came together and dipped forward as if bowing and returned to the kitchen.

In a moment, there was a bowl of warm soup in front of Yufitri, white and steaming. "Milk and potato are the main ingredients," the cat said comfortingly. "No mouse or rat has touched it." A purr snuck into its voice. "Though I can do nothing about the cat hair. A hazard of a cat-ruled kitchen, you see."

"I…also do not consume swine or cow, dear cat. Though I've no such objection to accidental fur." He smiled.

"I shall have a note made." Sure enough, it told the nearest set of hands to inform the kitchen. Yufitri watched, marveling, as two hands came together and reshaped into quill and parchment. Another hand wrote the note and, when finished, rolled it up, and flew off into the kitchen.

The potato stew was excellent. Two large birds served as main course, each carried by two sets of hands. Well-mannered cats cut slices off with their claws and took only small bites. The white cat, the politest of them all, patted delicately at its face and whiskers with the napkin from beside the plate.

After the meal, the rest of the cats leapt from their chairs and returned to whatever their business they had, leaving Yufitri and the white cat.

"Would you care to join me in the drawing room?" asked the cat.

"I would be glad to," he said.

It jumped off the cushion and landed primly on its feet, looking back at Yufitri. "I am curious about whatever quest brought you to this strange land, and I'm sure you have questions for me, though there is little I can answer."

The drawing room was small and dominated by a large table with a map laminated to the wood. The cat jumped up onto it and lay itself down across the smooth, waxy surface. "So," it said, flicking its tail from side to side. "Your father has you seeking out a pretty little dog. Why did you come all the way here?"

He shrugged and sat down on a long couch near the table. "I wanted to see the world, and across the sea seemed like the most interesting way to go."

"Do you want to win the competition?"

Again, he shrugged. "Being a king is a lot of responsibility and work. To be frank, I'd rather spend my time exploring."

"I enjoy your frankness." The cat purred, rolling onto its back and squinting its eyes at him. "And I shall help you in your quest if you will allow me to."

"I would be honored, dear cat."

"I do have a request though."

"You must only ask."

The cat purred softly. "Stay for a few more months. It has been so long since I had human company."

Yufitri readily agreed.

The next day, the cat showed him the hunt. Not exactly sure how the cat effectively rode the lovely gray mare, he wasn't about to ask. The cat explained that normally dogs were involved, but they didn't typically enjoy feline company, so the hunting animals were the cats from the previous day's gathering. Cats, Yufitri learned, hunted like hyenas—though they were much quieter.

The foxes and pheasant caught ended up on the night's dinner table from which everyone, cat and prince alike, ate with gusto.

That night when Yufitri woke in the middle of the night, he found the cat curled up in the curve of his legs and decided not to wake it.

It was gone by morning. So, it wasn't worth mentioning.

The next few months passed in similar pleasantness. Yufitri watched as autumn came and the plants in the garden turned brown, then were buried in the winter snows. He discovered snow was lovely—wet, cold, and exhilarating. The cat bounced its way through, its white fur making it disappear into the powder, only its green eyes and pink nose visible. And when they came inside to sit around the fire and warm up, he watched the snow turn to dew on its back, glittering like it had been dipped into a vat of diamonds.

The cat taught him the language of the land, purring in amusement when his tongue fumbled but gently correcting all the same. And in exchange, he shared the language of his people and told the cat their stories: of the violent god of storms and the desert, the usurper, keeper of swine; of the lord of the dead who died and rose again, and the loyal wife who saved him, goddess of magic; of the bull-headed god of war and righteousness, and others.

The cat listened well, sitting across from him or by his side, eyes following the motions of his lips or hands as he told his stories.

And every night, Yufitri would wake to find the cat on his bed, curled against his legs or his back, and said nothing.

But as spring came again, manifesting in new green in the trees and in the palace gardens, the cat grew somber. "You must leave soon, king's son," it said one morning at breakfast.

He sighed. "Yes, I'm afraid so, dear cat."

Ears back and tail agitated, the cat jumped down from its chair. "Come with me. I shall give you your gift."

Yufitri followed the cat to the drawing room where it leapt up onto the bookshelves and scaled easily up to a small chest sitting on top. From it, it retrieved a hazelnut and carried it gently back down to the floor before bringing it to Yufitri.

"Inside that," it explained as Yufitri turned it over in his hands, "is the prettiest little dog you will ever see. It is sweet natured and gentle. Take care not to open it before you reach your home, or the poor thing may catch cold."

He wasn't sure how a dog could possibly fit in such a place, but he trusted the cat. Besides, he didn't mind losing the competition. In fact, he found he didn't truly want to leave at all.

But leave he did.

The cat sent one of the tabbies with him into the forest to show him the way back to the village he had come from, its face impassive. But Yufitri knew it was sad to see him go. He almost promised to return, but what good would a promise do if he couldn't keep it? He kept it to himself, thanked the cat for the hospitality and gift, and bid it farewell. He turned to look back every few moments until the palace was swallowed up by the forest and disappeared.

The journey home began strangely. Upon arriving in the village and bidding the tabby farewell, Yufitri went to buy supplies for his travels. A few of the townsfolk recognized him, whispering to one another as he passed by, throwing a word around that he didn't quite understand, but he didn't know how to ask them to explain.

When he reached the sea once more, the sallow-skinned merchant was surprised to see him. "I have to say, I didn't expect your return. The northern mountains are a dangerous place. Did you succeed in your quest?"

Yufitri shrugged. "We shall see."

The merchant certainly didn't see any dog, but he wasn't being paid to ask questions. He did notice the quietness of his charge, as opposed to his talkativeness of the previous year, but said nothing about it.

When Yufitri at last came to the docks of his city, he found his elder brother. They embraced, shedding brief tears, and went to find the eldest. The brothers explained they had been coming to the docks every few days, hoping for Yufitri's return, praying that he would. They showed off their dogs—tiny delicate things with narrow muzzles and tall ears—but when they asked after his dog, he only smiled and bid them to wait until they were before their father.

Mystified, but curious, they agreed to wait.

Their father threw a feast to celebrate his sons' return, refusing to examine their dogs until after the festivities were complete. The elder brothers regaled the court with tales of their adventures, but Yufitri remained quiet, remembering his conversations with the cat, holding them in his mind so they wouldn't fade like a dream in sunlight.

"Come, Yufitri, tell us your stories," his father encouraged. "What is it like in the land across the sea?"

So, he told some stories of the people of the port cities, and of the red-eared people of the mountains, but the cat stayed locked away, too precious to share.

As they concluded the meal, the king sighed, rubbed his stomach, and leaned away from the table. "All right, show me your dogs, my sons, and let us see who shall take this challenge."

The eldest, Badis, went first, carrying in his dog from the east, thin-boned and ebony-black. The king held it carefully; it was delicate as spun glass.

Next, the middle son, Amestan, presented his dog from the south, a bit larger with mottled brown-and-black fur. Although friendlier and somewhat hardier than Badis's, the king didn't seem particularly impressed by it.

Finally, Yufitri stepped forward, removing the hazelnut from his bag. "Where is your dog, son?" the king asked.

Taking the nut by the seams, Yufitri cracked it open. Out fell a tiny, fluffy little thing, pale gold in color and too big to have fit in the hazelnut but still only the size of his hand. Scooping it up, he handed it to his father, who marveled. "What is this magic, son?"

Yufitri shrugged. "The magic of the northern lands is strange."

"It seems like it." The king was enchanted by the sweet little dog. It stood on his flattened palm, wagging its fluffy tail, tongue lolling happily from its miniscule mouth. It licked the king's thumb.

The brothers grumbled, knowing they had lost while Yufitri smiled, knowing he had been wise indeed to trust in his friend, the cat.

When the king formally declared Yufitri the winner, no one was surprised. "Now, your next task shall begin next week. You are to find me a skein of cloth so fine that it can pass through the eye of a needle. Not a large needle either. A proper clothing needle."

His sons looked at one another, all of them wondering where in the world they could find such a thing.

"I shall go north again," Yufitri declared as the boys left the dining hall. His brothers wondered if they too should go, but in the end, they decided not to. The finest cloth was made in the east, after all, so they went together and split at the great river. Yufitri only half listened as they spoke, already planning his return journey across the sea.

15

The merchant laughed upon seeing Yufitri again so soon. "Did you meet a girl, Your Highness?" he joked.

Yufitri only smiled and held out a pouch of gold.

After a month's journey, he found himself once again in the forest that hid the cat's palace. He wandered until the sun disappeared from the sky and only the red glow of sunset lit his circuitous path, but still the castle did not appear. As the near full moon appeared overhead, marking an entire day's desperate search, he fell to the ground and despaired. He was thoroughly and utterly lost now without any idea where even the end of the forest lay.

A rustle in the undergrowth. A large, fluffy black cat emerged from the brush, regarding Yufitri with large golden eyes.

"Please…" he said, reaching toward it. "Take me back to the palace. You can understand me, can't you?"

The cat stayed still, flicking its tail from side to side.

"Please," he said again. "Take me back."

It licked its nose and disappeared into woods. Yufitri tried to follow, but it was gone. Choking back frustration and tears, he sank once more to the forest floor, then wrapped his arms around himself as the night's chill settled around him. Perhaps the castle moved. It was clearly an enchanted thing. Perhaps the cat even moved it—obviously, it knew something of magic. Perhaps he wasn't allowed to return. The cat had been sad to see him go, maybe so sad it had left the forest along with the castle.

A while later, a new sound caught Yufitri's attention. Hoofbeats.

He leapt to his feet, looking toward the source, his eyes straining in the dark.

A gray mare appeared and seated on its back…a pretty little white cat. Another horse tied to the saddle walked obediently behind.

"Hello, king's son," the cat said in a warm voice. "I hadn't expected to see you again so soon if at all. Come, I shall see you fed and housed."

He clambered onto the back of the horse, a handsome tan gelding, and together they rode through the forest. The castle loomed into view after no more than ten minutes.

"Is the castle enchanted?" he asked.

The cat tilted its head. "Yes. It cannot be found by one seeking it who does not live within."

"Why?"

"I should be able to tell you in due time. However, for now, I can say only that."

"Even the castle is tied to your spell?"

The cat only nodded.

The horses walked freely to the stables where floating hands waited to put them away. They removed the saddles and other bits of tack after the cat jumped softly down to the ground.

"Come, king's son. You must be half-starved from your journey."

They supped in the kitchen, the cat perched on the edge of the servants' table while Yufitri ate his fill of fish stew and bread. The kitchen cats crept around them, directing the floating hands with outstretched paws and short, firm meows.

"I truly didn't expect to see you again," it said. "Your home is far from here, and there is no one here besides me with whom you can speak."

"My father has set us with an impossible task, so I wanted the excuse to come see you."

"Oh? And what task is that?"

Yufitri explained as he finished his food.

With a wave of the cat's paw, a small cake was brought over to him by a pair of hands.

"Did you have this made for me especially?"

"You are a dear guest. You deserve only the finest I can offer. And I can help you with your father's request. I only ask you spend more time here with me."

Knowing the cat regarded him as more than a simple distraction or entertainment warmed Yufitri's heart. With his brothers as overprotective as they were, it had never been easy for Yufitri to have a friend all his own.

He smiled. "That was my plan all along, dear cat."

The next day, he woke to the cat sitting on the end of his bed, its body upright and alert, tail flicking from side to side.

"Good morning, king's son," it said.

"Good morning... What's wrong?"

"I have a proposition for you."

Yufitri sat up, rubbing the sleep from his eyes. "I am listening."

"Shall I teach you something of magic?" The green eyes gleamed with excitement.

"I don't know if I am suitable."

"Magic is not a question of suitability, rather a matter of knowledge and practice. But if you have no desire to learn, I shall not force you."

He mulled it over. "It would be an honor to be given the chance to try."

The cat purred. "Excellent. Let me show you to my chambers."

Feeling a bit excited to see the cat's wing of the castle for the first time, he followed.

The cat lived in the east tower wing, through a heavy wooden door and up a winding staircase. Once they came to a landing, the stairs opened into a cozy circular sitting room. The fabrics and cushions were lush reds and purples, trimmed in gold. Not for the first time, he wondered who the cat had been before, to have such a regal bearing and lavish belongings.

"This is the parlor," the cat said. "Come, one more flight up."

Yufitri followed it up to another landing. This room, the same size as the last, was full of bound leather tomes on mahogany shelves and various jars and baskets full of what could only be called spell ingredients—dried plants, crystals, preserved bits of various animals. In the center, a vivid seal was painted on the stone floor in red. It looked like two squares painted on top of each other, enclosed in a large circle. Inside it, a six-pointed star's edges touched the interior octagon. A strange rune lay in the absolute center.

"What does it mean?" he asked softly, approaching it.

"It's a spell-circle. That's where I perform magic." The cat walked to the center of it and sat down. "But first, we have to go over the basics."

It bolted over to one of the bookshelves as cats do, Yufitri at its heels. "Take that book there, the green one."

He did so, looking at the drawings and careful lettering on the pages, unable to understand any of it.

"Do you remember how I told you knowing your name would allow me to do magic on you?"

Yufitri nodded.

"To perform a spell or enchantment on something or someone, you must first know its true name. For natural objects, generally they are called simply what they are. A stone is normally called 'Stone' in spellcraft, except, of course, if that stone contains crystals, which are highly magical and very capricious. Manmade objects are named by their creators. Functional objects are usually given the name of their function: 'Table,' 'Chair,' 'Pot,' et cetera. But some objects, usually ones that require more time and skill to craft, will have unique names—weapons being a prime example."

The cat paused, looking toward a longsword hung upon the wall. "That sword is named 'Spinecutter.' It has a bit of a history involving decapitation."

He didn't know what to say to that. "You're speaking in generalities. Can objects sometimes not have the name you expect?"

"Yes. It's one of those unpredictable parts of magic. An apprentice's first craft, for instance, will sometimes bear a name like 'Beginning,' 'Future Success,' or even 'Failure' should it not turn out as skilled as the master's. And for people, sometimes their true name is not the one given by their parents, though this is rare."

"I see." Though the explanation made sense, how it applied to the world beyond was unclear. He had no context for how the magic of this realm worked and frankly had no aptitude for even the magic of his homeland. But he'd always learned best by doing, so asking the cat further questions would be of little help.

"But," said the cat, quieting slightly, "for now, let's do some simple shrinking and growing spells."

Much to his chagrin, Yufitri had no aptitude for magic of all kinds, familiar or foreign. Still, when the time came for him to leave, he could at least grow and shrink simple objects, which the cat assured him was a normal level to be at for a beginner.

When the eve of his departure came, the cat brought him to its bedroom. Like the tower sitting room, it was ornately decorated with a large soft canopy bed wrapped in dark violet dominating the room. The cat fetched a walnut from the side table, laying it softly in Yufitri's outstretched hand.

"This holds the cloth which will pass through the eye of a needle. I wish you luck in the competition with your brothers."

He looked at the nut in his palm, rolled it around. "I find myself unwilling to go, dear friend."

"But go you must. Your family will think you dead. Do you wish for them to bear that burden?"

He sighed and put the nut into his bag. "No, I suppose not. But rest assured I will return when the final challenge is given, regardless of what it is. I trust you more than anyone to assist."

The cat was quiet for a moment. "You do me a great honor," it said at last, lowering its head.

Carefully, he reached forward, touched his fingertips to the cat's soft fur, and stroked.

After initially fluffing up in surprise, it leaned into his hand, purring, eyes closed.

Smiling, Yufitri brought both hands to the cat's head and scratched under its chin and across its jaw.

For a long while, they stayed like that. He scooped the cat up into his arms and cradled it against his shoulder. "I will return; I swear it."

The black cat from before led him back to the village, then mewed a small goodbye as it ran into the brush.

With months of practice, Yufitri was now comfortable with the language of the land, and he made conversation with the man he hired to take him to the coast. But when he casually asked about the castle in the woods, the man turned pale and quiet.

"We do not discuss that forest, sir."

"Why?"

"We do not discuss it, sir."

Thus foiled, Yufitri went back to pleasant small talk and silence for the rest of the journey.

This time he found his brothers already at the palace. They embraced and discussed their respective journeys, Yufitri keeping quiet about the cat, as before.

"Come, Yufitri, tell us about your lover!" Amestan joked. "She must be quite the beauty, for you to hold her so close to your heart."

He only smiled. "She is dear indeed, and so she'll remain a secret for now."

"Well," Badis said, "I ended up returning south after little success in the east. And I believe I've met my future bride." His face lit up, black eyes gleaming. "She is absolutely stunning. Her skin is polished ebony, her eyes full of stars, her lips full and—"

"Calm yourself, brother!" Amestan said, clapping him on the shoulder. "We believe you. There's no reason to wax poetic."

Their father approached from around the corner and greeted his sons warmly, a knowing smile hidden beneath his beard.

After the feast celebrating their return, the sons presented their cloth.

Badis went first, showing off the pale-white fabric from the south. But the king produced a tiny embroidery needle as the head through which to pass, and try as the eldest son might, it would not go through.

Amestan brought out a pale-red fabric from the east, so light it floated on the air as he pulled it from his bag. But even though the deep tan of the king's skin could be seen through it, it too would not pass through.

Finally, Yufitri stood and held up the walnut. With his knife, he cracked it open, revealing a hazelnut. Upon cracking that, he found another even smaller nut. His brothers looked at each other, concern on their faces. Sweat prickled on the back of Yufitri's neck, but he cracked the third nut as well and revealed a tiny millet seed.

But with the flat of the knife, he crushed it open, and pulled forth a length of cloth that could only be likened to air given form. It drifted as he lifted it from the table, fluttering on a near-imagined breeze.

The king handed him the needle. Carefully, so as not to rip it, he pinched the corner of the cloth and guided it to the eye.

It passed through smoothly, its form serpentine as it was pulled through.

Marveling, the king ran his hands over the beautiful cloth, his fingers making no sound as he stroked it. "Now, I know our Yufitri has won each challenge so far, but do not think you boys have lost yet. There is one more challenge, and it is a test of many skills: charisma, cleverness, and foresight, among others."

The brothers all stood in silence, paying the utmost attention.

23

"You must bring here your bride. A proper wife is beautiful, yes, but she must also be wise and clever enough to care for you and your affairs, and she must be well-spoken as she is to serve the people at your sides. I trust, after all your adventures, there is at least one woman you can think of.

"Tomorrow, you shall embark on one more journey. And after that, I will determine who best suits the throne I will leave behind."

Badis, thinking of his beauty, grinned. Amestan, a small, shy smile on his face, twisted his collar as he stood there lost in thought.

Yufitri, however, could think only of his dear friend the cat, and how on earth it was going to help him with this particular request.

When Yufitri arrived once more at the castle's forest, the black cat from before was waiting to greet him. It pranced slowly and carefully through the woods, looking over its shoulder now and again to make sure it hadn't lost its charge.

When they entered, the hands took his outerwear, and the cat scurried off, presumably to tell the white cat of his arrival. And sure enough, as he was warming his hands by the fire, the cat approached, purring softly.

"It does my heart good to see you again, king's son, though this will be the last of your visits," it said.

He leaned down to stroke the cat's face and neck. "You think I would not return? You are dear to me, my friend."

The cat purred louder. "The past has not been kind to me, dear prince. Please forgive my cynicism. You have done nothing that would merit it." It pulled away from his hand, but only so it could leap up onto the couch beside him and curl against his side. "What is your final task?"

With a sigh, Yufitri went back to petting the cat. "I'm to bring home a bride," he said quietly.

The cat stilled under his hand, suddenly tense. "I see."

"I didn't come here expecting you to be able to give one to me," he said quickly. "I wanted only to seek your counsel."

"I can help you," the cat said deliberately before it moved out from under his hand and slunk to the floor. "But first, you must trust me."

"I do!"

"Would you do as I ask without question?"

"Yes."

"Even if you don't understand the reason?"

"Yes, of course." He thought back to the cloth in the millet seed. "Were the nuts a test of trust?"

The cat's tail swished. "Had you given up on me, you would have not returned."

"I trust you, my dear cat. With my life, should you need it."

It shook its head. "I do not need your life; I need only your hands… Come with me."

He followed it to the eastern tower and up to the spell room. The cat sat down in the center of the circle, its eyes shining through the gloom of twilight. "Do you remember that sword's name?" it asked while indicating the longsword on the wall.

"I believe it is 'Spinecutter'? You said it had a history of… decapitation."

"I did. It is enchanted to do just that. My dear prince, I need you to cut off my head."

25

His stomach dropped, his whole body contracting with sudden nausea. "But…"

"Do you trust me?" the cat asked again. Its voice rang loudly in the small room, pressing against Yufitri's ears.

"I…I do… But…dear cat, I've no desire to kill you." His voice cracked on "kill." He felt limp and cold as if his blood had turned to mud in his veins. Why would the cat ask this of him? Surely the hands could wield a blade, if it *had* to be done. Why him?

"I cannot tell you what will happen. I may die, I may live. But I need you to trust me. Take up the sword and strike truly."

Closing its eyes, the cat stretched out its neck and waited.

Stilling his trembling hands, he took the sword from the wall, blood pounding relentlessly against his ears and behind his eyes. His entire field of view was shaking.

The cat's ears twisted, following his movements, but its eyes remained shut, its posture firm.

Yufitri stood before it, sword held in a white-knuckled grip. "Are you sure?" he whispered hoarsely.

"Do it."

The blow was eerily accurate, slicing cleanly through the notches of the spine. The little head fell to the ground with a soft thump, followed by the larger thud of the body.

Spinecutter clattered to the ground, drops of slick red blood dotting the floor around the growing pool. Yufitri sobbed openly, tears burning their ways down his cheeks. He fell to his knees, staring fixedly at the body before him, waiting desperately for something to happen.

For several agonizing moments—or were they eternities?—nothing did.

But then there was a twitch in the body, like something writhing within it.

Something was pushing its way out.

Like the dog from the hazelnut and the cloth from the millet seed, what emerged was far too big for its container.

It was a person.

The young man pulled himself free from the discarded skin, wiping blood and tears from his eyes. His skin was milky pale with short hair as white as the cat he had worn and eyes the very same vivid green.

The man stood shakily onto two legs. Then, in a fit of fury, he grabbed the head and threw it to the stone floor, smashing the skull to pieces.

Even in naked savagery, blood streaked across his white skin, marring that pale, pale hair, he was beautiful.

He met gazes with Yufitri and smiled, the anger falling from his face as quickly as it had appeared. Yufitri's stomach dropped again, but this time for an entirely different reason.

Smooth, cool hands touched his blotchy face and wiped away the remainders of tears. "Thank you," he said, his voice both like and unlike the cat's, a warm tenor that made heat bloom in Yufitri's chest.

"I don't—" Yufitri licked his lips. "—understand."

"Let me quickly clean and dress myself, and then I will answer every question you could even think of asking, my dear, sweet prince."

The man hurried up the stairs to his bedroom, something of the cat lingering in the elegance of his movement.

Bewildered and feeling a bit wrung out, Yufitri stayed in place on the floor, his eyes sliding over the carnage without really seeing it.

The former cat emerged clean and dressed in the same rich violets and reds Yufitri remembered seeing in his bedroom. Much more imposing now, the vulnerability of his nakedness and anger was carefully wrapped in gold-edged cloth.

Footsteps on the stairs. Yufitri turned to look. It was a young woman, thick black hair and a face that called to mind something of the sea merchant—dark, clever eyes and small features. She was hastily dressed in a loose sack dress and bare feet. "My lord," she croaked, tears welling in her eyes.

The man gave her a small smile. "Yes, Luisa, all is well. I trust you to take charge of the kitchen and arrange a celebratory feast? Something without mice would be lovely."

"Right away, my lord!"

She scampered back down the stairs and waited until the door latched closed to start directing the other servants.

The man smiled more broadly, looking down at Yufitri. "Should we talk in my room? I don't think the gore makes for an appropriate atmosphere for stories."

With a small nod, the prince got to his feet, ignoring the blood drying on his knees, then followed the man upstairs.

The man settled him in one of the armchairs, every accidental touch sending sparks across Yufitri's skin, and then sat on the bed. "Shall I start at the beginning?" he asked.

"Please."

"I am the prince of this kingdom, born twenty years ago to the king and queen. However, when my mother still carried me within her, she and my father went hunting in these woods. They had heard rumor of a fairy castle within, but they paid these flights of fancy no mind. But as night fell, they saw lights in the distance, and followed them to this very palace.

"When the fairies ruled here, the surrounding gardens bloomed year-round with exotic and unknown fruits and vegetables. My mother was amazed. She coveted the fruits and flowers and tried to scale the low wall to take some for herself.

"However, the elder fairy had no tolerance for thievery, catching her before she could take even one bite. My mother begged and begged. And the fairy agreed that perhaps a trade could be arranged. She pointed to my mother's stomach, which was only just beginning to stretch outward, and said she would trade as much fruit as my mother could carry for the child growing under her breast. She agreed."

Yufitri had such an expression of horror that the man stopped and leaned forward to touch his knee. "You must understand," the man said gently. "My parents had been assured by soothsayers and astrologers and prophets I would be a sickly little girl, one that would likely not live to see a year's life. Since my mother assumed the child would be lost to her anyway, I can understand why she would make the trade."

"That's still horrible." Yufitri thought of his father making such a trade, using him as payment for such a paltry thing as exotic food, and anger boiled in the pit of his stomach.

The man shrugged lightly. Clearly the hurt that had been there had long since scarred over—not gone, but no longer painful to touch. "So, deal made, she gathered all the fruit she could and returned to my father. After they'd gorged themselves, she revealed the trade she'd made, and while my father was angry initially, he came to see her reasoning.

"Several months later, I was born and was distinctly not a girl. And despite my pallor giving the appearance of illness, since both of my parents are dark-complected and dark-haired, I was perfectly healthy.

"But false predictions or not, the fairy came for her payment."

"What did she want with a baby, anyway? What exactly is a fairy?" Up until that point, Yufitri had been vaguely reminded of djinn, demons of the eastern merchants, but djinn had no use for children.

"Fairies are magical creatures, fully distinct from mortal ones like you and me. When I perform magic, I'm channeling the energy already in the object and in the objects I use to build the spell. Fairies fuel their spells from their own essence, and it's made more powerful by others' belief in them."

Yufitri furrowed his brow, trying to understand, but it was like trying to catch smoke—he could see it but not grasp it. "Why?" he asked.

"Something about the nature of magic being capricious and liable to backfire. For the spells I craft, most of the actual craft is channeling the magic into the right direction. Because fairies are so much more powerful, they need help focusing. So, fairies love children and fools, who believe in whatever the fairy seeks to do and so help direct the spell. Does that make sense?"

Yufitri thought about it but ended up shrugging. "Not exactly, but I believe you. So, they wanted you so they could…?"

"Practice spells with the extra focus my belief would give."

"I see." He paused, considering. "If they wanted you as a child, why did they turn you into a cat? Unless it wasn't the fairies?"

The man's eyes narrowed and turned cold. "Oh, it was them. My childhood was surprisingly happy. I was enchanted to never leave the woods, but the fairies treated me kindly, and they taught me magic to help pass the time. People came in and out of the woods, some of them runaways, some of them lost, and the fairies took them in, usually at the price of becoming part of my staff. For those with nowhere left to go, it was a godsend. And I was never lonely." His hands, resting in his lap, came together and squeezed tightly. "Then, one day, he came. A traveler like yourself, perhaps even from your own nation. He was...very much like you. A bit younger, perhaps, his beard yet a shadow on his chin. We met by chance in the garden, which he'd entered seeking food and shelter from the summer rain... I loved him madly."

Yufitri's heart stuttered in his chest.

"We met in secret because I feared the fairies would punish him. If only I'd known how severely... I would have told him to run, to leave this country behind him and never look back. But I did not.

"We were together only weeks before we were discovered. The elder fairy drove him from the palace in a fury, letting him think he could escape before she transformed herself into a fierce dragon and descended upon him with claws and flame and swallowed him whole."

For a moment, he stopped talking, throat twitching as he gulped back tears. "He was punished for coveting what was not his. And I was punished as well. My love meant I was no longer a child, and my defiance meant I was no longer of use. The elder fairy, my love's blood still on her lips, turned me into a cat and cursed me. I could not speak of it, and it could only be broken by convincing a man very like my poor beloved to cut off the head of the body in which I was trapped.

"Well, there are hardly men like you in this land, let alone in these woods, for the first spell remained. I thought I would be trapped here until my death... And yet, here we sit." He met Yufitri's gaze and smiled. "I am Calixtus. I give you my name, so you may know me."

"It's not as if I could do any magic with it... But I recognize your intent. I am Yufitri."

"Does it have meaning?" Calixtus asked.

Yufitri blushed a bit. "'Handsomer than a star.' My mother named me before she died. Yours?"

"Mine simply means 'beautiful.' My parents had planned for a girl after all." Another smile, but this one was edged in sorrow. "Your name suits you, Prince Yufitri."

"As does yours, Prince Calixtus." A thought hit him. "The cats! The other cats, where did they come from?"

Calixtus gazed up at the sliver of window behind Yufitri's head, eyes far away. "They were the human servants I had when I was turned. They were punished for not knowing sooner."

Yufitri balked. "That is entirely unfair."

"Fairies are not known for their fairness." Though his voice was light, Yufitri could see the bitterness in the tightness of his jaw and the way his hands curled and uncurled in his lap.

Silence. "So where are they now?"

Calixtus waved a dismissive hand. "Elsewhere. They went to find a new kingdom, free of the disgrace of this one."

Yufitri thought of the man from before who'd had such fear in his eyes when asked about the woods. "The villagers refuse to speak of this place. Do you know why?"

The answer was dry. "I presume because a man was eaten by a dragon here."

"Ah." Yufitri didn't know whether or not Calixtus expected him to laugh.

The silence was broken by the sounds of someone walking downstairs. "My lord?" It sounded like the woman from before. "The preparations have been made! Would you like us to begin serving?"

"Yes!" he called, getting to his feet. "Come, Prince." He held out a hand to Yufitri, who took it as he stood. For a moment, the touch lingered, but then he dropped Yufitri's hand like it was ice and smoothed his palm over his shirt.

Yufitri tried to ignore the way it made his chest hurt.

It was amazing how small the castle seemed with people bustling around. Though the hands lingered still.

"Those aren't also servants?" Yufitri wondered.

"No, they're spellcraft. They maintain the castle and carry things but cannot perform tasks like cooking or washing and mending clothes—things that require a certain amount of knowledge to do."

"I see."

When they entered the dining hall, Yufitri was surprised at how many people there suddenly were.

The woman, Luisa, stood near the door and greeted them as they entered. "My lord! And esteemed guest, of course." She crossed her ankles and bobbed, leaning her head forward. "Dinner will be a roasted goose and as many side dishes as the kitchen can handle." She grinned. "By God, it is good to hear my own voice again after so long!"

"Yes, I agree." He pecked her on the cheek as he passed her, eyes turning to Yufitri over his shoulder, but Yufitri couldn't read the emotion hidden there.

Dinner was amazing, and wine flowed like water. Yufitri ended the meal with a swollen stomach and a warm, sluggish head. As he made his way back to the guest room, he noticed Calixtus skulked behind him, padding silently.

Yufitri stopped and looked at him. Well, he sort of stopped. He got his legs to still, but his body continued to rock with the motion of walking. "Is something wrong?" Had talking always been so difficult? Why was his tongue suddenly so heavy?

33

"Your father's task. What is it that he's looking for?"

"Knowing my father, a pretty face and nice wide hips," he laughed. "My father, though I love him dearly, is a lecherous old goat behind closed doors." But he frowned and considered the question more seriously. "I don't know. He also said he wanted someone quick and well-spoken, able to handle household affairs and our subjects with equal ease."

"I see."

Finally sensing something was wrong, Yufitri frowned. Calixtus had grown still, his arms crossed tightly over his chest and his head bowed in some deep thought. "What is it?"

"I know a suitable candidate," he said stiffly. "Luisa, can you come here?"

The woman emerged from the dining hall, holding a stack of plates. "What do you need, my lord?"

"Would you want to marry our guest?"

Yufitri coughed in surprise, the sudden movement making his stomach roil in protest. She only narrowly avoided dropping the dishes. "Excuse me, my lord?!"

"P-prince Calixtus, hold on!" Yufitri stammered. "I wouldn't feel comfortable you giving me a person as if she were some sort of gift! And I'd much rather *know* the woman I marry."

"She knows you well enough," Calixtus said, his voice low and controlled. "She was the black cat who found you in the woods. She is exceedingly fond of you."

Yufitri stared at her. He remembered that cat, and yes, he had been happy to see it when he came across it in the castle—had probably petted its head once or twice. But marry her? Just like that?

"I… It's true," she said quietly. "But I would never! I mean… if you wanted to, of course. But surely you—" She stopped herself, eyes on her lord. "—I have to return these to the kitchen to be washed. Please excuse me."

She hurried away, leaving the two princes alone in the dark.

"Let's talk in the guest room, shall we?" Yufitri said.

Calixtus nodded.

"What in the world happened back there?" Yufitri asked, sitting down heavily on the edge of the bed and putting his hands on his knees. His head was spinning, both with drink (in which he had certainly overindulged) and with confusion.

"I was simply trying to help you as I always have." Calixtus stayed in the doorway, his hands held behind his back, legs spread in a warrior's stance.

"I don't need to win," Yufitri said emphatically. "I've told you this. I'd rather not marry under this kind of pressure anyway." He closed his eyes but still felt like he was swaying. He tried lying down, but that didn't seem to help either. He kept talking because he couldn't think of what else to do.

"The best part about being the youngest son is you don't have to be king," Yufitri mumbled. "And so, you get to choose who you want to marry unless you have to help make some alliance or whatever. But most of the time, you can do whatever you want. Of course, the only person I've met so far that I'd like to marry is you. Not that my father would ever approve of it. He wants an excuse to have some pretty girls around since it's all men at the castle since my mom died, not that you're not pretty—that's not what I'm saying." What *was* he saying? His head was swimming. Why was the bed moving like he was back at sea? Wait, what was this conversation about? He couldn't even remember. "I just…don't want you to keep troubling yourself for me, I guess."

Something warm nestled against his side, and he reached down automatically to stroke the cat, his hand meeting soft human hair instead. He petted it anyway. "I'd like to marry you too," came a whispered response, but Yufitri was already asleep.

With morning came a nail and hammer to Yufitri's head. He groaned as he came into awareness, his eyes squeezed tight shut against the morning sun. Something was set on the table beside him.

"Drink this," came Calixtus's voice. "It'll help."

He made a fumbling grab, eyes still pulsing red behind the lids, until Calixtus's cool hands rested on his, guiding the cup to his lips.

After a short while, the headache began to recede, and he was able to crack his eyes open. Calixtus sat at the foot of the bed, a scroll covered in black scribbles in his hands. "What are you reading?" Yufitri asked.

"A draft of an explanation to my father. I don't know if he'd still accept me as his heir, but I'm hopeful he will. Of course, if he's chosen another, it could become a bit of a political mess."

Even the mention of politics made the hangover worse. Yufitri slumped down onto the pillows. "Don't ever let me drink that much again, please."

There was amusement in Calixtus's voice when he spoke. "I shall do my best."

The memories from the night before were dark and jumbled. "What…happened last night? I remember you offered one of your servants to me to bring back to my father. But after that, I don't remember much."

Calixtus's face was impossible to read, his eyes half-lidded, mouth a blank line. Yufitri was beginning to realize he was just as inscrutable a man as he was a cat.

"You rebuked me for my actions and insisted once again I needn't help you with your father's challenge." His mouth quirked downward. "However, I don't know how else to show my gratitude for everything you've done for me."

Yufitri sighed and rolled upright before flopping over so he could look up at Calixtus, the crown of his head brushing against his hip. "You don't think you've done enough? You've fed and housed me for nearly two years. You've given me gifts crafted with skill and complex magic, and you think you have not done enough?"

Calixtus looked down at him, setting aside his draft. White fingers traced down Yufitri's nose, pressing softly when they came to the end. "You kept me company those two years, gave me hope I could one day wear my own face again, and then you turned that hope to reality. You gave me back my *life*. Nothing can ever repay that. Not even if I could pull the moon from the sky to give to you."

"I don't know what I would do with the moon. Power over tides of the sea and the tides of women…seems a heavy burden."

Calixtus gave a shout of laughter. "I speak such poetry for you! And yet you joke. You are strange and wonderful, my dear prince."

Yufitri smiled. "My head hurts too much to be serious."

"Well, then let me get you some breakfast. That should help too."

"You are a prince among men!"

Calixtus chuckled. "Yes, I am. I'd ask you not to go anywhere, but I trust you won't."

"I won't. This bed is much too lovely."

"I'll return shortly."

The door squeaked shut, and Yufitri rolled over to stare at the ceiling. His head, still sore, throbbed with a dull ache on either side of his eyes, but his heart was warm and full in his chest. It was the first time he'd seen the stoic Calixtus laugh.

With breakfast came something of a return to routine. But now, instead of lazily passing time with his friend the cat, Yufitri passed time with a beautiful man who, for all his honesty, still managed to be incredibly mysterious.

That night, Calixtus announced to the servants that those who wished to leave this place were welcome. Only a few ultimately took him up on the offer.

"We're here because there's nowhere else for us, my lord," Luisa said quietly as others agreed around her. "We will stay by your side."

And for a moment, his cheeks darkened with pride and perhaps love, but it was soon gone, replaced by the placid smile he hid so often behind.

It was strange for Yufitri, sleeping alone in the bed without the familiar warmth of the cat beside him. A fleeting urge seized him, and he was tempted to rush from his chamber up to the eastern tower and into that room of reds and violets where Calixtus lay asleep and join him, but the urge was quelled, and he fell into restless sleep until morning.

As the weeks went on, Calixtus continued to ponder what to say to his father, asking Yufitri for counsel from time to time. Neither of them spoke about his quest. Yufitri had given up, but he could tell Calixtus had not let it go. On the contrary, he was starting to suspect the silence was a cover for scheming.

A few times too many, Yufitri found himself "accidentally" running into Luisa. She was pleasant to be around and pretty, but if Calixtus hoped to spark something between the two of them, it simply wasn't to be.

It hurt, deep in Yufitri's chest, to think about Calixtus trying to make him fall in love with someone else. Truly, it became more and more difficult to ignore the fact that he was likely already in love with Calixtus himself.

He felt so warm and content in his presence, and he longed to run his hands through that pale, pale hair and kiss the tip of that long, straight nose, that mole under his eye, those pink lips.

Clenching his fists in impotent frustration, Yufitri bid Luisa another goodbye and returned to the guest room, then fell onto the bed with a heavy sigh. Now the question remained, what did he want to do?

He sat up. He was a prince and a warrior. Princes and warriors did not cower in fear of rejection; they went after what they wanted, consequences be damned.

The hallways were empty. Moonlight fell in stripes across the blue-black floors, and every suit of armor menaced from the shadows. Quelling the urge to return to his room, Yufitri pressed onward until he reached the eastern tower. The door opened at his touch, creaking in the heavy silence. He clicked it shut as quietly as he could and ascended the stairs.

His heart squeezed tightly as he passed through the spell room, flashes of blood, bone, and white fur assaulted him, but he climbed the final staircase.

Calixtus was sitting up in bed, posture alert as his eyes gleamed, catlike, from an opening in the canopy. He visibly relaxed as he recognized Yufitri.

"What brings you here so late, king's son?" he asked, pulling the canopy further aside. A whispered word and the sconces on the wall flickered to life, casting a warm orange glow.

"I have something I must tell you."

"And it could not wait for daylight?"

"No." Yufitri rubbed his arm. "I was afraid I'd lose my nerve."

Calixtus worked himself out from under the covers, the white fabric of his shift making no sound as it moved over the heavy wool. He sat on the end of the bed, expectant. "Then speak."

Yufitri drew in a shuddering breath, too aware of how it rattled hollowly in his chest. "Prince Calixtus. I... What I mean to say is...you are..." He felt like he was about to swoon. He clamped it down, rooting his feet, digging his nails into the skin of his arm, and pulled himself back. "You are the most beautiful person I have ever known, both within and without. I find myself captivated by you more and more with each passing day, and I want nothing more than for you to know my feelings. And for you to stop throwing poor Luisa at me. She is a lovely woman, but no one is lovelier than you." He stared at the floor, watching his shadow flicker in the firelight, waiting for a response.

Calixtus's shadow shifted and moved, then drifted forward until the two touched, and Yufitri looked up. There were tears shimmering in those spring-green eyes. "You have much to lose in loving me," he whispered.

"None of it matters if it means I get you in return."

Cool hands stroked his overheated face, drawing him up into a kiss. Deepening the kiss, Yufitri tried to lift him into his arms, but they ended up tangled together, unsure of whose hands were where until, laughing, they fell onto the bed. They broke apart, sighing into each other's mouths. Yufitri ran his fingers through Calixtus's hair, marveling at the softness of it, heat pooling near his hips at the soft gasp that action inspired. He did it again, a bit rougher, pushing his nails across the scalp.

Calixtus shuddered against him and pulled their hips together with his legs. Heat built between them, Yufitri moving his lips across Calixtus's jaw, moving down his neck, sucking at his pulse. Sharp fingernails pressed into his shoulders as Calixtus held him tighter and tugged at his shift.

At a gasped command, the lights went out, and Calixtus gently pushed Yufitri away. "One moment." He pulled the curtain fully closed and tugged Yufitri back against his chest until they were lying on the pile of pillows near the headboard. "I wouldn't want you to catch a chill," he said softly, sliding his hands up underneath Yufitri's shift, nails grazing tantalizingly across taut skin.

"No, that would be terrible," Yufitri agreed, nosing into the junction of ear and neck, hands braced on either side of Calixtus's chest. "It's getting so pleasantly warm in here. It would be a real shame to ruin it."

That night, Yufitri learned the miracle that was making love, the magic of watching Calixtus lose completely his stoic armor and careful words, dissolve entirely into low moans and sharp gasps as his nails painted stripes across Yufitri's back. As Yufitri fell asleep, he found himself wishing they would scar so he could keep them forever.

Morning came. Yufitri woke to the sound of birdsong and was surprised and pleased to find Calixtus lying half on top of him, breathing gently against his chest. He ran his fingers through that soft white hair and scratched lightly. Calixtus sighed happily and cuddled closer, leaning up to bump Yufitri's chin with his head. Just like a cat. Yufitri chuckled.

Too soon, there came the sound of movement beyond the bed curtains, the shuffling of someone opening trunks and bureaus to lay out clothes and the clink of dishes to serve breakfast. "It's morning, my lord," Luisa called.

Calixtus stirred, breathing in deeply before yawning and opening his eyes. For a moment, he appeared confused, but perhaps as memories from the night before returned to him, he smiled and sat up and looked down at Yufitri. "Thank you, Luisa," he said. "I shall dress myself today."

"Very well. The clothes are in the usual place when you're ready. Shall I go wake the prince?"

Yufitri stifled a laugh. Calixtus put a finger to his lips, eyes twinkling with mischief. "No need. I'll take care of it."

A pause. "Yes, sir. Have a pleasant morning." Footsteps, the shutting of the door.

The two princes looked at each other and burst out laughing. "So," Calixtus said, rolling over so he was fully on top of Yufitri. "Are you awake?"

"Hmmm, I don't know. Usually I'm not *really* awake until I've had a bit of exercise."

"Well then, what kind of host would I be if I did not oblige?"

By the time they got out of bed, breakfast had long gone cold. Despite this, they ate ravenously. With a contented sigh, Yufitri started getting dressed again and picked his clothes up off the floor, somewhat bemused as to how they had ended up so far away.

From his perch atop his clothing chest, Calixtus was suddenly grave.

"What's wrong?" Yufitri wondered if it was his fault somehow. Had last night not been as enjoyable for Calixtus? Was the before-breakfast, er, exercise too much? Was he about to be rejected?

"What are we doing?"

Yufitri tried to keep his voice light, but the fear of never having such a pleasant evening and morning again loomed in his thoughts. "Well, at the moment, we're getting dressed. Though I wasn't wearing much beyond a shift to begin with."

"You know I don't mean that."

With a long sigh, Yufitri went and joined him on the chest then put an arm around his shoulders. "We're being happy."

"But what about your family? Are you going to allow them to believe you dead or worse?"

"No, I suppose not." Yufitri tightened his hold. "Guess I have to bring you home and show you off."

Calixtus froze in the hug and looked at him with wide eyes. "What?"

"Did you think I would abandon you? What kind of man do you take me for?"

Calixtus shook his head, a smile on his lips. "I have no idea." They kissed, then kissed a little more before breaking apart to finish dressing and emerge from the bedroom into the afternoon sunlight.

As the time to return south approached, Calixtus took Yufitri by the hand and led him to the spell room. "I figured out how to break the spell that keeps me bound to these wretched woods," he said, looking smug. "I want you to watch me shatter it to pieces."

"I would be happy to."

Most of the ingredients were already laid out on key parts of the circle at line junctures or within the shapes they formed. Calixtus sat down cross-legged at the center and began to chant. As the ingredients glowed and were absorbed into the spell, a light appeared around Calixtus's neck. It glowed brighter and brighter until it was clear it was a collar, shining like moonlight.

Hands trembling with excitement, he clasped it tightly. Then he pulled. It did in fact shatter, the bits of light vanishing as they hit the floor.

The spell ingredients disappeared completely, leaving only cloying smoke. Calixtus sat still, breathing slowly in and out, hands, white-knuckled, pressed to the floor in front of him. "I…" His voice was small and shallow, suddenly very young. "I'm free."

Yufitri knelt beside him and gathered him into his arms. After a few minutes, when Calixtus's breathing returned to normal, he grinned. "So, we leave at dawn?"

Calixtus grinned back. "Yes. We leave at dawn."

.

After breakfast the next day, the servants made sure they were packed and ready, promising to look after the castle while their prince was away. Calixtus assured them he would return in a few months, and then the two of them made their way through the forest and into the village at the edge. The people recognized Yufitri by now; a few merchants even greeted him, but they eyed his companion with mistrust and fear.

Calixtus grew smaller at Yufitri's side. "They think me cursed or a demon," he said quietly.

"Why?"

"My hair and skin, I would imagine."

Yufitri frowned. "Is your coloring so uncommon?"

"It is," he assured him.

By noon, Calixtus's forehead and nose were violent pink and hot to the touch. Yufitri acquired some ointment like the red-faced man's so long ago and rubbed it into the burned skin gently.

"I have an idea," Yufitri said. "Wait here, and put more on when you want to, okay?"

Calixtus nodded and stayed where they were sitting outside another small town. Yufitri went to the marketplace and returned with a long piece of cloth. It took him a few tries to successfully imitate the nomads' head wrapping, and he was pretty sure he was doing it wrong, but it didn't matter. He pinned the cloth into place.

Now, instead of his skin and hair drawing attention and unwanted sunburn, Calixtus looked like a foreign traveler just like Yufitri. His eyes crinkled in a smile, then a wince as the tightness and soreness of the skin made itself known again.

"Thank you," he said, voice muffled through the cloth.

"Whatever you need." He pecked his lips to the slip of forehead he could see. "You ready to go?"

"Yes, I'm coming."

Calixtus became horribly ill the first few days at sea. His skin took on a gray pallor, and he spent hours gripping the railing of the boat, pouring the contents of his empty stomach into the water. However, after those first awful days, his nausea faded, and he was able to enjoy the wind in his hair and the view of the distant shore.

Calixtus kept his head wrapped as they approached the port. Yufitri thought he saw one of his brothers on the dock and waved, but they were still too far out. Calixtus was pensive as they drifted closer. "Say, Prince Yufitri...am I beautiful?"

"Fishing for compliments?" Yufitri smiled.

He smiled back, his eyes crinkling. "Yes, but also for a bit of a…mischievous purpose."

"Oh? Well, yes, you are stunningly beautiful. What's the mischief?"

"Well, your brothers are expecting a bride."

"Yes."

"So, why do we need to tell them I'm not one? At least not right away. After all, they can't see my face, and I can keep quiet."

Yufitri stifled a laugh into his hand. "Do you really want to?"

"I want to see if I can fool them." His eyes twinkled.

"All right. I'll play the game with you. Though they know enough of your tongue to know your name is masculine."

"You can call me Calliste then. That should be neutral enough to throw them off."

Yufitri laughed. This was going to be fun.

As they exited the boat and paid the merchant, Calixtus acted no different from his usual self. Yufitri half expected him to play up the role a bit, but maybe that would've made the jest too obvious. Amestan alone met him on the dock and embraced him. "Yufitri, I am glad to see you home and well. And I can't wait to meet your bride!"

Yufitri grinned and gestured toward Calixtus, who nodded his head.

"Um, brother, did you travel across the sea to find a well-dressed nomad?"

"The cowl is to protect her delicate skin. I told you of the northern people. They have skin that is milk white and turns violent red in the sun. We couldn't have that, could we, my dear?" He winked.

Calixtus gave him a blank stare as if he didn't understand. Yufitri had to bite back a shriek of laughter.

He turned back to Amestan. "Sorry. I learned her tongue, but she still knows little of ours." He slowed his speech, fully aware Calixtus had understood perfectly well. "The cloth protects the skin on your face, yes?"

Smiling as if he now comprehended, Calixtus nodded again.

"Well, she seems sweet," Amestan said approvingly. "Though you haven't met mine! You may have won the last two competitions, dear brother, but you shall not carry this day."

Yufitri shrugged. "I certainly hope not. I've no desire for the crown."

Amestan frowned. "Then why participate?"

"The chance to adventure, of course!" He grinned. "I have no regrets." He looked at Calixtus, who gave him a genuine smile.

"Well then, shall we return to the castle and wait for our brother?"

"Of course." He held out his hand to Calixtus, who took it happily and walked close alongside Yufitri as they made their way through the busy marketplace. The smell of spices, fish, and incense made Yufitri feel comfortable and at home, and he was sad that it would likely be a long time after this visit before he would be able to return.

Standing in the courtyard when they returned, a woman wrapped in beautiful red fabric—a long tunic over loose pants as well as a veil over her dark hair. Her clothing was patterned with delicate gold needlework, and gold jewelry glittered on her ears and, most intriguingly, on the side of her nose.

She smiled as they entered the courtyard, and Calixtus's grip tightened on his hand. "She's definitely pretty," he said quietly, whispering into the cloth wrapped around Calixtus's head. "But you are more beautiful still."

Calixtus chuckled, and said in his native tongue, "Keep flattering me and I'll stop believing you."

"Oh no," he said, smirking. "Then you're absolutely hideous. I can't even look at you right now."

Calixtus bit back a laugh. Amestan glanced over his shoulder at them, smiling before going over to his bride. His arms around her were gentle and kind, and Yufitri got the feeling she would be good for him, no matter what happened.

Then, with great excitement, Badis arrived. At his side was an absolutely stunning woman.

She looked as if someone had taken a blade to the night sky and cut her out of it, then placed stars in her eyes. She was tall, long-limbed, and absolutely gorgeous. Her dress was yellow and orange, and her curly black hair was wrapped in cloth of the same color, piled on top of her head like the crest of a waterfall.

Yufitri could see why Badis had heaped such praise on her. But with Calixtus's hand cool in his own, he found no envy in his heart.

After greetings and compliments, the three brothers and their brides entered the castle where their father stood in wait. He embraced his sons and greeted the women (plus Calixtus). "Why do you cover your face in the presence of a king?" he rumbled in displeasure.

Calixtus gave his best blank stare as Yufitri was quick to intervene. "Shyness, Father. You'll see her face at dinner, I promise."

He squinted his eyes suspiciously, grumbling to himself. "Then let dinner be served!"

Yufitri and Calixtus shared a mischievous grin.

The entire group gathered around the table, smiles and compliments given to the king as the centerpiece, a great pot of stewed lamb, was placed on the table, still steaming hot. Winking at Yufitri, Calixtus slowly unwrapped his head, folded the cloth neatly, and placed it beside him on the bench. "Thank you so much for your hospitality, Your Majesty," he said, his speech accented but clear. "This meal looks spectacular."

The king and the two brothers looked from Calixtus, to Yufitri, to one another, and then back to Calixtus.

"Um, Yufitri," Amestan said. "Do you know...?"

Yufitri roared with laughter. "Do you think so poorly of me, my dear brother? This is the man who helped me win the last two competitions. He is a fine enchanter."

Calixtus's smile dimmed at the corners. Yufitri took his hand and squeezed tightly. "And he will make a fine bride."

That got a laugh, but only from his beloved. His family looked concerned.

"But Yufitri, don't you want to be king? You need a bride who can bear your children."

"Then I won't be king. I didn't come here expecting to win. I came here to introduce my beloved to my family." He brought Calixtus's hand to his lips. "You all know I would make for a poor king, anyway."

"Very well; are you removing yourself from the competition?" the king asked.

"Yes, Father."

The two other brides sat up expectantly. The night woman was still the more eye-catching of the two, despite the other's finery.

The king asked them both many questions, and Badis's bride proved to act exactly as impressive as she looked.

So, in the end, despite the entire charade, the eldest son won the throne on a technicality. Amestan did his best not to sulk during the celebratory party.

After pleasantries and congratulations had been exchanged, Amestan pulled Yufitri aside out onto the balcony. "Brother, I worry for you."

"Why?" Yufitri asked, leaning against the stone railing. The air was dry and warm, and he was surprised how much it made him feel at home.

"It's just... You said he is a sorcerer. How do you know you're not...cursed to love him?"

Yufitri chuckled. "I appreciate your worry, but he showed me enough of magic to know that's not the case. The magic he does is tricky; I doubt he could spell me without my knowing."

"That does not inspire confidence, brother."

"Then trust in me. I never wanted to be king. Besides"—he grinned—"I think being a queen will be much more fun."

"What?" Oh, the worry on his dear brother's face! Yufitri had to restrain a childish giggle, covering it with a cough.

"He's an heir in his own right," Yufitri explained. "Hence, I shall be his queen." He couldn't help a wink.

Amestan's expression soured. "More like his concubine. Kings need heirs of their own, Yufitri."

"Then I'll be the second wife he loves much better than the duty wife." But the thought settled cold and wet in the pit of his stomach. "We haven't discussed that yet, to be honest."

"Sounds to me like that should happen soon."

"It will. Please don't concern yourself on my account. I'm happier than I've ever been."

And Amestan sighed and smiled. "Well, it's not my place to argue your feelings. I wish you all the happiness in the world."

"And I you."

The two brothers embraced, the stars and desert their only audience.

"Come," Yufitri said after a time. "We should return to the celebration."

Calixtus gave him a questioning look as he came inside, so he bid Amestan goodbye and went to join him. He bumped his lips against his cheek in greeting. "Miss me?"

Calixtus let himself smile before sobering. "What were you talking about?"

"He was worried about me as brothers do."

"Worried about what?" His expression grew dark.

"My happiness. Don't fret; I would never let him interfere with what we have between us."

Calixtus sighed and switched to his native tongue, then spoke quickly and quietly. "I'm just…scared someone here is going to talk sense into you and convince you to stay and settle down with some sweet girl instead and make me return to face my father alone, and I just…" He dropped his head to Yufitri's shoulder. "And I know it's horribly hypocritical because I was trying to foist Luisa on you, but that was *before*, and now I can't even imagine anyone else touching you without half planning spells that would involve their eyes turning to acid."

Yufitri laughed and hugged him close. "There's no need to melt anyone's eyes, dear. We'll go back north in a month or two. For now, let me show you the beauty of my homeland." He chuckled. "Hopefully without you turning a strange, yet attractive shade of scarlet."

Calixtus snorted. "We'll travel by night. The moon is safe."

"I don't know. You haven't seen a full moonrise over the desert." He kissed Calixtus's nose. "Well, not yet anyway. Give it a week or so, and then you will."

They did. The sight of Calixtus silhouetted against the great moon, his cape fluttering out from his shoulders like a pair of predator's wings, was one Yufitri would not soon forget.

A few days after the celebration as Yufitri and Calixtus were getting ready for bed, Yufitri's father sent for him. Calixtus looked worried, but Yufitri kissed him before he could raise a concern again. "My father can say whatever he likes," he said. "I am coming home with *you*."

Yufitri met his father in his sitting room. Divested of his kingly regalia, he was only an old man.

"Yufitri," he said slowly. "What are you doing?"

"With what, Father?"

"With a *man*, son. Do you not love women?" The king pulled unhappily at his beard, not quite meeting his son's eyes.

Yufitri sighed, coming forward to kneel next to his father's knee as he'd done so many times as a child. "You did nothing wrong in raising me, Father. I enjoy the company of women, but I love Prince Calixtus. He is good and kind and—"

"And going to take you away from me." It was then Yufitri saw the real reason his father was upset, and all of the righteous fury he had built up on the walk over died away. His father hadn't expected to have to say goodbye.

"It isn't forever," Yufitri said. "I will visit from time to time. I'll have to see all the nieces and nephews that will no doubt be filling the castle soon, won't I?"

The king pulled him up in a tight embrace. "I know you are a stubborn child. Any argument I could make would fall on deaf ears, and I saw Amestan already talked to you at the party. So, as your father, all I can ask is that you be well and never forget, this land is your home. And always will be, no matter what."

Yufitri smiled, returning the embrace as tightly as he could. "Thank you, Father."

The king wiped at the tears gathering in the wrinkles under his eyes. "Since I only have sons, I never imagined I would be giving away a bride."

"A bearded bride no less!" Yufitri added.

The king laughed and ruffled his hair. "You call that fuzz a beard, boy? You've got a ways to go before you catch up to your old man!"

They ended up talking for a while longer before the king retired for the night, and Yufitri returned to his room only to find an anxious Calixtus waiting for him.

He kissed the furrows between his brows. "We have my father's blessing," he said. "Now do you believe I won't leave you?"

Calixtus made a show of tapping his chin in thought. "I don't know," he said slyly. "Words are so cheap, after all."

"Then clearly we need some actions." Yufitri gave him a wolfish grin, putting the last of his clothes aside. "Come here. Let me *show* you how attached I've become."

After a month's time, Yufitri bid his family goodbye for the last time in what would be a long time. His brothers and father wished him all the best and saw them off, this time in a royal vessel of his very own.

Yufitri waved from the stern until they were completely out of sight.

"So!" He turned to Calixtus. "Are we returning to your castle, or are we headed for the capital?"

Calixtus, head wrapped once more, now in a proper cover of white linen, sighed wistfully. "In truth, I would like to go back to that castle. As much as it was a prison, at least it was a familiar one. And so, it is imperative we go to the capital, so I cannot later trick myself into not going at all."

"A wise decision."

"I hope so." He rubbed his arm. "I find myself afraid."

Yufitri rested his head against Calixtus's neck, his hands around his waist. "Of?"

"What if the fairies deceived me? What if there was no deal made? What if my parents simply abandoned me to the woods, and the fairies found me?

"I always told myself they had no reason to lie, but what if they did? What if a child who's told his parents left him to die isn't good enough for their needs? Or maybe they had no reason to lie, but by the same token, they had no reason not to?

"What if I'm not royalty at all?"

Yufitri squeezed him tightly. "Even if it was all a lie, what we have here and now is not. No matter what happens, I will stay with you."

"Even if—"

"No matter what! I think we've established you can't scrape me off that easily."

Calixtus sighed, relaxed into Yufitri's arms, and chuckled. "I hope not. What would I do without my lovely barnacle?"

The capital was a whirl of sounds and people. As his head and face were still shielded from the sun, Calixtus allowed Yufitri to do most of the talking. His accent was noticeable, but it served to make him interesting and exotic rather than a target for thieves.

Calixtus liked the way his mother language rolled off Yufitri's tongue, the auditory equivalent of adding foreign spices to a familiar dish, changing it just enough to be new and wonderful. They followed strangers' instructions to the castle entrance, the dark stone edifice looming over them like a great beast with a gaping maw.

The two entered, their hands clasped together for mutual support.

The guards on duty stopped their advance. "What brings you here, strangers? You are not from this land."

"Actually, I am." Calixtus removed his head covering, revealing his pale skin like that of the guards. "We're here to see the king."

The guards exchanged glances.

"There's been no king here for many years, stranger."

Calixtus frowned, his face turning ashen. "Then who rules this country now?"

"His widow. There was a rumor long ago that a son was born, but he disappeared. Died, I figure."

"We are here about that son," Calixtus pressed, his nails digging sharply into Yufitri's hand.

The guard raised an eyebrow. "The one I just told you about?"

Calixtus sighed, pinching the bridge of his nose. "I know how it sounds, I do, but tell the queen what I look like and explain it's about the son who was spirited away from her."

The guard looked to his companion, who frowned, eyebrows raised, and entered the throne room, letting the door shut behind him.

Yufitri could feel how strongly Calixtus trembled and had a fleeting urge to remove him from this nerve-wracking situation, wrap him up in a warm blanket, and give him gentle kisses until the shaking stopped. But Calixtus had to do this, and so Yufitri allowed him to use him as a lifeline, despite the bruises his hand would soon have.

The guard returned. "The queen will see you now."

Calixtus didn't move, his gaze fixed on the open door in front of him. Yufitri let go of his hand, grabbed his shoulders from behind, and pushed him forward into the room. "It'll be fine," he murmured in his ear. "Calm down. It'll be fine."

The queen was an old woman, though she perhaps wasn't quite as old as she looked. The years and sorrows she had suffered had scoured their way across her face and weighed heavily on her stooped shoulders. And yet, when she saw Calixtus enter the room, for a single moment, she looked young again.

She stood, leaning on an ornate cane, watching Calixtus and Yufitri enter. The front guardsman closed the door behind them with a thud that echoed through the chamber.

On unsteady feet, the queen hobbled to meet them halfway and brought her hand up to touch Calixtus's face. She ran her fingers across his cheekbones, around his chin. "These are my husband's," she said in a small voice. She touched his nose, his lips. "These are my sister's." Across his brow, his eyelids. "And these are mine."

And indeed they were. Straight, narrow brows and deep-set eyes.

"And you have the mark of my son's affliction." She ran her fingers through his pale-white hair, so like her own, despite his youth. Choking back a sob, she threw her arms around her son and held as tightly as her frail body could. He grasped her back just as tightly.

Yufitri took a few steps away, giving the two some space, and smiled to himself. After a short while, the queen pulled away and dabbed at her tears with a handkerchief. "Who is your companion, Calixtus?" she asked, looking toward Yufitri.

Calixtus introduced him. "Without this man, I would not be standing here right now," he said, touching Yufitri's arm.

The queen tipped her head forward. "This kingdom thanks you, Prince Yufitri. And I, as a mother, thank you."

He bowed in return. "It was nothing."

"No," she said sincerely. "It was everything."

Calixtus and his mother went to talk politics with her advisors, leaving Yufitri to his own devices for a few hours. He wandered the city, meeting people. He even met a fellow countryman and his wife, and they ended up talking for quite some time. The man advised Yufitri on what dishes to avoid, some of the holidays celebrated in this land, and what some of the stranger customs were. Some he already knew, but others surprised him.

As the sun set, Yufitri bid his new friends goodbye and returned to the castle. Calixtus was waiting in the entrance hall. "Did you get lost?" he asked.

"No, I met some of my kin, and the time got away from me. How did it go?"

Calixtus sighed and waved him over so they could walk to the guest chambers. "There's a lot to be done. I've never had formal training in politics or proper decorum, so that's the first thing the advisors want before I'm coronated. In addition, they want to use my reappearance as fuel for a marriage alliance."

Yufitri's heart stuttered. "What did you say to that?"

"That I'd have to think about it. In reality, of course, we need to discuss it."

"Of course." The atmosphere grew heavy around them, and Yufitri had to focus to keep his feet moving in the right direction. "Is that what we're going to discuss tonight?"

"I think we have to." Calixtus didn't sound excited by the prospect.

They arrived. The rooms were small with a fireplace in each as well as thick bed curtains and blankets. Calixtus undressed, hung up his clothes, and crawled into one of the beds. Yufitri joined him and curled up against his back.

"So," he said after a moment.

"So," Calixtus agreed. He took the hand resting on his arm and twined the fingers together. "I'm going to need an heir."

Yufitri sighed into the back of his neck. "I know... I don't suppose you have a sex change spell up your sleeve?"

Calixtus gave a small laugh. "No, that would require a fairy."

"Damn." He paused. "I would carry your child, though, if you needed me to."

Calixtus voice softened, and he rolled over so they were face-to-face. "As convenient as that would be, I would miss you as you are now." He skritched Yufitri's beard, enjoying the rough softness of it.

Yufitri smiled at the touch, and he grabbed Calixtus's hand so he could kiss the palm. Then he sobered. "So, what do you want to do, Calixtus? I can only share your burdens if you offer them."

Calixtus shrugged, his expression morose. "In a perfect world, nothing. But this country's position has been precarious since my father's death, so a marriage alliance would be the perfect opportunity to begin to repair that."

"What kind of woman would you want?"

He sighed, bumping his forehead into Yufitri's. "You."

"Come on, be serious."

"A woman who can conceive quickly and easily so I won't have to sleep with her again."

Yufitri chuckled, then kissed the tip of his nose. "I'm sure you'll be able to find a bride who's as disinterested in you as you are in her."

He laughed, and the tight lines of worry faded from his face. "One can hope," he said warmly. "But let's be finished with this conversation now."

Yufitri hummed his assent and buried his face in Calixtus's hair. "I will get jealous," he said quietly. "But I will love you no matter what."

"I will too."

The castle in the woods became Yufitri's domain and Calixtus's refuge. When life in the capital became hectic or unhappy, he would return to the woods and Yufitri's arms.

His wife, an older princess from a nearby kingdom, was given a small manse of her own after their son, Leon, was born and grown to young adulthood. Calixtus made sure she wanted for nothing and was free to do as she wished. The rumor was she had two lovers who were not her husband, but she would never allow such baseless accusations to sully her legacy.

Prince Leon enjoyed the woods and his uncle Yufitri's company. Yufitri taught him of swordplay, and of wrestling, of camping, and of hunting. They spent many summers together, exploring the forest and finding bits of fairy magic left behind. And when they would return, muddy and exhilarated, Calixtus would laugh and usher them into the washroom where he would listen to the full account of their adventures as the spell hands wiped them clean.

As a king, Calixtus was dedicated and conscientious. Despite his off-putting appearance, he soon won the people's trust and faith. Although whispers about his romantic life followed him his entire reign, he never let them distract from his work, and history would remember him fondly long after his death.

So, I suppose it could be said that Yufitri and Calixtus, and their various loved ones, all lived happily ever after.

A Step Apart and
a World Away

To those who have ever wished to become invisible.

Naomhan hated carriage rides. They were too loud, too smelly, too hot. "Don't lean out of the window like an unruly dog, Naomhan," his father said, his tone bored as he glanced up from the book he was reading. "And stop fidgeting."

Biting back a groan of discomfort, Naomhan slid down into his seat, putting his hands under his thighs exactly like his tutors taught him to constrain his restless wriggles. (But *why* couldn't he wriggle, here in this private space with only him and his father? His skin itched with restless energy.)

Naomhan was a young man of twelve, leaving the sleepy country estate of his childhood for the first time, bound for the castle town where his uncle, the king, reigned. His father, the Duke Diarmad, the king's younger brother, was to become a teacher to the Prince Fachtna, the king's only son and heir—Naomhan's cousin.

As the carriage rattled and snorted its way through the town's gate, Naomhan was thrust into a myriad of new sensations: yelling all around the carriage, the *thunk* of many wheels on cobblestone, and the acrid smell of too many animals in too small a space. He squinched his eyes shut, trying to block it out, but it was too much, too much, too much—

The carriage rumbled to a stop, and Naomhan forced his eyes open despite how the light made them burn and water. His body ached with tension, his hands sweating beneath the wool of his trousers. "Come, Naomhan," his father said and stepped out of the carriage, holding the door open for his son.

The sounds of the town were lesser here, within the castle gardens, but it was still new and overwhelming.

"You must be on your best behavior for the king and the prince, Naomhan," Diarmad said sternly, and they stepped into the castle proper while the carriage rumbled away behind them.

Naomhan watched it go before he nodded to his father and kept tight to his right side as he'd been taught. He kept his face pointed straight ahead, eyes darting around as he absorbed the chaos of sound and movement before him—servants bustling and busy, moving every which way in their various duties, like watching an anthill. It took Naomhan a moment to find his words. "Of course, Father. Is it true that the prince is very handsome?"

The duke smiled, amused by his son's enduring love of beauty. It reminded him of his late wife. "So they say. It has been many years since I laid eyes upon him myself."

"But you're the king's brother. Don't you get invited to all the balls?"

Diarmad chuckled. "I do, but I prefer our estate. Though I suppose this year you are old enough to begin attending yourself."

"Does that mean I'll have to get a new suit? And shoes?" Naomhan asked seriously. He squeezed his father's sleeve. He hated new clothing. It rubbed his skin raw, and he wasn't allowed to scratch.

"And a haircut," Diarmad said with a laugh, ruffling his son's hair even as the boy flinched away at the unexpected touch.

When they entered the castle, they were soon greeted by the king, who kissed his brother's cheeks and thanked him for coming. His gray eyes twinkled as they fell upon Naomhan.

"And look at the lad! I haven't seen you since your christening! The picture of your mother, you are."

Naomhan knew. There was a portrait of her in his bedroom. He bowed. "Thank you, Your Majesty. It is an honor to meet you properly."

"The honor is mine," he said warmly, patting him on the shoulder before pulling Diarmad away into a private discussion. Naomhan was free to wander, so he did, peering into open rooms and making a game out of staying out of the guards' sight. Blissfully unwatched, he walked on tiptoe through the halls, trailing his fingers over the tapestries he passed. The weave was soft and tight, his skin tingling pleasantly as he went. From the garden, his ear caught a woman's voice, little more than a gasp. "Oh, Prince Fachtna...we mustn't!"

Wondering what was going on, Naomhan crept through the garden and found Fachtna sitting on a bench with a pretty young woman, her blonde hair braided with flowers. It was she who had spoken, her voice high and breathy, almost a whisper.

The Prince Fachtna was indeed handsome with straight, red-gold hair and pink-white skin dusted with freckles. His nose was long with a single bend when viewed in profile. He wore his finery with ease without any of Naomhan's twitching.

Naomhan watched them from a bend in the path that kept him out of sight. Fachtna murmured something too low to hear, and that made the woman's face soften, a pink flush rising in her cheeks.

And then they were kissing. They kissed in a way that made something stir inside Naomhan's belly, something hot, prickly, and strange. He ducked away and hurried back inside, his heart pounding a staccato against his ears.

When Naomhan formally met the prince that evening at dinner, his ears burned as he bowed. Hearing his name from that handsome, well-kissed mouth turned his knees to jelly.

It took some time for Naomhan to understand what the strange feelings he'd encountered were, but when he did, it was with both the joy of revelation and dread of certain doom.

Fachtna did not like this interloper of a dukeling, nor did he like his uncle the duke. He was a young prince of fifteen, a proper man but for the growing he still had yet to do, but Duke Diarmad treated him as a child, yammering on and on about useless things like etiquette and "behavior expected of a prince." Pah, he was to be *king*; it was *his* behavior that determined etiquette. If he declared all people should address the duke as "the puke," he could *do* that.

"Of course you could!" his mother told him, stroking his hair as they sat in conference as they so often did, for Fachtna found public dining tedious.

"Can't you make him *leave*, Mother? I don't need him, nor Father's prattling. I'm going to be king! Then, everyone will have to do as I say!"

"Exactly so, my angel," she said and kissed his temple. "You will be a fine king indeed."

The courtiers, too, knowing this single prince would one day become their king, went out of their way to appease him, to ignore his selfish outbursts or rude behaviors, to the king's constant frustration. But his pleas to be stricter with his son came far too late, for Fachtna had already learned how not to listen.

And so, contented and coddled, Fachtna grew into a perfectly handsome terror.

Naomhan was seventeen when the Oster ambassador came, and Fachtna, twenty. He had been nursing his love quietly for those long years, despite Fachtna's frequent dalliances with the young noblewomen of court. After all, that was what it meant to be loyal, wasn't it? To love despite the frequent little hurts of seeing a new woman on his arm or the brief flash of a love bite upon his neck?

When the ambassador and his retinue arrived, it was Naomhan who greeted him at the entrance to the royal study, speaking the few words in Oster he knew as his interpreter left to meet with the kings to confer briefly. The ambassador was so pleased by Naomhan's disjointed, awkward Oster that he bowed and removed his hat. "It is pleasure to meet you, Prince Fachtna." He spoke with a thick accent, stumbling over unfamiliar sounds.

"Oh no," Naomhan said with a smile. "I am not the prince, my lord." But while he was speaking, Fachtna stood, his pale skin blotchy in anger.

"Of course he's not the prince! Look at the man before you, dressed in the royal colors, bearing the ring of his status!" He flashed his ring marking him as his father's heir before clenching it into a fist. "I should have you strung up by your toes for such an indignity!"

The ambassador, a man who had at first appeared jovial with his apple-round cheeks and broad belly, frowned deeply and turned to Naomhan, reaching for his hand. "Who this?" he asked, glancing from Fachtna back to Naomhan. "Prince, he have me fear. Call guarden?"

"My lord, I am *not* the prince," Naomhan tried again, but he patted the man's hand and gave Fachtna a wide-eyed, pleading look. "*This* man is Prince Fachtna."

"Yes, yes, Prince Fachtna. You help?" He was still addressing Naomhan.

Again and again, Fachtna raised his voice in anger, and the ambassador held tight to Naomhan in apprehension, asking him to call the guards.

At last, the king and the translator returned to the room. The king, in a stern voice, cut through the overlapping conversations with a firm, "What is going on here?"

"Your Majesty," the ambassador said with a bow before launching into fluent Oster, explaining the situation to his interpreter, who glanced between Fachtna and Naomhan as he struggled to understand.

"Which one of you is the prince?" the interpreter asked, and Naomhan immediately gestured to Fachtna, who simultaneously pointed to himself with murder in his eyes.

With the king's stormy expression making Naomhan's ears burn with the threat of punishment, the interpreter explained the situation to the ambassador, who raised his eyebrows with each word until they all but reached his hairline.

He turned to Fachtna and gave him a sharp once-over, then turned to the king, disapproval curling his lip. "You understand my confusing, Your Majesty," he said.

The king nodded slowly, his anger simmering below the surface. "I understand completely, my lord. And my son will *apologize* for his rudeness."

With the face of a man swallowing a lemon, Fachtna apologized, but his own glare fell to Naomhan. Pretty, perfect Naomhan, who had tricked the ambassador just to humiliate him!

After his father's meeting with the ambassador, Fachtna was summoned to his father's chambers where he was lectured for nearly an hour, his arms crossed, thinking only of how much he wanted to strangle his cousin for causing such an indignity. When the king finished his lecture, Fachtna burst into Naomhan's chambers. He grabbed him up by the hair. Naomhan gasped and twisted in the prince's grip, but Fachtna held tight, naked hatred in his storm-gray eyes. "You will no longer greet guests," he hissed, bringing Naomhan up to his face. "If you happen to be in the room, you shall say nothing. You shall pretend to be a mute, or I shall cut out your tongue myself. Am I understood? You are a duke's son, but *I* am your prince."

"I understand, Your Highness," Naomhan whispered even as his heart broke.

Without kindness, Fachtna threw him to the floor. "Good." He shook strands of Naomhan's dark hair from his hand and swept out of the room, leaving silence and sadness in his wake. Naomhan gathered himself up in his arms and wept.

When Diarmad heard of the prince's behavior, he was beside himself with anger. Swiftly, Naomhan was packed up and sent home to the forest estate, far from the castle and the prince's temper.

In many ways, it was good to be home. Naomhan had never grown used to the hustle and bustle of the castle, so it was also good to be back in the gardens his mother had planted, able to sit once again in quiet and peace. The garden was nicely arranged, full of pleasant smells and textures throughout the year. He wondered sometimes if his mother had been like him—so in tune with the tiny details of the world everyone else seemed to miss. As he sat beneath his mother's favorite willow tree, reading his books, he was free of the whirling confusion that was the court and Fachtna's hatred and was content.

One day, some months after his return, he was sitting in the garden, playing a soft tune on his flute when something curled tightly around his leg. Looking down, he was shocked to see a snake, its body mossy-green yet golden where the light hit it, wrapping itself around his ankle and up his calf. He almost screamed until the gardener came rushing by, yelling about a snake, which startled him into silence.

"My lord, have you seen a large green snake? I've been trying to catch and kill it all morning," the gardener said, walking up behind Naomhan's bench.

The snake stared up at him beseechingly with dark eyes.

"No, I haven't. I'm sorry."

Cursing under his breath, the gardener marched away. Opening his lunch basket, Naomhan set it beside his leg. "Go on, go inside," he coaxed. "I'll protect you."

To his surprise, as if it understood, the snake unwound itself and coiled into the basket, its dark eyes gleaming from the shadows. Naomhan closed the lid, picked up the basket, and brought it to his room.

Once there, Naomhan set to work making the snake a small nest in the corner of his bedchamber. He used his own too-small childhood clothing and some pillows in a basket that had once been a bed to a dog he'd had as a child.

He called down to the kitchens for leftover meat from lunch and fed the snake the scraps, smiling as he watched it eat. "There," he said once the snake had ceased eating and was curled contentedly over the pillow. He smiled sadly as he knelt there beside it. "A bit of kindness never hurt anyone." He thought of Fachtna, daydreaming about what kindness from the prince might look like.

The snake watched him with an unwavering gaze.

"If you permit, I shall keep you until you shed your skin. I would like to keep it."

Its tongue flickered. He took it as confirmation.

A t the king's court, the young women lamented the loss of Naomhan.

"He was such a gentle lad and so polite! Always keeping his face down, what a gentleman!"

"Why couldn't *he* be the prince instead?"

At every mention of him, Fachtna's jealousy twisted him more and more. It was he who held the power here, second only to his father the king. They should care nothing for a simple duke's son, especially when he was already gone! He went to his mother and complained bitterly that Naomhan had beguiled them all. Perhaps he had even used magic to turn people's hearts against his betters. He was related to the royal family, after all. Perhaps he meant to usurp the crown. Fachtna wouldn't put it past the twitchy little sneak.

The queen agreed as she always did. "You should go hunting in the forest with only your most trusted guards," she suggested. "And see the truth of whether it truly is magic he is using. If he means to turn the court against you, it is only fit you prevent him from doing so."

Fachtna nodded grimly. It was his duty to the kingdom to rid it of witches after all. Maybe that would make his father understand he was no longer worth lecturing like a lisping child.

Some weeks later, Naomhan said goodbye to the snake, which raised its head as he left, its tongue flickering, but he paid it no mind. He went for a walk through the forest. After some time, he turned, confused at the sound of the royal hunting horn and the baying of the hounds. As he approached the sound, he was surprised to see Fachtna bringing his horse to stop outside the gates of the estate. He looked at Naomhan and smiled.

"Naomhan!" the prince greeted. "It has been too long! Come, hunt with me. I have a horse for you."

Naomhan eyed the stallion warily. The prince had never before been so kind.

"Come," Fachtna said again and offered him a hand with a warmth and charm that made Naomhan's knees buckle. "I'm sorry for acting such a beast before."

Naomhan relaxed and smiled. "It's forgiven, Your Highness."

They rode deep into the wood, far past where he usually walked, the dogs barking ahead of them. It was too loud to speak, but Naomhan didn't mind, filled with the rush of excitement at spending this sort of time with Fachtna. The dogs sighted a hare in the brush and took off after it, yelping and howling, the horses thundering along behind. Then, without warning, Fachtna whistled, and he and his men pulled off into the woods, leaving Naomhan alone. Suddenly fearful, he glanced around, his horse slowing to a walk.

"Your Highness?" Naomhan called.

There was no answer but for the distant barking of the dogs.

Steeling himself, Naomhan followed the sound, dreadful anticipation clawing at his gut. He stumbled across a clearing where Fachtna's men stood, dismounted, swords drawn. There was no sign of Fachtna.

"Is something wrong?" he asked, sliding from the stallion's back. "Is His Highness hurt?"

They didn't answer, only advanced, raising their blades. Biting back tears that sprang unbidden to his eyes, he cast around for a stick, pointing it at them in shaking hands. "Stay away!" he ordered, though the tremble of his voice weakened his command.

A few of the men hesitated, their blades dipping toward the ground, but others still advanced.

Naomhan stumbled backward until the trunk of a tree stopped his retreat. His heart was beating so loudly that, at first, he didn't hear the roar rumbling through the forest, causing the men to stop.

With a great snarling and crashing, a lion appeared, huge and covered in shaggy golden fur. It wasted no time in leaping upon the men. Naomhan turned away from the gruesome sight but couldn't escape the warm wash of blood that splattered across his face.

When the screaming stopped, he dared a look, trying not to move for fear the lion would attack him next.

But instead, the great beast simply sat, observant, staring at him with dark, sad eyes for a long moment as it licked the blood from its maw.

His heart pounding, Naomhan stared back, then flinched as the lion stepped forward, with its mouth open. But instead of biting, it licked the blood from Naomhan's face, its tongue sandpaper-rough but warm.

"Th-thank you," Naomhan whispered.

The lion butted its head against his and once more bounded away into the forest.

It was then Naomhan saw Fachtna standing on the other end of the clearing, his eyes burning with rage and fear. "You *are* using magic," he hissed.

What? For a moment, Naomhan stared, mute. "I don't know why the lion saved me," he rasped, his throat dry as he turned his eyes to the blood-strewn leaves of the clearing, "but why did *your* men…" He trailed off, the realization dropping like a stone into his stomach. "You told them to kill me."

Fachtna sneered. "I wasn't expecting your bodyguard, but no matter. If you ever return to the castle, I will see you burned for the witch you are."

Naomhan dropped his head. "Once, I would have died for you gladly, Your Highness. But very well, you shall never see me again."

Scoffing, the prince departed, and Naomhan walked home alone, lost in thought. He could go to the king, but what if the king didn't believe him? He was certainly capable of frustration with Fachtna, but this…this was more than frustration. Fachtna had— Fachtna had tried to have him *killed*. What if the king decided Fachtna was in the right? He wasn't a witch, but the lion *seemed* to have obeyed him. Why would the king believe him over his own son? And surely that wrath could also fall upon his own father if he explained poorly. He tangled his hands in his hair and pulled the scalp taut, the pain releasing enough of the anxiety to keep him walking.

Listlessly, he returned to his rooms, deciding the best thing to do would be to depart this land entirely and never return. Fachtna wouldn't be able to kill him, and he wouldn't go after his father (hopefully) because Naomhan would still be out of his way. As he sat and removed his boots, he saw a light shining from beneath the door of his bedroom.

Slowly, warily, Naomhan crept forward and threw the door open. The snake sat on his bed, its body glowing and glistening. As Naomhan reached toward it, it wound itself around his arm, up to his mouth where it pressed itself against his lips. It was smooth and cool, pleasant to the touch, but startled, Naomhan flung it away all the same.

Gasping, Naomhan stumbled back, the snake falling to the ground. And yet, before it hit, something large burst forth from the snakeskin, then crouched on the ground as bits of the white fell around it.

Kneeling before Naomhan's bed was a shining, golden man, dressed in the sheerest, softest white silks, his body all but dripping with gems and gold.

Mouth dry, Naomhan's knees nearly gave way. But the man caught his hand and held him fast. It *hurt*. He kept trying to pull away, and soon, the man let him. "Be not afraid, dear Naomhan," he said gently, standing and fixing Naomhan with a dark, sad gaze. "I am the snake you rescued from the garden, and I am the lion that saved your life from the prince's assassins. I am the fairy Tairis, and you freed me from the cruel curse which prevented my speech."

"With a kiss?" Naomhan asked weakly. Unable to meet the fairy's steady gaze, Naomhan kept his own on the fairy's mouth.

"With a kiss," Tairis confirmed, a flush rising in his cheeks. "Forgive my boldness, but I wanted so badly to speak with you."

Dumbly, Naomhan nodded his forgiveness. He frowned. "How did you come to be cursed?" he asked.

Tairis smiled, but it was forced. Naomhan could tell by the stiffness in his jaw. "My friends believed they were being funny."

"Forgive me, but they do not sound like very good friends."

Tairis's smile turned radiant. "You are noble and kind, Naomhan. I wish to reward you."

"Y-you have already saved my life," Naomhan said, casting his eyes downward, unable to even look at his face anymore. "I need no further reward."

Long fingers rested under Naomhan's chin and tilted his face up toward the fairy. "And yet I wish to give one," he said, his dark eyes sparkling. "Shall I make you wealthier than the kings of the golden south? Shall I turn your handsome face irresistible, so you can wrap anyone around your finger with only a glance? I can make you a great painter, or singer, or musician—any skill you wish. Simply say the word, and it is yours."

"As lovely as those sound, I am content with myself as I am, Tairis," Naomhan said softly, trying not to stare too long into those familiar, dark eyes. Staring was rude. He remembered the painful stroke of a switch upon his knuckles when he had stared too long.

But Tairis didn't seem to mind and stroked the back of one finger over Naomhan's cheek, drawing his gaze once more.

"Then I can give you a bit of fey magic," he said, and Naomhan's heart leapt with excitement, despite a lifetime of warnings against a fairy bearing gifts. But surely those gifts were not the same as receiving only the magic itself? "You would be able to fly across the world with only a thought as well as pass through any obstacles in your path. Be warned: this power easily corrupts those not pure of spirit, but you, my dear Naomhan, I suspect you will be just fine."

And because it aligned so neatly with what he already wished to do, Naomhan said, "Very well. Please, give me some of your magic."

Tairis raised three fingers and passed them over Naomhan's eyes and down his face three times, then finished with a kiss in the center of his forehead. The tingle of magic seared through him, blooming from his forehead and down to his fingers and toes. A fierce joy bubbled up in his chest, and he found himself floating upward, anchored only by Tairis's hand.

"One more gift," Tairis said, and plucked a red cap from the air, three bright green feathers sewn into the brim. "When you wear this cap, you will be unseen by all but myself, including other fairies." He tugged Naomhan back to the ground and placed the cap upon his head. "Go, test your gift," he said warmly.

So, Naomhan imagined himself at a grove of wild roses he'd seen a few days before, and before he could think too deeply, his body was flying through the air, passing through leaves and branches without even leaving a rustle of wind.

When he found the roses, he plucked three closest to full bloom—one pink, one red, and one white—then wrapped them carefully in his handkerchief to protect from the thorns. He imagined himself home and flew off.

Tairis smiled as he returned. "So? What do you think?" he asked.

Naomhan grinned and held out the three roses. "A thanks, for the cap."

For a long moment, Tairis only stared in mute surprise before he smiled and took the roses from Naomhan's hand and breathed deeply of their scents before blowing into them. They opened until they were at peak bloom. With a touch of Tairis's hand, the thorns fell away, and vanished into the air.

Plucking the white one from the bunch, he tucked it into Naomhan's shirt. "This one will make sure you are never poor. Simply turn it upside down and shake it. Whichever land you find yourself in, that is what coin will fall." The pink one, he tucked into Naomhan's belt, a sadness coming over his face. "Hold this beneath your lover's throat, and you will know if they love you truly." The red one, he wound into Naomhan's dark hair. "This will allow you to call upon me, should you ever have need. Simply speak my name, and I shall fly to you."

"You give me too much. Please, allow me to give you something in return," Naomhan insisted, transfixed by the sadness in those eyes.

After a moment of thought, Tairis carded his hand through Naomhan's hair, drawing him into a kiss. Naomhan's heart thudded heavily in his chest, his eyes fluttering shut as the kiss deepened, Tairis's tongue flickering out for only a moment as if he were once again the snake. Warmth flooded through Naomhan, and he wrapped his arms around Tairis's neck. He had never liked to be touched, but Tairis somehow was an exception. His lips were soft as flower petals, and pliant as new spring leaves.

The fairy pulled back. "Be well and keep your heart. I hope to see you again," he said, his voice rushed, his gaze distant, and in a blink, Naomhan was alone as if there had never been anyone there at all.

He raised his fingers to his lips, a new sort of heat coiling deep within his belly.

At the castle, Fachtna seethed. He paced about his chambers like a wild man, clawing his fingers through his hair. Naomhan had slipped from his grasp, and now his men would fear him more than Fachtna himself since he had some witch's familiar in that lion.

He tipped over a nearby table, but the crashing of the fine crystal and shattering of porcelain gave him no satisfaction. He could imagine it. Naomhan, his father's men at his back, riding into town astride the lion, waving a rebel's banner. The damned courtiers would turn; Fachtna just knew it. They *fawned* over him for reasons Fachtna could not even fathom. The boy was *strange*, too polite, his gaze too knowing. Perhaps he was even a changeling, a curse upon the kingdom, meant to destroy them all.

Sure, Naomhan was gone, for now, so he said. But Fachtna needed to kill him, but *how*?

A thought stopped him in his tracks. No, he didn't need to *kill* Naomhan. If Naomhan sought the throne, all Fachtna had to do was prove his own worth. Then the courtiers wouldn't turn, nor would the people.

He would prove himself worthy of the throne, to his father, and to everyone of the kingdom. But the question remained of *how*?

He went, as he so often did, to his mother and explained his troubles. His mother confirmed his suspicions. "I never trusted that Diarmad," she said, her eyes narrowing. "He's always lusted after the throne, despite his words to the contrary, and he's the quiet, conniving sort. Maybe he even turned his son to black magic when he could not get the throne himself."

"What shall I do, Mother?"

She hummed thoughtfully, tilting her head from side to side, stroking her fingers through his hair. "You should go on a quest," she said after a long moment. "And I think I may know one perfectly suited."

Fitting the cap tightly on his head, Naomhan took one last look at his rooms and then one last walk through the garden. He would miss this land, and yet... He was excited to see the world.

He imagined the sprawling city he'd seen only in books, the towering, ornate cathedrals, and the intoxicating smell of fresh pastries. The city of Tateaux, the capital of Norance.

Beneath his feet, the wind rose, and he was off, streaking across the cloudy sky. Below him, trees rushed past, then abruptly gave way to sparkling blue ocean. He twisted around and saw the white-gray clouds encircling the Highlands as if locking them away from the rest of the world.

He flew for some time, just long enough to wonder how far he had yet to go before the city began to unfold beneath his feet. He landed without a sound on the cobbled streets, staring about in wonder. People unconsciously walked around him as they bustled here and there, attending to their daily business.

Smiling at the truth of being unseen, Naomhan held himself and rocked back and forth, giddy with the freedom from the tutor's switch. He did all of the things he'd been told not to. He scratched and rocked and shook his hands, enjoying their boneless flopping. But when he yelled, people turned to look in alarm, so he quickly quieted.

He wasn't a complete ghost. Still, he was unseen. Suppressing his excited laughter, Naomhan set off to explore.

He spent several days in the city, admiring the architecture and fashions, eavesdropping as people went by speaking a variation of the court tongue. When he hungered, the white rose provided the money to stop and eat at one of the many cafes and restaurants sitting along the river. It was almost as pleasant as his daydreams.

With money as no object, he hopped from inn to inn, experiencing the best luxuries the city had to offer. He imagined he acquired something of a reputation as a wayward prince. The thought made him smile until he remembered Prince Fachtna wished him dead.

Suddenly, a bustling city served only to remind him of a life he could never lead again. He departed Tateaux, enjoying the lush countryside and farmland of Norance. The weather was sweet and clear in the cooling rush of autumn. He kept his cap in his bag, letting the breezes tousle his hair and whisper over his face like the phantom touch of a fairy he might never see again.

He passed through villages and hamlets, always generous with his coin (he could always acquire more, after all), making friendly acquaintances in his wandering.

As he approached the wide river between Norance and its neighbor, Deurich, he passed through a thick, dense wood, blacker than any he'd ever known. As he traveled, he encountered a young man, hardly older than Naomhan himself, dressed in rich clothing, that was now torn and dirty, curled in the embrace of a tree's roots, sobbing.

Filled with compassion, Naomhan knelt beside him. "My dear man, why are you crying?"

With tear-streaked cheeks, the man flinched away, surprised by Naomhan's presence. And yet, he soon surged forward and took hold of his shirt much to Naomhan's alarm. "Please, kind lord, the woman I love, my sweet Agathe, is being married off to a rich but wretched man by order of her parents. I attempted to free her and was driven off for my troubles, forbidden to see her again. The wedding is tonight, and I am helpless to interfere. Is there anything you can do, my lord? Anything at all?"

Naomhan smiled and patted the man's shoulders, pulling himself free. "It so happens that I can. Tell me, where is the wedding being held?"

The young man, who introduced himself as Georges, gave him directions and descriptions of those involved, his eyes fever bright with hope. "Can you truly help, Lord? Forgive me, what might I call you?"

Naomhan pondered. His true name was perhaps best kept to himself for fear of attracting Fachtna's ire or the eye of his father—both of whom would undoubtedly try to seek him out. Instead, he considered the language of the Highlands, landing upon a word that perhaps described what the fairy Tairis had made him. "You may know me simply as Sìogaidh."

Georges tilted his head. "Chigé?" he tried to repeat in an accent that made Naomhan chuckle.

"Close enough," he said and walked off toward the estate. Once Georges was out of sight, he placed the cap on his head and imagined himself in the manor's dining hall. Despite the splendid music and the pleasant smell of the feast, he soon spotted the maiden in question, seated beside a man who must have been nearly three times her age. Fat with his wealth and happily partaking of the food behind him, he ignored the girl who dabbed silently at her tears.

Naomhan frowned and walked over to the high table. The bridegroom had great, swollen gouty feet, the joints too large to fit comfortably within the shoes laid beside him. Naomhan coughed at the sight, his stomach churning. Agathe turned at the sound, peering through him for the source of the noise.

Instead of addressing her, however, he turned his attention to the parents—the true villains in this drama. To her credit, the mother looked abashed, her gaze down as she pushed the food around her plate. However, the father banged his hand upon the table, hissing at Agathe, "Smile, girl; you are marrying tonight!"

Shockingly, the thought didn't seem to cheer her.

Naomhan leaned in close to her mother's ear. "Know that should your daughter marry this man, a curse shall fall upon your house and all of its descendants," he whispered, dropping his voice to its deepest, most threatening tone.

She screamed and fell, clutching her ear. "This marriage is cursed!" she shrieked. "I knew it from the start!" The cheery music suddenly stopped.

Her husband laughed at her distress. "It is only the wine, woman!"

Naomhan grinned and put a heavy hand on the man's shoulder before whispering, "It is truly?"

Now his turn to wail, he looked about for any possible source, but he saw no one. "A voice!" he gasped. "A voice from the air!"

Naomhan spoke loud enough to be heard by most of the people gathered. "This marriage is cursed! For this girl has already a man who loves her truly! Fetch him from the wood and bring him forth!"

For a long moment, no one moved or even breathed.

Finally, in a shaky voice, Agathe's father turned to his guards. "Fetch the young man and bring him here. Now!"

The now-former bridegroom was outraged. "Now see here—" he began, but as he rose, Naomhan stood upon his ugly, swollen feet and caused the man to howl in pain.

Seized suddenly by a fierce sense of power, Naomhan grinned, shoving the man to the ground. He could do *anything*. No longer was he cowed by his father's expectations or his tutor's switch or his love and fear of Fachtna.

Naomhan advanced on the man, enjoying the fright in his eyes. He could do *anything*.

From across the room, there was a flash of golden light, and a tiny little bird fluttered from the hall, out through an open window. Somehow, he was reminded of Tairis and paused, taking a deep breath.

This time seeing the old man, whimpering as he clutched at his feet, Naomhan was filled with compassion. He knelt and helped the man sit up. Tears leaked from the former bridegroom's eyes, his throat working as he looked desperately for the hands that had pushed him upright.

The door opened, and Georges burst inside, looking around frantically. There was rush of air as Agathe ran past to meet him. The two lovers fell into each other's arms, Agathe weeping and sobbing in relief and happiness.

Begrudgingly, her father gave his blessing, and the former bridegroom gathered his people and left.

Naomhan ducked into a hallway and removed the cap from his head once he was out of sight. He returned to the dining room and clapped a hand on Georges's shoulder. "Looks like I didn't need to do anything," he said.

Georges smiled at him and shrugged while he rocked Agathe gently in his arms.

"Take care, both of you," Naomhan said and left, replacing his cap as soon as he was around the bend.

Instead of continuing on into Deurich, which Naomhan thought of as a strict and colorless place, he imagined the city of Merenze, tucked away into the southern mountains. He imagined the ruins of an ancient empire, a lazy river and relaxed people, and a warm sun overhead.

And then he flew, the patchwork of farms rushing past beneath him, close enough to touch, though he passed through them without even a whisper. The mountains grew below, and he tilted upward to follow their path—snow beginning to swirl around him as he flew on and on.

Once over the mountain peaks, he slowed and sank as a city opened beneath his feet. He landed without a sound. Despite how far away it was, the ocean glittered blue on the horizon.

Naomhan stepped into an alley out of view, thinking about love. He wished to drive Fachtna from his heart and find a love as strong as Georges and Agathe's. Frowning, he touched the red rose, the one which could call Tairis to his side.

But the stories warned of such liaisons. The fair folk are fickle, they warned. The fair folk are never so generous as they seem.

He put it away and instead took out the white one, turning it over to pour fresh coin into his money pouch. When it was sufficiently heavy, Naomhan put the rose away and removed his cap, tucked it into his bag, and stepped out to explore the city and maybe find a new love.

Playing the wayward prince, Naomhan attended parties. Parties had never been something Naomhan liked, but being able to disappear and escape whenever he wished gave him a confidence like never before. And these parties were home to many beautiful people, men and women alike, but he found himself captivated not by the nobility but by one of the dancers.

He had long, fine limbs and a square, handsome face. As a dancer, he entertained at many of the noble parties Naomhan attended. For weeks, Naomhan watched him, falling in love with the way he moved and the way his long, black hair fell over his shoulders when he was still.

One party, seven weeks after he had arrived in Merenze, Naomhan announced it was his eighteenth birthday. The attendees toasted him, teasing that he should've told them so they could have made it a proper birthday feast. They plied him with drink and overwhelming attention until Naomhan was a giggling heap upon a couch, the room rocking pleasantly as he swirled the wine in his glass.

The dancer approached and took the wine from his hand to keep it from spilling. "Careful," he said, and *oh*, even his voice was lovely. Naomhan giggled helplessly. "I heard you are the guest of honor tonight."

"It's my birthday," Naomhan explained. He couldn't stop the staring any longer. The dancer was so beautiful; it was probably rude to look away. Or perhaps it *should* have been? Naomhan didn't know.

"Well, happy birthday, then. I've seen you at many of these parties, and yet I don't know your name." He was smiling still. Apparently, he didn't mind the staring.

"I don't know yours either," Naomhan said, fluttering his eyelashes. "You can call me Sìogaidh."

"Scighe?" he repeated, his handsome face wrinkled in confusion, and Naomhan giggled at the accent.

"Close enough," he said, patting the dancer's cheek. "And what can I call you?"

"Erasmo," he said with a charming smile. "Shall I help you home, my lord?" He offered a hand.

"Your help would be most appreciated."

And if Naomhan leaned on him a bit too much, well, he could blame the drink.

He was staying at one of the luxurious inns meant for traveling nobility, and Erasmo whistled appreciatively as they entered the fine chambers Naomhan called his own.

The drink made him bold. "You can stay if you wish," Naomhan said as Erasmo turned to leave. "I have admired your dancing for so long, but I've only just begun to appreciate the beauty of your voice."

Erasmo smirked as he walked to Naomhan and crowded him up against the back of a low couch with Naomhan's spine curling slightly as he leaned over it. Erasmo's hand came around to steady him. "Shall we only talk then, my lord Scighe?"

"God, I hope not," Naomhan gasped, his face afire.

Erasmo laughed as he brought their lips together.

They continued their kissing well into the bedroom until Erasmo had Naomhan spread out over the bed, his knees on either side of his hips. "Well, my lord, how would you like to continue?"

Naomhan trembled with excitement and anticipation. "I, I don't know. I am…inexperienced in this."

Erasmo smirked and lowered his head to nose and nibble along Naomhan's jaw. "Then shall I take the lead, my lord Scighe?"

Naomhan trembled and nodded. "Please," he whispered.

Erasmo was happy to oblige.

When Naomhan woke the next day, it was to a swollen, aching head. Erasmo had left, but there was a simple breakfast of bread, cheese, and grapes set out on the table when he emerged from the bedroom. He smiled and ate, eager for the next party to arrive.

However, that afternoon, as Naomhan was recovering from his hangover, there was a knock at the door. When he opened it, Erasmo walked in and pecked him on the cheek as he passed. "I'm happy to find you still here, my lord. I was hoping we could walk together before the sun passes and I have to work."

He offered an arm.

Grinning, Naomhan threaded his own through and leaned his head against Erasmo's shoulder. "That would be wonderful," he said.

As they walked through the city, Erasmo admired the clothing and jewelry in the shops they passed—never seriously, just window-shopping. Naomhan admired right along with him, enjoying the rich, glittering fashions of this part of the world, so different from the thick, heavy fabrics of the Highlands.

When they passed one shop, however, Erasmo gasped, his dark eyes sparkling as a shirt caught his eye. It was a dark, forest green, sewn through with bits of gem that glittered and sparkled like the distant sea. "Oh, if only," Erasmo sighed. "But the life of an entertainer is hard, and the money is poor."

Naomhan could agree the shirt was beautiful, and it would be gorgeous on Erasmo, bringing color to his dark eyes and olive skin. With a smile, he took Erasmo's hand and brought it to his lips. "Then allow this humble lord to give you a gift." Coin was nothing to him, after all.

Erasmo gasped in delight, and Naomhan flushed with the joy of giving.

And yet when Erasmo put it on, Naomhan could only imagine that dark hair as lighter, the skin paler, and the little lights of the gems becoming the glow of a fairy's power.

He kissed Erasmo to drive out thoughts of Tairis.

Soon, Naomhan was showering Erasmo with gifts. He took each with the delight of a child and answered them with kisses and the lingering promise of more to come.

And yet with each gift, Naomhan grew oddly emptier. Erasmo more and more didn't come to see him, only asking him to meet at some shop or restaurant, and then departing afterward.

After nearly a month of the widening gap between them, Naomhan drew out the pink rose, which could tell him truly of a lover's heart. He twirled it between his fingers, frowning. Truth was a terrifying thing under the right circumstances. He had seen Erasmo not two hours before at a party, and it had been as if they didn't yet know the other's name.

But eventually, he decided to do it and placed the cap upon his head. It was late at night, so Naomhan imagined Erasmo asleep, tired from the evening's festivities, his dark hair spread across his pillow.

Responding to his thoughts, his body rose and sped off into the night.

Naomhan flew into a tall, thin house, squeezed between two others and filled with sleeping people. He recognized other dancers and musicians from Erasmo's troupe. The magic led him to Erasmo's room where the man himself lay asleep, flat on his back, snoring slightly.

For a moment, Naomhan stared, admiring the curve of his neck, the straight line of his jaw, and the sharp bow of his lip before he took out the pink rose and held it beneath Erasmo's chin, a hair's breadth from his Adam's apple.

The rose, which had begun at full bloom, slowly closed until it was little more than a bud, and truth indeed was a wicked thing.

Tears stinging his eyes, Naomhan put the rose away and turned to leave out the window when the door creaked open behind him.

One of the musicians entered, a young man with plain, unremarkable features. His eyes were deep-set, color lost to the shadow of the night, and his hair was loosely curled, pulled back from his face in a short tail.

The musician bent over Erasmo's bed, touching his lips to his forehead.

In shock and rage, Naomhan prepared to attack the man assaulting his lover, but Erasmo woke and *smiled* at the man, pulling him into a proper kiss as Naomhan, invisible, watched in numb shock.

"Hello, lover," Erasmo said, sitting up so the man could sit beside him. "How went your private show?"

"Well enough. And your affair with the little prince?" The musician said this with a smirk. "Is he truly as innocent as you say?"

"He doesn't suspect a thing," Erasmo said with a laugh. "It's clear he's starved for affection. I feel almost bad for taking advantage. He's sweet."

"And rich," the musician added wryly.

"And rich," Erasmo agreed. He leaned contentedly against the man's shoulder. "Thanks to my little Prince Scighe, soon we'll have enough to leave this wretched place."

"Together." The musician wound their fingers together.

Naomhan's heart beat hot and cold, rage and despair warring. His fingers itched for Erasmo's throat to punish him for using Naomhan. And yet he wanted to scream and cry, love ripped from him once again.

Fachtna hated him; Erasmo loved only his money. What had he done to be so wretchedly lost? What sins had he committed?

Rage began to win, swelling within his breast. He had done *nothing*.

Slowly, he approached the bed, his fingers twitching, eager.

From the window, a moth fluttered into the room, catching Erasmo's eye as he stared through Naomhan. "Oh!" he gasped. "Look, it's beautiful!"

It was the color of burnished gold, four iridescent spots across its wings. It fluttered forward, and unconsciously, Naomhan reached for it, forgetting his invisibility.

And yet despite it, the moth landed on his finger; its long fuzzy antennae waved as it stared at him, its dark eyes fixed upon his. After a long moment, it fluttered away. Naomhan let out a breath he didn't know he'd been holding.

In confusion, Erasmo turned to his lover. "Did it land on something?" he asked, reaching toward Naomhan to feel. But his hand passed through unhindered.

Remembering Tairis's words about being the only one to see him when his cap was on, Naomhan's heart leapt. Frantically, he searched for the moth, but it was gone, leaving not even dust behind.

Naomhan looked back at Erasmo, content and happy with his plain-faced musician, and felt the pang of his despair, rage quelling. Erasmo had charmed him out of coin, sure, but coin was nothing to him just as Erasmo would be from now on.

Still, as the two of them fell asleep in each other's arms, Naomhan pulled out his white rose and quietly poured coins onto the nightstand. Finding a schedule book, Naomhan opened it and wrote, *So you can find a home away from this place. From the Prince Sìogaidh.*

Then he stepped out of the window and imagined himself away.

Fachtna stood in the audience chamber of his father's palace as if he were a common peasant instead of a prince. The king sighed as he surveyed his son, stroking his beard. "What am I going to do with you, Fachtna?" His voice was heavy with exhaustion. "You galavant off with soldiers and return with only their names. You ignore your tutors and disrespect our diplomats but turn around and demand their fealty."

The duke, wretched Naomhan's father, stood solemnly at his brother's side.

"And now your cousin, Lord Naomhan, has vanished without a word after an unplanned hunting expedition with *you*, who was happy to make his loathing clear." The king removed his crown and stared down at it in his hands. "Fachtna, my son, tell us truly, where is he?"

His anger flared. "I've told you time and again, I do not know! After the lion killed my men and refused to kill him, I left and returned here. That is all I know, I swear it!"

The duke's frown deepened, distrust in his gaze, though he still remained silent.

The king rubbed his eyes and set the crown down in his lap. "This cannot stand, Fachtna. Years and years, I have trusted in the man you would become, giving you the chance to prove yourself worthy of your title as prince." He set the crown back on his head, staring down at his only son. "And yet you have proven only your own foolishness and temper. As of this moment, the heir to my throne is Duke Diarmad."

Fachtna gaped. "Father, you can't!"

"I *can,* and I *will.* Your hand, Fachtna."

Gritting his teeth, Fachtna offered his hand. His father removed the signet ring marking his status as crown prince and held it out to his brother, who slipped it onto his index finger. "Thank you, Your Majesty."

"You are welcome, Diarmad. Now, I give you some troops to search the forest for your son. I pray we find him swiftly."

"Thank you." Diarmad bowed and left the room.

Fachtna and the king stayed for a long moment in silence before the king sighed and waved him away. "You still have your retinue to keep you safe. Use them wisely, and perhaps one day you will prove yourself worthy of the title of king."

Seething, Fachtna let the door slam shut behind him and went straight away to his mother's chambers. She commiserated with him and said she would speak to the king, that, of course, it was unbelievable he would do such a thing to his only son!

Somehow, her support only made him feel worse.

For the first time Naomhan traveled without a destination in mind. He followed the sun, gliding like a slow, swooping songbird over the snow-capped mountains. After some time, he spotted a city in the midst of celebration, and drawn by curiosity, he descended.

He removed his cap and joined the throng of onlookers clustered in the roads. A well-dressed young man, a hat pulled low over his milk-white face, was waving at the crowd from atop a white horse, a small, kind smile on his lips.

A bit behind him, on a black horse, was a man who Naomhan could only assume was from across the southern sea—his skin brown as freshly tilled earth, and his hair and beard a rich, black cloud of tiny curls. His full, dark lips were parted in jubilant laughter.

Guards followed behind, bearing some sort of violet and gold banner—a royal one, Naomhan assumed.

He couldn't recognize the language the people around him were speaking, but as the procession traveled up toward the castle, he assumed it was a coronation.

This assumption proved true when the white man descended from his horse and walked up to a richly dressed priest, who drew a crown and heavy fur cloak from a chest on the low table. An older woman—the queen mother, perhaps?—rose to stand beside the future king, murmuring in his ear, making his cheeks flush red.

Naomhan couldn't understand the priest's speech to the gathered crowd, nor the man's, but the crown was eventually placed upon his head, and the people burst into cheers. Curious about the southern man, Naomhan replaced his cap and slipped through the revelers, seeking him out again.

He was easy to find, walking with a pair of guards up into the palace. The three men were laughing and joking. Perhaps he was a guard captain of some sort? But it was odd he didn't wear the uniform.

Eventually, the man left the guards and went through a side door, whistling as he climbed upward into a tower. Halfway up, he stopped and placed a hand on a blank bit of wall, which was not a wall at all, but a perfect replica.

Naomhan followed, in awe of the casual magic the man displayed, wondering if such magic was common in his lands. More stairs led up into a secret part of the tower where he stepped inside a warm, red-toned room. The walls and floors were covered in red-and-gold tapestries, and a large bed across from a fireplace was draped in dark-violet curtains.

The man whistled as he divested himself of his outerwear and combed his fingers through his hair and beard. He unbuttoned his shirt halfway and pulled the bedcurtains aside, then settled himself against the pillows. His eyes flickered back and forth between the door and his body, which he kept rearranging, even looking down to fiddle with the dark hair across his chest.

Naomhan backed up toward the door, beginning to understand the man was waiting for a lover, and that he shouldn't become a voyeur. But before he left, the door opened, and the white king walked inside, still wearing his crown.

The man on the bed made some joke that made the king laugh, and he set the crown on the dresser, then removed the heavy fur cloak from his shoulders. As he walked to the bed, however, he brushed through Naomhan's arm.

Unlike Erasmo, who had not noticed anything when passing through Naomhan's form, the king froze, his eyes widening in fear. The southern man noticed immediately, jumping out of the bed, then reached out to touch, but he was waved away.

Naomhan hurriedly backed away, but the king's gaze seemed to find him, the man's wide pupils turning his green eyes black. He spoke a word and swiped his hand through the air. From nothing, Naomhan felt hands upon his person, holding him still.

His heart pounded, and he wracked his mind for anything he could do to escape as the king advanced, still speaking in a language he couldn't understand.

After a moment, the king frowned and touched his throat, then spoke again. This time, Naomhan could understand though the king's lips did not match the sounds he heard. "What are you, spirit? There is fairy magic at work, but you are not one yourself."

"I, I am called Sìogaidh," Naomhan stammered, tugging futilely at the hands that held him.

The king's eyes narrowed. "You are wise to conceal your name, but do you think it wise to call yourself a fairy when you merely wear one's echo?"

After the initial shock of his native tongue being understood by this strange king, Naomhan sighed, hanging his head. "I don't know how to call what I am, so Sìogaidh will serve."

The king stroked his chin, his gaze flickering to the other man, his lover. The man had drawn a sword from somewhere, and had it trained in Naomhan's direction, all joyous anticipation gone and replaced by resolve. The king touched his arm, murmuring something in a completely different tongue, and the man lowered and sheathed the blade.

"Young man, I believe you are being used by whatever fairy gifted you their power," the king said. "I know you do not want to hear that—perhaps you even think you love them and they you—but please know the fey are wicked and fickle creatures, who view mortals merely as playthings and sources of power. You will serve your purpose as entertainment or fuel, and then you will be abandoned and lost."

The man gripped the king's shoulder as he spoke, touching their heads together—a comfort. Naomhan didn't doubt the king spoke from experience. Perhaps that was why his skin and hair were so colorless. Even his eyelashes were pale blond, almost invisible against his face.

"You would be wise to give back whatever powers you have been gifted and return to the life you once led. A life touched by a fairy will never be normal, but perhaps you could mitigate whatever damage has been done."

Naomhan thought of Tairis and his dark, sad eyes. He thought of the lion that had saved him from Fachtna's wrath, and the moth that had stayed his rage in the face of betrayal. "This fairy is not the one who so hurt you, Your Majesty. Your warning is understood, but I shall not heed it."

The king sighed and shook his head. "They can be incredibly charming. They will wear any face they think will entrance. Why do you think they are so often beautiful? It is a mask, and nothing more."

"He's different!" Naomhan yelled, struggling once again against his binding. "He is generous and kind! He saved my life when I didn't yet know who he was!"

The king didn't appear angry at being contradicted. Instead, he only looked sad. "I cannot force you to listen to me, young man. I know what it is to be young and rash. I only ask you remember my warning when your heart is broken." He raised his hand and closed his fingers. Naomhan was freed, and he stumbled across the ground, trying to regain his balance. "Take care to whom you give your name, young man. You give them more power than you think."

Naomhan fled, the king's sad gaze haunting his thoughts as he took to the air, speeding away without care for the direction.

In the end, he realized he was going north, the trees thinning out and shrinking until there was only rock and brush. The air was cold, his breath foggy. There were those who said that was his spirit he was seeing, and he should be careful to call it all back. Maybe that had happened to him when he was young, which had made him so strange—he'd lost some of his soul as a child pretending to be a dragon.

His tears turned to ice on his cheeks, so he descended onto one of the snowy mountains far below, the bare rock devoid of life. He wiped his face and sighed out a cloud, staring up at the sky. The sun was near to setting, painting the sky in reds and oranges, stars beginning to twinkle in the east. The light was reflected in the still, cold water beneath his perch; a lake perhaps, for surely the ocean did not become so still? It was peaceful here in a place without people. Maybe this was the sort of place he truly belonged.

Naomhan removed his cap and put it away, then scratched his scalp, the sensation pleasant enough to give him goose bumps. Or maybe it was the cold. He didn't know anymore.

Below, a pale bird with curved wings dove toward the water before circling back skyward. It swooped toward Naomhan's perch and landed without a sound. Up close, Naomhan could see its black head, gray body, and its familiar dark eyes.

He didn't dare breathe, for fear of scaring Tairis away. If it even was Tairis. "Tairis?" he whispered.

The bird cocked its head, its cry sharp and a little hoarse, before it very distinctly nodded.

"Have you been following me?"

The bird shook itself, its feathers rising before smoothing back down. It turned its head about, perhaps thinking, before nodding again.

Why didn't he show himself properly? "Why?"

The bird fixed him with a stare, perhaps in frustration. But finally, it jumped up, flapping its wings once to drive it high into the air before Tairis himself descended to the rock. He was not dressed in the fine gold Naomhan had seen before. Indeed, there was still something of the bird in the silver-gray of his clothing. He was bare of jewelry. "I promised myself not to interfere in your journeys," he said softly. "But I couldn't let you…lose yourself. The power you wield is great, more than many mortals could bear. But you've done admirably so far." He smiled gently.

"Why didn't you tell me about Erasmo? Did you know he was using me like that?"

Tairis looked away, his expression hard to read against the darkening sky. "I promised myself not to interfere," he said again, "but you would regret hurting him in your anger."

Naomhan frowned, kicking his heels against the stone of the mountain. "Why are you here now then?"

"Do you regret the gifts that have been given to you, Naomhan? If you wish, I can take you home and leave with you whichever gifts you like."

Naomhan's brow furrowed, and he stared at Tairis's shadowy face. "What are you talking about? Why would I regret what has been so generously given?"

Tairis wouldn't look him in the eye. "Because I know the land from which you have come, and I know of the man who has become its king."

In his chest, Naomhan's heart skipped a beat. "Was the king right?" he whispered. "Did you do all this to try and... get something out of me? Some purpose beyond generosity?"

Tairis's fingers slid against the stone as his body tensed and color climbed in his cheeks, visible even in the darkening twilight. "I shouldn't have said anything. I'm sorry. You're not ready to hear it."

"Says who? Say your piece, Tairis."

But Tairis only shook his head. "No. Your heart is recovering from betrayal. I will not allow it influence over your mind."

Naomhan's brow furrowed, his stomach souring. "You're no different than Erasmo, are you? *He* only wanted my money, and *you* only want whatever it is you're not telling me!" What was it the king had said? "Entertainment or fuel"? Which was Naomhan?

Tairis's shoulders hunched, but he didn't answer. His expression was oddly *blank*, doll-like. It shook Naomhan to his core. He didn't know Tairis at all, did he? What was he even *doing*?

Without a word, Naomhan jumped from the mountain. The magic took him and swept him away. If he heard his name upon the wind, it did not give him reason to stop.

The sun set while he flew, unsure of where he was going. He slowed, staring at the stars as he went. He knew sailors navigated by the stars, but he hadn't the foggiest idea how. He tilted down toward the ground and let his fingers skim across treetops, the ocean glittering somewhere distantly before him. Perhaps he was over the great forest between Norance and Deurich again? Had he gone south, back toward home?

Before he could think more deeply on that, however, a scream cut through the peaceful night. Naomhan sped toward it, happy for something to distract him from his thoughts.

The scream had come from a young woman who was being accosted by ruffians. Her dark hair was pulled back in a braid, and her gown was sewn through with small jewels. "Let me go!" she yelled, struggling against the men holding her.

Checking his cap was well in place, Naomhan dropped to the ground and rushed at the nearest man and knocked him over. "You will leave this place!" he said in his deepest and most princely voice. "You have angered the fairies of this forest, and a curse shall fall upon you if you do not leave!"

"A ghost!" one of the men yelped, looking around in fear. "I *told* you! This place is cursed, and now we are too, oh dear Lord!" He dropped to his knees, a string of prayers passing his lips too quickly to understand.

"Idiot, it's just a trick!"

Naomhan grabbed his collar from behind, whispering in his ear, making sure his breath could be felt. "Are you sure?"

The skeptic became a believer. Shaken, he glanced at his men, one still gibbering on the ground, the two others frozen in sudden fear. "L-leave her; maybe they'll take her instead!" he yelled and bolted, his men scrambling to follow.

The woman was thrown unceremoniously toward the ground as they fled.

When Naomhan was sure they were gone, he stepped into the trees and removed his cap before emerging. "Miss? Are you all right?" he asked, offering her a hand.

Instead of taking it, however, she screamed again and scrambled backward, away from him.

"Miss! It's okay! They're gone," he said, trying to soothe.

She hesitated, fixing him with a wary, uncertain stare. "Was that your voice? But you sounded so close."

"I'm a ventriloquist," he explained quickly. "I can throw my voice."

"I. I see." Shaking, she took his offered hand and stood, her eyes searching his face. "You are a man, yet you are different from those who took me."

"Is that such a surprise?" he asked, concerned. "Surely you have met good men before?"

She shook her head, still watching him as if she expected him to bite.

He frowned. "Is there anything I can do to help?"

She pulled the braid over her shoulder, stroking it thoughtfully. "Could you, perhaps, escort me to docks? I don't know where I am, but they didn't travel more than a day while I was blindfolded and gagged."

"Of course," he said, remembering where he'd seen the ocean. "What can I call you, by the way? I'm Naomhan." As his name passed his lips, he remembered the white king's warning, but surely an innocent young woman would do him no harm?

"Forgive my manners, I'm Caoimhe."

Only after she gave her name did Naomhan realize that they were speaking the language of the Highlands. He swallowed, waiting for her to recognize his name, but she didn't seem to, looking only concerned when he ceased speaking.

"Do you know the way, Sir Naomhan?"

"I do," he said quickly, offering an arm. "Allow me the honor of escorting you, Miss Caoimhe."

She smiled a little and took his arm. "Very well. Thank you."

They walked for some time before Naomhan could contain his curiosity no longer. "So, Miss Caoimhe, how is it you have never before met a good man?"

She stroked her braid, her eyes flickering over to him before settling on the ground before her. "I live on an island across the sea, forever shrouded in mist. No man may enter that place.

It is the domain of a powerful fairy, and I am her daughter's maidservant."

It had taken time for Fachtna's mother to find the book, and she had kept it secret from his father, murmuring about how he couldn't be trusted with such things. She kept many such secrets from the king. And Fachtna believed her. His father was rash, after all, to turn so suddenly against his own son, and for what? For seeking to defend the kingdom from foul magic? Unbelievable.

But found it she had. Bound in dark leather, the words *The Faerie Amongst Us* elegantly written in the center of the first page. "There is a girl," his mother said, tapping the page she'd marked. "The daughter of a fearsome fairy. Seduce the daughter, and you win the fairy's allegiance."

Sitting beside his mother as the full moon hung outside the window, he read.

Across the sea lies a secret island, shrouded in mist. It is known as a woman's paradise where men dare not go. Fierce warrior women guard its shores, and any number of fey spirits guard its castle. But within that hidden place, there is a princess, born of a fairy, weak to men's charms.

The fairy was a pariah among her people for her affection for the Mad Prince of Ghairé, and so, she built the island to escape her scornful kin. And for a time, the two of them lived there happily.

But soon he tired of her constant, tireless attention. There are no secrets from a fairy wife. Wherever he went, she followed, no matter how high the mountain or how deep the cave, telling him again and again a child would soon be born. But he paid no heed and kept running. Until, at last, he turned upon her. He called her ugly names, his love long ago spent.

In a cold fury, the fairy grew to a great size, gripping the Mad Prince by the collar and hoisting him into the air. "My temper is greater than your patience, so you will not end your life as mewling cat or burping toad, but know you this: fairy magic leaves no human mind untouched, and without my love, you shall soon lose yours.

"I leave you to your dismal, petty life. You shall never meet your child."

And indeed, the fairy's curse came true. After a few months, the Mad Prince began to see and hear things that weren't there, grasping spirits at the edges of his vision. Phantoms gripped him in his sleep, so he was never rested. Voices from unseen mouths whispered cruelties.

He went mad.

The fairy retreated to her timeless island, calling upon her kin and those spirits she could control as well as any woman strong enough to wield a weapon. She took them all to her home and cloaked it in a thick fog, so none could ever spot it. There, she had her daughter in peace and named her refuge the Isle of Calm Delights.

It is said her daughter, the princess, is more beautiful than any woman but has a human heart to be won. Any man strong and brave enough to seek out this place and claim the princess will win her hand in marriage and perhaps even the fairy's loyalty.

Fachtna turned to his mother in excitement. "This is perfect, Mother. How did you know?"

She smiled serenely. "Why, the Mad Prince was my uncle. I heard the story from his own lips, but I knew you'd want to see the truth upon the page." She gestured to the book. "Surely, there are sailors and soldiers who can find this place, who could be paid enough for their silence and discretion."

Fachtna paced eagerly, drumming his fingers against the book cover. He would have one of the women kidnapped first, he thought. Then, once her assistance had been gained, he could send her back as a spy to find the princess and spirit her away.

If not, well, he could simply lead his men against the island itself. They were just *women*, after all; what chance did they really have against the might of his soldiers?

Fachtna set the book on his bedside table and lay down, his head overflowing with plans for the fairy queen's power. No one would ever say he was unworthy of the throne again. Naomhan *who*?

Serene, despite the gleam of madness in her eye, the queen watched on. Another secret to keep from the king.

"I was taken because I foolishly lost track of my mistress's parrot," Caoimhe explained. "Seeking to catch it, I waded into the surf. When I did, the fog..." She frowned, gesturing meaninglessly in the air. "It—it moved? I didn't go far, but the fog was suddenly behind me, and in front of me was a boat with those men on it."

"Do you know why they took you?" Naomhan asked.

"They were asking me about the princess and said they were taking me to meet someone."

"Princess? Your mistress?"

Caoimhe nodded. "She's *beautiful*." Her eyes glittered. "Long, gorgeous red hair and perfect pink lips and—" She blushed and covered her reddening cheeks with both hands.

"O-oh my, but she is. She is." She paused, turning to stare at Naomhan with something like fear. "What does love feel like?"

Naomhan stopped in his tracks, taken aback. "Uh, it feels like…" He remembered Tairis's burning kiss, the fluttering, dark-eyed moth upon his finger, and the red rose in his bag before it all went wrong. "It feels like warmth, protection, and a desire to protect them in turn."

Her hands still clasped to her cheeks, Caoimhe lost herself in thought, then gasped aloud. "*The Isle of Calm Delights*!" she shrieked.

Naomhan jumped at the sound, wincing. "What are you talking about?"

"The island! It—it does *something* to your emotions! I-I-I love my mistress!" Her blush burned from between her fingers. "I want to kiss her an-and hold her and—" Her blush faded, her expression becoming fearful. "She's lived there her whole life. I *know* what my emotions should feel like. I once again understand fear and love and distress, but she doesn't. Sir Naomhan, she *doesn't*." Caoimhe looked horrified. "Oh, sir, we need to save her!"

Naomhan stared, trying to make sense of what Caoimhe was saying. "I… Wait, what is the island doing?"

She lowered her hands, her gaze beseeching. "It—it *calms* you. You don't feel anything deeply; you just—just *are*. I was young when I found myself on that island, wandering through the ocean fog after the death of my mother, following a kindly voice. I didn't realize… Lord in Heaven, I *know* what it is to feel again, and I—I can't stand the idea of my mistress being so suppressed." Her voice trembled, tears swimming in her eyes. Naomhan wondered if this was an effect of the island—having gone years with her emotions smothered, now it was difficult for her to hold them back.

Naomhan put his hands on her shoulders, hoping to help ground her. "Okay, we'll save her. What would you have me do?"

Caoimhe blushed deeper and shifted from his touch, stepping away, but her eyes were wide in thought. "You can throw your voice. Perhaps you could come with me to the island and hide from the guards, and—and *lure* her out. She's very curious, my mistress. If she heard a man's voice, she'd try to investigate especially if I encouraged her to."

"And once we meet?"

Caoimhe shook her head. "You *must* stay hidden. Her mother is fierce and powerful and will not hesitate to kill you for piercing her sanctuary. You must lure her through the fog into the water. There, she should be able to *feel*. I'll be able to explain after that."

"Okay. Lure her to the water and you'll explain?" he confirmed.

"That does seem to be the best way," she said uncertainly. "Ooh, this could go so wrong." She squeezed her cheeks between her palms.

"Okay," Naomhan said, trying to interrupt her anxiety, "how do we go to the island?"

"Surely at the docks we can get a boat?" Caoimhe tilted her head, innocent confusion shining from her expression. Did she understand the idea of money?

He patted his bag where the white rose lay. "Yes, we can get a boat."

The boat they bought was a small one, little more than a rowboat, but it had a sail, and Caoimhe seemed to know how to work it, so Naomhan sat back and let her do so. There was a handsomeness to her face and body he could appreciate, but he was starting to understand he would never want to settle down with a woman.

They sailed on northward until the distance filled with white-gray fog. "We're almost there," Caoimhe said. "Can you feel the magic in the air?"

Naomhan sat and closed his eyes. Indeed, he could when he sought it out—a buzzing over his skin like static, like the sizzle in the air after a lightning strike.

At the edge of the fog, Caoimhe dropped the anchor, staring into the nothingness. "I don't want to lose this," she murmured, holding her heart to her chest. But she took a steadying breath and jumped out into the surf. "Follow if you can, but stay *hidden*. I'll draw the guards away, but I can only give you a few minutes."

They nodded to each other, and Caoimhe marched through the mist, her dress trailing behind her in the lapping water. After a moment, her voice echoed out, speaking with the guards, telling them her tale—without mentioning Naomhan.

He put his cap on his head and made sure it was well secured before slipping into the water.

As he walked through it, the fog was endless. How long had he been walking? It had taken Caoimhe only a few minutes; was he lost?

But the buzz of magic was ahead of him, and so he pressed toward it until at last he pushed through…into what could only be called paradise.

A rocky beach, covered in small, smooth gray stones surrounded him. Ahead, verdant green fields filled with food and flowers, and beyond *that*, a magnificent white stone palace, its towers edged in gold.

In a small copse of trees near the beach, Caoimhe talked with the guards, who kept their backs to the shore. They were the tallest, broadest women he had ever seen, though not unfeminine in their dress or manner. The swords on their belts were, however, no mere toys.

And yet, he could feel what Caoimhe had spoken of, the blanket covering his heart. He feared the warrior's blades, and yet he had no urge to flee. He thought of Tairis, and was concerned and confused, but it was no longer the storm of mixed emotions threatening to swallow him whole. It was absolutely smothering.

Despite knowing the guards couldn't see him, Naomhan kept his distance, especially as they finished their conversation with Caoimhe and started pacing the edge of the fields—their regular route, he imagined.

He dodged past them, falling in behind Caoimhe as she walked toward the palace. "Sir?" she whispered, keeping her gaze locked forward.

It was simple enough to come up beside her. "Here," he murmured.

Her shoulders relaxed a fraction. "The evening is such a nice time for a walk here," she said evenly, swinging her arms as she walked. "I shall have to bring my mistress."

Naomhan nodded, though she couldn't see him, and continued following. Closer, the palace was somehow even more beautiful, surrounded by lush gardens with plants Naomhan had never seen. The interior was just as impressive, filled with gold and velvet, all in rich, dark colors. He was reminded of the white king, and some of his excitement waned. This was a fairy place, he remembered, ruled by a fairy not like Tairis, but more like those the white king feared. (And maybe Tairis was just like her.)

He adjusted his cap, remembering Tairis's words that none but he would see him, trusting in them despite everything as he followed Caoimhe up a wide marble staircase.

"Caoimhe!" came a cry, and Naomhan turned to see a stream of red curls and a snow-white dress descending upon his friend.

Even with her emotions softened, Caoimhe embraced the woman tightly. "Mistress, it is good to see you again."

The woman pulled away, her blue eyes sparkling in the afternoon light. "Caoimhe," she said in slight reproach.

Caoimhe blushed. "Eilidh," she said instead.

The redheaded beauty smiled, perfect pink lips over pearl-white teeth. "That's better. Now, come, tell me what happened."

As Caoimhe began her tale, Naomhan followed, studying Eilidh. There was a fairylike quality to her in the slenderness of her body and the too-neat symmetry of her features, but she seemed human in all other respects. He wondered about the story of this place. Why had Eilidh's mother entrapped her daughter so, and why suppress her emotions?

Curiosity flaring when they arrived in Eilidh's chambers, Naomhan took a slip of paper from her desk and a pen, then stepped into another room to write a question. *Why do you live on this island away from the world?*

He returned to her room and allowed himself to float upward, then dropped the note, watching it flutter to the ground before her.

Stopping midsentence, Eilidh bent to retrieve it and read it. "Caoimhe, did you do this?" she asked, holding it up.

Caoimhe, who had taken up a pile of mending to be done, shook her head, as confused as her mistress.

Eilidh frowned at the question, looking up at the ceiling to seek the source, but Naomhan had returned to the ground, still wearing his cap. "My mother has asked me to," she answered simply and set the paper aside, returning to her conversation with Caoimhe.

He stole another paper, this time writing, *Why are there no men here?*

This note he left on her bookshelf, which she found as she rose to retrieve a book they were discussing. She frowned. "Caoimhe, this isn't funny."

"I'm doing nothing, Eilidh," Caoimhe insisted.

"Because men have been nothing but trouble for my mother," Eilidh said in mild frustration. "Though I suppose *your* mysterious rescuer is different, hm, Caoimhe?" At this question, the line between Eilidh's eyebrows deepened before smoothing over as if the anger had passed.

"He was so kind," Caoimhe said. "Shall I draw you a picture of him, mistress?"

"Eilidh," she said.

"Eilidh," Caoimhe repeated.

"If you wish to show me this storybook hero, go ahead, so long as you aren't attempting to marry me off." This was said with a smile, a private joke.

"Those men are foolish and greedy," Caoimhe said. "This one was kind."

Naomhan leaned into Eilidh's ear and whispered, "If you come to the shore tonight, you may find out for yourself."

Her eyes widened, her head snapping toward his voice. "Who spoke?"

He wrote one last note. *I am neither angel nor demon. I am a man, though not a brute. I wish only to help you learn something of yourself that your mother has hidden from you. Come to the southern shore when the moon rises.*

This he placed upon her nightstand, which she found after supping for the evening and watching Caoimhe draw Naomhan's face in charcoal.

"Caoimhe. Come with me. We'll get to the bottom of this note business."

"Eilidh, is that wise? Should we bring the guards?"

Eilidh shook her head, holding hairpins in her mouth as she drew back her long tresses. "No, I wish to meet this note sender myself."

Caoimhe held out her hand. "Then I shall go with you, Eilidh, and keep you safe."

Eilidh took the offered hand and squeezed it tightly. "Come, we shall face him together."

Naomhan flitted out the window and down to the shore where he stood in shin-deep surf, waiting for the women to arrive. When he spotted the gleam of Eilidh's dress, he looked around for the guards. Seeing none, he backed into the fog and removed his cap. "Eilidh," he called to her. "Follow my voice."

He couldn't see them, but he heard Caoimhe's voice. "Perhaps we should, mistress."

"Mother said to never trust anything through the mist." But despite her words, there was an edge of excitement. "But, if it's only a *look…*"

"Yes, only a look, Eilidh," Caoimhe said.

He walked further backward, continuing to call her name, until at last he emerged from the fog, only feet from his boat. He took a deep breath, savoring the emotions of excitement and anticipation.

And shortly after, Eilidh and Caoimhe appeared through the mist as well. Caoimhe smiled at Naomhan, but Eilidh was suspicious. "Who are you? How did you find this island?" she demanded before hesitating. "Caoimhe, he looks like your picture."

"That's because I'm the one she drew," he said with a bow. "It is a pleasure to meet you, my lady."

"How did you—" She cut herself off, staring in horror over Naomhan's shoulder.

As he turned, he saw why. A great ship in the distance sailed against the moon, flying a very familiar flag. "Fachtna," Naomhan whispered.

"What did you do?" Eilidh demanded, her voice rising to a shriek as she grabbed Naomhan's shirt. "Who have you brought to my mother's sanctuary?" She swallowed, gasping for breath. "What's *wrong* with me? This. This *burns*. It turns my stomach to acid; *what did you do?*"

"Eilidh!" Caoimhe cried, pulling her back. "This isn't his fault. What you're feeling is *anger*, properly for the first time. This fog, it blankets not only the island but also the hearts of those within."

"My—my mother did this to me?" Eilidh whispered, tears springing to her eyes and cascading over her cheeks. "But why would she do such a thing?"

Caoimhe wrapped her in her arms. "She only thought to protect you, I'm sure. But now you understand, don't you? We have to go."

"But"—Eilidh turned to the approaching fleet—"who are they?"

Naomhan blanched. "They are soldiers of Prince Fachtna. But what would they want? How did they know to come here?" His heart thudded painfully. Had Tairis done it? Had Tairis perhaps been working with Fachtna this whole time, luring Naomhan away from the kingdom and thus the eyes of his father and uncle?

Caoimhe frowned. "There are stories about this place. Perhaps he was why I was taken. Which would mean"—she turned to Eilidh—"they mean to take you, perhaps to win the cooperation of your mother."

Many expressions raced across Eilidh's face too fast for Naomhan to catch until she settled on grim determination. "If they wish the wrath of a fairy, then perhaps we should give it to them." Her skin glimmered in the starlight.

"What happened to your mother? Why did she make this place?" Naomhan asked. "If we know the story, perhaps we'll know what he wants for sure."

As Eilidh shook her head, helplessness creeping into her eyes, Caoimhe put a hand on her arm. "I know the story."

It was a sad tale about a fairy who gave too deeply and was abandoned in return. It deserved a better retelling than three people standing knee-deep in cold ocean. "As I said, he likely seeks to take Eilidh and thus force her mother into cooperation," Caoimhe finished, putting her arm around Eilidh's waist.

Naomhan nodded, looking at the distant ship still several hours away from shore. It appeared to have stopped for the night, the sails drawn, preparing for the dawn. Taking a deep breath, he took out his cap and jammed it on his head. "I'll be back," he said, ignoring their shocked expressions. "Wait on the shore. Don't tell Eilidh's mother yet. I'm going to see if I can convince him to leave."

From the shallows to the lead ship took almost no time at all, though surely it would have been hours swimming. He landed without a sound, peering around. The sailors on duty were attending to the sails and rigging, murmuring to one another in low, serious voices. They were scared, but the love of their king rose above it, and Fachtna, as his son, received that love as well.

It churned Naomhan's stomach. After some time away from home, he couldn't stand the idea of his own kinsmen being hurt in defense of Fachtna's childish need for validation. When he ascertained the prince wasn't on deck, he walked through the locked door to the captain's cabin where Fachtna was pouring over a book, muttering to himself.

It was strange, seeing him again. Naomhan had been only months away, and yet Fachtna was significantly changed. He'd thinned out, the bones of his hand rising under the skin from knuckle to wrist. His hair was longer, wilder—wiry where he'd combed through with his hand. Perhaps it was the love he had come to know, but Naomhan could hardly remember what he'd seen in Fachtna besides a handsome face.

"No one will again say I'm unworthy," Fachtna whispered fervently. He touched his knuckle to his lip as if kissing his ring, but… Naomhan stared. It was gone. The mark of the heir was *gone*. What had happened in his absence?

"Prince Fachtna," Naomhan said.

Fachtna whirled around at the sound of his voice, his eyes wide as they scanned the room. "Am I to become mad now for hatred of you?"

Even now, the words stung. "I am here but shall remain unseen, for fear of your violence," he said softly.

At this, Fachtna seemed to shrink, shifting his weight onto his hands, pressing against the table before him. "I think my father might have made *you* the heir had you been there," he said, his fingertips turning white where they pressed against the wood. "He's always loved you best."

Naomhan hesitated, unsure of what to say. He had never seen Fachtna like this, his heart bare and shaken. He kept his distance but moved to stand before him, touching the table. "What has happened, my prince?"

"I am wretched. My own father has seen fit to deny me my birthright," Fachtna said. But he raised his head, staring through Naomhan with burning eyes. "But I will be redeemed. With a fairy's daughter as my wife, and her mother under my thumb, no one will think me unworthy of the throne."

Overcome with sudden anger, Naomhan slapped Fachtna across the face. Fachtna recoiled with a snarl while Naomhan shook the pain from his palm. "Listen to yourself!" he said furiously. "Kidnapping an innocent woman will do nothing to prove your worth as a king! Who in the world would think that proper behavior for a prince? Or even a man?"

The wheels turned in Fachtna's head, his expression shifting from rage to confusion. "But it is a quest like the old tales of yore. It's the perfect chance!"

"No one cares for quests. Did you honestly think yourself unpopular because you had not completed a *quest*?" Naomhan would have laughed if he weren't so incredulous. "No one likes you because you're quick-tempered, foul, and see people as pawns in your imagined, paranoid games." Naomhan wondered if anyone had ever put it so plainly to his face.

"I will see you ha—" Fachtna began to yell, lifting his fist to strike, but he cut himself off, staring at his knuckles. He lowered his hand, tracing it over the pages of the book before him.

Naomhan tried to take advantage of this opportunity, now that Fachtna's guard was down. He paced around the room, squeezing his hands together. "If you wish to impress your father, wouldn't it be better to actually listen to what he has to tell you? He wants you to be a good king one day. It's all he's ever wanted from you—even I know that. Why are you so resistant to it?"

"Because... Because my mother is."

Naomhan frowned, caught off guard. The queen was a known recluse, hardly ever leaving her chambers. It hadn't been possible to avoid hearing the whispers that the reason the marriage had produced only one child was the king did not like her. And indeed, even in all Naomhan's years at the castle, the number of times he'd seen the queen could be counted on one hand, and he'd never seen her with the king. He didn't realize Fachtna was close with her. "Your mother...is resistant to your father's advice?"

Fachtna nodded, rubbing the stubble of his beard, his gaze on the book, but he wasn't reading it. "She always told me to not listen to him, that he was foolish, and his brother was a schemer."

"My father?" Naomhan furrowed his brows, thinking of Diarmad. Distant perhaps, stern and too fond of protocol certainly, but a "schemer"? "What sorts of things was he supposed to be scheming? How to get your head out of your own ass?"

Fachtna tossed a cork at the sound of Naomhan's voice, but it passed harmlessly through him and bounced off the wall. Naomhan chuckled. It was nice to be immune to his temper. "She was never so specific," Fachtna said quietly. "But she probably meant the throne."

This time Naomhan laughed aloud. "My father, after the throne? He'd rather be left alone to tend to the estate. The only reason we came to court was for him to tutor *you*."

"Liar! *You* want the throne!"

Naomhan stopped laughing in shock, then clutched his stomach in great heaves of mirth. "*Me*?! By the gods, Your Highness, you really don't know me at all, do you?" In truth, it hurt, for Naomhan had spent much of his adolescence pining for Fachtna, yet it was clear Fachtna didn't understand the first thing about him.

Fachtna puffed up, his cheeks blotchy in embarrassed anger. "You're doing black magic right this second to obscure yourself! Clearly you seek power!"

"I sought and gained *invisibility*, Your Highness." He picked up the cork and tossed it back to the prince. It rolled in a circle as it landed. "I would imagine that is the opposite of what you want."

Fachtna, his anger slowly draining, sat in his hammock, pushing it back and forth with a foot. "My father took my ring because he believes me a murderer. *Your* murderer," he said softly.

"You did intend to be." But Naomhan found only pity in his heart now. Fachtna was a man who had been nursed on lies and paranoid delusions. Was it any wonder he had turned into a terror? "But, no, I am not dead."

Taking a deep breath, he lifted the cap from his head and became visible. Fachtna looked him up and down but made no other move. "You've grown." His gaze dropped to his foot, still rocking, moving the hammock. "I know I am in no position to beg favor, but…would you return and clear my name?"

Naomhan crossed his arms. On the one hand, it was just for Fachtna to be punished for what he did. But on the other hand, he did at least *seem* to have begun to examine himself with a careful eye. Such introspection could begin a slow process of his becoming a better person. "Turn this ship around and leave the inhabitants of this island in peace, and I will," he said.

Fachtna stroked his beard, casting his eyes to the floor. "Very well. I suppose you're right. I can't imagine how my father would have reacted had I returned home with a crying woman as a prisoner."

"Poorly," Naomhan said flatly.

"Mm." Fachtna didn't disagree. It was clear he was lost in his thoughts. After a moment, he stood. "Well then. I suppose I'm turning this ship around. But before you go, Naomhan."

Naomhan turned from the door, stopped in the middle of raising the cap back to his head.

"Are you truly a witch?"

Naomhan chuckled. "No, I think I'm something of a fairy now."

"Somehow, that doesn't surprise me." Fachtna ran his fingers through his wild hair, wincing as it snagged. Relief filled Naomhan's heart. Tairis hadn't interfered with this. If he had, surely Fachtna would have reacted in some way.

At the door, Fachtna hesitated, staring at the handle. "For what it's worth, coming from me, I'm sorry, Naomhan. You didn't deserve the blame I foisted upon you, nor the cruelty."

Naomhan smiled. "I never hated you, my prince."

Fachtna's lips twitched upwards. "Well, that's something. When you return to the palace, you will be a guest of honor. We missed your birthday, after all."

"Thank you, my prince. I will see you soon." And with a bow, he placed the cap on his head and departed.

After a moment, Fachtna called Naomhan's name but received only silence. Had he truly been there or a figment of imagination? Still, Fachtna had given his word, and he supposed it should mean something. He stood and left the cabin, shouting orders to turn around to the ship's captain. He didn't miss the relief that softened the sailor's faces.

Before he could be questioned, he returned to his room. The book, that damned book, still lay open across his table. He moved to slam it shut but instead found he had no anger left to burn. He closed it instead and brought it with him to his perch, then ran his fingers over the leather as he rocked himself.

Their conversation echoed through him, a throbbing bruise of a blow richly deserved. He remembered Naomhan's arrival to the palace—a small, pretty lad with the courtly manners of someone much older. It was little wonder the nobles had been charmed, next to a boy who strutted about drunk upon his own ego.

He could still feel Naomhan's curls gripped in his fingers as he raged over his humiliation after the incident with Oster. His mother had assured him of Naomhan's fault

"Too courtly, that boy. And like anyone at court, he surely meant to slight you."

And despite Fachtna's violence, Naomhan had trusted him, followed him on his "hunting" trip. He curled his lip and stopped his rocking. Yes, Fachtna's men had died to the lion, but *he* had been the reason they were there. (And he hadn't even sought out their families to apologize. He had left that unpleasant task to his father. Was it any wonder he was considered irresponsible?)

He stared blankly at the door, listening to the calling voices of the sailors outside it. They were his father's men, loyal to him only by virtue of his blood. And yet, an hour ago, he would have seen them all perish upon a fairy's shore—if only he could return the royal signet to his finger.

Fachtna pulled his palm over his beard and set the book aside. He stood and then fell to his knees with a heavy heart and clasped his hands to his chest.

And for the first time in his life, he prayed for forgiveness.

And meant it.

Naomhan flew back to the shore, looking over his shoulder as he went to watch the great ship turn, the oars on its side cutting into the water. He landed on the shore, removed his cap, and approached the two women standing together, speaking softly.

"You surprised us," Eilidh said as he came into view, her voice flat with the fog.

"Forgive me. But the prince is leaving."

Eilidh leaned against Caoimhe's shoulder. "I'm glad."

"So, what happens now?" Caoimhe asked.

"I don't wish to stay here," Eilidh said. "Knowing my contentment is a farce created by my mother is…unpleasant. I wish to travel the world. With Caoimhe, of course." She put her arm through the other woman's.

Caoimhe returned Eilidh's grasp, leaning her head against Eilidh's shoulder. "I have no objections, Eilidh. Shall we leave tonight?"

Naomhan gave them both a small bow. "Please, allow me the honor of escorting you, my ladies. I would worry, should you travel alone."

"Thank you, Sir Naomhan," Caoimhe said with a smile.

A voice boomed across the island. "*Who is this man who walks upon my shore?*"

Eilidh's eyes widened. "Fly, my friend, as fast as you can!"

Nodding, Naomhan rose upward, not bothering to put on his cap in his haste. But even as he moved, hands clasped his ankles, pulling him down, holding him in place. He struggled and fought, but they held fast.

A woman appeared on the shore, and Naomhan's blood ran cold. *The fairy. Eilidh's mother.*

Confirming his suspicions, she placed a hand on Eilidh's shoulder. "You should have told me you had a guest," she said coldly. "Naomhan, was it?"

He remembered what the white king had said about names and closed his eyes, trying not to let his fear show too clearly on his face. As she walked forward, Naomhan's hand darted into his bag and pulled out the red rose—the one to call upon Tairis. He grasped it tightly. "Tairis! Tairis, *please!*"

The fairy looked perplexed, tilting her head even as a rush of wind picked up. Without warning, Naomhan was released and fell into the shallows with a splash. And there before him, undisguised, was Tairis.

Naomhan was almost shocked to see him there. He was dressed simply in white, contrasted with the gold of his hair, glowing in the light of the moon. He glanced back at Naomhan for only a moment, long enough for a reassuring smile that was somehow still sad, before he walked to Eilidh's mother.

"Aoife, it has been too long."

The fairy flared at the sound of her name, suddenly wrong-footed. "Why does this mortal bear your magic, Tairis?" she asked.

"A gift freely given," he explained, then clapped his hands together with a charming smile. "It has been too long since last we met."

She sniffed and was not distracted. "And yet it is to the call of a mortal brat you come."

"Naomhan, what is it you want?" Tairis asked, ignoring the jab.

Naomhan stood, his wet clothes sticking to his skin. "Let Eilidh be free to travel with me. Stop smothering her in this fog."

Tairis nodded, his back still to Naomhan, his focus only on Aoife. "Very well. That is my request. When I helped you make this place, you promised me a favor. I spend it now."

"You would waste it on this? You do not even profit of it!"

"You have heard my request, Aoife."

Frowning, Aoife snapped her fingers, and the fog dissipated. A rush of longing hit Naomhan like a hurricane, pulling an audible gasp from his lungs.

"Eilidh, my darling, if this man does not make you healthy and happy, I will wear his intestines as a shawl." She kissed her daughter's cheeks. "If you need anything, simply speak my name, and I will fly to you." Her gaze slid to Naomhan, her eyes narrowing. "If you hurt her, physically or not, I will make you pray for death, boy. Make her happy."

Eilidh and Naomhan shared a confused glance. Naomhan was simply to be a bodyguard; how would he hurt her beyond physically? Caoimhe's lips pinched, but all she said was "Come, mistress, we've been through a trial. Let us prepare for bed."

"Of course, Caoimhe. Sleep well, Naomhan. I'm sure one of the brownies have already made you up a room." And with a whirl of her red curls, she walked arm in arm with Caoimhe back up toward the palace.

Aoife watched her go, then turned a shrewd gaze to Tairis. "My friend, walk with me; we need to catch up."

Tairis, his eyes still avoiding Naomhan, gestured her forward. "Of course. Is your garden still the envy of the worlds?"

"As much as it can be on a mortal plane," she said, pleased, offering an arm.

Concerned and confused at being ignored, once Aoife had turned away from him, Naomhan put on his cap and followed. He knew Tairis could see him, so he kept as quiet as he could, creeping slowly behind, eavesdropping on their soft conversation.

"Tairis," Aoife said sadly. "You cannot keep pinning your hopes upon these mortals. I learned long ago they are not capable of making the proper choice. Either take them as is tradition or leave them be."

Tairis didn't answer, absently tucking a lock of golden hair behind his ear.

She sighed loudly. "I know it distresses your sensibilities, but *you* were taken, and you turned out fine."

At this, his voice became wry. "Ah yes, a pariah among my so-called kin. I turned out perfectly well."

She had the decency to look a bit abashed. "Yes, but I'm a born fairy and a pariah too."

"Our ostracizing has the same cause, my friend," Tairis said. "Only you have the bloodline to defy it."

The two fairies embraced, and Aoife kissed his cheek. "You are always welcome to stay here with me," she said. "Should their tormenting grow too fierce."

Tairis pulled out of her grip, hunching his shoulders. "If only it were that simple. But this world no longer feels like home. It has no place for something like me."

Naomhan hesitated, no longer following. This conversation was becoming heavy, far heavier than he could have expected. They had come to the palace gardens, and Tairis paused to turn and pluck a rose from a bush beside him, smiling at the coral-pink blossoms.

He saw Naomhan out of the corner of his eye.

Naomhan froze, as did Tairis, their gazes locked. It was Tairis who moved first, straightening up and looking once more at Aoife, rose in hand. "Perhaps I *will* take you up on your offer, Aoife," he said. "At least for a night. Please, show me where I shall be laying my head."

And his hand curled behind his back, beckoning Naomhan to follow.

He did.

Aoife and Tairis discussed more things as they walked into the palace, mostly telling stories about people and fairies Naomhan didn't know, but eventually Aoife left to attend to Eilidh, and Tairis and Naomhan were alone in the room.

"You can remove the cap if you wish, though it makes no difference to me," Tairis said, rubbing his face as he sat beside the fire.

Naomhan did and sat across from Tairis in the opposite chair. Tairis looked tired, no longer the shining beacon he had presented himself as when freed from the snake's form or even the quiet elegance of a traveling sea bird. Still ethereally beautiful, of course, but the glow had dimmed, and his eyes were dark and sunken in his face. He appeared almost mortal.

"It's rude to eavesdrop, you know," Tairis said, and Naomhan dropped his head.

"I know. I tried to leave when you began discussing more private things, but…"

Tairis nodded. He didn't seem to be too upset. With a sigh, he leaned into the chair and crossed his legs at the ankle. "So, I imagine you heard everything."

Naomhan winced. "Yes. I'm sorry."

"Ask your questions, Naomhan. I am not angry." And indeed, he wasn't, as far as Naomhan could tell. But there was a melancholy to his features that made Naomhan's heart ache.

The first came easily. "What did Lady Aoife mean by 'taken'?"

"Fairies have long been interested in mortals," Tairis began, closing his eyes as he pulled together his thoughts. "They came to this land from their own long, long ago, and mortals could not escape their notice."

Venture not into the fens, the elders said. *For within rest the homes of gods. Disturb not their mounds nor their trees, and perhaps they will leave you be.*

But the young man was brave and foolish with youth. One

night in his sixteenth year, he crept from his home and into the fens, determined to bargain with a god or else acquire a treasure, something he could bring back to woo the one he loved—a shepherd's son with hair of golden wheat and eyes the blue of the sky.

He walked slowly through the marsh, wary of sinkholes. In the distance, lights flickered in and out of existence, making his heart pound in sudden fear. But his foolhardy bravery pushed him on until he found a god sitting in a clearing even more beautiful than the shepherd's son.

The god glowed like the moon and beckoned the young man to his side, smiling as he inquired about his name. And as the god repeated it, the young man felt something shimmer around him, a shifting of the world, and his name was gone.

The god brushed a hand over the young man's soft, curly hair and lifted his chin up to better examine his face appraisingly.

"You are a fine boy," the god said in a voice like home. "I would like very much to keep you."

The young man could not refuse, still frowning as he tried to recall his name.

The god took his hand, and they fell into starlight.

In the land of the gods, they supped, the god laughing as the young man was overwhelmed by flavors he could never even have imagined. And the god took him to a beautiful manor where they tasted of marriage. For days, the young man was lavished upon, overwhelmed by the attention but not abhorring of it.

Until he sought to return home to his shepherd's son.

Rather than being angry, the god merely laughed. "That is not your home anymore, gentle boy. But go, look, if you don't believe me."

So, the young man went. His village was changed.

Once-familiar faces were gone, and when he inquired about the people he'd once known, he received only confusion. Though he could not recall his own name, he knew the names of his family, repeating them again and again until a kind baker woman brought him to his old home now painted anew with different plants growing around it.

And within, a brother once known, age heavy on a familiar face. He looked like their grandfather.

For a long moment, the two stared at each other, the brother in shock. Then, rage. "You dare to come to me wearing that face!" he yelled, tears falling from his eyes. "Demon! I cast you out, begone!" And he warded his heart, slamming the door shut between them.

The young man wandered to the shepherd fields where an old man with a crooked staff stared at him with eyes as blue as the sky. "You remind me of someone I once knew," he said with a sad smile. "But he vanished long ago. Spirited away, they said."

And the young man nodded, not trusting his voice to speak.

He returned to the land of the gods and became one himself. The god who took him called him Tairis, the tender-hearted.

"Fairies can be born two ways," Tairis explained. "They can be made and birthed as any other creature, or they can begin life as a mortal being. A mortal being who is brought to the land of the fairies and partakes of the food and drink will start to become fey themself. So, for some, it is a matter of finding interesting mortals and taking them, often through seduction, to our world for the purpose of changing them. Changed fairies are considered somewhat lesser, lacking the bloodline of the so-called 'true' fairies." He drummed his fingers against his stomach, his eyes opening to watch the ceiling.

"I was one taken by such a seduction, but when I attempted

to return to my home here, I found half a century had passed while I remained ageless. You see, our worlds are alike, but they are like two rivers, side by side." He held up his hands, illustrating. "This world is like a swift mountain stream flush with snowmelt, burbling down a mountainside. But the world of fairies, it is a long, ancient river, slow and mighty in the mountains it has cut.

"When I crossed from river to stream, though I had been only days away, most of my family had died, and those who had not viewed me only as a monster wearing their brother's face." His fingers stopped as he laced his hands together. He sat up and looked at Naomhan. "I returned to the land of fairies, but in defiance, I retained many of my mortal habits."

He shifted his weight and stretched his arms, and only then did Naomhan realize Aoife had remained unnaturally still beyond the necessary motion; even her expressions had been nothing but purposeful. It had the effect of making her seem inhuman and strange, a trait Tairis did not share. Except on the mountain. Perhaps the fey's natural expressions did not come from the face and body, so to move them took conscious effort.

As if following the shape of his thoughts, Tairis yawned, his jaw popping, and rubbed his eyes. "In truth, my life is a lonely one, so I have tried to find another changed mortal to spend it with me. But I refuse to do what was done to me. Anyone who comes with me must do so of their own will." He smiled sadly. "I had hoped to ask *you* the question when the time was appropriate, when we'd spent more time together." Bitterly, he chuckled. "I should have asked you on the mountain. But I didn't want you to choose on a broken heart, for they can lead so quickly astray. But now you have the lovely Eilidh here. I know what your answer will be."

Many emotions at once threatened to bury Naomhan, so

much so that he struggled to find words. "Why me?" was all that came out, squeaking past his lips.

Tairis regarded him. "I fear I will perhaps cause offense, but you seem...distant from the other mortals. You do not dislike them, but you also do not quite live among them. It seemed to me perhaps you would not mind turning this world into one to visit, rather than live in. And you are kind and brave, traits I cannot help but admire." He gave Naomhan a small smile.

Naomhan considered his words. He had never thought of himself as being distant from humanity, but as he considered it, he wondered if it were true. Indeed, he wasn't unhappy flitting from city to city, playing the part of a wandering, mysterious prince. He had never even thought to imagine his father would think him dead. If he were a fairy, that could be his relationship with this world forever.

Of course, he would miss his father and uncle and maybe even Fachtna one day, but would it truly be so terrible?

Tairis sighed and stood. "And now my heart is empty of secrets. You may answer my request truly. Indeed, I am prepared for your refusal."

"Could I give you an answer later?" Naomhan asked, looking up at him. "I want to give it the consideration it deserves."

Tairis frowned, but a glimmer of hope sparked in his eyes. "Of course. But what will Lady Eilidh say to such an abandonment?"

Naomhan shrugged. "She and Caoimhe can find other bodyguards, ones even better than myself."

A long silence filled the room. "Is... Do you *not* intend on marrying Lady Eilidh?"

"M-marry?!" Naomhan fell backward into the couch, his eyes wide.

"You wanted to take her from this place! You asked only for

her freedom!" Tairis stammered.

"Yes, of course! To live in a place where your very emotions are smothered?! Madness! I don't need to desire marriage to want to free someone from such a fate! And indeed, Miss Caoimhe would be upset with me if I even proposed such a thing."

Tairis sat back down, his eyes wide as he gawked. For a long moment, the two stared at each other. Then, in a small, hopeful voice, "So, you're truly considering it?"

Naomhan smiled. "Yes, I am. First, I must return home. Prince Fachtna has promised me a birthday celebration."

The red rose tugged itself out of Naomhan's bag and settled inside his hand. "You can call upon me when you have decided on an answer," Tairis said. "I admit I am anxious to hear your reply, but take as much time as you need."

It took a few days for Eilidh and Caoimhe to gather their things for travel. Naomhan had hoped to spend the interim with Tairis, but he was still skittish. It was frustrating when the kiss they had shared the year before still burned bright in Naomhan's memory, but the kinder part of him could understand Tairis's hesitation. After all, he could still say no.

Not that he was especially planning on it. As he watched over Eilidh and Caoimhe, he started to understand what Tairis had said about his distance. Though he had been well-liked at court and had known the important names and faces, he had never been able to forge friendships. In truth, and with few exceptions, he was content to reflect what others needed him to be. A rock settled inside his stomach as he wondered if even his father knew the boy beneath the mirror. Did Naomhan himself even know?

Naomhan *liked* people certainly. He enjoyed spending time

with them and helping them, but he came to the uncomfortable realization that such feelings were more often given to a treasured pet than others who were equals.

On the final day of the women's preparations, Naomhan took a brief trip to the kingdom of the white king. He found the king in what must be his actual chambers, a large office with many books and papers stacked neatly around the room. The king sat alone, frowning at a particular stack as he took notes on a spare sheet.

Naomhan stood well away from him, in his direct line of sight, and removed his cap.

The king was startled, of course, and bound Naomhan once more, holding him fast. But when he didn't struggle against his bonds, the king frowned and tapped his throat, his voice once more in the language of the Highlands, though his lips spoke something else. "You are the boy who was here before," he said.

"Yes, I wished to speak with you, Your Majesty. My name is Naomhan."

After a moment of wary suspicion, the king waved his hand and Naomhan was freed. He drifted harmlessly to the floor. "Then speak, Naomhan. I will listen."

"I understand better now the dangers the fairies pose, but I have been offered the chance to become one myself."

The king raised an eyebrow. "Do you seek my approval of such a thing?"

With a wry twist of his lips, Naomhan said, "I do not think I would ever get that. No, I wish to hear an argument against it. I do not trust myself to be objective when my heart is already swayed."

"To become a fairy, you will throw away *anything* binding you to this world. All the people, all the familiar places. You will place yourself into a nest of vipers, who will see you forever as inferior and beneath their attention."

"Will I not be a viper myself?"

The king scoffed. "A hatchling, perhaps. It will likely take you centuries to learn the extent of your powers, and until that point, you will be mocked and pitied, as will the fairy that brought you to their land."

"He already is. I'd rather he not have to face such cruelties alone."

The king sat, steepling his fingers together. "There is a belief the fairies are lawless, but in truth, their laws are simply without reason as we conceive of it. You may be asked to behave in ways that are anathema to you."

Naomhan thought of his tutor's switch and the myriad laws of the court—who he could speak to, who could be looked upon, who could not. He thought of the itchy discomfort of the clothing he was made to wear and the longing for the clothing he could not. His smile was brittle as he said, "I fail to see how that is any different from our own realm."

The king knit his brows together but did not respond to the joke. "Then, it seems to me I cannot change your mind. I will ask only one thing. Do not forget who you once were. Too many of the fey see themselves above the lives of mortals. We are power and entertainment—useful pets. Do not allow yourself to become so corrupted. We do not need one more hungry fairy preying upon our world like it is their right."

Naomhan nodded. "Thank you, Your Majesty. I appreciate your help and advice."

"Even if you ignore it?" The king's voice was dry.

Naomhan grinned. "Even so."

And so, Naomhan escorted Eilidh and Caoimhe to the Highlands and introduced them to his uncle's court simply as friends he'd made on his journey. His father, so pleased to have him "back from the dead," made sure no especially probing questions were asked of them.

At the grand feast celebrating his return, Prince Fachtna stood, quieting the room with a few taps of knife to table. "Lord Naomhan, I wanted to take this opportunity to formally apologize for my behavior to you. I was immature and blamed you for my own failings and insecurities. Though I have yet more maturity to gain, I wanted you and everyone here to know how deeply I regret the man I have been, and I'm determined to one day make things right."

Naomhan led the hall in applause. There were a few titters of disbelief, but he believed in Fachtna. He watched as, after the meal, he and the king fell into quiet conversation, much of Fachtna's characteristic temper gone. One day he may even make a good king.

But perhaps Naomhan would not see it with his own eyes.

After the meal, Naomhan met with his father. For a while, they chatted about whatever came to mind until Naomhan could conceal his true purpose no longer. "Father, I may not return to this place."

Diarmad frowned. "What do you mean, Naomhan? Was Fachtna's speech simply for show?"

"No, I think he will do his best to live up to his father's example. However, I did meet someone else beyond the Ladies Eilidh and Caoimhe." He hesitated, unsure of how much to tell his father. The proper truth would only cause him pain and heartbreak. But then again, Naomhan's leaving at all would do that. "I have fallen in love with someone from a distant land, far out of reach of even our swiftest ships. I have been asked to journey to that homeland, and I…wish very much to accept the invitation."

Diarmad sighed and sat heavily upon his chair. Uncertainly, Naomhan sank to his knees and perched beside his father's lap as he'd done as a child. "I'm sorry, Father."

Shaking his head, Diarmad rested a hand upon his son's face and ran his thumb over the curve of his cheek. Naomhan closed his eyes, willing himself not to pull away. "When you were born," Diarmad explained, "your mother lived only a few days. But in those days, she was blessed with prophesy. She clutched you to her breast whenever she could, crying that the fairies would come and take you. We set wards and charms, and when she passed, you were hale and healthy, no sickly changeling." His eyes were sad as they gazed upon his only child. "But now you have become a man and shall leave me still."

Naomhan leaned his head against his father's thigh, unsure of what to say.

"I am no fool, Naomhan, nor was your mother, it seems. I must ask—are you sure? There is a home for you here, and perhaps"—he touched the signet ring upon his hand—"perhaps this kingdom could one day become yours to rule."

"Heavens above, I would never wish for such a thing," Naomhan said before he could stop himself.

Diarmad smiled and put his hand on Naomhan's head. "Precisely why I think the crown would suit you far more than your cousin, but there is enough of your mother in you I know you are informing me of your choice, not seeking to be swayed."

Naomhan tried to apologize again, but Diarmad hushed him. "For the first days of your life, I thought I would lose both wife and son. Instead, I have watched you grow from babe to man, carrying your mother's spirit. I have already been given more than I expected to receive." He stroked Naomhan's hair. "But if I may ask a boon, introduce me to the fairy who will spirit you away at long last."

Naomhan took an uncertain breath but nodded and stood before removing the red rose from his bag. He spoke without preamble. "My father wishes to meet with you."

There was a heart-stopping moment when Naomhan feared he would not appear, but soon there was a shimmer in the air, and Tairis was there, wearing the finery of their first meeting—with one dramatic difference. This Tairis was wearing a woman's guise.

Naomhan placed a hand on his arm. "I appreciate the attempt to protect my honor, but I wish my father to know *you*."

Tairis looked at him, uncertainty in his gaze, but his form shifted—still regal, still beautiful, but undeniably male once more. Diarmad surveyed them both, silent but for the soft rush of his breathing. Then, he stood and held out his arm to Tairis. "Promise me you will care for my son. He is the greatest gift I have ever been given."

Tairis bowed his head and gripped the curve of Diarmad's elbow—an ancient motion of pact-making. Diarmad did the same, laying the flat of their forearms together. "I shall swear it in blood, should you ask it of me."

Diarmad shook his head. "I wouldn't. But lean down, give me your head."

Bemused, Tairis did. Diarmad kissed the tip of Tairis's proffered forehead, right at the edge of his golden hair. "Even if we never meet again, you have my blessing for whatever it is worth to your kind. If my son loves you, then I shall as well, for family is nothing without bonds of love as well as blood. Tell me, what is your name?"

Tairis stared wonderingly at Diarmad, still gripping his arm. His gaze was far away. "Once, I was Eoghan," he said softly. "I remember now. I was Eoghan."

"Care for my son, Eoghan," Diarmad said and released his hand. "And we shall never be at odds."

"Yes, my lord."

Diarmad patted Naomhan's shoulder. "Thank you for indulging your father, Naomhan. I need to rest now. Please don't leave until tomorrow morning."

"Of course, Father. Sleep well."

As the door closed, Naomhan turned to Tairis, who was still wondering. "Should I call you Eoghan now?"

The fairy smiled sadly. "No. It is a mortal's name, not a fairy's. But I had thought it lost. It is…pleasant to remember. As a reminder of who I once was. I may no longer *be* Eoghan, but I have never wanted to forget him." His expression brightened. "So, if your father is giving me a speech like that, does that mean…?"

Naomhan held out his hand. "If you will have me, I will follow."

Tairis surged forward and grabbed Naomhan's waist, then lifted him up and brought their lips together.

It was even better the second time.

The morning dawned, and Naomhan bid his father farewell. In the garden, Eilidh and Caoimhe waited, their beauty rivaling the flowers'. Eilidh kissed Naomhan's forehead. "I don't know if I'm fairy enough to give you a blessing, but I can certainly hope to," she said warmly. "May your days be sweet and your nights sweeter, my friend."

Naomhan blushed even as he smiled. "Thank you, Lady Eilidh. I shall carry your good will with me."

"Farewell, Sir Naomhan. Fortune favor you."

The wind rustled as Tairis appeared, shining white and gold in the dawn light. He tapped Naomhan's nose, and as Naomhan glanced down, he watched his old clothing transform to match Tairis's finery.

Eilidh clapped her hands. "Oh, white looks so lovely with your dark hair!" she cooed.

Tairis offered his arm for Naomhan to grasp and brushed his lips against the crown of his head as he did. "Hold tightly to me. Do not let go until I tell you."

Naomhan nodded. His heart fluttered with nerves and breathless anticipation.

"Take care, my ladies," Tairis said, and the wind picked up, shifting from blowing against him to blowing *through* him. Around him, the world faded.

When Naomhan's sight returned, it was like he was seeing color for the first time. "*Oh,*" he breathed, looking at Tairis in wonder. "I didn't know it would be so beautiful."

Tairis plucked a tray of fruit from the air, each piece gleaming and succulent. The food of the fairies, which would make Naomhan one of them. "Are you sure?" Tairis asked once more. "This is your last chance to turn back."

Naomhan took an apple from the tray and kissed its skin. "Yes, I'm sure."

And with one bite, Naomhan *became.*

Name Pronunciation Guide

Naomhan (NEEV-awn)

Fachtna (FAHKT-nah)

Tairis (TA-rish)

Caoimhe (KWI-vuh)

Eilidh (EH-li)

Aoife (EE-feh)

Diarmad (DYEER-mad)

Sìogaidh (SHEE-gih)

Eoghan (YO-un)

In the Shade of the
Tree of Life

To those on the outside.

When Innes met Crown Prince Kenneth for the first time, he knew he was doomed.

The prince was quiet, known for being thoughtful and a bit distant, a scholar king-to-be. Some of the courtiers even called him cold, arrogant—the sort of man who saw himself as above the rabble. *He would rather hole himself up for months than deign to interact with even the nobility,* some of the visiting lords and ladies tittered.

Of course, as the heir, he was required to show his face at meals. Prince Kenneth was handsome enough, from a distance, tall and broad-shouldered, his hair coppery-gold, swept away from his face, but his expression was always oddly still, his mind far away.

The prince being such, Innes, the tailor's apprentice, didn't even meet him when he first came to the castle with his master.

For months, Innes was happy to work with the various other nobles who lived in the palace while his master exclusively attended to the royal family. Innes was personable, but easily distracted, so it was all the best he didn't approach the royals.

Therefore, of course, his master fell ill during the winter festivities and asked Innes to attend to Prince Kenneth's feast wear. His heart in his throat, Innes approached the prince's chambers, his basket of supplies held tightly in his sweating palm. After a swift knock, the prince himself answered the door and ushered him inside.

The prince's rooms were surprisingly messy, books and scrolls scattered haphazardly around, spread across the floor and bookshelves. With a blush, the prince moved a few of the books with his foot. "Forgive me, I was caught up doing research."

And indeed, the desk was spotted with the wax drippings of candles burned long into the night, and there were dark bags under the prince's red-rimmed eyes. He was not at all like Innes had been told to expect. Indeed, he was reminded of his elder brother, and Innes couldn't help a teasing smile. "I hope you made a grand discovery, Your Highness," he said lightly.

Prince Kenneth laughed and rubbed the blond-red stubble over his chin, the blush darkening. "I wish. I was reading about the royal family of the Highlands prior to the invasion of the Saxtish warlords. Nothing groundbreaking, but a bit sad. Did you know one of the cousins of King Fachtna the Humble was supposedly spirited away by fairies? Scary to imagine."

The prince was modest and the sort of sentimental man who'd get caught up in reading about history he already knew the outcome of as well as latch onto strange little anecdotes. Innes was immediately drawn to him, which he had to stop in its tracks. He opened his basket. "I'm sorry to hear that, Your Highness," he said primly. "Shall we begin?"

"Ah, yes, of course." Prince Kenneth's amber-brown gaze slid away from Innes. "Forgive me, I know you're busy with your master sick."

Innes removed the new cotte and helped the prince into it, falling into his routine—"Arms up, please," "Back straight, please," "Watch the pins." The prince, quiet and compliant, no longer made conversation. Thinner than Innes had expected, the prince would need his cotte taken in quite a bit to fit. He frowned to himself, debating whether or not to comment. He decided to frame it as a question. "Would you like me to pad the waist a bit to make you look a bit more substantial, Your Highness?"

"Have I lost weight again?" he asked, frowning.

"I've no idea, Your Highness. I've not measured you before. Do you often lose weight?"

"I have an ill-tempered stomach, and winter suits it poorly," the prince said, running a hand down his torso.

Innes focused his gaze on the velvet of the cotte, keeping his head down. "That is most unfortunate, Your Highness. I am sorry to hear that."

He could feel Prince Kenneth's eyes on the top of his head. "Please, pad the cotte," the prince said after a long moment. "There is no reason to worry the kingdom needlessly."

"Of course, Your Highness." Innes helped him out of the pinned and marked velvet, then folded it to return it to the basket. Innes chanced a glance upward and caught sight of the prince's eyes, looking at him. A blush crept up his cheeks. "If I may ask"—his heart thrummed; he shouldn't—"what sort of fare suits Your Highness's stomach?"

The prince was caught off guard, his face lovely in confusion. "Soup and bread rarely trouble me, but why do you ask?"

Innes gave him a smile. "Surely an educated man such as yourself could guess." And to keep himself from even more impertinence, Innes bowed, stepped back out of the room, and closed the door. He kept his hand on it for a moment, heart pounding in his ears. Oh, this was bad.

He returned to his and his master's chambers to make the alterations.

Oh, this was *bad*.

A week passed before Innes returned to Prince Kenneth's rooms, basket in hand. This time, the floor was clear and neat, books in straight lines on their shelves. The prince sat behind his desk, writing out something with a fresh quill.

He perked up as Innes entered. "I'm glad you get to see me more at my best," he joked, setting his paper aside as he rose. "Though, I must admit, it was not my doing." He was handsomer with a good night's sleep, more like the portrait of him that hung in the public gallery.

Innes bowed and reached into his basket, producing the fresh loaf of bread he'd requested with his morning breakfast. "I worried about you losing more weight, Your Highness," he said.

Prince Kenneth's smile shifted from polite to gentle, his eyes sparkling. Innes's heart fluttered in his chest even as his stomach clenched in fear of what that meant. "You are very kind. I hope it wasn't any trouble." He took the bread and wasted no time in ripping off a piece. He offered it to Innes first. "I know you are no assassin, but if you could."

"Oh, of course." He was stupid. Of course, the prince had to be careful of unexpected food and drink. He took the piece of bread and stuffed it into his mouth, embarrassed and awkward, wishing for ale to wash it down.

Once Innes swallowed, the prince ate a piece of his own. "You must forgive me, but I forgot to ask your name."

"Innes, Your Highness. I apologize for not introducing myself properly." He bowed.

"It's fine, it's fine," Prince Kenneth said, waving his hand. "Are the alterations done?"

"Yes, of course, Your Highness." Innes knelt to open the basket, then pulled the cotte free and helped the prince into it. It looked wonderful. A small twinge of regret lanced through Innes's stomach; he should have dragged out the tailoring process for more excuses to see the prince. (No, he definitely should *not* have done that. It would've reflected poorly upon his master and himself.)

The prince walked before his mirror and turned this way and that to better examine his reflection, a smile on his face. Despite being sad their brief time together was ending, Innes allowed himself a moment to admire his work—a pleased client was a joy all its own. He was only an apprentice, and to know a prince, the *crown* prince, was happy with his journeyman's stitching? It was a confidence in which he didn't often let himself indulge.

Prince Kenneth ran his hands over the fabric, over the padding around the torso, his expression filled with emotions Innes couldn't quite understand. He was pleased, of course, but sadness lurked too—a well-worn sadness, nearly threadbare with how often he had worried it. Innes saw it because he knew it as well. But it would be improper for him to speak of it aloud.

Prince Kenneth turned back to Innes. "This is lovely," he said warmly, offering a hand to help Innes to his feet. When their hands touched, Innes's heart raced and his knees weakened beneath him. It was like falling into a sunset as the prince's gaze turned honey soft. For a long moment, they stayed like that, holding hands until the prince turned away, tucking his hand behind him as if he meant to sit on it. "I'm sorry, Sir Innes." His lips drew tight, the apple of his throat bobbing as he swallowed.

Innes closed his hand, trying to recapture some of that warmth. Then, Innes made a foolish choice, one he knew full well would lead only to tragedy. He took Prince Kenneth's other hand and held it to his chest, drawing the prince's gaze. Deliberately, he raised the prince's hand to his lips and placed a kiss upon his knuckles, keeping their eyes locked.

Kenneth's eyes widened in surprise, his fair cheeks darkening beneath his freckles. But innocence lasted only a moment.

When their lips met, Innes was filled with an absurd urge to say a blessing. *Blessed is the Lord, our God, who has allowed me to reach this joyous day.* He didn't though; he was a bit tied up. He didn't think the Lord would mind, for surely it was He who made such a perfect mouth, soft and shy but oh so wanting. Inexperienced, Innes could tell, for he rushed and fumbled. Innes held the back of his head and guided him while embers burned in the pit of his stomach, desire swiftly stoked.

Kenneth, almost a head taller than Innes, was bent at an odd angle, his arms coming around the small of Innes's back. Kenneth walked the two of them toward his desk, then ran his hands down Innes's thighs. "Sit," he said breathlessly.

Quick to comply, Innes settled on the desk, uncaring of the papers upon it. Kenneth stood between his legs and looked up into Innes's face. Innes smirked and wrapped his legs around Kenneth's thighs, pulling them flush together.

They kissed for a minute—or was it an hour?—before finally pulling apart, Kenneth's face flushed, his lips swollen and wet. Innes swallowed heavily, his thoughts indecent. Both were breathless, the moment still unbroken—like a snowflake upon a scarf.

Kenneth smiled and tangled his fingers in Innes's dark beard. "You wear it quite long," he commented, scraping his nails along Innes's jaw, which made a shiver run down his spine.

"Ah, yeah," Innes said and caught Kenneth's wandering hand and twined their fingers together. "It's religious. We're not supposed to shave the 'corners,' which I never understood, but my father wears his beard like this, so I suppose it must do."

"What *is* the corner of a beard?" Kenneth wondered, now stroking the length of it with his other hand. "Is it the line of the jaw? Or along the bottom of the beard itself?"

"I couldn't tell you," Innes said with a laugh.

Kenneth hummed thoughtfully while kissing along the underside of Innes's jaw, using their still-joined hands to move his head to the side. The stubble tickled.

"What are you doing?" Innes asked, resisting the urge to squirm.

"Looking for the beard corners," Kenneth teased and placed a sloppy kiss upon Innes's pulse.

Innes laughed and pushed him off, then gripped Kenneth's face between his hands, smiling. He kissed his nose.

Kenneth wrinkled it before resting his hands on Innes's thighs. "So, tell me of your religion," he said. "You've made me curious."

Innes sighed. "Do you have a lifetime? Because that's what it will take me to explain. Suffice it to say, it's not much different than yours but with more rules."

"What sort of rules?" Kenneth's hands moved up to Innes's hips, warm through his linen trousers.

"About what to wear and what to eat and such things." Innes found it hard to concentrate on the words coming from his mouth as Kenneth's fingers slipped beneath his tunic and touched bare skin. They were cool and smooth, different than the rough pads of Innes's needle-pricked fingers. They were big though, a man's hands indeed. Innes shivered. It had been a long time since he'd felt small.

"Sounds difficult," Kenneth said, his fingers finding the dips in Innes's spine as if he were playing a harp.

This time, Innes couldn't resist the urge to squirm, knocking his knees into Kenneth's hip. "No more difficult than any other rules really."

"Mm." Kenneth gave up on any pretense of conversation, planting small kisses down the side of Innes's neck, his hands teasing at the top of his trousers.

"I should," Innes breathed. "I should return. I don't know how long I've been here."

"Not long enough clearly," Kenneth said, his mouth—still swollen with kissing—quirking up in a wicked smirk. "You're still thinking."

Innes laughed and rested his head against Kenneth's shoulder. "I'm afraid *that* will take a bit more than kissing."

Raising his eyebrows, Kenneth asked, "Is that a challenge?"

"Not…at the moment." Innes looked away, the burn of embarrassment in his ears. "But maybe soon."

Kenneth stepped away and into his bedchamber, then returned with a small, brass key. He pressed it into Innes's hand. "There is a servants' stair," he explained, pointing to one of the walls. Indeed, once Innes had stared long enough, he could see the outline of the door, blended into the pattern of the wall. "At the bottom of the stair, there is a door. This is the key to that door. When you can, I'd appreciate a visit."

How could anyone have thought this man cold? His smile was like the sun after a long winter, radiantly warm and kind. There was a soft dip in the center of his bottom lip—it called for a return to kissing.

In part to help control himself, Innes stared at the key, a sinking, swirling uneasiness unfurling in his stomach. Of course, this was to be a secret affair; it couldn't be anything but. He rolled the key between his fingers. He could refuse. He *should* refuse. This was the crown prince, heir to a *kingdom*. He was a tailor's apprentice and a man whose people were doomed to be forever unwanted.

He closed his hand around the key and smiled at the prince. "I shall listen closely and knock before I enter."

Prince Kenneth stroked his cheek. "Will you come tonight?"

"I will try, Your Highness." He stood and retrieved his basket and tucked the key inside.

Before he left, Prince Kenneth caught him around the waist and kissed the top of his head. "I shall wait for your knock."

When he returned to his master's appointments, he strung the key upon a leather cord and tied it around his neck. He rubbed his thumb against the cool metal and dropped it into his tunic to keep it from view.

After the key settled there, gooseflesh spreading across his chest, Innes pressed the heels of his hands to his eyes, harder and harder until he saw stars. He mouthed a blessing, the one for new beginnings, and prayed when (and it would be *when*) this went wrong, they both came out okay.

Oh, this was so very bad.

That night, after his master had gone to bed, Innes slipped out of his bed. He went through his clothes, checking his underthings for stains before pulling on a nice vest. Emptying his tailor's basket, he placed in two egg pies he'd saved from the evening's supper before putting on his softest and quietest leather shoes.

He left the room, rubbing the key through his tunic. He padded through the hallways, watching for guards, practicing his "oh no, this isn't the way to the privy!" drunken slur in his head.

He needn't have worried. He had no issue entering the servants' door near the main staircase for the wing. From there, there were a lot of stairs upward until he came to three doors, all locked. He tried his key in each, right to left, before the leftmost one opened.

As he climbed the stairs, he kept his ears open, listening for voices. When he heard nothing, he rapped on the door, his heart in his throat.

The door opened, and Kenneth offered him a hand, grinning. "You look lovely."

"I brought food," Innes said, holding up the basket.

With a surprised laugh, Kenneth took out one of the egg pies. "We'll have a snack for afterwards." His face fell a bit. "Unless you'd prefer we…?"

Innes shook his head and stroked the stubble on Kenneth's cheek. "No, I want to," he said with a smile. "So long as you'll have me." Even if it was only until the morning. Even if it was only this night, this tryst. Innes was already here, after all.

And so, Kenneth and Innes went to bed, locking the bedchamber door behind them.

It was silly and a little awkward as all first times are, but as they lay together in the bed, bare but for the warm covers, a deep, heavy sense of peace—one he'd felt only a scant few times before—filled Innes's heart.

The bed was warm and safe, silent but for their breathing, nearly synchronous in the dark. Beneath his head, Kenneth's heart beat, deep and steady—the sound of being alive. Innes did not often know a peace like this; his mind preferred a life of worry and anxiety, spiraling from worst-case scenario to worst-case scenario until Innes nearly popped like too-tight stitching. But here, in the afterglow, a languid, lazy weight in his limbs, and a heartbeat in his ear, he found peace.

It was a shame it was soon to end.

He sighed against Kenneth's chest, trailing his finger through the red-gold hair. "I should go," he said softly. A small voice, the part that still dared to defy reality, wanted Kenneth to insist he stay.

Instead, Kenneth frowned and stroked his hand over Innes's hair. "Yes, you should. But I shall miss you."

So dismissed, Innes got out of the grand, four-poster bed and shuffled about, gathering his fallen clothes, redressing quickly. His thighs and back ached with exertion, but he didn't have any need for regret. "Farewell. Shall I come again tomorrow?"

Kenneth smiled, his head resting in the crook of his arm. "If you can," he said.

Innes would certainly do his damnedest.

Nightly visits lasted the next week. On the seventh night when Innes entered, he found Kenneth already asleep. Unwilling to wake him, and recalling it was the Sabbath, Innes lit a candle and murmured the blessings under his breath as he covered his eyes. He pulled out the bread he'd kept from dinner and blessed that, too, before eating it.

He sat beside Kenneth in the bed, imagining constellations in the galaxy of freckles that covered his cheeks. After tying back one of the curtains, he picked up the book Kenneth had been reading from the nightstand. It was another history book, written in Senatin, this one detailing the Norench invasion of Saxtain nearly three hundred years prior.

It had been a long time since Innes had been able to sit and read, so for a time, the words came frustratingly slowly, but he kept at it, bending his lips to each letter as it came until they smoothed out in his mind.

After an hour or so, Kenneth yawned and woke up, bumping his head into Innes's hip. "You're here," he said sleepily, smiling.

"I am," Innes said, ruffling Kenneth's hair. "I didn't want to wake you."

"Mm, you're so kind," Kenneth mumbled, wrapping his arms around Innes's waist. Then, his eyes opened in a realization. "Wait, you're reading. Are you literate?"

Innes nodded. "I'm out of practice, but it's a well-learned skill."

His eyes sparkled. "Does this mean we can talk about books together?"

Innes laughed and set the history text aside, then slid down under the cover to cuddle with Kenneth properly. "It does."

"I shall have to share all of my favorites," he said, wrapping Innes in his arms, his voice softening. "Forgive my exhaustion. I spent much of the day hunting with Ellar."

Innes imagined it—the thin, waifish Kenneth beside Prince Ellar, who was younger and stronger, a man who would be considered "strapping." Prince Ellar was blond and broad, the picture of his father in his youth. "You poor thing," he teased and kissed Kenneth's forehead. "Sleep. I'll stay a little longer."

After some time, the candle winked out. As Kenneth was asleep again, seeming younger in his repose, Innes got out of the bed and closed the bedcurtains. It was getting harder and harder to leave. He sighed and pinched the bridge of his nose. This was so bad. He needed to separate himself before this went too far.

But the rational, logical thought filled him only with emptiness.

He managed to stay away for three days, throwing himself into work, determined not to think about the prince. So, of course, he thought of him constantly, like a toothache, tonguing the hurt again and again. Was Kenneth upset by his sudden disappearance? Was he worried? Did he miss Innes? And if he did, did he miss *him* or just his "company"?

Innes scowled as he pricked his finger, drawing blood. He licked it clean, staring at the perfect round spot of red that had fallen upon the white undershirt he'd been sewing. It was no use, he realized. It was already too late. It had been too far for quite some time. It had been too far the moment Innes had used the key still strung around his neck.

"Oh dear," his master said, peering over his thick spectacles. "Let's get that in some cold water and get you a bandage."

"Yes, sir. I deeply apologize."

"No harm done, my boy. It's not as if anyone will see it under the outer clothes." With fingers nimble despite their age, he whisked the shirt away and set it in their water basin. Against Innes's chest, the key burned.

He returned to Kenneth's room that night. If he was going to be hidden and scrubbed from history someday regardless, he might as well enjoy his moment. But the way Kenneth's face lit up upon seeing him made it worthwhile.

Once Innes had accepted the inevitable, the two of them fell into a routine. Some nights they made use of Kenneth's large, warm bed for a variety of activities, but other evenings saw them reading side by side, Innes occasionally interrupting to ask about a word or sentence he didn't understand. Afterward, they'd talk about what they'd read, anything from discussions of current politics or long dead history to religious debate that would leave the castle's cardinal with heart palpitations.

Kenneth was fascinated by Innes's people and had a surprisingly open mind about his own beliefs. "There was a great philosopher who said, 'The unexamined life is not worth living,'" he explained when questioned. "If I do not approach my own beliefs with the same rigor as I do others', then I will forever trap myself in hypocrisies."

"I think I'd like this philosopher," Innes said. "Do you have any books about him?"

And so it went.

One day, Innes brought Kenneth the worn, hand-me-down copy of the Ketuvim that had been a gift for his bar mitzvah, only a few short months before his people's expulsion from the neighboring country of Saxtain (on charges amounting to little more than "they're different and that makes them evil"). It was a small leather book, and the inside held only translations in Senatin, not the original text itself, but it was still a treasure to Innes—a connection to his people even if their traditions were slowly being leached away by the pressure of living among those who were hostile toward them.

Kenneth examined the book with interest, a smile on his face. "This is well-loved," he commented, rubbing his thumb over the places were the leather had been worn smooth.

The two of them sat together in Kenneth's bed, the book held between them as Innes pointed out some of the most interesting or beautiful passages. Kenneth was familiar with the contents, though he did not know the translation, not written by a monk of the Church.

In the Song of Songs, Innes ran his fingers over a few of the lines, over which were written some of the original letters. "*Ani l'dodi, v'dodi li,*" Innes read softly.

Kenneth translated the Senatin. "I am my beloved's, and my beloved is mine." He lifted Innes's hand to his lips, kissing the back softly.

"I am my beloved's," Innes echoed, setting the book aside to roll into Kenneth's lap, his arms around his neck. "And his desire is for me."

For months, their courtship continued until they grew from new lovers to comfortable ones. Innes was no longer struck dumb by the way candlelight glinted off of Kenneth's late-night stubble, nor by the smooth lines of his back. Instead now, he saw home in those things—like the taste of his mother's soup or the scent of his father's pipe. More often than not now, their nights together were spent in the sitting room of Kenneth's chambers, surrounded by his book collection, their ankles hooked together as they sat and studied. Sex still had its appeals of course, and they did plenty of that as well, but some of the immediate ardor had cooled. There was time enough, they felt.

Which of course was their death knell.

When people are comfortable, they become less attentive to detail. Innes stopped making sure his master was truly asleep before he slipped away. Kenneth stopped confining liaisons strictly to his bedroom behind door and curtain.

And so it was, one night, Prince Ellar burst in with important news from their father and found himself staring at his brother and a bearded man locked in a passionate embrace upon the sitting room sofa.

For a long moment, silence rang through the room as Kenneth and Prince Ellar stared each other down, and Innes tried desperately to hide his face from view.

"The servants thought you were seeing someone," Prince Ellar said quietly, his eyes still wide in shock, "but *this*." His lip curled. "Have you no shame?"

Kenneth tightened his grip upon Innes's back, comforting and seeking comfort both at once. "Can I ask you to keep this a secret, brother?"

For a moment, Innes wondered if the prince would do it. His face pinched, jaw working in thought. After a long, breathless moment, Prince Ellar sighed and shook his head. "I'm sorry, brother, but I can't. You're *betrothed*. And this"—he gestured toward Innes, who ducked his head in supplication— "is something that will make it much more difficult for Father and Mother to finalize that agreement."

Kenneth frowned, narrowing his eyes. His grip tightened on Innes's torso. "Then Princess Elodie has accepted?"

Innes's blood ran cold, hearing that name. The eldest princess of Saxtain. If the Highlands were to unite with such a place, would Innes and his family be driven out once again?

Ellar gave him a sharp nod. "I thought you might want to know," he said, lip curling.

"All kings take mistresses. So long as I am discreet, what is the harm?" Kenneth's hands were trembling—or maybe that was Innes? He couldn't tell.

"He's an outsider, lower than a commoner. His people were *expelled* from Saxtain. Such things must happen for a reason," Prince Ellar spat. "If it were *only* a man. If it were *only* an outsider, perhaps. But *both*? No, brother."

Innes closed his eyes, breathing Kenneth's scent, savoring what would be their last embrace.

Kenneth kept arguing. "Again, I ask you, so what? Who is being harmed by this relationship?"

"Your integrity!" Prince Ellar's voice rose in pitch before being clamped down into a sharp hiss. "Have you no care for that? It's bad enough you're hardly better than a recluse, and now you want to add that you are warped?" He buried his hands into his short, blond hair, tugging at the roots. "You are the *heir*, brother! You represent our kingdom to the world!"

Innes glanced at Kenneth's face and spotted the glimmer of tears in his eyes. He had stopped arguing.

Prince Ellar sighed again. "I will give you a day," he said softly. "Because you are my brother, and I care for you. Do with it what you will." And with that, he left, shutting the door firmly behind him.

For a long moment, neither Kenneth nor Innes spoke. Silently, Innes untangled himself from Kenneth's arms and straightened his clothes before reaching up to smooth down his hair. Kenneth stood after him, looped his arms around Innes's waist, and pressed a kiss against the crown of his head.

Innes relaxed against Kenneth's chest, resting his hands atop his. "We knew this would happen," he said, forcing down the ache in his throat.

"I hoped it wouldn't." Kenneth's voice trembled. Innes pretended not to feel the dampness sinking through his hair.

"Hope is for children and fools," Innes said, looking at their joined hands. "I shall have to tell my master there's been a death in the family. I can leave tomorrow morning."

Kenneth's grip tightened. "You're going to leave the castle?"

"It's the best way," he said. "If I am here, we both may be tempted." Slowly, he pulled free, unable to look at the man who had once been his lover. The man who was now betrothed to an enemy. "You shall not see me again. Your brother will likely keep his discovery quiet to maintain the polished appearance royalty must wear. You will marry. You will beget heirs of your own. The world will continue on." He glanced at his hands. Not shaking. Good.

Kenneth's voice was soft, still thin with tears. "And what of you?"

Mirthlessly, Innes smiled. "I will survive. It's all my people are good at." Like mice in the larder hiding from a cat perhaps, but survival all the same. In the scheme of history, this hurt was nothing. Taking a deep breath, Innes turned and bowed to Prince Kenneth. "Take care, Your Highness."

"Wait!" Prince Kenneth ran into his room and returned with a handful of plain gold jewelry. "Please." He held it out in offering. "To—to help you."

Innes looked at the gold. It would be useful, to have money to help his family while he sought new work. And yet, would he be questioned about its origins? Plain they may be, but perhaps they held some small maker's mark, which would paint Innes a thief, taking advantage of his position. *Greedy.* He shook his head. "Your help is appreciated, Your Highness, but I can take care of myself." He bowed low once more and opened the servants' door.

And with that, Innes left and hurried down the stairs. It was only when he arrived at his master's appointments that he realized he had kept the key. He pressed his palm to his chest, feeling its outline. It was to be a memento, then. So be it.

Under his breath, Innes said a blessing, all but meaningless when his heart was so shaken. But it did the job of holding back tears, and that was enough.

In the morning, Innes returned to his parents' home down in the city. They shared it with the family of his father's friend, who had graciously offered them a place to live when Saxtain turned against them.

He murmured the day's prayers under his breath as he walked, taking comfort in the ritual. As he walked down the cobbled streets, away from the castle on the hill, he watched the city wake, stirring to life like a beehive in spring.

Carts and carriages rumbled around him, coming and going from the palace. A small piece of him wondered if Prince Kenneth would step out of one of them and bring him back to the castle.

But of course, he didn't. He reached his parent's home without issue, down in the bowels of the city where the sky was small, and the light was dim. Before knocking upon the door, he touched the mezuzah affixed to the doorpost, taking comfort in it. He hadn't hung one in the castle, for fear of standing out. (It wouldn't have mattered since Prince Ellar had known what he was regardless. He should have. It felt like betrayal now that he had not.)

He knocked. His younger sister, Ruth, answered it, her dark eyes wide. "Isaac!" she said, hugging him tightly. "What brings you home all of sudden? Is everything okay?"

He had underestimated how hard it would hit him to hear his home name after so long away. Tears prickled behind his eyes. He had chosen the name Innes so he could travel easily in this strange land. He liked the name Innes; it felt like him.

And yet, it still made his chest warm to hear his familiar name from a familiar voice.

At Ruth's exclamation, their mother, Hadassah, appeared in the entranceway, concern and joy warring in her expression. Isaac sighed and wrapped his sister up in another hug, squeezing her tightly. "It—it's a long story. Suffice it to say, I won't be working at the castle any longer."

Hadassah clucked her tongue, narrowing her eyes. She would get the full story out of him later, whether he liked it or not. But for now, she said, "Well, come into the kitchen then. Let's get you fed."

While he ate, his mother worked. She was a seamstress, and it had been from her he'd first learned to sew. When his bowl was empty, she set the mending aside and took his hands, rubbing her thumbs over his knuckles. "Now, tell me what happened and what you plan to do next."

Behind the doorway, Ruth hovered. With a sigh, Isaac waved her in as well. "You mustn't share all the details with Father and David, please." He worried more about his older brother than his father. His brother had been an example to live up to Isaac's entire life; he hated the idea of him seeing Isaac brought so low.

Hadassah pinched her lips. "So, it *is* about sex. Isaac, my boy, what have you gotten yourself into?"

Isaac told her everything, spilling his heart across the small kitchen table to the crackle of the stove and the scent of simmering soup. Ruth had her arm around his shoulders while his mother still held his hands.

"Oh, my darling," she sighed. "What a fine pickle you've found yourself in. I'll see what we can do about getting you a new job. I actually may know of one… I'll have to ask Mistress Lithgow down the road. Ruth, sweetheart, go nip down to the market and get some sugar? Pastries are best for asking favors."

With a last squeeze to Isaac, Ruth was up and away, the door creaking as it shut. Hadassah contemplated her younger son, turning his hands over to rub circles into his palms. "We'll spin a story. Perhaps an argument. Or plain bigotry. It seems this land is not so free of prejudice as we'd hoped." Her smile was bitter. "The Church is everywhere and has declared us its enemy."

Innes sneered, freeing his hands to wipe the tear trails from his cheeks. "Are we not the source of its Savior?"

Hadassah threw her hands up in exasperation before taking up her mending once more. "Something they seem eager to ignore. For now, you can make yourself useful." She pointed the basket.

Shaking his head fondly, he helped his mother. When Ruth returned, Hadassah took to baking while Isaac did her work. While he did, Ruth sat with him, helping him as she could, but mostly reminding him she was there. "No matter what, I love you, Isaac," she said softly.

He kissed her cheek. "You too, Ruthie."

At the end of the day, his father, Mordecai, returned along with David. Isaac told the story he and his mother and sister had crafted from truth—that the Prince Ellar had taken issue with his being close to his elder brother. David looked ready to march up to the castle, but Mordecai put a heavy hand on his son's shoulder and pushed him down to sit at the kitchen table. "We'll help you find new work," he said, tugging thoughtfully on his salt and pepper beard.

"I'm on my way to Mistress Lithgow's now," Hadassah said, scooping the still-warm pastries into a basket. "Soup is ready. Bread is baked. Help yourselves."

Ruth and Isaac served the food, doling it out across the table. David began a long tirade against the crown and the prejudice their people faced while Isaac made dismissive grunts at all the right places. If Mordecai noticed his younger son's uncharacteristic silence, in his kindness, he did not bring it up. Instead, he engaged David in debate, leaving Isaac to eat his meal in relative peace.

Partway through the meal, Hadassah returned, her basket empty. "You'll meet with a messenger tomorrow for a Lady Keita," she said proudly. "She's from the south!" Her smile turned to a grin.

"Saxtain?" Isaac asked warily.

"No, further south." His mother's grin widened.

"Ibern?" David asked.

"Further." Hadassah took the bowl of soup offered by Ruth and sat down.

"Amhassinia?" Mordecai asked, his gray, bushy eyebrows rising to meet his hairline.

"South enough but move westward." She swirled her bread in the broth before taking a bite.

"The Mandali Empire?" Isaac asked, his eyes widening. "What is such a person doing all the way up here?"

He had heard all manner of stories about the Mandali Empire. Its people were said to be so dark skinned their teeth glowed. The land was so rich with gold its people plated their dishes with it and wove it into their hair like wildflowers. Its prince had once traveled to the Holy Land and along the way had spent so much gold that entire economies had crashed in his wake.

"I was told she was married to its ambassador, but he died. However, the lady decided to stay as she had money enough to do so."

"And…her messenger needs a tailor?"

Hadassah grinned and lifted the bowl to her lips before she answered. "No, *she* does."

Isaac's head swam with images of golden clothing and with the riches that could be his. Unbidden, his mind gave him an image—years in the future, himself dressed in gold, marching to the castle in finery and before the entire court, proclaiming himself the lover of the king.

It was a pretty image, but its ridiculousness made him laugh. Such a stunt would end only in his robbery and execution. Still, money enough to care for his family would be good. Mordecai worked only as a barber and David alongside him. If Isaac could save good coin from this job, perhaps his family could buy their own home, higher in the city where the light was better, and the smell was sweeter.

"I will meet with her messenger," he said.

"Of course you will," Hadassah said with a snort. "You'd be a fool not to."

"But I am only an apprentice still." Isaac felt the need to blunt the hope that filled his mother's eyes.

"And you'd be shocked how few people want to work for a foreigner," Hadassah said evenly. "Eat."

Innes had no trouble finding the man at the tavern the next day. His dark skin and bare head, along with his neatly trimmed black beard, made him a cow among sheep. He was dressed in sumptuous velvet with little glimmers of gold thread showing in the embroidery of his surcoat. He stood and bowed to Innes. "It is a pleasure to meet you, Sir Innes," he said with a wide grin. His teeth were stark against his skin, but they certainly didn't glow. He spoke with an accent Innes had never heard before, in a rich, deep voice that sent a thrill down Innes's spine. "You may call me Musa."

Innes returned the bow. "Thank you for meeting with me so soon."

"I was told you worked at the palace," Musa said, gesturing for Innes to sit as he did. "Mistress Lithgow was happy to provide examples of your work. It is exquisite. My lady was pleased."

Innes blessed his mother. "Thank you so much. I'm happy she enjoyed my work. And I did, yes. I was the apprentice of a master who brought me with him."

"Why did you leave?" Musa asked, raising his eyebrows.

"I'm afraid there were some…religious tensions." He tugged on his beard, the half-truth burning on his cheeks.

Musa, to Innes's surprise, smiled. "You are not of the Church then? This is good. My lady is not as well. It is lonely, in this land, to be apart from it."

"Oh." He blinked. Foolish of him, perhaps, to imagine the Church had spread so far.

"Though, I must be forthright. My lady will not allow herself or her daughters to be touched by a man unrelated and unmarried to them. Do you have a woman who could serve as your hands for such tasks?"

He thought of Ruth. Like their mother, Ruth knew her way around a needle, and could take measurements and place pins. "My younger sister. Will she do?"

Musa clapped his hands together once. "That sounds perfect! Very well, there shall be a trial period of one month—paid, of course—during which you and your sister shall live in my lady's home and attend to her and her daughters' clothing. If all goes well, such placement shall be made permanent."

Innes was a little overwhelmed. "Ah, yes, that is an agreement I can make. I shall have to discuss with my sister, but can I send a message back to this inn when I have confirmation?"

"Of course," Musa said, removing a small book from his pocket and making a note. "I shall wait for your confirmation, and if all goes well, we can meet here, say, around noon tomorrow? And I will escort you to the estate."

"Is it far?" Innes asked, tugging on his beard, overwhelmed by the speed of this transaction.

"About one hour from here," Musa said, pointing toward one wall. "Eastward."

Innes was impressed he had even the faintest idea of direction in this part of the city where the sun was only visible when directly overhead. "Very well, I shall speak with my sister and send word."

He returned home with a light heart. He touched the mezuzah on the doorpost and kissed his hand, smiling at the little box. For once in his outside life, his family and his faith had not been an obstacle to overcome or hide away. It was a marvelous feeling.

Ruth was, as he had thought, excited by the opportunity. Her eyes gleamed as she clasped her hands. "Oh, Isaac, that sounds amazing!"

"And who knows, perhaps you shall find yourself a husband," Hadassah said lightly from her seat in the living room.

"Mama," Ruth groaned.

"It's bad enough your brother is determined to deny me a wedding; I won't have you doing it as well!" She pointed her needle like a dagger.

"Shouldn't you be harassing David over that?" Isaac said. "He's the one who's almost thirty."

"What makes you think I don't?" She snorted and returned the needle to her work. "I've been trying to get him to have a sit-down with Miriam, you know, Abram's daughter, but he keeps dodging me." She pursed her lips. "My children are cruel to an old woman."

"Mama, you're not old," Ruth said with a sigh, but she went over and kissed her mother's temple. "If an opportunity arises, I shall at least hear the man out."

With a smile, Hadassah patted her daughter's hip. "You're a good girl. Watch out for your brother."

"Yes, Mama." She turned to Isaac, rolling her eyes so their mother couldn't see.

Isaac smothered a laugh and went to go send the message.

That night was the Sabbath, so they supped heartily and bathed in the glow of the candles. Mordecai and David congratulated the two younger children on getting such a lucrative job even if it was to be on a trial basis.

As the family laughed and talked, Isaac retreated into his thoughts, sipping his wine. Despite the bustle of his family around him and the promise of a good job, he still missed the prince.

It was a futile endeavor, missing the prince, like mourning a limb lost. It wasn't going to come back, no matter how fervent the wish. Noticing his distance while the evening wound down, Ruth sat beside him on the couch. "Here," she said, placing a ball of yarn into his lap. "Hold it for me while I knit."

On another night, he would have protested, but on this night, he was happy to do anything helpful. The rest of their family had retired to their rooms, leaving only the two youngest by the fire. "Do you imagine you will need a scarf?" Isaac asked wryly. "It will hardly be cold a mere hour from here."

"No, just something to do," Ruth said, the soft, familiar scrape of her needles soothing. "You'll be doing most of the work, after all. I'm only an assistant."

"What will you bring?"

"My clothing, of course. And a few trinkets. My Haggadah. You?"

Isaac thought about it. "Clothing, of course. And my book of Ketuvim."

She nodded, humming a bit as she did. "We are so alike, you and I," she said softly. "We shall both make Mama cry, I think."

Isaac saw his sister in a new light. "You as well?"

She did not take her eyes from her work. "David should marry soon because I have trouble imagining more weddings to come."

"You won't marry just for appearances?" he asked.

With a sigh, Ruth set her knitting into her lap and tucked a stray curl of hair behind one ear, turning her dark, clever gaze onto her brother as she raised an eyebrow. "Will you?"

He looked away, shame burning in his ears. "I wasn't planning on it, no. Sorry."

"Apology accepted." Satisfied, she resumed her work. "I'll help you pack when I've done a few more rows."

He nodded. For a few minutes, they sat quietly until Isaac murmured, "I appreciate you telling me, Ruthie. I'll help you if you need it."

She smiled and leaned her head against his. "Thank you, Isaac. I feel the same. Say the word, and I'll be there for you."

They both packed and prepared as best they could for the day ahead.

Musa met them at the tavern entrance. He gave both siblings a grin and a bow. "It is good to see you again, sir, and a pleasure to meet you, dear lady."

She chuckled and curtsied. "The pleasure is mine, sir. I am Rose."

He waved to a carriage nearby, driven by a man just as dark skinned, though his hair was wound into thick coils he had pulled back into a ponytail. "This is Adama. He speaks little of the tongue of this land, but he is an excellent driver."

Musa opened the door and gestured them inside, then climbed in behind them. "You travel lightly!" he said, gesturing to the two bags they had between them. The carriage began to move, wood clacking against the cobblestone.

"Habit," Innes said. "We've suffered a lot of upheaval."

Musa frowned. He was incredibly expressive. "That is sad to hear. I hope you will find stability with my lady."

"What can you tell us about her?" Innes asked. "You speak of her fondly."

With a grin, Musa leaned back into the seat, rubbing his chin. "My lady's name is Isatou Keita. She is the widow of Baboucar Keita, an ambassador to this land from Mandali. The Lord saw fit to take him home late last year, and we hope his soul is at peace." He bowed his head in a moment of sadness before raising it once more. "My lady decided to stay in this land. The weather is pleasing to her, and she has a fondness for the peculiarities of its people."

"I see," Innes said. He tried to picture Lady Keita, but he couldn't even begin to imagine what she might look like or how she would hold herself. He would have to wait and see.

"My lady has two beautiful daughters, the young ladies Kadiatou and Sira. They are beautiful in face but also in spirit." He touched his chest, closing his eyes. "My ladies are very important to me."

"Could you tell us of your homeland?" Rose asked, leaning forward. "We have never been."

And with sparkling eyes and articulate hands, Musa regaled them with stories from the whirling sand and the oases within. He was just finishing a story of a young man and a magical lamp when the carriage came to a stop. "And here we are!" Musa said, hopping out so he could open the door for Innes and Rose.

The manor was splendid, the walls so white they seemed to sparkle, and colorful stained-glass panels decorated the top of the windows along the face of it. Adama pulled the carriage away, down a winding dirt path around the house that presumably led to the stables.

Musa led them inside, which was even grander than the exterior. Rich, colorful tapestries depicting stories Innes didn't know adorned the walls, oil lamps infused with exotic scents hung between them, giving the corridor a sweet smell, and the grand staircase leading up to the second level had gold leaf patterns swirling up the railings.

And standing at the foot of the stairs was the grandest, most magnificent woman Innes had ever seen. She was draped in fabric, a colorful, lightweight linen that shimmered with golden thread, tied expertly around her body. Her dark hair, barely visible at the hairline, was enclosed in a wrap, made of the same cloth. Around her neck were beautifully beaded necklaces, in bright, charming colors.

In the afternoon light streaming through the windows behind them, the woman's dark skin glowed golden. As she approached, Innes bowed. "It is an honor to meet you, my lady. I am the tailor, Innes, and this is my sister and assistant, Rose." Beside him, Rose curtsied.

Lady Keita smiled, her full lips stretching wide. "The pleasure is mine." Her voice was rich and warm, like honey.

"I was impressed by your work, and Musa tells me he believes you shall be a good fit here in my home."

"His confidence is appreciated," Innes said, which made Musa laugh.

Lady Keita turned and spoke loudly toward the second floor. "Girls! Come and meet our new servants." She gestured to one of the servants nearby and waved toward Innes and Rose's bags, which were quickly grabbed and taken up the stairs.

The two young women, who appeared at Lady Keita's call, were dressed similarly but without the hair wrap. One was taller, maybe fourteen or fifteen, while the other still had growing left to do, maybe eleven or twelve if Innes had to guess. The older sister's black hair was bound in thin, intricate braids, which were decorated with beads and small, milky pearls. The younger sister's hair was left mostly loose, floating like a cloud around her head. Innes wondered how it was so weightless.

"This is Kadiatou," Lady Keita said, placing her hand on the older girl's shoulder. "And this"—she did the same to the younger one—"is Sira."

Innes introduced himself and his sister once more. Kadiatou gave them a small curtsy while Sira nodded and immediately tucked herself behind her mother.

Lady Keita patted her cheek fondly, to which Sira wrinkled her nose. "She is shy. Now, you have had a journey, so let us eat, and then Musa will show you around the manor."

Lunch was a large bowl of flavored rice with seared and salted fish and vegetables. Spice sizzled across Innes's tongue, surprising at first, but soon addicting. Rose had a similar reaction, her cheeks pink but her smile wide.

At their faces, Lady Keita laughed, deep from her belly. "Forgive me. Is it too much?"

"No, my lady. It was just surprising." He sipped some of the sweet drink she had provided. It was floral and sugary—a perfect counterpoint to the spice.

"I can request your meals be made specially if you need," she said, the laughter giving way to seriousness.

"We request only that the food be made without pork or shellfish, my lady," Innes said.

"Oh, of course no pork," she said easily. "Pork is forbidden. And shellfish is hard to find in this land, so it is easy enough to avoid them." She waved one of the servants over and spoke to them in a melodic, unknown language. Innes assumed it to be the language of her country.

The servant bowed and walked into the kitchens.

"It is done," she said and sipped her drink.

After everyone was done eating and the dishes quickly cleared away, Musa stood and bowed to Innes and Rose. "Shall I give you the tour now?"

"Yes, thank you." Innes made sure to bow to Lady Keita before they left. "Thank you again, my lady."

"Your work shall begin tomorrow," she said airily. "Now, go, enjoy my home."

The rugs and tapestries were gorgeous throughout the manor, and Innes soon lost count of how many rooms the place had. Musa kept up a steady stream of commentary as he showed them around, explaining where certain furniture pieces were from or who the artisans were who created them.

It was a little overwhelming, and Innes found his mind wandering, remembering the finery of the palace as well as the homey touches that had marked the prince's chambers. He had largely eschewed fine decor in favor of well-made, simple pieces in dark woods. And books, of course. When Innes let his mind drift, he could still smell ink, parchment, and worn leather, cut with the soft musk of Kenneth's skin.

He snapped himself out of it just as Musa gestured widely to an open doorway. "And this, finally, is to be your chambers. There are two rooms, connected by a single door, which can be locked from either side if you need privacy from each other."

"This is perfect. Thank you, Sir Musa," Rose said sweetly, putting her hand on her brother's shoulder to pull him out of his wandering imagination.

She steered him inside, closing the door behind them. "I see your bag here," she said, pointing to the bed. Indeed, Innes's bag sat at the foot, unopened. "So, mine must be in the other room. I'm going to go unpack."

And with that, she was gone, leaving Innes to his thoughts. He examined the room. It was larger than the quarters he had shared with his master in the castle with thick, warm-looking curtains over the windows and a large, intricate rug at his feet. He slipped out of his shoes before stepping on it. One side of the room was set up as a workstation with a frame for clothing forms as well as a long, broad table with shelves on one side already stuffed with fine fabrics. He opened one of the drawers to find a neat assortment of threads and a pincushion of needles along with a thimble.

He chuckled at the thimble. The skin of his thumbs was already leather enough to not need it, but he appreciated the consideration of it.

The other side of the room, separated by a folding screen, was the bedroom proper with a large bed and bureau. He fetched his bag and began to organize his clothing in the wardrobe. At the very least, this was to be his home for a month. At the bottom of his bag, the book of Ketuvim.

He picked it up and brought it to his lips before setting it carefully into the drawer of the nightstand. With a sigh, he sat on the bed, surrounded by finery and comfort, and longed.

The next day, Innes put together a plan. The first step, as always, was to make a dress form for each of the women he'd be making clothing for, so he and Rose went to each woman's room in turn—beginning with Lady Keita, of course—and took their measurements. Rose was the only one to touch, as agreed, and Innes oversaw and wrote down the numbers as they came.

He also took the opportunity to ask what kind of clothing Lady Keita wanted him to make. "This land is my home now," she explained as Rose finished. "So, I want clothing befitting a noblewoman of my station. The clothing of my land is good, but I want to show I am of this land now, not that one."

Innes nodded. "Would you prefer something classic, or more…daring and trendy?"

At this, Lady Keita laughed, delighted. "Daring, of course! If I am going to stand out regardless, I want to do it with *drama*." She paused, considering. "But it must not be risqué," she said. "My body is not meat, to be displayed for all to devour."

"You have a talent with words, my lady," Rose said with a chuckle.

Lady Keita patted her cheek with a warm smile. "And you are very sweet."

Innes took some notes as well as beginning some half sketches. He had rarely been afforded the opportunity to make full outfits under his master, especially not for a noblewoman as wealthy as Lady Keita. This was a fine chance to test his skills, and he found himself eager to undertake the challenge. "And for your daughters, my lady?"

"Much the same," she said. "Though, of course, I defer to their final judgment. They are old enough to dress themselves. Sira, I know, would prefer not stand out if she could." Lady Keita sighed and rubbed her cheek. "I wonder if, perhaps, she would be happier returning to Mandali, but I also know she would not want to go alone."

For a moment, Lady Keita was quiet, contemplating perhaps how her choice to stay had affected her children. But she quickly set her thoughtfulness aside. "I know you two do not share my faith in truth, but if you wish, you are welcome to join us for prayer."

"That would be lovely, my lady, thank you. We shall."

They had both heard the call to prayer the day prior, beautiful and somehow familiar despite the strangeness.

"Then come along," Lady Keita said, leading them to a central hall, divided by a screen down the middle. As the call to prayer began, servants filed in. "This way, dear," Lady Keita said to Rose, offering a hand. "Women on this side."

Musa spotted Innes and took him under his wing similarly. "This way. If you like, you can kneel here in the back."

Innes watched with interest as another man knelt at the front of the gathered people, reciting prayers and folding forward. Innes didn't bow, but he did pray. He recited his own words, covering his eyes and seeking out that thin thread of connection to the divine he had felt during his bar mitzvah so long ago. He had not felt it since, but he still tried to find it now and again.

It continued to elude him, of course, because life was capable of great cruelty, but it wouldn't stop him from trying. He pressed his palm to his chest, feeling the key.

The prayer session didn't last long, but it left Innes feeling refreshed and rested and ready to continue the day. And at the end of the day, what else was prayer meant to do?

He and Rose met at the door. She was smiling. "I missed praying in a group," she said softly. "It's... There's something about it, you know?"

He nodded. "I know what you mean." And he supposed he really did. "Let's go measure the daughters."

Kadiatou was much like her mother in terms of what she wanted. She was a bright and vibrant young woman, eager to make an impression. "Since I am not married," she explained, "I need to stand out even more than my mother. Though I suppose I should not upstage her."

Innes laughed. "I do not think she would stand for it, no, but I can make you vibrant."

Her dark eyes glittered. "I look forward to seeing what you make me," she said, clasping her hands in excitement.

But Sira, like her mother had said, was more reserved. She took some time to even speak to Innes, choosing instead to murmur softly with Rose, but at last she looked at him, her cheeks dark with nerves. "I want to be pretty," she said softly. "But if people look at my sister instead, that would be good."

"I can do that, my lady," Innes assured her.

And that won him a tentative smile.

As the day finished, Innes and Rose joined prayers and then dinner where Innes ate half-heartedly, sketching with his free hand.

Rose rolled her eyes at him, chatting with Musa as they ate. "Don't mind him," she said. "He's a hard worker."

"Seems so!" Musa said brightly. "I think it will be appreciated."

Innes could certainly use some of that.

Innes got to work. Dress forms came first, stuffed with wool and horsehair. He and Rose got them made quickly with neat lettering along the base to indicate which of the Keita women each was.

184

Bases complete, he began designing in earnest. It had been a long time since he'd had the chance to work from scratch, and he relished it. He started with chemises for the women since the clothing of their homeland seemed to lack them. Rose worked on main stitches while Innes sewed in delicate details—lace along the neckline and sleeve ends for Ladies Keita and Kadiatou and some cute ruffling for Lady Sira—along with their initials, so they weren't mixed up in the wash.

Then, kirtles. For Ladies Keita and Kadiatou, bright, vibrant colors that contrasted beautifully with their dark skin and embroidery over the bodice where it would show beneath the gown. He agonized over the patterns before deciding on ones that reminded him of summer. Bright-green leaves and white flowers, along with sun-yellow circles.

For the demure Lady Sira, he chose darker colors, which would not stand out as much against her skin, and details that needed a careful eye and the right light. She, too, received flowers, but night flowers, pale against the darker fabrics, and star-white diamonds.

The month flew by on the kirtles alone. He had yet to begin the gowns, even with Rose's assistance. But when, at the end of the month, he presented the ladies with his works in progress, he was buoyed by their joy.

"Oh, I *do* love the design!" Lady Kadiatou exclaimed, tracing her fingers over the embroidery on her kirtle. "Rose! Help me change!"

"Of course, my lady," Rose said warmly and gestured for her to enter her room.

Lady Keita beamed as she held hers up to the light, admiring the shimmer of the embroidery. "This is fine work, Innes."

"Thank you, my lady. I apologize I was unable to finish some gowns to go over top."

She waved her hand dismissively. "For this quality? I am happy to wait." She turned to her younger daughter. "What do you think, Sira?"

Lady Sira smiled shyly, covering her face with the kirtle, her black eyes sparkling. "Thank you. It's very pretty," she mumbled, her voice muffled.

Her praise was the one that made Innes's heart the lightest.

"That settles it. You and your sister shall stay," Lady Keita said.

Innes bowed. "We are honored, my lady."

She waved her hand again. "An honor well-earned."

Lady Kadiatou emerged from Rose's room. She had changed into her chemise and kirtle. Innes could see alterations to be made—dress forms could only ever capture so much—but he was pleased with his work, and Lady Kadiatou was as well. "What do you think, Mother?" she asked with a laugh, curtsying.

"You are a fine lady in such fine clothes," she said warmly.

"Lady Kadiatou, if you would not mind staying dressed for a short while, there are some changes to be made," Innes said.

"Of course," she said easily.

"I shall need both of you for the same," Innes said, bowing to the other ladies. "Sometime later. I realize it is almost time for prayer."

Lady Keita smiled. "Whatever you need, Innes. You need only ask."

And that day, after prayer, Innes and Rose—no, Isaac and Ruth—hung their mezuzot on their door frames. The talismans were too old, technically, saved from the home they had been forced to leave, their paint chipped, their scrolls faded. But as Isaac drove the nail deep into the wood, securing it in its proper place beside the door, he felt an echo of rightness. *We live,* the mezuzah said. *And you will not destroy us.*

As he finished, Isaac stepped back and admired his work, the hammer hanging from his hand. Ruth, similarly finished, came to stand beside him, threading her arm through his. "Home," she said. It was more than a word. It was a declaration.

"Yes," Isaac agreed, leaning into her embrace. "Home."

He closed the door and returned to his work.

The next few months saw the creation of gowns. For these, Innes had to dig deep into both the current trends—which were always changing at court—as well as a good tailor's knowledge of flattering body shapes, timeless designs, and, of course, color.

Ladies Keita and Kadiatou wanted shades of the latest trends, to stop a room when they entered. Dramatic gowns were a joy to design and create. And since their basic color palette was so different from the ordinary noblewomen of the Highlands, dramatic came easily.

Lady Sira, however, in her desire to be outshone, proved more difficult to please. More and more, she oversaw his work at every stage, making comments and suggestions. Had she been overbearing about it, Innes might have been annoyed, but Lady Sira was never impolite, and her comments were usually helpful.

Rose taught her how to sew, and soon Lady Sira was a permanent fixture in their chambers.

One day, as Lady Sira was working on an embroidery sampler, she asked, "Innes, why did you leave the castle?"

Innes paused in his work to tug on his beard. Across the room, he felt Rose's gaze. "There was a disagreement I had with Prince Ellar," he said neutrally. "So, I deemed it prudent to leave and avoid further conflict."

Lady Sira chewed her lip. "Do you miss it? Do you like it here?"

Innes smiled at her, which led to her ducking her head behind her canvas, the tips of her ears ruddy. "I like it here very much. It's quieter, more relaxed than the palace. And the people are kind."

Her returning smile was shy and sweet. But she soon frowned. "You didn't answer my first question. Do you miss it?"

Innes sighed and stroked his hand over the velvet of the gown he was working on. "Sometimes. I had a…good friend there. I miss him."

Rose's gaze burned into his ear.

"Was he a servant too?" Lady Sira asked, swinging her feet under the chair she was sitting on.

"He works in one of the libraries," Innes answered, sweat prickling on his neck. The prince's room certainly contained a library, and he did often work in it. Lady Sira didn't seem to notice the evasion.

"I wish you could visit him," Lady Sira said and popped an injured finger into her mouth.

"That would be nice," Innes agreed. He allowed himself a daydream of Kenneth—the prince, rather—living in Lady Keita's estate. He'd be a scholar, maybe, of religions. Innes smiled to himself. *Kenneth would like it here.* Some of the servants carried small talismans of an unknown purpose (to Innes, at least). Kenneth would ask about them and listen respectfully to the answers. Lady Keita would be charmed by him.

He closed his eyes and pulled himself out of the dream. Lady Sira was watching him. He gave her a reassuring nod and returned to his work, and she did the same.

Some weeks later, Innes and Rose took a trip to town to visit home and to do some shopping. They visited the market first, which was bustling in the early afternoon. Innes made his way to the fashion pamphlets at the cloth vendor's stall, showing off the latest designs. With a jolt to his heart, he recognized Prince Kenneth in one of them. He was wearing a pale tunic, uncolored in the cheap pamphlet of course, with straight buttons across the front, draping beautifully around his thin legs.

The pamphlet was labeled "bridegroom." Innes's stomach clenched.

Noticing his attention, the vendor approached. "Ah, looking at the prince? You know, he called the marriage off with the Princess Elodie."

"What?" The man now had Innes's full attention.

He shrugged. "That's what I heard. There was apparently a huge shouting match between the prince and his father over it in the dining hall."

Innes boggled. He couldn't imagine it. In all the time he'd seen Prince Kenneth, he'd never been one to raise his voice in anger. The closest he'd gotten was when the Prince Ellar had caught them.

"It's a huge scandal of course. The rumor right now is she slept with someone, but who knows? Not me. It's a nice tunic though."

Innes set the pamphlet down. "It is. However, my current clients are a lovely trio of ladies." He smiled and picked up a few of the women's papers instead. But the question nagged.

Why had Prince Kenneth broken the engagement? It had been planned for years and had been poised to smooth tense relations between Saxtain and the Highlands.

Why had the prince seen fit to throw that away?

He met Rose outside the stall. As they made their way down to their parents' home, he looked up toward the castle, his thoughts swirling. Saxtain was no friend to his people, but surely that was nothing to break such an important engagement over? No, there had to be a different reason.

He touched the mezuzah at the door and entered.

Soon after, Lady Keita swept into their chambers. "I have received a message from the palace," she said grandly. Rose walked in from her room to listen. "There is to be a series of balls!" Lady Keita continued, smiling. "The elder prince it seems is seeking a bride of any of the eligible ladies in the kingdom. And he shall marry her at the end of the year!" She pinched Lady Kadiatou's cheek. "Why not you? Surely, the king would see that a good match? Mandali and the Highlands? Perfection."

Lady Kadiatou laughed. "I am too young for him, Mother."

"Then the younger prince," she teased.

"*Mother.*"

Innes couldn't help a smile, reminded of his own mother. "Rose and I will make sure your gowns are prepared, my ladies," he said, cutting in with a bow.

"Thank you, Innes," Lady Keita said. "I believe I will wear the orange, blue, and red dresses."

"And I the yellow, blue, and orange," Lady Kadiatou said.

He swept another bow. "As you say. And for Lady Sira?"

Lady Keita tapped her chin in thought. "I shall have her come and tell you," she said at last. "I do not know what she will want. Oh! And it is to be a masquerade as well, so we shall need masks. Is that in your capability, or shall I buy them elsewhere?"

"I can make you masks, my lady," Rose said.

"Wonderful! You both are lovely." She kissed Rose's cheek. "I shall let you work!"

The door shut and quiet filled the room. Innes let the smile fall from his face. Kenneth was to be married by the end of the year? He didn't have the right to be upset, but his heart wasn't interested in rights.

Rose squeezed his shoulder. "You knew it would happen," she said gently.

"I did," he said stiffly. "Let's just…work, okay? We have a lot to prepare. Three balls means three outfits."

"Of course. But if you want to talk…"

He nudged her shoulder and gave her a smile. "I know. Thank you, Ruthie."

*B*lessed *is the Lord, who has given me work to drown out my thoughts*, Innes reflected glumly. He refused to go into town. The fashion pamphlets would be all about the upcoming wedding, speculating on outfits and new trends and how the new princess would wear her hair. It made his stomach hurt.

Rose, in her kindness, went in his stead, only buying the ones relevant to their work and giving him no gossip.

As the day approached, Lady Sira came to visit. She sat in her usual chair, swinging her legs. "They look very pretty," she said, gesturing to the gowns up on the dress forms.

"Thank you, my lady. I'm glad you like them," Isaac said warmly.

She smiled back shyly and looked down at her feet, her slippers popping in and out of view. "Do you think your friend will be at the balls?" she asked.

Innes's heart twinged. "I'm sure he will be. Such a grand event is fun for everyone at the palace."

"Do you want to come along?"

His hands stopped, and he glanced up. "What?"

"You could be my valet," she said, her eyes twinkling. "And so, you could come and dance and see your friend!" She lowered her voice, conspiratorial. "I don't really *need* a valet anyway."

Innes's thoughts warred. It was going to be a masquerade anyway. He didn't need to *talk* to the prince (Lord only knows what they would even say), but it would be nice to *see* him. Was he doing well?

But he may well see the prince with his future bride.

"Can I think about it, my lady?" he asked.

She nodded. "I understand. You'd have to make an outfit for yourself too."

"Exactly." He was grateful for her innocent misunderstanding. "We'll have to see if I can finish up all of these for you and your family first."

"Can I help?"

Innes looked over at what needed to be done. "You know what, you can. You remember how to do a satin stitch, right?"

She mimicked the motion of it with her fingers. "Like this!"

"Exactly so. Then can you fill in the leaves on the flowers on your gown for the first night?" He'd already done the outlines.

"You'll have to be *very* neat. If you're not, Rose or I will have to redo it."

She nodded eagerly. "I can. I swear!" So, he gave her the spool of thread and the pincushion of needles, and the two of them worked quietly until dinner.

I saac discussed Lady Sira's offer with Ruth. "What do you think, Ruthie? I want to see him, of course, but I can't shake the thought it's a bad idea."

She chewed on her lip. "It might help you move on. 'Absence makes the heart grow fonder,' you know? Maybe you'll see him and realize it was for the best."

"Maybe." Isaac combed his fingers through his beard, remembering suddenly Kenneth's touch against his jaw. He couldn't imagine it, but perhaps it was possible? After all, a Prince Kenneth who would yell at his father in public and break an important engagement was also foreign. Perhaps he'd never known the prince as well as he thought.

He decided to sleep on it.

And when he woke, lying in bed as he said his morning prayers, the sun warming his face, Innes watched dust motes dance in the light and imagined, someday, being able to enjoy this with someone else at his side. He'd given up on a marriage of romance, but perhaps he could have one of friendship.

In his imagination, he saw a woman—average looking, dark haired perhaps—waking up beside him, both in nightshirts. They wouldn't have sex, but that would be okay; he could simply tell his father he was impotent when questioned about children. And by that point, David would likely have children, so it wouldn't matter too much. And maybe they would smile at each other as they woke and dressed and went about their days—together, partners, but not in love.

It wouldn't be the end of the world, that sort of marriage, he reasoned.

But he couldn't settle into that life until he had moved on from impossibilities.

"I'll go," he told Ruth.

She patted his cheek. "I'll make you a mask."

The days leading up to the first ball were a flurry of activity—last-minute decorations or alterations and bursts of chaos from accidental rips or stains. Still, the day arrived, and Innes was trembling from nerves.

He climbed into the carriage after Ladies Kadiatou and Sira, sitting across from them. Their mother was traveling separately to make the biggest splash. Lady Kadiatou was radiant in her yellow gown, her skin glowing with health and sparkling with the jewels and gold that adorned her ears and neck. Lady Sira was dressed more simply in a midnight-blue gown, trimmed with stars—embroidered herself with silver thread. They varied a bit in size and shape, but so too did the stars in the sky.

They were both excited, chatting in their native tongue as the countryside rolled past them out the window, red and yellow in the light of the setting sun. Innes tugged uncomfortably on the cuffs of his chemise, fixing the line of his cotte. It hugged his chest in an unfamiliar and not altogether pleasant way. Rose had worked on it while he had focused on the ladies. It was simple black and white—suitable for a valet—but he wasn't used to such a formal outfit. His mask—black with small, irregular pearls—sat in his lap.

As they arrived, Innes put it on and stepped out before bowing to each lady as he helped her descend. Castle guards came to help escort them up the grand staircase. Innes was struck with sudden fear that Prince Ellar had banned him from the palace, that he would be dragged away. But no, either they had no such order or they did not recognize Innes in his mask because they happily showed Innes to where the other servants and valets had gathered in the hall as the lords and ladies were announced in the ballroom.

Fearing discovery now and chastising himself for not thinking of the possibility of having Prince Ellar as a true enemy, Innes kept away from the other servants—a few of whom he recognized—in favor of joining the throng of people eating and dancing. Lady Keita, surrounded by fawning admirers, appeared splendid in her orange gown. Innes smiled. The joy of a job well done.

Far behind her, a line of women snaked its way through the crowd, and at the head, wearing a simple but elegant mask of green and gold, was Prince Kenneth, recognizable instantly by his red hair and freckles.

And *oh*, Innes had forgotten how handsome the prince was.

His shoulders were visibly tense, even with how far away Innes was. Each bow and polite smile tensed them further. He wasn't happy about being here. Behind him, the king and Prince Ellar sat, keeping careful watch. Innes looked away, tugging on his beard as he sought out the buffet table.

His hand trembled as he brought a pastry to his mouth, nervously picking at the crumbs that fell into his beard. Why had he come? This was stupid. He glanced back at the prince.

Oh, he was less tense. The lady he was speaking with was pretty from behind, her dark hair wound up in an elaborate braid at the crown of her head, and her gown was a lovely sapphire blue. She had a hand on the prince's arm. Her shoulders shook with genuine laughter as the prince returned the touch.

It was a simple thing, touch, but when Innes glanced toward the king, he was watching with an approving gaze.

The ballroom was too loud. Music, laughter, and conversation piled up around his ears like snowfall. He was cold.

Lowering his head, Innes made his way toward one of the servants' doors and escaped into the hallway, his heart in his throat. *Stupid,* he berated himself, refusing to let tears fall. *You should have listened to your instincts.*

Searching for a distraction, Innes wandered the corridors, stopping at the entrance to the gallery. He had never seen it empty before. Walking in, he took his time examining the portraits and tapestries on the walls, detailing the royal family's history.

Kenneth resembled his great-grandfather, King Fachtna the Humble. There was the red hair, of course, but something about the curve of the jaw was also familiar. Looking at the portrait, Innes wondered if the prince should wear a beard like his ancestor. Somehow, this innocuous thought, imagining Prince Kenneth older and bearded, triggered the tears.

He pulled off the mask and tossed it aside, burying his face in his hands, afraid of being seen despite the empty room.

For a long moment, he got to cry in peace, but then a soft voice said, "I don't think I've ever seen someone cry over a portrait of Fachtna before."

Innes jumped, an undignified yelp escaping his throat.

There was a young man beside him, maybe twenty at the oldest, holding his mask out to him. He had a messy mop of dark hair and an impish look to his features. Hanging from his belt was a red cap, decorated with a red rose.

He took the offered mask, hastily wiping his eyes. "Forgive me."

The young man shook his head. "There's nothing to forgive. I wasn't saying no one cried over *him.* I did that plenty myself."

His smile was rueful. "Do you know how long it's been since his coronation?"

"Uh." Innes scratched his head, perturbed. "I guess about a hundred years? That sounds about right since his grandson is now king."

"Oh wow, it's been a while," the stranger said. "The castle's almost the same though except for the decor. Interesting."

"Uh, if you don't mind my asking, who are you?" Innes's voice was small in his bafflement.

The young man stared at him with wide, storm-gray eyes and grinned. "Forgive me for not introducing myself. I am Naomhan." He bowed. "And you?"

He had not heard someone with such a traditional name since he'd arrived in the Highlands, especially not around the palace. "Innes," he answered.

"And what brought you to tears about the dead king?" He was looking at the portrait of King Fachtna now, his body unmoving.

"It's a...long story."

"I don't have anywhere to be. Do you?" Once that intense stare returned to Innes's face, he wished Naomhan would look back at the portrait. "I would like to help, if I could."

"You cannot, but I appreciate the sentiment." Innes put the mask on again and moved to pass Naomhan and return to the hallway.

In front of him, the door swung closed on its own. He turned back to Naomhan in alarm, but the boy was still smiling. "Sorry, sorry, I keep forgetting. I don't want to scare you."

There was something deeply unsettling about Naomhan.

"You can go if you want. But I do think I can help." He waved his hand and the door opened again, without either of them touching it.

Innes's first thought was *sheyd*. He felt locked in place, but he didn't know if it was Naomhan's influence or his own fear.

"Damn, you're afraid," Naomhan said, frowning. "How can I fix that?"

Innes gaped, his heart pounding. He didn't know how to answer.

After a moment of consideration, Naomhan sat down on one of the couches, crossing his legs under him. "How's this? I'll stay over here, and you can stay over there, and we'll talk like this. If Fachtna is a hundred years gone, why cry over him?"

Innes licked his lips and found his voice. "What *are* you?"

Naomhan held on to his feet, rocking absently. "The people of this land call us *siogaidh* or 'fairies' in this tongue," he explained. "I used to be human though. I wanted to visit those I left behind, but I waited too long." He looked sad for a moment, but his expression soon reset to neutral. "Still, it is good to visit. So, I came here to get an idea of how long it has been and saw you crying. And I would help if I can. Opening and closing doors is just the merest magic I can wield."

Innes frantically thought of any stories he could think of about fairies. They didn't often come up in Saxtain, though the people of the Highlands seemed to have many traditions around them. He suddenly remembered King Fachtna's cousin supposedly had been spirited away. "Are you the sort of fairy I'll need to pay with my firstborn?" he asked. If so, he had a pretty good loophole since he would not have any children.

Naomhan laughed. "No, no. I'm not that sort of fairy, though I understand the trepidation. My help is free, no strings."

Innes doubted that very much.

Naomhan continued. "How about this? You tell me your problem. I tell you how I can help, and if you want it, you have it. If not, you don't."

"No strings," Innes asked, still suspicious.

"No strings," Naomhan confirmed with a nod and grin.

This was still a bad idea, but Innes had already made so many mistakes; what was one more so long as the fairy didn't demand to be treated as a god? "Fine then. I'm upset the prince is going to marry one of the women at these balls."

Naomhan rocked side to side, still holding his feet, his stare unblinking. "Why?"

Innes faltered, almost afraid to say the words aloud. "*I* love him," he whispered.

"Then, go to him," Naomhan said, cocking his head. "Why stay away?"

Innes stared. "He's the *prince*," he said slowly. "I can't. He has to marry and produce heirs and be king."

"Oh, right." Naomhan resumed his rocking. "That is trouble. Does he love you too?"

Innes combed his fingers through his beard. "I don't know. Maybe not anymore," he mumbled.

"*Hmmmm*." Naomhan leaned back, staring up at the ceiling. "I could give you the ability to bear children, but I don't know if it would last long. Permanent magic is difficult."

"Please do not."

"But then you can't be together." Naomhan sat up again.

"My body is my own. I will not alter it so fundamentally."

Naomhan frowned deeply. "Well, what if it's superficial? I can make you look like a woman, but it would only be a guise."

"Still no heirs," Innes pointed out.

With a heavy sigh, Naomhan bent forward over his legs before sitting up straight again. "Then, I don't know how to help you," he said.

Innes resisted the urge to say he'd told the fairy that from the beginning. He glanced toward the door, thinking of the ballroom and the line of women. "I wouldn't be able to marry him, but... Perhaps we could have a better parting," he said thoughtfully. "You said you could change my appearance without altering my body, yes?"

"Yes, easily."

"If I looked like a maiden, I could approach him without suspicion. We could...have some time together before he has to marry." Innes's heart lurched at the thought, torn between present pleasure and future pain.

Naomhan's face pinched. "If that's what you want."

"I do."

Naomhan nodded. He got up and paced around Innes, eyes squinted, lips pursed. He was taking this quite seriously. "Do you want to be beautiful? Look totally different, or more like yourself?"

"Like myself. I...would like for him to be able to recognize me."

Naomhan nodded. "Okay." He stretched out his hand and touched Innes's nose.

Heat rippled over Innes's skin like sitting too close to a fireplace. He winced at the sensation. When it passed, Naomhan was holding a mirror. "What do you think?"

He examined his reflection. His beard was gone, his jaw softer than it had been in his youth, and his cheeks rounder. But it was still his own face. His cotte and chemise were unchanged, but the black surcoat had become a beautiful white gown, flaring out from his wider hips as it brushed the ground. "This is...very good," he said uncertainly, his voice coming out in a delicate falsetto. "Thank you, Naomhan."

Naomhan smiled. "Go enjoy your party. Your appearance will change back at the stroke of midnight."

Innes returned to the ballroom and joined the line. It was much shorter now that the party was in full swing, so it was only a few minutes before he was nearly there. What could he say so the prince recognized him? He looked enough like himself, but there would need to be some sort of trigger, something to help the connection be made. The key to the prince's room burned against his chest, but no, that would have to be a confirmation, not a clue.

He was running out of time. His mind was blank.

And too soon, the prince stood before him. "Thank you for coming, my lady," he said politely, bowing. As he rose, he looked over Innes's shoulder and smiled. "It seems you are the last one. What is your name?"

"I-Irene," he stammered, aware of Prince Ellar's gaze.

The prince gently patted Innes's arm. "No need for nerves, Lady Irene."

"Have you," Innes began, his voice weakening. "Have you done any interesting research lately?"

The smile became a little more genuine. "You know my reputation then," he said ruefully. "Yes and no. It's interesting definitely, but the more I learn, the more I realize I don't understand."

"Ah, that is the curse of the scholar," Innes said with a chuckle.

"Indeed."

No, he was turning away! "Would you like to dance, Your Highness?" he said quickly, offering a hand.

Prince Kenneth was taken aback at being the one invited. "Well, you *are* forward, aren't you?" But the words were teasing. "Very well since you asked."

He took his hand, and Innes led him into the crowd. Around them, murmurs stirred. Apparently, the prince had yet to dance. Cold sweat broke out on Innes's neck. As they took their starting positions, Innes's stomach dropped. Oh no, he only knew how to lead! The first few steps were horribly awkward, Innes having to mentally reverse everything he remembered in real time, terrified of stepping on the prince's toes.

"You don't dance often, I see," Prince Kenneth teased. "It's okay. I don't either." He guided Innes in a spin. "If I may, I have a question you may think impertinent."

"You may ask," Innes said, trying to keep up with the dance as well as figure out what to say to get the prince to recognize him.

"Are you one of the *b'nai yisrael*? You bear some of the features."

So startled to hear such a polite reference, Innes stopped moving completely, staring at the prince. He hadn't taught him that, he didn't think. How did the prince know that phrase? "I—yes, Your Highness. You seem quite knowledgeable."

His smile was definitely genuine now. "That is what I have been researching, you see," he explained.

Oh, did Innes love this man. "Is that why you broke your engagement to Princess Elodie?" he asked. "It was quite a scandal."

Prince Kenneth sighed and ran his hand over his head. "In part. Come, let's step outside and get some air. It is warm in here."

They walked out onto the balcony. In the moonlight, the white gown glittered like a star. Prince Kenneth leaned against the railing, taking deep breaths as he stared up at the sky. "Princess Elodie had many unkind words for your people, among other things. I could not marry such a woman."

"Even for your country?"

He frowned and rubbed his chin. "You sound like my brother," he said wryly. "But if I am to marry someone, I believe our values, at the very least, should align."

Innes joined him against the railing. "Such as?"

"Kindness, curiosity, a certain…open-mindedness about our world. I do not believe the Lord created differences just so we could attempt to quash it."

"That's an elegant way to phrase it," Innes said.

Prince Kenneth chuckled. "Well, I spend a lot of time thinking about it," he said.

They stayed quiet for a time, listening to the distant sounds of revelry before them and the chirping of crickets behind them.

Innes took a steadying breath and eased the mask from his face. "Your Highness, I am going to tell you something. And you may not believe it at first, but I swear it to be true."

Prince Kenneth turned, curiosity in his eyes. "Go ahead, Lady Irene."

"My name is not Irene. My name is Innes." He reached down into his chemise and pulled up the key.

Kenneth's mouth opened, his eyes wide. "Innes?" he breathed. "But your face, your voice, your *beard*." He held Innes's face between his palms.

"A fairy helped me."

Rather than being placated, Kenneth became more alarmed. "A *fairy*? Innes, are you *mad*? Why would you do such a thing? What did you trade away?"

Innes shook his head. "The fairy asked for nothing, I swear it. And the illusion shall fade at midnight. I am still myself, only disguised."

Kenneth didn't seem completely reassured, his hands moving over Innes's face as if trying to make sure he was real. "Innes, how have you been? Well?"

"Very well. I work for Lady Keita of Mandali. She has been more than kind to myself and my sister."

Kenneth knit his brows together, his expression uncertain. "Why did you come here, Innes? Why disguise yourself?"

Innes took Kenneth's hands in his, closing his eyes. "Since I had heard you are to marry by the end of the year, I just... wanted to see you. We parted in such stressful circumstances, I thought it would be nice to have a proper farewell."

"Innes... You could stay if you wanted. I could convince my family."

Innes chuckled. "Your Highness—"

"Kenneth. Please."

"Kenneth," Innes repeated, looking into his eyes. "You know that isn't possible. This is a goodbye. Let's have it be a pleasant one this time."

For a moment, Kenneth looked like he would argue, but instead, he bowed his head. "Very well. May I kiss you then, Innes?"

"You may."

Kenneth took off his mask, set it aside, and then pulled Innes into his arms.

It was a homecoming, like falling into a warm bed at the end of a winter's day, like sipping wine on the night of the Sabbath, the candle flames dancing in the window. When they broke apart, there were tears sparkling on Kenneth's lashes. "It's strange," he said with a small laugh. "Kissing you without a beard."

"I'm sure you'll get used to it," Innes said with a smirk and pulled him in for another.

They stayed long enough on the balcony that Prince Ellar came out, looking for Kenneth. This time, when they broke apart, Prince Ellar was smirking. "And you said you'd *never* get over that one," he said.

Innes gave him a curious look as Kenneth turned dark red.

"You'll get no shame from me," Prince Ellar said, raising his hands in mock defeat. "What is your name, my lady?"

"Irene," Innes said, ducking a bit so the prince wouldn't see his face clearly. He hoped he just came off as shy.

"Well, Lady Irene, I'll make sure these doors are shut properly, shall I?" With a wink, Prince Ellar stepped back inside and, indeed, shut the balcony doors.

Innes and Kenneth stared at each other and then collapsed into each other with laughter. "I would have never expected to get that reaction," Innes chuckled, wiping tears from his eyes.

"Well, he's given us plenty of privacy," Kenneth said quietly before moving his lips to Innes's neck. "Shall we take advantage of it?"

Innes's stomach flipped. "So long as you don't stain my dress," he said, suddenly breathless.

Kenneth stroked his hand down the front of the gown, cupping what he found at the apex of his legs, drawing a gasp.

"No stains," Innes repeated as Kenneth palmed him.

"I guess I'll just need to go underneath," he said with a wicked smile, and true to his word, he was soon on his knees.

Innes was overwhelmed in more ways than one, heady with pleasure and the knowledge *he* was enough for a prince to kneel. He placed his hand on Kenneth's head and curled his fingers into the short, red hair, smokey in the moonlight. "You told your brother you'd never get over me, hm?" he murmured.

Hiding his face but unable to hide the darkening of his ears, Kenneth pressed his face into the crook of Innes's thigh.

Innes stroked his finger over one ear. "You are a fool, but I love you, Kenneth."

Slowly, Kenneth's gaze rose, his eyes gleaming with too many emotions to name. "And you are cruel, Innes, to tell me so when you plan to say farewell."

Innes lowered his head, closing his eyes. "I'm sorry. I won't say it again."

Kenneth trailed his fingers down Innes's thigh, thoughtful and sad. "I will never forget you. I hope you know that," he said softly. "No matter who my parents foist upon me in the end."

Innes tried to find words he could give in answer, but in the end, Kenneth buried his face between Innes's thighs and swallowed any further conversation.

As midnight approached, Kenneth escorted Innes inside, arm in arm. They had both put their masks back on. "Will I see you again tomorrow?" Kenneth asked.

"I will be here, but I do not know if I will be able to play the Lady Irene," he said uncertainly.

Kenneth placed his hand over Innes's. "Is there somewhere we could meet then? If you don't have your disguise?"

Innes considered it. "The gallery, perhaps. There was no one there earlier." Aside from the fairy.

"Very well. If I do not see the Lady Irene, I will meet you there. Shall we say at ten?"

Innes nodded. "I will see you then." He slipped his arm free, and with a small curtsy, Innes left through one of the servant doors and made his way to the now-empty gallery as the clock chimed midnight.

The room was empty when he entered. And when the final chime sounded, his body burned hot and then cold, and when he looked down, the white gown was a black surcoat once more, and there was again a beard upon his face.

He left the gallery and returned to the ballroom, seeking out Lady Keita and her daughters. He found Lady Kadiatou sitting in one of the side rooms, Lady Sira fast asleep in her lap. He smiled as he entered and gave her a small bow. "It seems she had a good time," he said quietly.

Lady Kadiatou stroked her sister's hair. "Yes, she did. One of the young noblemen taught her to dance. She had a marvelous first night." She winked at Innes. "How was yours? Did you find your friend?"

"I did. We plan to meet tomorrow as well. But I think for now, we should head home. It's a long ride."

Lady Kadiatou hummed an agreement and gently patted Lady Sira's cheek to wake her. "Come, Adama can take us home."

"Your mother?" Innes asked, helping Lady Sira to her feet as she yawned.

"She has her own carriage for a reason," Lady Kadiatou said with a small laugh. "*Nà yan*, Sira," she said to her sister.

"*Ne bɛ nà, ne bɛ nà…*" she mumbled and yawned again.

Innes offered her an arm as they made their way to the front door. He risked a glance back into the ballroom and saw Kenneth talking with his brother, his cheeks flushed red. Unable to stop himself from smiling, he turned away and escorted his ladies to their carriage.

Of course, Innes didn't have any other outfit for the next night, nor for the next. He hadn't planned on needing one. So, he donned the same clothing and returned the following night, feeling underdressed.

Ladies Kadiatou and Sira both looked thrilled to be back, rushing down to the ballroom hand in hand. Innes followed at a slower pace, then slipped into a side hallway so he could return to the gallery and look for Naomhan.

The room was empty. "Naomhan?" Innes asked in a whisper, looking around.

There was no answer.

With a sigh, Innes turned and headed back to the door, only to stop in his tracks because a dark-haired young man was blocking the way. "You called?" Naomhan asked.

"Can you disguise me again?" Innes asked.

"Of course!" Naomhan tapped his nose, and warmth tingled through Innes's body. When he looked down, his gown tonight was sapphire blue. A quick rub of his face revealed his beard was once more gone. "Are you sure I can't do anything else for you?"

"No, thank you. Midnight, yes?"

Naomhan nodded. "Midnight."

With a small bow because it seemed right, Innes left the gallery and hurried to the ballroom. It was easy enough to spot Kenneth, milling around the food, politely entertaining his guests.

But when he and Innes locked eyes, Kenneth's smile turned soft and genuine. Excusing himself from the courtiers, Kenneth made his way to Innes's side where he lifted his hand to his lips. "Lady Irene. It is a pleasure to see you again."

Innes blushed, pleased. "The pleasure is mine, Your Highness."

"I had hoped you would come tonight. I have something to show you."

Giving him a conspiratorial wink, Kenneth led Innes to one of the side rooms where several books had been piled onto a low table, a loveseat placed behind it. "I wanted to show you my research, and you could help me sort which sources were credible or not."

Innes, stunned for a moment, laughed. "You get me in private but only to read together!" he gasped, his stomach aching. He collapsed against Kenneth's shoulder, tears escaping his eyes. "I love you, Kenneth," he said, then suddenly chilled, remembering this was only temporary.

Kenneth smiled sadly. "I know," he said, but soon brightened, only a slight tremble in his chin revealing anything other than happiness. "Come, I have a lot to show you."

So, Innes and Kenneth whittled away several hours poring over books as they had done before. Innes scoffed at several of them. "Outsiders," he said, indicating several misunderstandings or outright falsehoods. "Anything that claims we do anything involving human blood can be burned or used for scrap," he said. "We haven't done sacrifices of any sort since the destruction of the Second Temple, and even when we *did*, they weren't human. That's the entire point of the story of Abraham and Isaac; human sacrifice is evil. It was a condemnation of the other religious groups in the region that did."

Kenneth nodded and set the offending books aside. "I understand. So, nothing involving blood."

"Not even meat," Innes confirmed. "We have to cook it thoroughly"—he winced—"not that I follow those laws strictly. It is difficult to do so without the aid of a community."

Kenneth frowned and kissed his temple. "I'm sorry, Innes."

"It's not your fault." He reached back for the book pile. As he brought the cover closer, his eyes widened. "Oh," he breathed, tracing his fingers over the cover. It was decorated in delicate golden embossing with the old language in calligraphy. "*Oh*." He carefully paged through it, tears filling his eyes. "Where did you *find* this?" he asked.

In his hands was a complete copy of the Torah. It was not a proper scroll, but it had both the old text and a Senatin translation side by side. Throughout, there were notes in the margins, one set in Norench and another in Saxtish. Kenneth drew his brows tight. "Princess Elodie had it," he said seriously. "She... Her people took it from a-a place of worship before torching the building. She brought it with her for me to, apparently, laugh at and then burn it together. As a 'show of proper faith,' she said."

Innes's eyes burned, his happiness subsumed completely by rage. "Is *that* why you broke the engagement?" he asked, wiping the acid from his eyes.

This time, Kenneth answered directly. "Yes. I could never *live* with someone who would delight so completely in another's suffering, let alone marry them."

Innes stroked his hand over the book's text, feeling the contrast between parchment and ink. In the front was a list of names, former owners of the book, Innes assumed.

"Let's study together," Kenneth said softly, nudging his head against Innes's. "Please, teach me."

Innes sighed and rubbed his eyes again. "I'm no scholar, nor is my father. My knowledge is limited."

"Then we'll learn together. What better place to start than the beginning?" Kenneth took the Torah book and turned to the first page of text. "The beginning of everything?"

Innes was finished crying. With a smile, he took Kenneth's hand in his. "Very well." He closed the book. "If we're to start at the beginning, we don't start with the book. Instead, we begin with our most important prayer. Repeat after me."

They were words he said every day, words he could not remember learning, words that were more a part of his soul than his mind. He taught them to Kenneth, their hands clasped as Innes covered his eyes. Kenneth repeated uncertainly at first, but as they chanted together, he began to learn.

רָחָא הָוֹהִי וּנֵיַהֹלֱא הָוֹהִי לֵאָרְשִׂי עַמְשׁ

דֶעָו סָלוֹעָל וֹתוּכְלַמ דוֹבְּכ םֵשׁ ,ךוּרָבּ

When Innes deemed his pronunciation acceptable, he kissed him. "And now, we can begin the book." He opened it and traced his fingers over the familiar letters. "I do not know if I will remember how to chant properly, but I can read."

Kenneth settled in. "I'd love to hear. I won't know the difference if the chanting is right or wrong." He chuckled. "Can you point to the text as you read? I want to try and follow."

"Of course." Licking his lips, Innes began, stumbling at first, but swiftly gaining comfort as the sounds became familiar again. "*Bereshit bara Elohim et hashamayim ve'et ha'aretz…*"

After a few verses, they discussed what they'd read, seeking meaning beyond the surface words. Time slipped quickly away until the clock began to chime midnight.

"Oh no!" Innes gasped. "I'm going to change back." He kissed Kenneth goodbye, ignoring his cry of "Wait, Innes!" and hurried out, just getting into an empty servants' stair before the magic swirled over his skin once again.

He stood in the stairway, trembling. *One more night.*

He pressed the heels of his hands into his eyes, angry at himself and at the cruelty of the world.

At the third ball, Innes went straight to the gallery, murmuring Naomhan's name. The fairy soon appeared. "Prince Kenneth is very sad today," he said.

"Did you help him too?" Innes asked.

Naomhan shook his head. "No, I didn't show myself to him." He rocked back and forth of his feet, holding himself. "I didn't want to scare him when he was sad."

Innes raised an eyebrow. "You didn't mind when it was me," he commented dryly.

"I'm still learning how best to do this," Naomhan said, closing his eyes. He soon opened them again. "One more disguise, I assume?"

Innes's stomach was in knots. "One more."

This time the gown was silvery blue, shining like moonlight.

He entered the ballroom and immediately went to Kenneth's side. But before they could talk beyond teasing pleasantries, Prince Ellar approached them, clapping his hand to his brother's shoulder. "Well, well," he said warmly. "It seems you have found your bride, brother! Come, let us meet her properly."

Innes stared, wide-eyed, suddenly full of panic. He had a name, but no identity to use as cover. He couldn't use Lady Keita; he hardly looked Mandalian.

"Allow us a short walk in the garden first," Kenneth said quickly. "It's quite frightful to meet the king and queen for the first time."

Prince Ellar laughed. "Very well, very well. But don't fly away, little bird." He patted Innes's cheek and strolled away.

Kenneth and Innes went to the garden. It was lit with tall, curving lanterns, casting a soft flickering glow around them. "I'm sorry," Kenneth said softly. "But we have some time to spin a story if you want. Or…or you can leave. I'll claim not to know where you went. I'll play the role of abandoned suitor with admirable aplomb." His smile was melancholy even with his playful bow.

Innes leaned into Kenneth's arm, bitterness on his tongue. "The latter would be the safer option," he said quietly.

"I thought so," Kenneth murmured, and Innes's heart broke. "Let's have a nice long walk. And then—" He swallowed.

Innes nodded against his shoulder.

After a few minutes, Kenneth said, "You gained the aid of the fairy Naomhan. Are you sure you could not…take Irene forever as your disguise?"

"No heirs," Innes said with a sigh, not looking forward to rehashing the conversation he'd had with the fairy. "After a few years, we'd be forced to annul the marriage, especially since I would give you no political gain, no matter the story we spin."

"Could—could the fairy make it possible for you to—"

Innes stopped walking, staring deeply into Kenneth's eyes. "I love you, I do, but, Kenneth, my body is *mine*, given to me by the Lord. I will not *change* myself just to be with you. I would rather miss you."

Kenneth looked away, shame burning in his ears. "You're right," he mumbled. "I'm begging you to change yourself for me, but that's not fair. It isn't fair for me to ask you to sacrifice your body, your *life*, for my happiness." His expression shifted in profile, becoming thoughtful. "Not without changing something of my own in turn."

"Kenneth?" Innes asked.

A whistle broke through the quiet night. Prince Ellar was on the balcony overlooking the garden. He waved at them, gesturing for them to come inside.

With one last lingering look, Innes bowed. "Farewell, Kenneth," he said softly. And hating himself for putting them both through this agony a second time, he ran from the garden and disappeared into a servants' hall.

After a few minutes, he could hear the guards clamoring around, calling for Lady Irene. Slowly, quietly, he crept to the one place they wouldn't look. Removing the key from his neck, he opened the prince's stair and climbed up into Kenneth's chambers.

He closed himself into his library, suddenly overwhelmed by the familiar scent. He sat on the sofa where they had read together many a time, laughing and cuddling. On the table beside him was the Torah book from the night before. Tears welled up and fell, coursing down his cheeks. Innes clutched the key tightly as he cried. Soon, he was out of tears, and sat, numb, waiting for time to run out.

And as the distant clock struck twelve, Innes wiped his eyes, pressed his lips to the metal, and set the key down on top of the book.

Bearded once more, Innes left the room and went to find his ladies. Missing the weight of the key, his chest felt bare.

He nearly ended up tripping over Lady Sira. "Innes!" she said, happy at first, but soon frowning. "Your eyes are all red," she said, knitting her eyebrows together. "Are you okay?"

He wiped his eyes. "Of course, my lady. It's...hard to say goodbye sometimes."

She nodded seriously. "It is. Do you think the prince will find Lady Irene?" she asked.

Innes shrugged. "*Inshallah*."

"*Inshallah*," Lady Sira agreed and took his hand. "Kadiatou is waiting outside with the carriage."

"Lead the way, my lady."

And she did.

A way from the castle town, Innes could sink back into his work and avoid the royal gossip. He wasn't interested in whatever saga had been crafted from his disguise. He ignored Rose's attempts to talk about what had happened.

As the balls slipped from being days prior to weeks, they started to feel more dream than reality. Lady Keita had enjoyed herself and had made many connections with other nobility, which meant she was planning balls of her own, the first to be held in two months.

Innes was happy for the task of designing and creating her and her daughters' new gowns. As busy with work as he was, Rose stopped bringing up Prince Kenneth, and life went on.

Then, one day, Rose returned from the town, having gone for supplies and a quick visit to their parents. Her expression was troubled.

"What's wrong?" Innes asked, only glancing at her quickly before returning to hemming.

Rose set the fabric she'd bought across his work bench, brushing stray threads off her apron. "Prince Kenneth has abdicated the throne," she said. "Apparently, it happened only days after the balls. It was a *huge* scandal. I'm surprised we didn't hear about it before now."

Innes's hands stilled. "What happened? Is he still at the palace?"

Rose shook her head. "No, he left soon after. He didn't say where to."

With a sigh, Innes sat back into his chair. Kenneth had left his throne…for him? But it had been weeks, and Kenneth had not come to Lady Keita's manor though Innes had told him he was there. He rubbed his eyes. No, Kenneth had not left his throne for him. Perhaps he had left to be free to pursue other desires, whatever those might be.

"Well, good for him. He was unhappy as a prince. Prince Ellar will do a fine job," Innes said, aware his voice was flat.

"Are you okay, Innes?" Rose asked, rubbing his shoulder.

He shook her off. "Fine. I'll be fine." He shut his thoughts away and returned to his work.

W eeks turned into months. Lady Keita held her parties. Rose and Innes returned to their parents' home for the High Holy Days and for Pesach. They did not have a synagogue, but those around them did gather to recite what prayers they could remember, and to come together as a community. Innes and Rose celebrated Eid with Lady Keita, talking and laughing as a seemingly endless stream of food emerged from the kitchens.

After nearly a year, Innes felt reasonably good alone. He entertained his little fantasy of a marriage of friendship again, writing out letters to his mother, trying to find the words to explain what he wanted. He hadn't found them yet, but they would come. He wrote letters to Kenneth as well, asking what had transpired, where he had gone, and what he planned to do. Those letters were burned. He liked to imagine the smoke carrying his wishes to wherever Kenneth had gone, but he knew it was foolish.

Lady Sira's body was shifting in her adolescence, and so Innes and Rose had to stay on top of her clothing, keeping them comfortable and modest. It was a new kirtle for her he was working on when there was a knock on the door.

"Come in!" he called, shifting the straight pin from his lips to between his teeth to keep it from falling as he spoke. He glanced over, expecting to see Rose or Lady Sira.

Instead, the pin fell from his mouth. "Your Highness!" he gasped.

Kenneth smiled awkwardly, rubbing the back of his neck. "Not really anymore." He'd grown out his beard, the red-gold hair now several inches long. "How are you, Innes?"

Innes stared, unable to speak, his mind swirling with the impossibility of Kenneth *being there*. "Uh," he said eloquently, leaning down to pick up the fallen pin. "I'm—I'm fine." As he set it on the workbench, he risked a glance at Kenneth's face. Blood rushed into his cheeks and ears, and he looked quickly away. "And you? Where have you been?"

Kenneth shifted in the doorway, letting the door close behind him. "Deurich," he said. He rubbed his hands together, then massaged his palms with his fingers. "I—I wanted to find a proper teacher. Since it would be unfair to put the burden on you. So, I sought out the rabbi who had owned the Torah book."

Frowning, Innes ran his fingers through his beard. "Why would you go through so much trouble?" he asked, baffled.

Kenneth rubbed his hands again, his gaze on the floor. "I wanted to learn, and the more I learned, the more I wanted to be a part, not merely an observer. I found the Rabbi Shlomo after some time searching. He has been very gracious— probably more than I deserve." He fiddled with the hem of his surcoat, his ears scarlet. "He kept discouraging me; saying I didn't need to change myself, that it would give me nothing I did not already have. But, still, I wanted to. Again and again, I asked to be taught. Until eventually...he agreed." He looked up through his pale eyelashes. "Innes...can I ask you what your true name is?"

"*Yitzchak ben Mordechai,*" he said softly, looking at him now. "And what is yours?"

Kenneth smiled. "*Chananyah ben Avraham Avinu,*" he said.

"So, you are a convert now?" Isaac asked, bewildered.

"It will be the rest of my life before it feels real, but...yes." Hananiah rubbed the back of his neck, blushing still. "Rabbi Shlomo agreed to come here with me, and I convinced my family to allow the building of a synagogue. There...will be a true community here if you wish to join it."

Isaac breathed slow and deep, his mind spinning too fast to keep track of. He sat down in his chair, dragging his fingers through his beard. "I—yes, of course I will. Yes. That's—" He stared up at Hananiah, tears clouding his vision. "*Why?*" he breathed.

Hananiah shifted his weight from foot to foot. "It wasn't only for you, but it would be false of me to claim you were not on my mind. I saw how you struggled to keep your culture without roots to hold you. I admired it, and I longed to do something. But I feared the act of change. I didn't realize how much a burden I had placed on you—how I kept pushing you to change yourself for my sake." He closed his eyes, his hands folded around each other. "It was wrong of me. And I apologize. I will never ask it of you again. Can you forgive me?"

For a long moment, silence stretched between them until Isaac rose and walked to Hananiah's side and took his clasped hands in his own. "I forgive you. But you do not need to be so extreme as to never ask again."

Hananiah looked up, their gazes meeting, a question in his eyes.

"Relationships are not one-sided," Isaac continued, turning over Hananiah's hand to trace the lines of his palm. "They are a dance, a give-and-take. I ask instead you promise all important decisions between us will be discussed and compromised, so we may both participate." He winced. "I must apologize to you as well. I was selfish in coming to see you when I had already left you once. It was cruel of me to do it a second time. Can you forgive me?"

"I forgive you," Hananiah said. He shifted their grips and entwined their fingers, his blush creeping back. "I do notice you are discussing a relationship. I hope it can be with me?"

"If you can still trust me after that whole fiasco," Isaac murmured, shame burning his ears.

"I can. I do!" Hananiah said quickly. "I do, trust you, that is."

Isaac stood on his toes and touched their lips together. "Then let us celebrate the Sabbath together."

With a grin, Hananiah wrapped him in a tight embrace. "Currently there is no dedicated synagogue, of course, but my father gave Rabbi Shlomo a fine home at my request. It is large enough that he will be conducting services there until the proper building is completed. Will you come with me?"

"Of course, I will." Isaac rested his head briefly against Hananiah's shoulder. "I will have to bring my family. Are you prepared to meet them?"

Hananiah's smile was radiant. "I am."

"I have a blessing to say," Isaac said with a small laugh. "Would you like to join me?"

"Of course, though you may need to help me with the words," Hananiah said tentatively.

Isaac laughed again. "Don't worry; you'll be hearing it a lot soon."

And together they chanted the blessing of new beginnings.

Rabbi Shlomo was a tall man and old, his gray beard streaked with white. His eyes were dark and deep-set, almost hidden behind his bushy brows. He had set up his sitting room as a sanctuary with two sets of seats clustered around a small, raised platform that served as a *bimah*. And in a tall cabinet, glass-fronted with the inner shelves removed, there was a set of Torah scrolls, lovingly covered in embroidered velvet.

Filling the room were Isaac's neighbors. Abram the woodcutter and his daughter, Miriam, whom his mother was determined would marry David. Old Eliezer and his wife, Leah, flanked by their two sons and their wives. The merchant Levi and his son, Reuben, whom Isaac had once fancied. It seemed he was married now to Sarah, the cobbler's daughter, who leaned on his arm. On his other side, he held the hand of a young girl, no older than four, who gazed around the little sanctuary in unabashed wonder.

And around Isaac, his family with one important addition. Hananiah placed a hand on Isaac's arm.

Isaac had expected to tear up. He hadn't expected to sob, overwhelmed by the feeling of coming home. His mother and sister laughed, embracing him as the rest of the community clustered around him, offering handkerchiefs and gentle teasing. But as he laughed with them, he saw tears sparkling in many an eye.

"Thank you," Isaac said to Hananiah.

"Thank you," the little crowd echoed.

Suddenly surrounded by sincere gratitude, Hananiah flushed scarlet before dropping his head. "I did only what was right. Please, do not give me more credit than is my due."

A warm laugh cut through the chatter. "Let the boy be," the rabbi said. "He may well melt if he blushes anymore." Something of Deurich had crept into his voice, sharpening his *W*s, roughing his *R*s. "But as sundown nears, I think we should sit."

Ruth squeezed Isaac's hand and left with their mother to the women's side.

Candles were lit, wine and bread were passed around, songs were sung, and prayers were chanted, familiarity sending pleasant chills down Isaac's back. As the Torah was carried around the room, Isaac stroked his fingers against the velvet of its cover, transported to the day of his bar mitzvah when it was he who had carried it against his chest, pride and fear of dropping it filling him in equal parts.

"You're crying again," Hananiah murmured, dabbing at Isaac's eyes with his handkerchief.

On his other side, David muffled a chuckle.

As the chant of the Torah echoed through the small room, Isaac closed his eyes, listened, and let the words wash over him. His chest filled with light, the same feeling of *connection* he had felt only once before.

As the rabbi finished, he raised his head. "In this week, the children of Israel have ceased their wandering in the desert and come to the land of milk and honey," he explained. "Just as we here today have found a new home, driven from the land of our ancestors. Like our forefathers, we, too, wander this world in search of a home. But it is always important to remember homes are not always given by powers on high. Sometimes, they must be made." He looked around at the tiny congregation. "Today, we make this our home. Perhaps it is a Promised Land, or perhaps it is only a stop in our wandering in the desert, but look around you, at our community." They did. Isaac squeezed Hananiah's hand. "*This* is our home. As is this." He gestured to the Torah scroll before him. "It is a tree of life to those who hold fast to it."

With more prayers and blessings, the Torah was put away, and the service was concluded with food and drink.

"So, Isaac," David said, nodding toward Hananiah, "I guess you made an impression."

Both of them blushed. Isaac laughed and put his arm around Hananiah's waist. "I suppose you could say that."

221

Ruth nudged his shoulder from the other side and gave him a knowing smirk.

He nudged her back. "I don't want to hear *anything* from you," he warned.

She laughed and pinched Hananiah's cheek. "Be good to my brother, Hananiah."

"I would dream of nothing else," he said sweetly.

Hadassah joined them, putting an arm through David's. "My dear, now that we're all here, you can meet with Miriam!"

"Help me," David mouthed as he was pulled away to a chorus of laughter.

Hananiah helped with the establishment of the synagogue and devoted himself to study full-time. "Why isn't your family upset by any of this?" Isaac asked one afternoon after he'd come into town to shop.

Hananiah scratched his beard, his cheeks flushed. "I sought out the fairy Naomhan," he explained. "And asked only that my parents accept my choices and that enemies of the crown could not find me. He gave me this." He pulled down the front of his shift, revealing a silver chain at the end of which was a delicate flower pendant. "So long as I wear this, I will be hidden from my family's enemies," he explained. "Or so the fairy said. And he accomplished my other request, though I dare not ask how."

"He seemed kind," Isaac said, running his thumb over the flower's enamel petals. "I don't think you need to worry."

Hananiah grinned. "If *you're* not worrying, it really must be fine."

With a laugh, Isaac helped tuck the necklace away. "Is the synagogue almost finished?"

Hananiah nodded, looking at the building with a fond smile. "You know, I would love it if you moved back into town." He took Isaac's hand in his and rubbed some of the white scars dotting its surface.

"What would I do?" Isaac wondered. "I have a good job with the Lady Keita."

"Maybe you could open up your own shop?"

Isaac snorted but then paused, thinking through his salary from Lady Keita. "I…could, I think," he said slowly, his heart lifting. "But I would hate to leave her in the lurch."

"Maybe you could take an apprentice? And she could always commission you for something extravagant."

"That's true." He looked over to his sister where she was chatting with the cantor. She was quite a seamstress in her own right, even more so now with nearly two years of steady work. "Ruth!" he called. She turned her head toward him and held up a finger before turning back to finish her conversation.

Eventually, she walked over. "Yes, Isaac?"

"How would you feel about a promotion and an assistant? I promise I'll help you find a cute one."

She grinned.

"It is a shame to see you go," Lady Keita said, touching her chest. "You have become a part of our family."

Innes bowed. "I feel the same, my lady. But this opportunity is one I have only before dared to dream of. Know that whatever work you need from me, you are entitled to a significant discount."

Lady Keita reached into her sleeve and removed a golden chain at the end of which hung a pendant in the shape of a hand with a jeweled eye in the center of the palm. "To protect you," she said.

"Oh, I couldn't take something so valuable," he demurred.

"I insist," she said firmly and held it out to drop into his waiting hand.

He took the necklace and fastened it around his neck. It replaced the key quite nicely. "Thank you, my lady. I will treasure it."

She smiled, her full lips gleaming in the sunlight. "You are welcome, Innes. I wish you all the best."

Buying the little building was simple. Furnishing and getting it set up was more complicated, but in the end, he was proud. The ground floor had two parts, a front-facing area for meeting with customers and selling accessories such as belts, stockings, and gloves (and masks if there was to be a masquerade again). It was arranged neatly with the items on display marked with their prices as well as a counter for conducting the transactions. Through a door was the work room with various dress forms, two workbenches, and towering shelves for fabric, thread, and supplies. His scissors hung from small hooks over the main workbench, and his needles were tucked away in a wooden drawer on top of it. The main workbench also had drawers for storing bits and bobs. Isaac smiled at the brass knobs, fully aware of plans he had for the first of those drawers.

As he stood in the workroom, his labor finished, he took a deep breath, enjoying the scent of wood and cloth. Soon, sweat would add an unpleasant undertone to that smell, but there was a window, so it would not be unbearable in the summer months. Through an archway, his kitchen, made of stone and well away from his supplies.

In the back of the workroom, a staircase wound up into the second floor where there was a comfortable apartment. His family had helped him furnish it, calling in favors with the various members of the community to make sure it was exactly what he needed. He had a spacious bedroom and a small office for doing his accounting as well as a sitting room, which had two empty bookshelves.

He retrieved his book of Ketuvim from his bag and set it on one of the shelves. He looked forward to filling them together with Hananiah.

As if summoned by the thought, the floor creaked, and Hananiah himself entered the apartment, then put his arms around Isaac's waist. "Hello, my love," he said before pressing a kiss against Isaac's cheek. "Are you happy with it?"

Isaac placed his hands over Hananiah's, leaning into his embrace. "I am," he said softly. "Are you? In the end, you are the one who gave up the most."

Hananiah hummed thoughtfully then pressed soft kisses against Isaac's neck, the shell of his ear. "I am," he said after a moment. "Being in the public eye distressed me as did knowing I needed to put my country over my own happiness. In the end, I think this is what I was always meant to be. A quiet, private scholar, living with a fussy tailor." He chuckled.

Isaac wanted to dispute the "fussy" descriptor, but he found he didn't know how. So instead, he turned to kiss Hananiah properly. After a few moments, they broke apart, and Isaac smiled. "Speaking of readiness, how are your studies coming along?"

Hananiah laughed and groaned as he leaned into Isaac's embrace. "It is so much to learn, I fear I'll never find the bottom, but I can't help but chase it. But my portion has been chosen, and the rabbi is helping me to learn it."

"That's wonderful! When will you have your aliyah?"

"In three weeks' time. I'm simultaneously excited and terrified."

Isaac remembered that feeling well. "You will do a good job," he said, stroking Hananiah's swiftly lengthening beard. "And even if you stumble, we will catch you. That's what it means to be part of a family."

Hananiah smiled and leaned down for another kiss.

There was a secret project, hidden in Isaac's workbench drawer. An unassuming sheet of wool into which Isaac had embroidered blue stripes and a pattern reminiscent of the palace ramparts. At each corner, Isaac had made a small hole.

The week of Hananiah's aliyah while Hananiah was absorbed fully in his studies, Isaac acquired long strings and sorted them out, one long string and seven shorter ones for each corner. Putting them together, he drew the threads through each hole, then knotted the threads five times and wrapped the long string around between them.

He murmured prayers as he worked, aware of the weight of history upon his shoulders. His own father had wrapped *tzitzit*, as had his father before him, and his father before him—an unbroken thread stretching back into the Promised Land.

He finished the final corner, folded the shawl, and touched it briefly to his lips before tucking it back into its hiding place, now complete.

The Sabbath morning of Hananiah's first aliyah, Isaac woke early. Hananiah was already awake of course, his hair askew as he sat in the front room, curled around his book of prayers, murmuring to himself.

Isaac kissed his temple as he passed by. "Good morning, Hananiah."

"Morning, love. Where are you going?"

Isaac smiled and said, "You'll see."

He retrieved the shawl and returned upstairs with it folded behind his back. When Hananiah opened his mouth to ask, Isaac said, "Stand up and close your eyes."

Smiling, Hananiah made a show of setting his book on the table and rising to his feet, arms outstretched and eyes closed.

Isaac approached and chanted the blessing, unfolding the shawl carefully before he wrapped it around Hananiah and laid it over his head.

His mouth visible, Hananiah smiled and held it for a moment before adjusting it properly so the fringes fell against his body. He looked down, admiring the design, tears sparkling in his eyes. "Isaac, it's beautiful. Thank you."

"I received my first on the day of my bar mitzvah," Isaac explained, running his fingertips over the embroidery laying on Hananiah's shoulder. "So, it seemed only right for you to receive yours on the day of your first aliyah."

After wiping his tears with the heels of his hands, Hananiah wrapped Isaac into an embrace. "I could say a million prayers of thanks, and they would never equal the blessing you are to me," he said.

Isaac blushed and laughed, squeezing tightly. "You stole the words from my mouth," he said.

"Shall I steal your breath as well?" Hananiah asked, his cheeks darkening. "We still have an hour until the service begins."

"Not in your tallit, we're not," Isaac laughed.

With a grin, Hananiah removed it, folded it neatly, and set it beside his book of prayers.

As the years went on, Isaac maintained his contact with Lady Keita, who often sent work his way. Her patronage kept his name in the mouth of the court, and he never lacked for money.

Hananiah continued studying, eventually becoming the cantor of the synagogue. His red hair had grayed, and his voice had thinned, but he never lacked for energy, even in the winter months when his stomach plagued him.

Isaac's hands remained steady, and he took apprentices, passing on his skills to a younger generation—including to his darling nephew, Joshua ben David.

If the community passed judgment on the two bachelors living as brothers, they never said, whether out of a sense of gratitude or genuine love, Isaac could never decide. And perhaps, in the end, it didn't matter.

They lived their lives in love with family all around them, repairing the world each in their own small ways. And when they departed, they left behind their names and a legacy that would follow them long after they had turned to dust.

It was the grandson of Joshua, named Daniel in David's memory, who saw him next. Tensions in the city had risen to a fever pitch as the Highlands and Saxtain vied for status in a shrinking world. Daniel was afraid. In his six years of life, he had known too much violence.

Hidden beneath a willow tree, he sat, his gaze hard and fixed as his parents argued in the distance. There was a rustle of wind, and there was a man sitting beside him, a red rose cap in his hands, storm-gray eyes winking out from behind a mop of dark hair. "My name is Naomhan," the man said with a smile. "How can I help?"

Cultural Notes

This is not comprehensive, but hopefully it provides some context for things that may be unfamiliar!

Blessed is the Lord, our God, who has allowed me to reach this joyous day.

A translation of the Shehecheyanu, a prayer said on special occasions or new experiences

Mezuzah, plural mezuzot

a small wooden box containing a parchment scroll of the Sh'ma that is hung on the doorpost of a Jewish home. Some people also put them on the doorposts of all living spaces as well, such as a bedroom or kitchen.

Sheyd

roughly the Hebrew equivalent of 'demon'

B'nai Yisrael

Children of Israel, i.e. Israelites (the ancient tribe, not modern Israelis)

Nà yan - Ne bɛ nà, ne bɛ nà

Bambara language, spoken in Mali. Translates to "Come here/I'm coming, I'm coming"

הֵעוּ סָלוֹעל וֹתוכלמ דוֹבֶּכ בֵֹש דֹוֹתָב / הָחָא הָוֹהִי־וֹנֵיֵהלֵֶא הָוֹהִי לָאָרֹשִי עָמֹש

Sh'ma Yisrael, or the Sh'ma. A declaration of the one-
ness of G-d. The most important prayer in Judaism.

Bereshit bara Elohim et hashamayim ve'et ha'aretz...
The opening lines of Genesis

Inshallah إِنْ شَاءَ ٱللَّٰهُ
Arabic, 'if G-d wills it'. Because it's used in the Qu-
ran, it's a common phrase even among non-Arabic
speaking Muslims.

*Yitzchak ben Mordechai/Chananyah ben Avraham
Avinu*
Hebrew names are patronymic or matronymic (de-
pending on the gender of the child), so Isaac is "Isaac,
son of Mordecai". Converts to Judaism traditionally
are spiritually considered children of the Biblical
Abraham and Sarah, and so use "Avraham Avinu",
Abraham our Father, or "Sarah Imenu", Sarah our
Mother. This is only true for the first generation of
convert. So if Hananiah were to have a son named
Noah for Naomhan his great-great uncle, Noah's full
name would be *Noach ben Chananyah*.

Hamsa
The pendant gifted to Isaac by Lady Keita, an amu-
let of protection used by both Jews and Muslims to
ward off the evil eye

Aliyah

During the Sabbath services Saturday mornings, different members of the congregation are invited to come read from the Torah. Typically a Jew's first aliyah is their bar or bat mitzvah.

Tallit

a prayer shawl worn during services that have tzitzit or knotted fringes. In Jewish wedding custom, a tallit is often used as the chuppah, or wedding canopy.

Repairing the world

Tikkun olam, a Jewish concept of our role in the ongoing process of the world's creation.

From Stars
They Fell

The first thing I became aware of after the crash was pain. The sky burned my eyes as I opened them, my limbs ached and smoldered where bits of burning metal had stuck to flesh like hair in paint, and something was stabbing me in my shoulders, right at the base of my wings.

I groaned and rolled over. I raised the wings on the skyward side until they were perpendicular to my body to stretch them and check for breaks or tears. I was lucky. They were sore as anything but intact.

I rolled onto the other side and did the same thing. It felt like there was a noticeable tear in the smaller set—it twinged painfully as I opened it—but it was an injury that would heal up fine given time. Satisfied, I folded them down again and rolled back to face the sky.

It was an eye-searing blue with fluffy white bits of condensation suspended in air. I was lucky twicefold; I could breathe normally. The ventilation slits at my joints creaked as I opened them further to let the atmosphere in. Deep breath achieved, I steeled myself and peeled the bits of metal from my skin, hissing through all my slits as I tried not to cry out. They left angry welts behind. They would blister in a few hours, I was sure. But I got them all and sucked on my fingers where they had gotten slight burns from the heat.

Suddenly, the peaceful sounds of blowing air were interrupted by voices. They were low and rumbling, reminding me of the great beasts of the plains. I could feel the translation chip in my ear whirr to life while the embedded screen in my contact lenses blinked on to provide written transcripts.

Well, one side did. The left side had apparently been damaged.

With a groan, I removed that one in case there were ruptures or anything else that could damage my eye. I did not want to be stranded on a strange world half-blind. My life was already torturous enough, thank you very much.

I could now see the voices belonged to much smaller creatures than I'd been expecting. They maybe came up to my lower thorax, though they were twice as wide and covered in long hair of various colors, ranging from gray to red to brown. I counted perhaps six or seven in all. They exuded warmth so much I had to conclude they were mammalian or some equivalent.

The translation chip was working, so clearly, they were intelligent.

"What do you think it is?" one with light-brown hair said. The hair parted in the middle to reveal a mouth and short, flat teeth. When the mouth closed, the line of hair was complete once again. I was fascinated.

"I don't know. Clearly, it's alive, but I've never seen anything like it," one with red hair replied. A five-fingered hand appeared from behind the hair only to grab and stroke it in what I assumed was a thoughtful motion.

They all turned to one with silvery-gray hair and a pair of lenses perched on what I could only conclude was a snout of some kind. I wondered if they indicated some sort of status or if the creature just had poor sight.

"The first thing is to see if it understands us," ze said. They all turned to me. "Can you understand us?"

I sat up so we were at eye level. Possible responses flicked across my right eye.

yes/no question asked: response needed

nonverbal:

   affirmative: forward motion of head toward thorax

   negative: horizontal turn from side to side

   double blink to view verbal responses

I chose to nod an affirmative because I did understand hir and didn't have any reason to lie. I directed it at the one with lenses since ze seemed like the leader. Ze had hir eyebrows furrowed in…surprise? Confusion?

"Can you talk?" ze asked.

A long string of instructions for proper sound production scrolled across my vision, and I rolled my tongue around my mouth in anticipation.

I took a while though. They were murmuring to each other quietly, wondering if I had understood them or if I was mute. Finally, I got enough input to croak, "Yes, I can. It will take me some time, however."

"Do you have a name?" one of the others in the group asked.

I tried to think about how I could adapt it to this language without wing buzzes. "Veniaki?" I tried. I couldn't think of a way to render the jaw click of the final consonant, so I swapped in the velar stop. And there was no realistic way to convey the wing tone. But it would have to do.

"Nice to meet you, Veniaki," said the one with lenses. "You can call me Patience. And these are Chastity, Temperance, Charity, Prudence, Kindness, and Humility."

My head swam. I wasn't going to be able to put faces to names for a good while, but I thanked hir for the introduction anyway.

"So," Patience said. "Can I ask where you came from?"

I blinked up at the sky, but the brightness of the solar star combined with the atmosphere drowned out anything I might use to orient myself. Instead, I just indicated upward.

"From the sky?" ze tried to clarify.

I nodded.

This perplexed hir. "I see you have wings, but even birds live near the ground."

I didn't know how to respond, so I shook my head, which had the unfortunate effect of making the world sway and my headache return in force. I held my head in my hands, trying to make the pain subside.

Patience grabbed my arm before I could topple and helped me stay straight. "Are you all right?" ze asked.

"No," I responded. "But soon."

Patience looked around, then back at the rest of hir companions. "If you need shelter and food, we will happily provide."

"Truly?"

"Of course. Dwarves are nothing if not gracious!"

I didn't know what dwarves were except it was apparently a word for what Patience and hir companions were, but a roof over my head and food in my stomach would both be appreciated. "Thank you," I said.

I stood up, took a moment to adjust to the new gravity (it was slightly more than what I was used to), and followed the dwarves. I took this time to look at the landscape in more detail. There were many plants, though most of them were green rather than the reds and violets I was used to. They stank of chlorophyll, but it didn't take long to adjust to it.

In the distance, mountains rose into the sky, brown and green up close, fading to purple as the colors fought through the air. As we walked, the yellow star overhead sank low behind the mountains and disappeared, leaving the once-blue sky vivid with oranges and reds.

I could learn to love such a place.

We arrived at night after I had tripped over what seemed to be every plant, root, and rock the forest had to offer. The living structure was surprisingly small for such a large enclave of dwarves. The walls were rough-hewn stone with a straw roof and cutouts for windows. Inside, seven beds lined one wall with a small kitchen with a wood-burning stove taking up an opposite corner. The remaining corner had a worn couch and large, hinged containers that were apparently for storage.

The dwarves filed in and moved toward their respective beds, mumbling to one another as they removed what turned out to be garments hidden under their hair. The rest of their flesh was surprisingly sparse of fur with the same pale-brown skin as around their eyes. Heavy boots clunked to the floor as they climbed into the beds and buried themselves in blankets. Patience had the largest bed, taking up the back corner across from the kitchen. Ze got a fire going in the space beneath the chimney (I wondered about the safety of a flammable roof over a fire) and shuffled over to the bed.

"It should fit you if you sleep sideways," ze said to me. "I have spare blankets somewhere around here." Ze opened one of the storage chests and rummaged around, pushing aside things that glittered to access the areas beneath. "Ah, there we go." Ze stood and shook out a blanket, raising a cloud of dust from the floor. "This and a spare pillow, and you'll be set. Chastity, give the poor thing one of your pillows. You know you've got the most."

Chastity, one of the brown-haired dwarves, grumbled from under hir blankets but begrudgingly offered one of the pillows from behind hir head.

I took it gratefully.

"You can fold those wings of yours up nice and tight?" Patience asked.

I demonstrated.

"Excellent. Then we shouldn't have a problem. All right, everyone, ready for dinner?"

I sat on the couch while Patience made something in a large pot on the fire. Prudence and Charity helped hir—fetching water from a well behind the house and more wood for the fire. I watched, observing and recording important parts. I knew I should've asked permission, but I didn't think ze would understand what I was asking.

Besides, who would I show? It wasn't as if there was a computer around here to which I could upload them.

Once the food was prepped and simmering, Patience turned to me, wiping off hir hands. "So, Veniaki, how should we have you earn your keep? You're too big for the mine tunnels, and I get the sense you wouldn't do well in them, having watched you in the dark earlier."

I looked around, gestured at the dust and cobwebs, then to the pot on the fire. "I could do this?"

"What, cook and clean? Do you know how?"

"If you show me, I will know."

Patience laughed. "I like you. Very well, Charity, you'll stay here tomorrow and show Veniaki the ropes. Looks like we've got us a housekeeper!"

The dinner was good. Mostly it tasted hot, but I didn't mind it. I was glad it settled well enough into my digestion.

I thanked whatever deity brought me to a place where I could attempt to build a new life. Considering everything else that had gone wrong up until now, it was nice to know *somebody* still cared enough to look out for me.

After dinner, the dwarves told stories as the fire burned down, and when it was nothing but embers, they went to sleep. I lay down at the foot of Patience's bed, my wings folded tightly against my back. Hir feet barely rested against me, and after I was wrapped in the blanket, I hardly felt hir at all.

Morning came quickly, and soon, I was roused by Patience shaking my shoulder. The sunlight spilling into the little house was beautiful, highlighting the dance of dust motes I supposed was universal. My burns had in fact blistered, the flesh swollen and painful. I resisted the urge to poke at them.

I watched the dwarves dress and gather their bags, then waved goodbye as they took several round baked dough loaves from the kitchen and left. Their whistling hung in the air for some time after they departed, carried on the wind.

Charity remained as Patience had asked. Ze was a red-haired dwarf with bits of gold and glass woven into the braided hair under hir mouth. "So!" ze said brightly as ze fidgeted at the fireplace to get the fire started again. "What do you know about keeping house?"

I shook my head. "Only that it must be done."

Ze laughed. "An excellent start. All right then, let's go over the daily chores. The first thing is dusting. You take the duster from its trunk over here. Oh, do you mind if I call you Veni? It's just that Veniaki is sort of…long."

"That's fine. I like it." The wrong consonant had been unsettling me. At least chopped in half, the name was more or less correct. I recorded videos of the lessons, though everything was ultimately simple. It was mostly a question of remembering which tools were for which tasks, where to find the tools, and to which location they needed to be returned. Charity was forgiving of my slow speech and kept up a friendly stream of chatter as we worked.

"So, I never did get the chance to ask, Veni. Are you a man or a woman?"

I tilted my head to express my confusion. "I do not understand."

Ze was perplexed as if I'd just said I didn't understand that things fall when dropped. "You know… Are you the sort to carry the baby or the one to put it there?"

My head remained tilted. "My kind lays eggs."

"*Well*, are you the kind to lay them or not?"

"Everyone is capable of laying eggs."

Ze stared at me. "Then how do you divide up your kind? You know, how to behave and such?"

I didn't understand the line of questioning. "Well…we are 'divided' by wing size, I suppose. There are those with long wings and those with short. Long-wings are better suitable for some lives than short-wings and vice versa."

Ze brightened up. "Oh! Okay. Are you a long-wing?"

I shook my head and raised up my wings to their full horizontal width, showing them the short second pair of wings that ended at the top of my abdomen. The injured one burned as I stretched it, so I quickly put them back down. "A long-wing's second pair ends near the ground." I held up a leg to demonstrate.

"I see! And what kind of rules are there about the two?"

I had to think about it. "The traditional rule is that short-wings are more...wild? Short-wings were first. Long-wings came about because long wings were fashionable, so they became popular. Or that is the story anyway. Now it's pretty even between short and long. There are also those in-between, of course. Long-wings are considered more...civilized? Better at things like accounting, diplomacy... Things that would not cause their wings to get in the way."

Charity tugged at hir hair thoughtfully. "So, long-wings are female, by our standards, I suppose. And that would make you male! So, you're a man."

I didn't understand the importance of classifying me as such, but I nodded.

"And I'm a woman, by the way," ze (she? The pronoun was scrolling across my contact. Apparently, this language modified for gender? Strange.) added. "Humans can't tell because their women don't have beards, the poor things." I added the vocabulary. The hair on a dwarf's face was a beard; a human is not a dwarf. Women are those who bear young, and they are considered less wild than the opposite, which was a... male? Man? Was that related to *hu*man? Ugh, vocabulary.

"What is a human?"

Charity tugged her beard again. "Well, they're a bit like dwarves, but taller, about your height. Their ears are smaller than dwarves' though, and their noses too. And they come in all kinds of browns, not just the little range of tan to beige we got. Patience's seen humans who are white as snow with hair to match, and she's seen humans who are near black as pitch. There aren't too many of those around here though. They live far to the south where the sun burns hotter."

I tried to imagine it, but I didn't know what the dwarves' faces looked like beneath their beards. I made a note of Patience's gender since apparently that was important to this culture.

"Will I see a human?" I asked.

Charity laughed. "I'm sure you will! We sell to them often, so on not-mining days you might see some. Master Wystan is here plenty, at least."

"Master Wystan?"

"Come, come, let us clean *and* gossip," Charity chided, bumping my arm in what seemed a good-natured way, but she knocked one of the blisters, and I hissed in pain. "Oh goodness, are you all right?" She took my arm and turned it gently in her grip. "Oh no, are those blisters? Why didn't you say anything? Come and let's get those bandaged up!"

She pulled me into the couch corner and pulled a small chest out of a larger trunk, then set it on top. Inside, there were bandages and packets of sweet-smelling plants. She pressed one of the pouches (they looked like the kind of cloth tea bags were made of?) to the largest blister. The skin felt strange where the dried plants touched it, almost like it was sizzling, but there was no pain. After a few moments of that, she removed it, wrapped a short bandage over it, and secured it with a pin. No adhesive, I supposed.

She turned my arms over, then repeated the series of actions on all the blisters she found, including the one on my upper thorax where she had to wrap the bandage around my shoulder to cover it. I'd had to lift my wings up out of the way, which caused the injured one to twinge again.

But as sore as I was, I was blessed to have lived through the crash at all, so I didn't complain. Charity, after she had finished wrapping, stared interestedly at my ventilation slits. Smirking a little, I blew air at her out of the center joint one on my arm. She jumped, her eyes going wide.

244

"That is amazing," she murmured. "How do you do it?"

I struggled to explain. "It's how I breathe."

She shook her head but smiled. "You are an astonishing creature. All right, any other injuries you haven't told me about?"

"My wing, but you cannot bandage it." I showed her the tear with my hand. "I don't want it to be crushed."

She tapped her finger against her lips, eyes bright and curious. "Yes, of course. Are you okay to work?"

"Yes. Thank you for your assistance."

"You're quite welcome." She beamed at me, then turned around to face the greater room. "Now, where did we leave off?"

After the chores were explained and finished, Charity made lunch. Another soup, it seemed. I didn't mind. It was salty and filling and hot, all good things.

"So," Charity said, having slurped down her meal with gusto, "does your kind wear clothes?"

I looked down at myself and smiled at little in embarrassment. "Yes, normally. I didn't really think about the lack until now."

"Nudity is fairly acceptable?" She was making some connection. To another species of this planet perhaps? Maybe humans? Something else?

I nodded. "For children, yes. I am young, so I'm yet unused to much ornamentation." In truth, I started being expected to dress regularly about two cycles ago, but I'd spent most of my time indoors modding my internal computer, so I hadn't ventured out much. My siblings had fed me.

I pushed the memories away. They still burned like citrus on a wound.

"Well, since we've some time before the others return, should I make you something?"

"That is kind of you to offer."

She beamed again, her cheeks becoming round like large fruits. "It's no trouble. What can I make you? If it's simple, it won't take long."

I thought about it. "Something like what you are wearing, I guess?" I pointed at the circle of fabric peeking out from under her beard. It seemed to sit at the waist and fall open, which would be perfect.

"A dress?" she said doubtfully for some reason.

"Well, I do need to breathe." I hissed my leg slits a bit.

"Oh, right! I guess everyone wears skirts on your world."

Skirt. Dress. Synonyms?

"Yes, I can make you a simple dress. Won't take more than a few hours. I've got some fabric lying around here somewhere." She got up to rummage through a trunk. "Ah, yes, Master Wystan traded us this! Feel how soft it is." The fabric was pale blue, like the sky, and was indeed very soft. "Got it from the Near East. Rare here but he said it was commonplace there and not expensive to buy. Does this suit you?"

I nodded.

"All right, up you get! Time to measure you."

She was quick with the measurements and laid the fabric out on the floor to mark it with a piece of chalk. "I'll make you a simple little sack dress. Nothing frilly, nice and airy, which I bet will be important for you." She grinned at me over her shoulder, then closed one eye in what appeared to be a jovial, conspiratorial gesture.

I watched in fascination as clothing appeared from plain fabric. First as an outline, then as a shapeless cutout, and then finally stitched together. Two hours hadn't gone by when she finished, holding it up for me to see.

Tucking my wings down, I knelt so she could put it over my head and settle my arms through the openings on the sides. It was very comfortable, except for my wings being trapped against my back. I buzzed them a bit to indicate the problem.

"Oh goodness, I didn't even think!" Charity smacked her forehead lightly, then picked up the scissors. "Give me two shakes of a lamb's tail."

I pondered that image as she pressed gently down my back to feel out where my wings were. Her scissors brushed against me as she removed a large chunk of the back of the dress and then tied the top pieces of the shoulders together. "There," she said slowly. "How's that? Now you'll put it on by tying it here at the back of your neck." She patted the spot.

I buzzed my wings appreciatively. "Thank you, Charity."

"Wasn't anything," she said, but I got the impression she was feigning modesty. "I'm glad you like it. Now, let's get this mess cleaned up before the others come tromping in and step on it, all right?"

"Of course."

It was only after the others returned, supped, and lay down to sleep I realized she never had explained who Master Wystan was.

The next day, I was left to take care of the house on my own. It was a bit lonely at first, but after the chores were done, I was able to sit outside and enjoy the sunshine. I thought about my former life on my homeworld with my eggmates. They had abandoned me—no, *sacrificed* me—and yet I still found myself missing them.

I listened to the sounds of the forest. Some of them were familiar; many of them were strange. I hummed in harmony with the insects that passed by, my wings making a much lower tone than theirs, but I sensed friendliness emanating from some of them all the same. It was probably all in my head.

I sighed and lay on the ground, smelling earth and chlorophyll, wondering if I would forget how to speak my native language, given time. I certainly couldn't return home. Even if I wouldn't be killed upon landing, my ship had been destroyed.

But this place was peaceful, the inhabitants were kind, and it was similar enough I could survive.

In the end, I could ask nothing more of the universe.

When the sun rose on the following day, I was awakened by Patience, telling me that since it was not a mining day, she was going to show me sales work. Many of the other dwarves were rising at the same time, then washing and dressing as Charity passed around bread and cheese.

Several of the dwarves planned on going to market, so they were loading bags with gold coins and sparkling gems. They were led by Prudence, a black-haired dwarf with white beads strung into the hair of hir beard—tied in a single thick braid down hir chest.

The remaining four, including Patience and Charity, stayed home and turned some of the trunks into a table outside by putting a cloth over them to hide the seams, then laid gems and metal goods out on top.

"Prudence, Temperance, and Humility go and buy food and goods we cannot make," Charity explained. "And the rest of us set up shop here, and people come to us! Dwarves are known for mining and metalwork, so that's what people look for. Chastity makes a lot of the jewelry, Patience does the armor-forging—you'll see that in a day or two—Prudence and Temperance do weapons, and Kindness does detail work on everything, like you can see here." She pointed at some sort of war hammer, which had delicate filigree work across the side of the head.

I was impressed. I had never seen the process of making physical tools before, the same as I had never seen clothing being made before, and I had never seen many of the types of pieces before at all. I was looking forward to seeing the "armor-forging." Some of the armor pieces appeared to be designed to cover the thorax and abdomen, which made sense, though they were impractical for beings with ventilation slits and wings.

It didn't take long for people to start arriving.

Charity bumped my arm gently as a tall dwarf approached the table, eyes fixed on me. "That's a human," she whispered to me as I tried to look away from hir stare. "See how tall he is in comparison? And how small his ears and nose are?"

I glanced between her and the human. Now that I was really looking, I supposed I could see the differences, though they were not so stark as she had implied, leaving aside the height. He was still a bit shorter than me, and his flesh was the same pale brown as the dwarves' skin.

"I say," the human said. "What do you have here, Patience?"

"This is Veni. He fell from the sky."

"An angel?" He tugged his short beard. "I wouldn't believe it, and yet—"

I didn't know what an angel was or why I would or wouldn't be taken for one.

"If he's an angel, he doesn't remember it," Charity cut in. "Let's keep him between us, shall we?"

"If you insist." The human started talking money with Patience, gesturing at various goods.

That conversation was repeated in various iterations throughout the day. I met a number of humans, though not the mysterious Master Wystan, apparently.

As afternoon approached, however, two men came through the trees, leading a large, four-legged beast between them.

And now I saw what Charity had said about variation in colors. This man was dark, darker than any of the previous humans or the dwarves, a warm deep brown, with black, black hair curling tightly to his head instead of bowing out in large waves as Prudence's and Humility's did. What was most striking, however, was the shock of white in his hair just above his eyebrow, which was black on the ends but white in the middle, in line with the streak. And the eye beneath it was sky blue. The opposite one was dark brown, only slightly lighter than the rest of his hair.

All in all, he was amazing to look upon. His mouth was free of a beard, revealing dark, soft lips that were pulled up in a friendly smile. Patience waved to him and to his companion, a reedy, pale man with flat, brown hair.

"That's Master Wystan," Charity told me with a small laugh. "He's something, isn't he?"

"Master Wystan is the dark one, yes?" I said quietly. "Because the pale one is much the same as the rest."

She laughed harder, clutching at her abdomen. "Yes, Master Wystan is the dark one."

I was too busy watching the man to wonder what she found so funny. As he approached, his smile turned down as he spotted me, looking with curiosity. I found myself averting my gaze, embarrassed by my strange appearance and my simple dress. I thought of the golden ornaments of the well-off adults of home and their rich, dark-dyed skirts, and was ashamed to be seen by such a beautiful person.

He and his companion reached the table. Master Wystan gestured a bit, definitely toward me, then turned to his fellow expectantly.

"Master is inquiring about your new helper, Miss Patience," the reedy man said.

She smiled in return, looking first at Master Wystan, then to the man. "I figured. He came from the sky. He's called Veni."

The man made gestures to Master Wystan, who returned different ones and turned his gaze back to me. He waved. My translation chip whirred to life again.

nonverbal language detected

horizontal wave: greeting

possible response: return wave/greeting

A nonverbal language? I waved back. He gave me a warm smile that made my thorax feel strange, then returned to speaking through his companion.

This time, though, I forced myself to watch, letting the chip pick up and analyze the gestures being made.

right hand making half circle in center of thorax: chest, chest ornament

first finger tapped to temple: thinking

first and second fingers circling twice in front of nose: quality

furrowed brow: expressing uncertainty/question

And so on and so on. At first, my brain was having trouble keeping up. But the chip worked as quick as synapses, and soon I was able to follow the conversation without listening to the companion speak.

Master Wystan was debating between a gold chain with an emerald pendant and a silver one with a sapphire. I got his attention with a small wave in his periphery, touched the sapphire pendant, then my chest, before flattening my hand to swipe across to the left. *I prefer this one.* I tapped the corner of my eye, then pointed to his chest, nodding slightly with a smile. *It suits your eyes.*

My choice became even clearer when his eyes widened, causing both to sparkle beautifully in the afternoon light. He gestured very quickly. *You understand me?*

I am learning. I learn fast. I had no idea how to explain the idea of a translation chip implant to a culture lacking even basic bandage adhesive.

You must! He was grinning now. *I had heard that [???] could speak all languages, but I never would have thought that included something like this!*

A language is a language. I shrugged. I didn't know the distinctions. He was too excited for me to stop him for the word I'd missed.

Do you have a signed name? he asked.

I shook my head. *But I can spell my name.*

Master Wystan tapped his chin in thought. *No, you need a proper signed name. This is mine.* He made the gesture for the letter *W* and touched it to his white streak. *It's funny because my name* W-Y-S-T-A-N *and the color white* W-H-I-T-E *both begin with* W, he explained. *But for you…*

After a moment of deep contemplation, he crossed his arms and waved the first two fingers outward, raising his arms up slightly as he did so. At my expressed confusion he spelled D-R-A-G-O-N-F-L-Y, but that didn't mean anything to me.

He frowned, then asked his companion for a pen and paper. He bowed over the dwarves' table to draw something. It appeared to be an insect of some kind with two pairs of long veined wings similar in structure to my own. Master Wystan made the sign again after showing me the drawing, pointing at the drawing's wings and my own. *Dragonfly. Your wings are like a dragonfly's. So, your signed name could be Dragonfly.*

I liked that much better than Veni. *Thank you*, I signed. *I like it a lot.*

I will show you a real dragonfly, he promised. *Will you be here next week?*

Of course. I felt giddy. *I am staying with the dwarves.*

I will come see you next week. And we will go find some dragonflies. For a moment, he hesitated, and then he took my hand into his and ran his thumb across my palm. I smiled at him to make the awkward uncertainty fade from his expression.

Okay, it's time for me to make my purchases. Don't distract me now. Or she'll be angry. His eyes flicked to Patience, who was watching the conversation with interest and confusion. I bit back a laugh, but obediently put my hands behind me and looked away. I still caught his grin in my periphery though.

He purchased a set of "cufflinks" and wrote out instructions for a custom order, which Patience tucked into a pocket of her vest. He waved goodbye to me with an exuberant grin that melted me inside, then left.

Once he was gone and out of earshot, Charity gaped at me theatrically. "You know *his* language too?"

"I learn quickly," I said.

"Apparently you do," Patience said. "Seems like you could be a real help. Think you could learn goblin speech?"

What in the world was that? "Yes, probably."

"Little buggers are always trying to cheat us. It would be good to have someone to listen in on their conspiring," Charity explained.

"I will gladly help in any way I can."

Patience got up from her seat and stretched. "The goblins will be coming with nightfall. We should take a break for food and rest while we still have the sun."

So, we ate and napped, and that night, I met goblins. They were the same height as dwarves, but with skin that ranged from green to brown and bodies that seemed to be mostly skin and bone, compared to the dwarves' broadness. They had sharp teeth and a language that reminded me eerily of predators I'd thought long left behind.

I was glad to see them go and lose myself in memories of meeting Wystan.

L ater that week, I was treated to the sight of metalwork.
Patience, true to her name, was very patient in showing me each step, breaking everything down into words and slowed actions. I watched how ore became liquid metal, and how that metal was poured and shaped under her deft hands.

Her gray beard was tucked into the thick apron as she worked, and she told humorous anecdotes about it catching fire in various mishaps over the years.

It was amazing watching the red-hot metal curve into shape under her ringing hammer, listening to her explain about thickness and weight distribution and a myriad of other details I wouldn't have even thought to take into account.

And when she finished, I watched Chastity make jewelry. It was a much more delicate process than armor-forging, taking different tools and a more careful eye. I watched her sit and make chains of gold and silver, a magnifying lens over one eye as she worked, using long pliers to snip and fold each link into place.

She worked at an astonishing speed, finishing five chains within the hour I sat there, then set to work on pendants to hang from them. These were even more amazing, watching her twist and shape the metal around pristine gemstones that glimmered in the light of the forge.

When she finished with her work, she asked me what kind of jewelry my people wore.

I described to her the grand chest plates of the elders, half circles of metal with ornate patterns and inlays, and the various rings that were worn around arms and wrists and fingers.

I ended up drawing on a piece of paper, trying to convey exactly how they looked. She nodded thoughtfully as I did, twirling the end of her beard around a finger. She ended up keeping the drawings, storing them in the chest at the end of her bed. I wondered what she meant to do with them.

I counted down the days until I could see Master Wystan again. Charity teased me about it, but it was clear she was happy for me too. When the next sale day came, I found myself preening in the little looking glass Kindness kept at her bedside table.

Charity laughed at me, but she also licked her thumb and rubbed away a bit of dirt that had gotten smeared on my arm while I had been working on the previous day's chores.

She had altered my dress a bit, adding personal touches and designs. I was happiest with the embroidery she'd done on the shoulder. The stitching was white, and it spelled out my name. My proper name.

I touched it, solemn as I remembered I would likely lose my first language someday. It was a lonely feeling.

But Charity nudged my hip, and we went outside to help set up.

Wystan arrived much earlier than he had the week before without his companion. His smile was dazzling. *Are you ready to go?* he asked.

I nodded and waved goodbye to the dwarves as I joined him.

"Be back by nightfall!" Patience called. "We'll need you for the goblins!"

"I will!" I returned and hurried to Wystan's side.

How was your week? I asked.

It was dull as rocks. I must confess, I was excited to see you again.

I smiled. *I was excited too. I'm still excited, in fact. Where can we find dragonflies?*

Near water. Can you listen for it for me?

Of course. I returned to paying attention to my hearing, trying to pick out the sounds of trickling water. It was tricky, for the forest was full of all sorts of noise, but soon I was able to hear something.

I waved my hand at Wystan and motioned for him to follow me toward the sound. As we got closer, I was happy to discover I'd been right in guessing what it was. We'd happened upon a stream that fed a pond. Insects of all kinds buzzed across the surface. I couldn't help but buzz back a little. Wystan touched my arm and pointed at my wings, smirking.

Are you talking to them? he asked.

I laughed and shook my head. *They don't speak my language.*

The touch on my arm turned to a grip, and Wystan pointed eagerly toward the pond. At first, all I saw was a blur of movement, but the creature paused over the water, then zipped over to a different spot.

It was the largest insect I'd seen here, nearly the length of my finger from head to the end of the abdomen. It was bright blue with a startlingly green head and thorax. I watched it dart and hover a bit more before zipping forward and snatching another insect from the air in an impressive show of speed. It ate as it flew away, almost too quick to see.

I looked back to Wystan, who asked, *Do you like it? Or would you like a new name?*

I like it, I said. I twitched as there was another one, this one with a black-and-gold-striped body instead of blue and green, darting quickly over the water. *Where does the name come from?*

Wystan rubbed his chin similar to how the dwarves tugged at their beards. *Well, a dragon is a mythical creature. They're giant flying lizards, essentially. Sometimes in legend they breathe fire. I suppose the "fly" part is because they buzz like flies do. So, the name would break down to something like "flies that resemble dragons"?*

Returning my gaze to the dragonflies on the water then back to Wystan, I asked, *Do they breathe fire?*

He laughed, his voice deep and breathy, rough around the edges. *I don't think so. It's probably the colors more than anything.*

I turned my attention back to the pond. They were remarkable hunters, dragonflies.

I don't know how long Wystan indulged my watching the dragonflies. Each time I asked him if he wanted to leave, he asked in return, *Do you want to?* And when I replied I didn't, he would smile and say, *Then we'll stay.*

We ended up sitting on the banks of the pond for a long time. After it was clear I was done watching dragonflies, Wystan motioned for me to sit next to him. *Tell me about the place you come from.*

So, I did. I described the towers with doors for windows, stretching up high into the sky. I described the bustling day-to-day in the capital where I'd lived, the ceaseless humming of the inhabitants even when the sun had long since set. My dwelling had been small and shared with four of my hatchmates. At first, I told Wystan amusing tales: About the time the second hatchling and I got lost and had to ask directions from no less than six passersby to get home. And the time where the eldest and I had a contest to see who could get from the ground to our home the fastest, and I'd slammed right into a person leaving hir home, knocking us both back into hir house.

But thinking about my family was bittersweet since it made me remember how they'd betrayed me.

So, I switched tack and told Wystan about my friend Dakiz, the shipbuilder whose craft had allowed me to come to this planet. Dakiz was a master of ships, and the one ze'd given me had been a personal project. I couldn't describe properly that the ship had lacked a functioning navigation system due to being an older model, reconstructed from the skeleton up, but I was able to convey I'd gotten lost and crashed my ship in this place.

Wystan looked up at the sky in wonder. *I never would have thought of* [???] *in such a way.*

I repeated the sign that I'd been unable to translate. *What is that?*

He seemed surprised. *Is it not the place you came from?* He spelled it out. *H-E-A-V-E-N. Heaven. The place where* [???] *dwell.*

It was that sign from the other day I hadn't understood. I repeated it. *This one is?*

A-N-G-E-L, he spelled. *Servants of God.*

I serve no god of yours, I said uncertainly.

Wystan frowned. *Then how do you understand me?*

I learn quickly, I told him again. *That's all. My people have mastered all kinds of tools, including ones to improve the mind. My ability is not given by a god but by people.*

I see. He looked out at the water. He felt distant now, out of my reach.

I touched his arm to regain his gaze. *Is it all right I am not an angel?* I asked.

Of course, it is. It's just that I had hoped you were.

Why? What's wrong? Do you wish to hear?

He shrugged. *I lost my hearing very young. When I was born, only one ear worked.* He touched the one beside the brown eye. *But it ceased when I was seven years old. I have been speaking with my hands and body for a long time. I think it would feel strange to suddenly not need to.*

Then what do you need an angel for?

He sighed, and I confess a small thrill of excitement when I heard the edges of his voice again. *My mother is dying. She tells me she needs the sun of her homeland, but I cannot give it. My father is too old to make such a journey, and my interpreter does not speak my mother's native tongue. And neither do I, of course.* He smiled sadly. *An angel could take her there or else heal her sickness.*

I wished I could turn away and stop looking at his sad expression, but he needed to see me to understand me. *I am sorry. There is probably nothing I can do.*

He tilted his head. *Probably?* he repeated.

Well, I do know something of medicine. Though your kind differs from my own, I imagine the principles are similar. Mostly

259

I had medical databanks downloaded, but again, I couldn't exactly explain that without having to explain a computer.

You would do that for me? Wystan asked, hope shining on his face.

I have to help a person in need if I can, don't I?

He pulled me into a tight embrace, his hands brushing the bases of my upper wings. His warm fingers on the delicate membranes made me shiver.

He pulled away, the brown of his cheeks darker than they had been. *Could you come with me tonight? I know the dwarves need you for some time, but I can wait until you're finished.*

I nodded. *I'll ask and make sure, but I don't see why not.*

He put his hand over mine, signing, *Thank you.* **Thank you**, with his free one. I hoped I could help his mother. Both for selfish reasons—to make him like me more—but also for more altruistic ones. What was the use of having such advanced knowledge if I wasn't going to use it to help others? I didn't know how much longer the databanks would be accessible when disconnected from the network except that I knew the program would degrade with time, so I had to make the most out of the time I had left.

After I finished with the dwarves and their goblin customers, Patience gave me a cloak to cover my wings. "Keep yourself secret as best you can," she said. "Be safe."

I thanked her, bid the dwarves good night, and followed Wystan into the woods.

Wystan and I couldn't talk much as we journeyed as the night was dark. This planet had one moon, but it shifted form nightly so it was little more than a sliver on this one. Wystan knew the way very well, however, so we were not lost.

Soon, we emerged from the woods to find a stone wall. Wystan showed me to a wooden gate. The guard standing there recognized him and let us pass.

Fires flickered in lamps along the streets. Everything seemed so short to me, but humans could not fly, so of course they would not build too high. The homes were largely wooden and painted with simple designs. Wystan took my hand as he led me along the winding paths, and I squeezed it tightly. He looked back at me and smiled.

Almost there, he said.

We stopped at a house much larger than some of the others. It had three rows of windows, indicating three levels within. I wondered how they moved between them, but I would soon find out.

When we entered, a person met us at the door, and another ran off. Ze was dressed neatly but simply, and I suspected ze was some sort of staff. The second one returned with the reedy man, Wystan's interpreter.

Why have you brought the angel? he asked.

Perhaps to help my mother. Is she awake?

The man asked one of the staff, who nodded. "Yes," ze said. "She is in the middle of getting ready for bed."

I translated before the reedy man could. Wystan chuckled at his offended face and led me deeper into the house. Around a corner, there was a series of tiny floors, each one slightly higher than the next, leading up to the second floor. Wystan used them to ascend, and I marveled a bit at the simplicity and engineering of it.

After another set of them, we were on the highest floor. The wood beneath our feet was covered in woven wool, decorated with geometric colors in various patterns. I understood in a rush that each one had been made by hand, without the aid of machine or computer, and marveled. The same was true of the portraits on the walls, which depicted various humans with pale skin and ornate clothing.

At the final door was a portrait of a darker human. Judging by the dress and types of jewelry, I guessed it was of a woman. Her black hair was braided into a series of tiny ropes that were pulled back and wrapped around her head, and her skin was darker than even Wystan's. I glanced between the portrait and his face, noting the similarities.

Your mother? I asked.

He nodded. *Yes. She's in here.*

He pointed at the door beside the portrait, then knocked on it before entering.

It was certainly the woman in the portrait who lay in the bed, though in person she was much older with wrinkles etched across her face and hands. Her hair was also loose, though still done in those tiny braids. She smiled at her son as we entered, but it was muted compared to his. I could see the sickness in her demeanor.

Hello, Mother, Wystan said as he approached. *This is the one I told you about. Dragonfly.*

How unexpected. Had I known my son would bring a guest, I would have gotten dressed. She gave him a sour look, but the effect was a bit ruined by her amusement.

It was unexpected for me too, he explained. *But perhaps they can help you.*

She looked at me with curiosity. I removed the hood of my cloak so she could see my face. She seemed to be comparing my features to her son's, looking at how long and flat my nose was, how high my cheeks, how wide my eyes, how thin my lips. My wings buzzed nervously, and she took in the sight of them as well, peeking behind the cloak as best she could.

Hello, ma'am, I said as politely as I could. I shifted uncomfortably away from her gaze. *Wystan asked me to examine you and see if there was anything I could do.*

She looked at him and shook her head. *He is a good child, looking after his mother so. What sort of examination?*

I mentally flicked through some of the files quickly. I pulled up the ones on mammals, hoping they'd be of use. I hesitated, my hands hanging limp in the air. Then, *Perhaps a bit of blood? I will need healthy blood to compare though—*

Before I even finished, Wystan was holding out his hand.

Something to cut with? I asked weakly.

He produced a small knife from his jacket.

I took it and held his hand in mine, examining it. His skin was lighter on the palm, covered in a multitude of tiny lines that seemed to cut across it at random. I touched the knife to the meaty part near the base of the thumb where there was a shadow I hoped was a vein.

Wystan's hand twitched at the pain, but I quickly bent over it and licked up the red blood that beaded up at the wound.

I held it on my tongue, letting the computer analyze it for its makeup. Mostly water, but also bits of sugar, fat, and salt. But overwhelmingly, I tasted iron. The blood was rich with it. This matched my databanks about mammals, so that was good.

I nodded to myself and swallowed, sucking on saliva to clear my tongue. Then I wiped the knife clean and brought it over to Wystan's mother. I worried about blood-borne disease for a moment, but she had given birth to him and suckled him, so I doubted there was much to worry about. She looked doubtful but held out her hand all the same. I made the same small cut and licked the same red droplets.

Her blood was different. It was missing iron. Not completely, but enough to be noticeable. I let the medical documents on iron deficiency in mammals scroll across my contact as I swallowed and rinsed my tongue.

Wystan, who was holding a handkerchief to his mother's palm, watched me warily.

I think, I began, only half signing while I read. *I think your mother should increase how much meat she eats. Especially liver.*

Why? he asked.

I shook my head. *I think it may help. I don't know for certain.*

He looked at his mother. She was concerned, judging by her furrowed brow. *I will try it,* she told him. *It can't hurt.* She patted his cheek. *Now get your guest situated in one of the spare rooms, and let's all go to sleep.*

I will. He kissed her forehead. *Sleep well, Mother.*

You too. Thank you.

I followed Wystan out, feeling useless. I wondered if she would listen to my advice and if it would even work. He touched my arm to gain my attention. *Thank you,* he said.

Thank me if she improves, I returned.

I'll do so then as well.

He showed me to a different room on the hall, this one with a portrait of a pale human on a gray horse beside the door. Within was a small room. Wystan pulled a cord next to the door on the inside, and a bell rang somewhere deeper in the house. The room was ornate with woven wool on the walls and floor. The bed was curtained, and there was a full mirror hanging on one wall. A small white basin sat beneath it on a stand.

Wystan indicated a small bowl beneath the bed. *For needs that cannot wait until morning,* he explained. *A servant will clean it; don't worry about using it.*

As he spoke of servants, one came through the door, bowed, moved to light a fire in the grate, and then gathered sheets and blankets from a tall, upright storage trunk near the bed. Once ze was finished, ze bowed again and left.

Wystan waved me toward the bed. *I will take you back to the dwarves' cottage in the morning. Please sleep well.*

I nodded. *You too.*

He hesitated, looking as if he had something else to say, but he didn't. With one final good night, he left the room, the door clicking shut behind him.

I sighed and hung the cloak on the trunk and slipped out of the dress as well before crawling into the bed. The sheets were soft and warm, and though my mind was far from tired, I fell asleep almost as soon as my face touched the pillow.

Upon my return, Charity was bursting with questions. I told her in detail what had happened and how awkward I'd felt afterwards. It was as if I had offended Wystan and his mother somehow. Wystan and I had barely talked on the journey home, our exchanges limited to only what was essential.

After speaking with Charity, I concluded that it was taboo to taste another's blood for some reason, and so I had disturbed them both with my actions. Filled with regret and shame, I sat quietly behind the cottage and watched Prudence working the forge.

I had missed the opportunity to watch her make weapons before, and the steady ringing of the hammer was soothing. Occasionally, there was the hiss of hot metal into liquid as she quenched the blade before taking it to the whetstone to sharpen. I watched as her black eyes looked unflinchingly at the sparks flying from the metal, marveling at her courage.

"Hey, Veni," she called. "Want to make yourself useful?" She tossed me the hilt she'd shaped and polished from bone. "Wrap the grip in some of the leather strips over there. When it's wrapped, put a pin from the box into the end, and hammer it in. Think you can do it?"

I looked at it, then at the materials I would need. "Do I need to hammer the first end in as well?"

"Yep. Good eye. Don't get your thumb. Hurts like the devil." She returned to sharpening the blade.

The leather and bone were both soft enough I didn't need much strength to drive the pin in until it was flush to the hilt. The wrapping was easy, and the final pin was only slightly more difficult than the first.

I handed her the finished hilt.

"Good man," she said, turning it over in her hand. "Now watch the fun part."

She took the blade back over to the forge and stuck the nonpointed end inside. "This part's the tang," she explained. "It goes into the hilt, so the blade doesn't snap off the minute you try and hit something with it." She pulled it out, the tang glowing red. Working fast, she pressed the hilt onto it, and the bone hissed at the metal's touch.

Smoke billowed forth as she fit the hilt down to the end of the tang, grinning at the smell of char. "And now it won't be coming off." She turned the sword over, so the hilt was facing me. "See?"

I gripped it and tried to pull, but it was indeed stuck fast.

"Thank you for the help," she said, taking it back to the whetstone. "I might make use of you again in the future."

"I would like that, I think."

She gave me a small smile. "Feeling better?"

I blinked. I did. Huh.

"Nothing like a good accomplishment to free your mind from the past's grip," she said, settling back in her chair. "That and hitting things with a hammer."

I found myself returning the smile. "I appreciate your advice. I will keep it in mind."

"See that you do." And then her friendly banter was gone, subsumed by her metalwork. I felt like I'd learned more about her than she'd meant to let on.

The next market day, Wystan didn't come.

I waited from when the sun rose, winking pink and yellow between tree leaves, until after the goblins departed, their purchases and trades clutched in their spindly hands as they disappeared into the dark woods.

That night, I shared a bed with Charity. It was too short for me, and I had to curl up almost double to fit, but her warmth and soft hair were enough comfort that the only tears I shed were silent. They dripped into her red beard and vanished almost as soon as they touched it.

Over the week, when the dwarves were away doing their mining and I was alone in the cottage, I felt hollow like a great beast had sliced me open and removed my insides for its breakfast.

I tried to make sense of it. What did we mean to each other anyway? We hadn't known each other long. And what had I been expecting? I'd been so full of delusions of courtship and the flush of new love I hadn't seriously considered about how he felt about me.

I'd thought I was special to him. An angel. A dragonfly. Someone who could talk to him without the medium of his translator. But what was I, really? A strange creature from a stranger place who did bizarre and sickening things without so much as blinking.

I longed to fly away, find a new place to settle, and lick my wounds in peace. I wondered how far away the lands were that Charity had told me about. Places where mountains scraped the bottom of the sky, or where the sun burned hot, turning the people's skin black. I wanted to see them.

But the dwarves had been kind to me. And my wing was still injured. Though I could hover a bit, I wouldn't be flying anywhere any time soon.

I leaned against the handle of the mop and wished I was home.

One evening, three days until the next market day, Chastity came and sat beside me by the fire, something wrapped in soft fabric in her hands. "Look," she said in her quiet voice, light glinting in her warm gray eyes. She opened the fabric to reveal a golden chest plate just like I'd shown her. She had embedded gems of blue and green into the metal, which sparkled along the edge. She slid it over my head and let it fall lightly against my thorax. "Blue and green, the colors of this land in springtime," she explained. "I hope this shows you are welcome here."

I hugged her tightly, too emotional to speak, overcome with how much I already considered this strange place as home.

When I went to bed, I wrapped the plate back in its cloth and held it to my chest through the night.

The following market day, Wystan came. He waved upon seeing me and grinned. *My mother's condition has improved!* he signed excitedly. Then he hesitated and glanced away. *I admit, I was skeptical. I had never seen a doctor drink a patient's blood to determine sickness, and it was...disgusting to me. And to her.* He looked at me, his gaze serious. *But I encouraged my mother to listen to your advice because I trusted you, and I am happy it was well-placed.*

There was a smile on my face and warmth in my cheeks. *I am only happy I was able to help.*

Forgive me for doubting you?

I shook my head. *There's nothing to forgive. I should have explained before doing.*

I want to make it up to you though. Is my order finished?

I turned to Patience and asked.

"Ah, yes, it is." She removed a small box from under the table and set it in front of her. Wystan walked the rest of the way toward us and picked it up, then looked inside.

He smiled at her and nodded. Reverently, he removed a long golden chain and a dragonfly pendant. The dragonfly was made almost entirely of gemstones and glittered magnificently in the sunlight.

Wystan set the box down and bade me approach. I did so, bemused, until he put the chain over my head. The dragonfly bounced lightly as it hit my chest.

For me? My hands were shaking. *But you...you ordered this when we first met.*

Wystan's face darkened, and he grinned nervously. *I wanted something as impressive as you are to offer before I began to court in earnest. Not seeing you last week... Even though I was scared of you, I still wanted so badly to be here. So, I know I made the right choice.*

I walked slowly around the table and folded myself into his open arms. He hugged me tightly, being so careful of my wings. I could hear the thudding of his heart, feel the echo of it in his arms. It felt like a sunset looked from space—a single perfect moment suspended in time on gossamer thread.

"Heaven above, what's happened?" Charity yelled impatiently. I heard someone, probably Patience, lightly smack her. I laughed and turned to face them, keeping my arms securely around Wystan's waist.

"I'm being courted," I said, perhaps a mite smug.

Charity gasped and clapped her hands, obviously overwhelmed with glee. Patience didn't seem surprised, her eyes twinkling knowingly behind her lenses. She held out a hand to Wystan, who shook with laughter and placed a bag of coins into her waiting palm.

Payment for my order, he explained.

"Could I have the rest of the day to myself?" I asked.

Patience chuckled through her nose and waved us both away. "Take your time, dears."

W̲e returned to the dragonfly pond, but this time we held hands on the way there, comfortable with the lack of conversation.

Will you tell me why you had to escape? Wystan said after a time.

I sighed. *It's mostly politics. There is a powerful bloodline in my country, and its scion is called the Royal. I'm not sure what the selection process is among each clutch of eggs, and I don't really want to know.*

The Royal of my generation is rash and extremely vain. They have made a number of poor decisions since coming of age but will hear nothing against them. Several of my siblings spread rumors, calling for a coup for the end of the Royal line.

A Queer Little Fairy Book

Those rumors were traced back to our home, and to save their wings, they placed the blame on me.

Wystan was frowning in distress and confusion. *Did you have anything to do with it?*

I shook my head. *But I was well-known in some treasonous circles, more for my*—covert communication programs—*code-breaking skills than actual treason. I wasn't a fan of the Royal and their policies, but I wasn't saying anything against them. But my name was already black, so it was easy enough for my siblings to use me to take the blame off their shoulders.*

Wystan's hands trembled as he confirmed, *So, you escaped to save your life?*

I nodded, turning my gaze back to the water and the peaceful buzzing of its insects.

Wystan didn't say anything else, but he did take my hand and scooted closer so he could put his head against my shoulder. His thumb rubbed idly against my knuckles.

We sat like that for a long time in silence, resting against each other. Then, Wystan sat up straight and asked, *Have you ever* [???]? He touched all his fingers to each thumb, flattened the center, and brought them together at the tip. He was blushing.

I repeated the sign with a question.

He blushed deeper and scooted closer until our noses were nearly touching. I still didn't know what he was doing.

There was a burning question in his eyes. He was waiting for some response from me, and I had no idea what to do.

He slumped and pulled away, dejected.

In a panic, I asked him what had happened.

Do your people not [???]?

I guess not?

He pursed his lips and, taking up a fallen twig, drew in the mud along the pond. Two figures made of simple lines and circles. He drew a symbol. *Heart,* he explained. *Love.* Then, another drawing, the circle heads touching. He repeated the unknown symbol, then spelled the word. *K-I-S-S. Touching lips to show affection.* Explaining it in such a clinical way seemed to make him sad.

I thought about it. Lips were sensitive, so I could possibly see the appeal. I got up onto my knees and touched my lips to his.

Oh, heaven above, he was warm.

I didn't know how long this action was supposed to last, but he was happy to take the lead, touching his lips to my own and also to my cheeks and my nose and my chin and back to my mouth, and it was dizzying, that heat. His lips were so malleable. I had noticed before in the dwarves' speech, but I never would have imagined they could be put to a use like this. He pulled my lower lip into his mouth and sucked and *oh.*

I gasped into his mouth, and his tongue flickered out, tasting me like I was something delectable.

Somehow or another, staying upright became too difficult, so he lay on the ground with me flush against his chest, my fingers digging into the fabric of his top. His hands stretched up across my back, and his nails ghosted across the sensitive flesh at the base of my wings.

By the time we were too tired to continue, the sun had set, and stars were visible overhead. I lay on his chest still, carding my fingers through his thick hair. It was soft and springy under my hand. He smiled as I scratched his scalp, so I did it more, eliciting soft sounds of contentment. It was sort of thrilling, hearing his voice.

I climbed off him to lie next to him and situated my wings carefully so they sat flat on either side of my back, rather than being crushed. I held his hand, and we gazed at the stars.

He tapped my arm for my attention and signed, *Did you come from a star?*

I chuckled. *Not as you're imagining. But I can tell you from which direction.* I looked up, telling the computer to label the stars I could see. *There,* I told him, pointing. *I came from past that star.*

But I frowned. There was something there, something not on any of my star maps. It took me a moment to realize it was moving—quite rapidly, in fact.

A low roaring began as the object got larger and closer and turned from white to red. The roar became a scream as it flashed by over our heads and crashed hard less than a mile away. The screeching and rustling of disturbed animals had us scrambling to our feet and running to investigate.

Instinct screamed at me to fly, and I kept instinctively taking off and hovering before I hit the ground when my injured wing howled in protest. I couldn't shake a painful knot in my gut, telling me I should turn, run the other direction, and never look back.

The smoke was cloying and familiar. I remembered lying in a field, looking up a blue, blue sky, pulling hot metal from my skin and smelling that smell.

Sure enough, the wreckage was all too familiar. And so was the pilot, half of hir body sticking out of the doorway.

"Dakiz!" I screamed, pulling free from Wystan so I could run and fly and run some more to my friend's side. "Dakiz!! By blessed Nqʌsa of the Eastern Sky, please don't be dead!"

Hir ship was more intact than mine had been; obviously hirs was a newer model. I touched hir face, buzzing with worry. "Dakiz, please wake up."

To my relief, ze stirred and opened hir eyes. "Vɛniaqi?" Ze blinked. "Vɛniaqi!" Ze embraced me as best ze could while ze was still wedged into hir pilot seat. Ze grunted. "Help me free?"

I helped as best I could until finally Dakiz wriggled free, standing up and coming face-to-face with Wystan. Dakiz jumped. "What is that?" ze asked.

"A human. They're mammals and sexually dimorphic, so there's a distinct 'male' and 'female' and they're different shapes, and it's *weird,* and their language *modifies* based on that difference, and it's *weird.* This one is named Wystan. Ze can't hear."

"All humans can't hear?"

"No, no, just this one. Well, likely not *just* this one, but this one is the only one I've met. Ze uses a signed language." I realized I should've been translating. *Sorry, Wystan,* I said quickly. *This is the friend I told you about, the one who lent me the ship.* I wondered how to spell it, and decided on *D-A-K-I-Z.*

Can they understand me too?

Probably in a little while, yes. They'll need time to adjust. I can translate in the meantime.

Wystan nodded. *Tell them it's nice to meet them.*

"Ze says it's nice to meet you," I said dutifully. "But what are you doing here? Are you all right? Did they exile you?" I signed while I spoke, so Wystan could follow.

Dakiz winced. "Something like that. The Royal wasn't happy about my aiding in your escape."

I gasped. "Dakiz, I am so, so sorry. I should never have come to you for help."

But Dakiz was frowning. "No, I don't regret helping you. I'm so happy I found you alive."

"How *did* you find me, anyway?"

Dakiz sighed. "It's a long story, and I am exhausted. Do you have a place where you lay your head?"

"I—" I hesitated."—I do have a place where I stay, but it is not mine, and it is quite crowded as it is."

Wystan, who had been silently following along as I signed, waved to get my attention. *You can stay with me,* he said. *Both of you. We'll return to the dwarves' cottage so you can disguise yourselves, and then you can stay at my home.*

Are you sure? I asked, but it was a relief.

Of course. It is a large house with many empty rooms. It's better than trying to cram someone else into the dwarves' place.

I hugged Wystan tightly, wings buzzing with happiness, thanking him without words.

He was smiling as I let go and turned to lead the way. I looked to Dakiz. "Did you understand?"

"Not a word. I never was as good at using the internal software as you are."

"We'll be staying in hir home," I explained.

"Ah, I see. Are we going there now?"

"A brief stop for clothing first, and then yes."

Dakiz buzzed hir confusion. "But we're wearing clothing." Indeed, Dakiz was dressed in proper attire since it hadn't all burned to ash like mine. It was a simple belted *gɛkuɪv*—a skirt-like wrap around the lower thorax, rough cloth on the outside, soft on the inside. A pouch and belt were around hir waist.

"Humans do not have wings. It would be bad to draw unnecessary attention," I explained. "Wystan's home is in a city where many humans live."

"I see," Dakiz said thoughtfully. "Have they not come into contact with other planets?"

"I don't think so, though the cursory knowledge of their mythology I've obtained might indicate it has happened in the far distant past."

"Hm, okay."

Wystan looked at me, his expression a little lonely.

I glanced at Dakiz and said, "Don't get lost, okay?" and jogged up to walk next to Wystan and took his hand in mine.

He blushed. *You didn't have to do that,* he signed one-handed.

I gave him a smile and squeezed his hand tightly. *But I wanted to.*

We walked hand in hand the rest of the way to the dwarves' cottage where I introduced Dakiz once more and explained the situation. We both donned the long cloaks and followed Wystan the short way to town.

Dakiz didn't seem particularly engaged with what was going on, but ze had just been in a ship crash, so perhaps ze was only tired.

Wystan brought us to the room where I'd spent the night before with the portrait of the pale human on the gray horse. As I went to follow Dakiz inside, Wystan caught my hand. *Would you like to spend the night with me?* he asked nervously.

I glanced at Dakiz, who was looking at me in weary confusion. *I'm sorry,* I said sincerely. *But my friend has been through a lot. I think they need me tonight.*

Wystan's face did something that made my chest hurt, and he looked away. He signed a quick, *I understand. Good night,* before making his escape.

Clearly, I'd missed something, some important cultural nuance. Did spending the night entail something other than the sharing of a room?

I sighed and went inside, shutting the door behind me. There was already a fire in the grate. Had Wystan been planning on inviting me over prior to the crash?

I decided not to dwell on questions and focused instead on Dakiz. Ze was stroking the soft fabric on the bed uncertainly. "This is to sleep on, right?"

I laughed. "Yes, it is. You sleep under the first two layers with your head on the soft squares at the top."

Dakiz slipped out of hir clothes and folded them neatly before setting them beside the bed. "Will you be sharing with me?" ze asked.

"Do you see another bed?" I joked. I removed the dress and hung it from the upright storage trunk and placed Wystan's token carefully over top.

"What is that? The sparkling thing?" Dakiz asked as ze settled under the blankets.

I joined hir, lying on my side so I could see hir face. "A courtship token," I explained excitedly.

Dakiz smirked. "I always knew you had exotic taste, but a different *species*? That's bold, my friend."

I covered hir face with my hand. "Shut your useless mouth."

Ze smiled under my touch and moved my hand with one of hirs. "I missed you, Veniaqi." Ze paused. "Oh! I completely forgot." Ze got out of bed, went to hir bag, and came back with a small bottle. "I brought some of your favorite honey wine."

I gasped in delight, holding out my hand for the bottle. Dakiz gave it easily. "You never did say how you found me," I said, sitting up so I could uncork it and inhale the sweet aroma.

"You think I don't have tracking chips in my ships?" Dakiz sat beside me, drinking nothing. "When the Royal came to me, knowing my role in your escape, I took my stealthiest ship and escaped myself. I decided to come and find you."

I held the open bottle, the smell no longer so appetizing. "Your family?" I asked.

Ze stared down at hir hands. "Abandoned me. Much like yours. No one wants to be on the Royal's bad side, though I suppose I understand why."

I recorked the bottle and set it aside so I could wrap my arms around my friend and hold hir close. "I'm sorry," I said, though my voice crackled at the edges. "I'm sorry; I shouldn't have involved you."

Ze hugged me back. "I did it because of our friendship. Don't be sorry." Ze rested hir head on my shoulder, our breaths mingling as hir lips rested near one of my ventilation slits. "Did you not want the wine?" ze asked.

"Wine is for celebration," I said. "Let us save it for another day."

Ze made a noise of assent and moved to put hir head on the pillows, then slipped down under the covers. I smiled and did the same, taking the hand that lay between us.

"You saved my life, Dakiz," I said, squeezing it. "And you suffered for it. You are truly my greatest friend, and I thank you. I hope one day I can do the same for you."

"I did it gladly, my friend. Now, we should sleep."

"We shall."

And lulled by the crackling of the flames and the soft rushing of the wind outside, we did.

I woke to Wystan's hand on my shoulder. I took a deep breath and slowly uncurled the fingers that had been wrapped around Dakiz's hand. *Good morning,* I signed sleepily.

His expression was one of…hurt.

I frowned, sat up, and reached for his face. Wystan stepped back, his lips tight. *What's wrong?* I asked him. *Are you feeling well?*

He gestured at the bed. *Naked in bed with someone else? I had thought we were courting. I had thought—!* He turned his hands to fists and held them stiffly at his sides.

I got out of bed, being careful not to wake Dakiz, and approached Wystan. *I think this is a misunderstanding. Please, can we speak plainly?*

I don't know how much plainer this can be! Unless the concept of loyalty is as foreign to you as kissing! His gestures were sharp and accusatory, his eyes burning with emotion.

How have I been disloyal to you? I asked in bewilderment. *We had to sleep. There is only one bed.*

But naked? Facing each other, holding hands?!

The only thing I could think to say was, *But I always sleep naked. And I share a bed with Patience at the dwarves' cottage. I don't understand how I've hurt you.*

Wystan sucked in an angry breath. *Dwarves stick to their own. But this one... They're like you. You're close. They understand things about you I never will.* The anger drained away, replaced by raw hurt. *They know your voice. They can speak to you in your own language, and they won't start stupid fights like this one because of irrational jealousy.*

I didn't know what to say. Instead, I walked forward and hugged him. I touched my throat to his and spoke, reciting old rhymes, nonsense verses, just so he could feel the buzzing of the sounds. I pulled away. *Now you know my voice. More intimately than anyone else, Dakiz included. And you speak perfectly well. That's what we're doing, isn't it?*

He gave me a weak smile, tears brimming in his eyes, and nodded. After a moment to collect himself, he smirked and asked, *So, do you want to show me how your body works since you're already naked?*

Heat bloomed in my face, and I hurried to put my clothes on, putting the necklace on first so it wouldn't fall to the floor. I fished it out as I tied the back of the dress around my neck.

Wystan turned the dragonfly over in his fingers, his hands brushing the front of my thorax as he turned it over in his fingers. I wondered if he could feel the thrumming of my blood under my skin, flushed at his proximity and the implications of what he'd asked.

I'm sorry for doubting you, he said after a moment. *It's just… It* looked *like you two had, well. Mated.* He made a disgruntled face.

Dakiz and I? I laughed so loudly that Dakiz woke with a snort behind me.

I tapped Wystan's nose with a finger. *My taste has never run toward hulking short-wing shipbuilders,* I explained with a smirk. *My loyalty is to you and no other.*

"By Vingid the Windruler, if you're going to screw, could you at least go somewhere else? I'm trying to recover from a very rocky landing here!" Dakiz griped from the bed.

I blushed and laughed at the same time, making a rude gesture at my disgruntled friend.

What? Wystan asked.

They suggested we find a place to be intimate in private.

Wystan grinned. *I could make that happen.*

Then why are we still standing here?

Giggling like children, we ran through the hallways, hand in hand, Wystan leading me to a room I hadn't yet seen. *Mine,* he explained, opening the door.

It smelled like him, which was the first thing I noticed. There was a desk along one wall, covered haphazardly in papers and books. Beside it, a row of bookshelves. Across from them, the bed was grander than the one in my borrowed room, the wood dark and carved into elaborate shapes. The curtains were heavy and a rich, dark red. I touched them, marveling at how soft they were under my fingertips.

Velvet, he explained. *Excellent for the winter, but in the spring and summer, I have to leave them open for fear of overheating.*

He motioned for me to sit on the bed. It sank underneath me, infinitely soft. I sighed contently and lay back, spreading out my arms to take in the luxuriousness. Wystan smirked and joined me, placing his hands carefully to avoid my wings. I tugged at the collar of his shirt. *If we are to be learning each other, shouldn't we undress?*

Wystan nodded and stood up. I watched with interest as he undid the ties on the shirt and his belt, removing both and tossing them aside. I drank in the sight of his dark skin, the black hair that grew over his chest and along the center of his stomach, leading down into the garment that covered his hips and legs. Trousers, I believed Charity had called them. He stared at me, his cheeks flushed. *How's this for now?*

I gestured him closer so I could touch. The hair on his chest was short and soft, and his skin was springy under the touch. But I was soon distracted by the two discs on either side of his breastbone. They were darker than the rest and looked like teats, but surely males did not feed young?

I brushed a thumb over one and was surprised to feel it harden at the touch. Wystan made a small noise, so I did it again, then pinched the flesh between finger and thumb, watching his face for a reaction. He gasped, but judging from the way he moved closer rather than away, I suspected he liked it. I did the same to the other one, and the muscles in his chest flexed restlessly under his skin.

Thinking back to the wonderful experience of kissing, I brought my mouth to his chest, tongue flicking out to lick. I regretted my lips were not flexible enough to suckle, but he didn't seem to notice the lack. Wystan's hand grabbed the back of my head, pulling me closer as I ran my tongue over his chest. His heart was thudding against my lips, making my head dizzy.

Then his hands were on my shoulders, pushing me against the bed. *Your turn,* he said, face flushed. I smiled and untied my dress, letting it fall forward.

Wystan had seen my naked body before earlier of course, but now he was touching it too. My flesh was not soft like his, covering a layer of warm fat. Instead it was stretched over hard bits of exoskeleton. But the junctions between the plates were soft and sensitive, and it didn't take Wystan long to figure out. His touch was gentle as he traced along the edges, pressing down where skin met muscle. I lay back on the bed again and raised my arms so he could see all of my thorax and all of my soft spots. Adventurously, he licked one of my ventilation slits, and I nearly went out of my mind with pleasure. Heaven above, why had we not done this straight away?

He pulled the rest of the dress off and sat back on his heels to speak. *Will you show me what to do?*

Embarrassed but eager to continue, I reached down to the slit containing the ovipositor and worked it open, not quite aroused enough for it to happen on its own. But it opened quickly enough, revealing the egg cavity underneath.

I pushed inside it, pressing at the base of the ovipositor at the same time, feeling the familiar shivers of pleasure. It had been a long time since I had done this, and I'd never had an audience before, but the body does not easily forget.

Soon my fingers were slick with lubrication, and I ached for more, but I didn't want to climax alone. I moved my hand back up to thorax level.

Can I? he asked.

I nodded eagerly and gasped when his hand slid into the opening, his fingers so *warm* inside me. First one, then two, then three, which was definitely my limit, the membrane around the entrance on the edge of pain.

He crooked them inside me as if searching for something. When he pressed on the base of my ovipositor from the inside, my hips rose of their own volition and a strangled chirp of pleasure escaped my throat.

He smiled, leaning over me to kiss me while he pressed into that spot again, playing me like an instrument. When I was mere seconds from climax, I pushed on his shoulders and backed away from his hand.

He immediately withdrew, looking concerned and scared. *What's wrong?* he asked. *Did I hurt you?*

I shook my head, too dazed to process what the computer was telling me about how to respond.

Your turn, I managed and rolled over onto my side to grab at the tie on his pants before tugging it loose.

It largely resembled my ovipositor though it was shorter and thicker, nestled in dark hair at the base and sheathed in soft skin. It was spongy to the touch, but it hardened quickly when I wrapped my hand around it.

Wystan licked his lips. *Let me show you,* he said, wrapping his hand around mine. He guided my movements, a steady up and down, firm but not squeezing. As we did so, it hardened further and drew up to rest against his belly, clear lubrication beading from the small hole at the top.

Breathing heavily, he pulled our hands away to ask, *Do you think we could...? That it would...?* I was able to guess what he meant and lay back on the bed to give him my answer.

He knelt between my legs and pulled my hips up to rest in his lap, then positioned his sex at my entrance, which still ached for him. He slid inside easily, and I made small noises of pleasure. When he rocked his hips, I rocked back to meet him, the wet sounds somehow both amusing and arousing. I didn't know whether to laugh or scream for more.

He wrapped his hand around the base of my ovipositor and pressed against it with his thumb just as I had. I couldn't stop the shivers of ecstasy that threatened to overwhelm me. My wings buzzed beneath me, causing me to rise up from the bed a bit.

Wystan laughed, his voice breathy and a little strange, and then gasped, his body jolting as I felt a shudder run through him. He had climaxed.

The thought was enough to send me over the edge as well, my ovipositor wasting itself over my thorax as the egg tract in me contracted around his sex, trying to draw out eggs I was pretty sure he didn't have. Spent, I fell flat onto the bed, the slight pain from my injured wing blurring into the waves of pleasure that still rocked through me in ever-decreasing waves.

He winced and pulled himself free but kept my legs in his lap. Gasping for air with every orifice available to me and feeling limp and noodle-like, I asked, *Are you all right? Did I hurt you?*

He shook his head, giving me a reassuring kiss to my nose. *The squeezing was a bit too much. It's too sensitive right after the climax.*

I nodded my understanding and sat up so I could lie on my side. I held my arm outstretched, asking for him to join me.

He did, leaving lazy kisses along my neck and jaw. *You're sticky,* he commented dryly, raising a playful eyebrow.

You're sweaty, I returned, pushing my thorax up against him out of sheer playful spite.

He made that wheezy, breathy laugh again, wrapped his hand around the back of my head, and pulled me to his chest.

I smiled into the hair that smelled so strongly of him and hooked my leg over his, tangling us together.

We both fell asleep like that, sticky and sweaty and happy.

After a short nap, Wystan untangled himself and left the bed, drawing the curtains behind him. I cracked open my eyes, making some sort of garbled noise to ask for him to stay. The servant bell rang.

In a few minutes, after hearing the door open and the sound of efficient footsteps coming and going, Wystan returned to the bed with a shallow bowl and a cloth. He kissed my forehead and then dipped the cloth into the warm water and used it to sponge away the dried seed splattered over my thorax.

I thanked him, then took it before he could use it on himself, insisting on returning the favor.

He'd put his shirt back on, but not his pants, so it was easy enough to lift it up and wipe his stomach and chest. He blushed at the contact, and his sex stirred hopefully.

I grinned and gave it a small kiss, hardly aiming to discourage it.

After the second round (and the third), we did truly get out of bed. Wystan yawned and stretched and then went to sit at his desk. He let me glance at the accounting he was working on. I was astounded to learn he did most of the arithmetic by hand with slight assistance from something he called an "abacus," which appeared to me to be nothing more than wooden beads on a stringed frame.

But he seemed to make sense of it easily enough, flicking the beads from side to side and gesturing to himself over the results. *These are the import and exports that my father has overseen in the last week,* he explained. *I make sure everyone involved is paid in full and that my father still makes a profit. Sometimes we cut it a little close, but I can always pull through.*

It looked like important work. I watched for a bit, then kissed his cheek and bid him good luck on his work before I dressed and returned to the room I was beginning to think of as mine.

When I made it back to the guest bedroom, I was floppy and a bit sore but exhilarated. I found Dakiz lying in bed, hir eyes moving back and forth as ze stared upward, clearly reading something. Ze looked over as I closed the door.

"You stink of mammal sweat," ze said dryly.

"I stink of carnal affection," I amended. "Very pleasurable carnal affection."

Ze made a gagging sound. "You haven't told me much about this creature yet. You should if ze thinks ze's good enough to be your lover."

So, I told Dakiz the whole story. It felt good to speak my native tongue again, the sounds natural in my mouth instead of strange. When I told hir about my wing, ze insisted on taking a look and ran hir fingers gently over the tear.

"I have some wing tape in my ship," ze explained. "We could go get it." Ze grinned. "But before that—" Ze leaned off the side of the bed and retrieved the bottle of honey wine I had neglected to drink the day before. "—we should celebrate your sexual awakening!"

"You are a deviant," I said, rolling my eyes.

"Says the one who literally just slept with an alien who's also a furry, sweaty mammal."

I smirked at hir, taking the bottle. "That high core body temperature is something, I *have* to tell you."

"Oh, heavens, please don't!" Ze covered hir ear flaps.

I laughed and opened the bottle. The smell brought back memories, and I sighed as I drank it in.

I took a swig from the bottle, too tired to worry about bothering a servant for some glasses. It tasted different than it used to, but perhaps it was an effect of the journey.

I sighed as I finished my drink, then held out the bottle to Dakiz.

Ze shook hir head. "You know I've never been much of a fan."

"Not even for old time's sake?" I asked.

"No. No, I'm fine. Do you want to go to the ship now?"

I recorked the bottle. "Sure." My head was buzzing slightly. It had been too long since I'd imbibed if I was feeling the effects of only a few sips. Then again, I had exercised pretty heavily. "I have to go tell Wystan we're leaving."

Dakiz nodded. Ze was being oddly quiet. Or perhaps the alcohol was making me paranoid?

I returned to Wystan's room and found him still at his desk. I approached from the side, trying to avoid startling him. I succeeded, and he smiled at me. *Hello, Dragonfly.* He continued, but it was garbled in my translator.

I frowned, trying to bring up the signs to say, "Wait, can you repeat that?" but I kept getting an error message. I tried to use just my natural memory, but all I could bring up was, *Sorry. Problem.*

He signed questioningly at me.

I shook my head, fully starting to panic. I pointed at my head. *Problem. Not understand. Problem.*

He was standing now, trying to slow and simplify his language, I could tell. I understood *you okay?*

I wanted to cry. Everything had been wonderful. Was my program breaking already? It hadn't even been a full season cycle.

I pointed at Dakiz. *We go,* I explained. *Fix problem.*

Wystan nodded, his face so worried and sad I just had to press my lips briefly to his. *I okay,* I told him. *Everything okay.*

I hoped I wasn't lying.

We traveled to the ship quickly. It was pretty much intact, though a bit banged up. Leave it to the shipbuilder to know how to crash land a ship without destroying it.

Dakiz took the broken door off its hinges, and we went inside. It was cramped, little more than a pod really, but ze started going through hatches to find the first aid bundle, and I sat down in front of the ship's main computer monitor. I touched my wrist slit, which contained a small metal connection disc, to the input pad, and it began to sync.

I was assaulted with error messages about being unable to connect to the home server for updates, but I ignored those and brought up my personal programs. I swore under my breath.

I'd gotten a worm. I was able to freeze it quickly, but the damage was extensive. It had taken a huge bite out of the language databases as well as several other files like my personal recordings, star maps, and scheduling.

I thanked the skies above for my backups and got to work restoring. I'd lose a few hours of language acquisition, but I was sure Wystan would be more than happy to help with that.

But where had it come from? It wasn't like this world was full of unsecured networks and hackers. I found myself looking over my shoulder at Dakiz.

It could have been in food. A little digging, and it turned out the source had been microbots, which had latched onto the implant and injected the malicious code.

Had Dakiz known the wine was laced? Or had ze been tricked by the seller? Perhaps the seller had been loyal to the Royal, and thus wanted to cripple Dakiz's ability to navigate. Ze just hadn't counted on Dakiz having no taste for it.

I nodded to myself and disconnected from the computer when the restore was complete. "Don't drink the wine," I said. "There's a nasty bug in it."

Dakiz turned, the first aid bundle in hir hand. "Truly? Veniaqi, I'm so sorry. Is everything okay?"

"Yes, I have backups, but that was terrifying for a while. Did you find the wing tape?"

"Yes, it's here. Along with some healing gel." Ze held up the roll of tape and a small tube. "Turn around and I'll apply them."

The gel was cool as ze used it to reconnect the split bits of wing, then used the tape to hold it. The gel tingled as it set. "There you go," Dakiz said as ze finished. "Here, I found some immune boosters too."

The pills were small and white, and Dakiz pressed a bottle of water into my hand as I swallowed them down. I sighed as they left my throat, washing the bitter chalkiness out with the rest of the water.

"Do we need anything else from here?" I asked as I got up.

"Not that I can think of. It will still be here later, I'm sure."

I laughed. "That's the truth. The people here are smart though. I can see them achieving this sort of technology faster than we did. It was... What? About nine hundred season cycles from the harnessing of electricity to space travel? I can't see it taking them so long."

Dakiz made a face. "You know them best, I suppose."

"Only of the two of us," I laughed. "They confuse me still in many ways." I was exhausted. Probably all the day's excitement catching up to me. "Let's head back. I'm tired. And hungry, wow. I could eat a ʝɯʒ."

"I don't think this planet has those," Dakiz said with a snort.

"I will accept a substitution of similar size."

We left the ship, and I led the way, growing more and more tired with every step. By the time we arrived back in town, I was half asleep on my feet, relying on my computer navigation to find our way even though I could've sworn I knew the way by rote.

The man at the door waved us in and directed us to return to the guest room. The whole house was buzzing with activity, more so than usual. Wystan met us as we reached the second floor.

Are you feeling better? he asked.

Feeling myself fill with energy at the sight of him, I smiled reassuringly. *Yes, it was a problem easily fixed.*

Wystan grinned in relief. *Excellent. My father is arriving home early. Would you care to join me for dinner?*

Despite the second wind, I was still tired. The exhaustion crouched on the edge of my consciousness like a deadly predator. But I got the feeling dinner with progenitors was one of those cultural traditions important to humans (at least these ones). So I said, *That sounds lovely.*

Dakiz returned to the guest room, and I went with Wystan to his mother's room. Under her watchful eye, Wystan decorated me with gold and jewels. *I wish we had time to give you a new dress, but it would need a lot of modification to fit your wings.*

Is there something wrong with this one? I asked with concern.

He kissed my forehead. *No, dear. It's just a little plain. It just means you need more accessories.*

He wrapped a gold chain around my bare head, the metal cool where it rested against my skin. Something dangled from the front, tapping lightly against my head when I moved. When he declared himself finished, I ventured a gaze in the mirror. There was gold on my arms and around my neck, and I glittered in the red light of sunset. The stone on my forehead was deep blue and almost glowed against my pale skin. I wished I'd known to bring Chastity's beautiful chest plate.

Unhurried and intimate, Wystan brought his chest to my back and touched the dragonfly that still outshone all the finery his mother had lent me. *You are beautiful,* he told me in the mirror. *My angel, my Dragonfly.*

I blinked slowly, each time a bit harder to stay awake. But I took his hand in mine, allowing myself briefly to wish for the warmth of him wrapped around me in his bed as I slept off this abysmal exhaustion.

I breathed deeply, taking in air on all sides, then releasing it in kind.

Ready? he asked.

Yes.

I wasn't sure what I had been expecting from Wystan's father. He was a tall man who had none of his son's darkness. His hair was gray, and he had an impressive beard, though it was nowhere near the length of a dwarf's. But something of his son lingered in his lines of his mouth, in the way his eyes crinkled at the corners and the way it made an otherwise severe countenance suddenly approachable.

Dinner conversation was pleasant, Wystan's interpreter standing at the father's side to translate. I was surprised the man hadn't learned to speak with his son, but some people have trouble with languages, so I tried not to think too much into it.

The fatigue crept closer and closer until I could no longer focus on what anyone was saying or on the food in front of me.

I didn't notice I was drooping forward until Wystan took my shoulder and pulled me upright before my face hit the full plate in front of me. I opened my eyes wide, trying to keep them from closing.

But the world slowly faded to black.

I woke later, my head pounding and my mind disoriented. I was in a bed. The guest room bed I had been sharing with Dakiz. I was lying on my stomach, my head turned to one side. I could see Dakiz through a gap in the bed curtains. Ze was facing away from me, hands busy with something in front of hir.

When ze turned around, ze saw my open eyes and sighed. "You were supposed to stay asleep until I was ready. You're not making my job very easy."

"Job?" I asked, trying to sit up. My limbs were too heavy to move.

"Did you honestly think the Royal was going to let you escape?"

My blood turned cold. No, Dakiz was my friend. We had been friends practically since we'd hatched, closer than any sibling. My family might have betrayed me, but Dakiz would never...

Ze sighed again and pulled the curtain aside. There was a syringe in hir other hand.

I knew what it was.

It was known as the Glass Prison. It froze the body, leaving the mind awake to see everything that happened. A victim, left alone, would live for weeks until starvation set in.

I yelled and managed to roll off the bed on the other side with a wince as my injured wing cracked through the gel and tape holding it together. "Those immune boosters you found…" I croaked.

"Sleeping pills. I didn't give you enough of them, apparently." Ze was advancing on me casually as if ze had all the time in world.

And ze did. Ze was between me and the door, and I still could only barely move. "Why?" I begged. "Why?"

"The entire underground decided to use you as a scapegoat, my friend. They thought you were in the wind, safe, but of course, the Royal in all their wisdom knew how to find you. And how to make me cooperate."

I got to my feet, swaying. "Your family didn't abandon you. They're hostages."

Dakiz didn't answer. It was the only answer I needed.

"Please. Stay here with me. Don't return. Don't do this."

Dakiz shook hir head, coming closer so ze could grab ahold of the shining chains still wrapped around my neck. "You don't think they planned for that? If I don't return within a cycle, they all die."

"Just *tell* them you did it and leave then. Don't do this. Please."

"You *know* they're going to go through my memories, Vεniaqi." The needle was sharp against my throat as it rested at the joint of two pieces of exoskeleton.

I pulled futilely at hir grip. "I could fix that! Write new ones! They'd never know!"

"*I* would know. And it would be enough. You're grasping at straws, Vɛniaqi. This is the least painful way they gave me. I'm sorry."

I gasped as the needle punctured flesh, and the cold liquid forced its way into my veins. Dakiẓ put me on the bed on my back, wings limp and flat on either side.

The poison worked swiftly until I could no longer feel my limbs. My eyes were the only things still in my control. I directed them toward the door, but I didn't know what I was hoping would come through it.

Dakiẓ picked up the dragonfly that lay on my chest and turned it over in hir hand. "My ship will need repairs before it will be ready for deep space again. I'll come and visit you before I go."

I glared.

"Who knows, maybe your lover will figure out how to feed you when your throat doesn't work." I watched hir open the door and walk away, hir wings twitching out of the way as the door swung shut. And I was alone.

I felt tears well up in my eyes and overflow down onto the pillow under my head. I couldn't even open my mouth to sob.

I was going mad.

How long had it been? Minutes? Days? Hours? Seconds?

I tried to sleep, but my thoughts buzzed angrily around my head, screams that could not be released building up like pus in an infected wound.

At some point, when the light from the fire had faded to embers, Wystan came. A servant built the fire up, and he came to my side. He sat down beside me and cradled my face in his warm hands.

You okay? he asked. *You were really asleep. Even your friend couldn't wake you.*

I wanted to sob. Impotent tears fell instead.

Dragonfly? Wystan squinted in the semidarkness, then felt the wetness on my face. *You're crying. What happened?*

He waited, but I couldn't so much as twitch. More tears fell.

Talk to me. He was about to panic. *Do you understand me? Is there a problem like earlier? I don't know where your friend went. I thought they were here.*

He picked up my hand in his. I couldn't feel it. It was as though he were holding a fake that looked exactly like mine.

You're cold, he said, touching more of me with increasing concern on his face. *Please, move for me. Hold my hand. Show me you're okay!*

I couldn't. I wasn't.

He was taking deep breaths now as he tried to stop the trembling I could see beginning. *Can you blink?*

I did so.

His chest swelled as he took a deep breath, and he freed his hands to speak clearly. *Good. Blink once for yes, twice for no. Do you understand?*

I blinked.

Can you move at all?

Two blinks.

Just your eyes?

One blink.

Are you sick?

Two blinks.

He furrowed his brow. *Did you do this on purpose?*

I wanted to grind my teeth, but my jaw felt like it was floating away. I blinked three times.

So, it's complicated. Did you do this?

Two blinks.

Did someone else?

One blink.

Was it something I did?

Two blinks. How could he think it was something he did? All of this was Dakiz's fault. All of it.

My chest hurt.

Wystan frowned. *Your friend?*

One blink.

Why? he asked, aghast. *Wait, sorry, you can't answer that.* He made some sort of gesture I was pretty sure was a swear. *Can I help?*

I didn't know. It was possible Dakiz had the cure with hir, in case of mishap. I didn't answer.

You don't know if I can, he guessed. His expression grew grave. *Well, I'm going to find out.*

I wished I could grab him back, prevent him from doing anything stupid, but he got to his feet and leaned over to press his lips to mine. *I'll be back soon, I promise.*

The door opened and shut, and once again, I was alone with my thoughts and the crackle of the fire.

Wystan's feet pounded on the floor as he walked at speed straight to Oswin's room. His interpreter was probably getting ready for bed, if he wasn't already asleep, but he got paid good money to be Wystan's voice, and right now Wystan needed it most.

He pounded on the door until Oswin opened it, half-dressed and clearly tired.

Get dressed, Wystan told him. *We have somewhere to be, and time is short.*

What's happened? Oswin asked, growing more alert as he noticed more and more his master's uncharacteristically serious mood.

Something dark and something serious. We're going to consult the dwarves.

Oswin nodded and went back into the room to put his clothes on. A few minutes later, he was fully dressed, and his face was damp with the cold water he'd splashed on it to wake himself up.

Wystan led the way, lamenting to himself that he couldn't take a horse. The path was treacherous at night, and it wouldn't be any faster in truth, but being on horseback *felt* faster.

There was light spilling out of the cottage windows, and he was grateful.

His pounding on the door brought Prudence, the black-haired dwarf who wove beads that looked disturbingly like bones into her beard. She was intimidating, even in her underclothes.

Wystan signed quickly at Oswin. *I need to speak to Patience.*

Oswin relayed the message and the reply. "Why? It is late and we've nothing to sell you."

It's about Dragonfly. About Veni.

That got her gesturing for them to enter and take a seat in the corner. Wystan preferred to stand.

A few moments later, Patience, setting her spectacles on her nose, took them back outside into the cool air. "It seems serious," she said through Oswin. "I don't want the others eavesdropping so obviously." She looked at the windows where several dwarves ducked out of sight at her gaze.

Wystan and Oswin explained what happened, Oswin having to stop Wystan to ask for clarification several times before he could believe it enough to properly convey it.

"What would you have me do?" Patience asked. "Provide you weapons? Tools of interrogation?" Wystan knew which word was the last even before Oswin's translation because her expression, even in the murky dark, was vicious.

I want to communicate better with Veni first. Do you know of anyone, any creature, who could do that?

Patience ran her fingers through her beard. "Yes. There is one." She reentered the cottage, leaving the door ajar, and went to one of the trunks, a small one sealed with an iron clasp. She produced the key from around her neck and removed a paper bird.

Once outside again, she cut a nick into her thumb and smeared it over the bird's wing, her lips moving so quickly that Wystan knew Oswin could understand no better than he could.

The bird shifted, its head twitching and turning like the real thing for a moment. It took off from Patience's hand and disappeared into the woods.

What are you calling? Wystan asked.

"A creature you have never seen before," she replied enigmatically.

As they waited, Wystan watched the moonlight ripple through the wind in the trees and the clouds overhead. He didn't speak, even to Oswin. All he could think about was his

Dragonfly, his poor lover, who had been betrayed by someone who was so dear. Dear enough to share a bed, dear enough that Dragonfly had trusted them to save them when their life was at stake. Dear enough that the betrayal would cut deeper than any knife.

It turned Wystan's thoughts dark, remembering the way his father had turned away from him when he had lost his hearing for good, never attending the lessons Oswin's master had given him and his mother. Or of watching his parents' shadows as they fought the night the doctor said his mother was never going to be able to give birth again. He had still been able to hear then, though only when sounds were loud enough and only on the left side. But his father's yelling had been plenty loud enough.

It wasn't pleasant to learn at the age of six that his own father considered him an unworthy heir because of something he couldn't control.

Wystan shivered in a sudden chill, crossed his arms across his chest, and squeezed tightly. Oswin gave him a worried glance but didn't say anything.

Patience turned sharply toward the woods. The one called by the bird had arrived.

It was a man, or at least man-shaped, with blue-black skin and unnerving white, slit-pupiled eyes. He was clothed in black, his whole body swathed in it, the darkness stark against his bone-white hair. When the moonlight hit him, it highlighted raised lines and dots drawn across his skin.

The man-creature's lips moved, and Oswin translated automatically, though his eyes never left the stranger.

"It has been a long time, dwarf. You have aged."

Patience nodded. "And you are much the same as when we last met, Calder." Oswin spelled the name as best he could determine.

"What bids you to use the favor so hard-won?" Calder asked. Wystan wondered idly what his voice sounded like. It would have to be deep and measured to go with the rest of him.

"My friend is in danger. He is trapped as a prisoner of his own body. I figured you would want to provide aid since you know the taste of stoneflesh."

"I do indeed. How can I be of assistance?" He swept an elegant bow.

"His lover wishes to speak with him, and so touch his mind. You who know the old magic could facilitate that."

"I could. Bring the prisoner here, and I shall connect them together." He turned to Wystan, those near-empty eyes making Wystan's skin crawl. "But be warned, lover—an unfettered mind is full of secrets you may not wish to see."

I don't care. And Wystan wasn't bluffing. He trusted his Dragonfly. *We'll return shortly.*

I woke to the touch of Wystan's hand on my brow and his lips on my eyes. *We're going to be taking you to the dwarves' cottage, all right?*

I blinked once for assent.

Wystan and his interpreter picked me up and dangled me between them. My wings drifted over the ground noiselessly as they carried me out into the night and then tied me to a horse. It smelled like earth and sweat and rocked uncomfortably as Wystan led it into the woods.

I thanked heaven for the short distance we had to travel as they carried me into the cottage, then laid me across Patience's bed. I thought of the first time I'd been in it and wondered if this would be the last.

A tall figure loomed into view, humanlike in shape but with flesh the color of the night sky and eyes that blazed as white as stars but for the slit pupil of a snake sliced up the middle. Ze had long pointed ears decorated with silver jewelry.

"So, you are the prisoner," ze said in a deep rumble of a voice. "I admit, I was not expecting a friend of the dwarves' to have wings." Ze looked me up and down, and I got the creeping sensation of being analyzed like a laboratory experiment. "Your lover wishes to join your minds briefly, so you can tell him what should be done. Blink twice if you object."

I didn't blink at all. Join our minds? How? What sort of technology did this strange creature have access to?

The bed compressed, and then Wystan lay next to me, holding the hand I knew was mine.

The stranger stood behind us and put a hand over our eyes, throwing the world into darkness. I felt the briefest twinge of electricity and feared for my computer before light burst behind my closed eyelids, and I realized I was seeing a dream.

Or at least it seemed like a dream. I had full control of my body again, and as a bonus, my wing was healed. I flew for a bit, examining the woods that made up the dreamscape. The trees appeared real, but they were the familiar reds and violets I had grown up with even if the bark resembled that of Earth.

A cloud appeared before me, and I found myself falling *into* it, bombarded with images of myself through another's eyes and a strange voice calling, "Dragonfly."

I shook off the images and headed toward the ground where Wystan was waiting. We embraced, our touch cool instead of warm. Another sign of the dream.

"Dragonfly," Wystan said, the strange voice coming from his mouth. It was high and soft, far too delicate a voice to belong to such a large man. Until I realized, he had last heard his voice as a child. Perhaps his internal voice, the one I was hearing, was the one he remembered.

"Wystan," I said, brushing my hand over his hair. "I miss you."

He stared at me in what seemed like awe. "I can hear you," he said slowly. Though he spoke with his voice, his hands moved with him. "Your real language. It's so strange. I hear the buzzes and clicks, but I understand them. I guess this is what it means for minds to touch."

The stranger's voice echoed through the dream. *This is a difficult spell to maintain, so please be brief.*

"Spell?" I asked skeptically. "Like 'magic spell'?"

Wystan raised an eyebrow. "What did you think it was?"

Images of computers and uploading cables attached to an opened skull that popped up around me. Wystan stared in confusion and revulsion.

"Sorry," I said and refocused on the task at hand. "Should luck be with you, Dakiz will be at hir ship. But ze will not just give you the cure." An image of the vial with the name of the cure wrapped around the glass in small text appeared in front of me. I grabbed it to show him. "It should look something like this." Around me, the scenery was shifting as my thoughts moved, showing the ship, the interior, where Dakiz would be—the engine hatch. "You will probably have to kill hir before you can get it." A flickering image of Dakiz lying on the floor of hir ship, blood oozing from a wound in hir neck came into my vision, making me feel ill.

"Can you show me how to do it quickly?" Wystan asked quietly. "So they don't suffer?"

I touched the gap in the exoskeleton below my heart. "Up through here. Try to thrust clean under the plate. Otherwise you may miss and hit a lung instead. Or else from behind, between the shoulder plates and down."

Wystan nodded grimly. "How do I give you the cure?"

I showed him a syringe and how to use it with the vial. "Do you understand?"

He nodded again and wrapped his arms around me. "I'll save you," he said, squeezing tightly. "I *will*."

But I could feel his fear. Because I felt it too. A vision of Wystan dead flickered across my eyes, and I shuddered.

Your time is up. I hope you have everything you need, came the stranger's voice.

A wall flew up between us, rising higher and spreading broader so quickly that in mere seconds I was once again alone with my thoughts.

The dreamscape faded as the hand was removed from my eyes. Overhead, the stranger looked tired, hir pupils blown wide and hir posture sagging. Ze took several deep breaths and walked away.

I listened to hir voice as Wystan slowly woke beside me.

"My debt to you is repaid, Patience," the stranger said, hir voice not quite as heavy and intimidating as before. "It has been a long time since I cast a spell that great."

"Here, I got you some water," Wystan's interpreter said.

The stranger's voice was surprised when ze replied, "Oh, thank you…?"

"Oswin." So that was his name.

"I am Calder. It is good to meet you."

Further eavesdropping was interrupted by Charity coming and laying her head on my chest. "Veni, I know you'll pull through this. I've been designing so many clothes for you; you *have* to try them on, all right? I mean, Lord, if you had to go to a formal event in this silly little sack dress? Oh no, you would be ruined, just ruined, I tell you!"

I wished I could smile and inform her I had, in fact, attended a formal dinner in this dress. Though I'd ended that evening falling asleep at the table, betrayed and poisoned by my dearest friend, so maybe she was on to something with the "ruined" bit.

Wystan waved at his interpreter over me impatiently. *Tell them I need a sword!* Eventually he had to make an angry, guttural sound to get the man's attention. *A sword,* he repeated, punctuating the gesture with a grunt.

"My master requires a sword," Oswin said stiffly.

There was a scraping sound and a great many shuffling footsteps. With a click, Prudence placed a blade into his outstretched hand. "Use it well," she said.

Wystan nodded as though he'd understood. Maybe he didn't need to hear the words to understand the sentiment.

He kissed me one last time and left, the sound of the door shutting once more shuddering through me. There was shuffling and the slam of the door for a second time. Charity rolled over to sit next to me, took my hand, and stroked the back. I couldn't feel it, but I could see it. "Prudence and Temperance went with him. It'll be all right," she said gently.

I wished I could at least help Wystan. I hated being stuck here like this.

The strange creature, Calder, appeared in my vision again. "I understand your frustration, denizen of the sky. Allow me to help you fly."

Hir hand came down once more over my eyes, but this time, I was filled with the sensation of *rising*. Before I knew what was happening, I was floating above my body.

"Go, but return before dawn," Calder said.

I wasn't about to pass up the chance to fly. I took off in the direction of Dakiz's ship, shocked when my "body" passed right through the walls of the cottage without stopping. It didn't take me long to find Wystan since he was on foot and corporeal. Prudence and Temperance flanked him, their expressions grim.

I drifted along behind, then streaked ahead to where Dakiz was. Ze was right where I'd imagined ze would be, half sticking out of the engine hatch. It was a mark of how close we once had been, and it made me sad.

I watched hir work for a while, deciding to enjoy the last moments of seeing my best friend alive. Was I worth saving? Hir family would miss hir. Unlike mine and myself.

Was my happiness worth their sadness?

But I thought of Wystan and the dwarves, my new friends. Their happiness was at stake too.

I wished I could take down the Royal, but I was just one lone insect, exiled from my home planet, condemned to die—though I was determined to live on. I noticed the small communication device used by the Royal's guard sitting on Dakiz's worktable.

It was used to send messages to all who served the Royal. Most of their guard had it implanted, but they must have wanted to send Dakiz as soon as possible.

I flew over to it, and though I couldn't pick it up, I was able to examine it.

My friend had to die so I could live, but perhaps we could be the last.

"Hey!" Prudence's voice cut through the night's quiet. Dakiz straightened and watched the three approach. "Give us the cure, and we'll let you live!"

I could see Dakiz trying to process the words. The program was better with oral language than written or signed, so ze did eventually understand.

"No," ze said.

Prudence took the heavy sword from the sheath on her back, and Temperance did the same with her axe. "Last chance," Prudence growled.

I watched Dakiz's eyes dart around before falling upon the wrench in hir hands. "No," ze said again, hir gaze sliding back to the dwarves, burning with challenge.

Prudence gave a cry, and she and Temperance charged forward. Dakiz took to the air, fending off their blows with swiftness and a well-placed whack with the wrench. Ze went to Wystan, leering in the dark. "You won't fight yourself?" ze taunted him. "Coward."

I wondered what Wystan was doing, standing still instead of joining the fray. But when Dakiz turned to fend off the dwarves, hir back to Wystan, I watched in horror as Wystan jumped to the side and thrust his sword right through Dakiz's top pair of wings, which flung hir forward to the ground as ze screamed.

Wystan put a heavy boot down on Dakiz's lower thorax, crushing one of the shorter wings with a sickening crunch. Had I been in my body, I don't doubt I would have felt bile rise in my throat. Already, I burned in sympathetic pain. But I forced myself to watch. Ze had watched as ze sealed my fate. It was only right I return the favor.

Dakiz was begging in hir native tongue, but Wystan was deaf to hir cries, both in the literal and figurative sense. I'm sure he could see the frantic movement of Dakiz's mouth, but he paid it no mind.

He pressed the tip of the blade to one of the weak spots I'd told him about between the shoulder plates. Dakiz realized, hir eyes widening.

"Give us the cure," Prudence said again.

"Kill me," Dakiz spat. "The Royal will torture first."

"Where is it?" she pressed further. "Or I'll get Patience and her dark elf friend here. I'm sure they'd love to peel off your skin and see what lies beneath."

Dakiz stared her dead in the eye. "No."

Prudence thumbed across her throat, and Wystan leaned forward to drive the sword in and down, squelching into soft tissue. Dakiz twitched once and then was still.

Despite how much I'd told myself it had been necessary, my incorporeal body still convulsed in grief and painful sobs spilled from my throat. Unable to watch anymore, I returned to my physical body, and we were rejoined with a single touch.

My heart ached, and tears fell anew as I fell back into my statue's pose, and Calder pulled hir hand away. The light of the fire burned my eyes, and I could do nothing but close them, pray for sleep, and wait for Wystan's return.

The next thing I knew, Wystan's face was above mine, his hand holding my neck as the other slid the needle into soft flesh. Sensation returned in a gradual ache, muscles screaming for movement after their forced stillness. I winced as my body burned and prickled, every bit of flesh feeling like it was being stuck with a thousand needles.

Wystan held my face, his expression worried. I touched his cheek, trying to reassure him it would pass. Nudging him to get off, I sat up and stretched every part of me I could.

Eventually, the pain subsided, and a wave of exhaustion and depression slammed into me with enough force I staggered from the blow. I collapsed onto Wystan's shoulder, crying for my friend and the life that had been taken to save my own.

Wystan held me until there were no more tears to shed. When I pulled away to wipe my cheeks dry, Charity was standing there in her nightclothes, holding out a cup of spiced cider. I smiled, just a weak upturn of the edges of my mouth, took it, and cradled it in my fingers.

I looked around at the other dwarves, all of them awake despite the late hour, watching over me. I drank the cider, feeling the warmth of the drink and the warmth of the room. Of my family.

Behind me I heard, "It seems the crisis has passed. I think I will take my leave." Calder walked to the door and turned. "I wish you luck, sky-dweller. It is a difficult path to walk, being the only one of your kind left alive." And after a brief farewell to Patience, ze swept out of the cottage.

"Goodbye," Oswin said after a moment.

Charity tucked herself into the side not occupied by Wystan and rested her head on my shoulder.

The next day, I left the dwarves' cottage early and slipped out into the soft haze of morning, Chastity's gift heavy in my hands. The ground was wet with dew, glittering like stars where the light touched it. I made my way to where Dakiz's ship lay, the metal gleaming despite the darkness it had seen.

Dakiz lay where ze had fallen. I picked hir up, struggling with the bulk of hir, and put hir on hir back. I arranged hir wings and limbs into a classic funeral pose, lamenting I didn't have the ability to carry hir up into the peaks that loomed above the horizon. That would have been right, but it was impossible.

So, I did what I could. I unwrapped the golden chest plate and settled it over hir neck against hir thorax. It gleamed in the colors of this land, this little planet in the blackness of space, and I prayed for my friend, calling upon distant gods to guide hir home. I sent hir on with my tears.

When I finished, it was nearing midday, so I went to the ship. It had clearly been ransacked. But I found the communication device, and the computer mainframe was intact. It was a simple matter to crack the device open and get at the software inside.

Attention all guards, said the beacon I wrote. *The Royal is not to be trusted. Their word is tainted by greed. Return to your friends and family and hold them dear. The Royal's power lies not with them, but with you. - The Dragonfly.*

There was no word for "dragonfly" in my language. But it was easy enough to craft one. Zɛg the Destroyer, a great and terrible reptilian beast of lore. Iʃi, a word ending denoting smallness. Vinuusɛ, a worshipper of wind, i.e. one who flies. Zɛkiʃi-finuusɛ, a small deadly beast that flies.

I imagined guards lowering their weapons and going home, leaving their victims the chance to do the same. I imagined an uprising. But perhaps my actions would do nothing. I had no way of knowing.

I left the ship and stared up at the blue sky, only able to dream of what was happening so far away on a homeworld I could no longer claim as mine.

I went to the engine hatch to find and destroy the locator beacon that was surely there, only to find it already disabled, lying uselessly on the floor. Dakiz had wanted to be the one to kill me, so the Royal and their followers couldn't torture me.

I'd thought I was out of tears, but I found a few more to shed for my friend.

When I exited the hatch and turned around, Wystan was there, his expression sad. *I'm sorry,* he said when our eyes met. *I know they were important to you.*

I nodded. *They were. But they should rest peacefully now.* I looked back to the sky, feeling the wind on my skin, the cool air in my lungs and in my limbs. This was a good place; I would enjoy my life here.

A dragonfly buzzed past me, off on some important mission of its own. I watched it dart away beyond my sight. Somehow, it brought a smile to my face. A small one to be sure, but a true one.

Come on, I said to Wystan. *Let's go home.*

And walking hand in hand, we did.

Echoes of the
Dead

It had been a long time since Oswin had contemplated the idea of being alone.

He had been hired to translate and speak for Wystan, a deaf man who had been taught to speak with his hands by Oswin's master. Barring a miracle of God or a spectacular falling-out, Oswin had assumed his job was secure. Not many people knew how to translate his master's signs, so it wasn't as if he was easily replaceable.

And it had been a nice job. He'd been paid mainly in room and board, but that had meant he got a very nice room in a very nice manse with actual servants he could ask to do things like fetch him a snack or draw him a bath. And the monthly stipend had been enough to keep his clothes up-to-date and well repaired. Wystan had been a dear friend, a confidante. They'd relied on each other. They'd *needed* each other. Oswin liked being needed.

But the unthinkable had happened.

No, Wystan's hearing had not returned.

An angel had fallen from heaven and fallen in love with him.

Him, Wystan the deaf man. Not him, Oswin.

And since the angel *was* an angel, albeit a strangely insectoid one, for the first time Oswin had had competition for his skills.

And Wystan's father, being a cheap man even on a good day, had decided he only needed one translator and turned Oswin out into the early winter chill.

Do you have everything you need? Wystan asked, bringing Oswin out of his reverie.

In answer, he patted down his pockets and belt. Money, food, water... Yes, everything he needed for the short journey to the capital. He nodded.

Wystan bid him a tearful goodbye and promised to write him via his former master in the capital and made Oswin promise—twice!—to tell him when he found a new job so Wystan could continue to write. But privately, Oswin didn't know if he could handle another position that was meant to be for life, only to once again have the rug pulled out from under his feet.

Wystan took off his warm woolen coat and offered it to Oswin. *I have more, and true winter is fast approaching. Stay warm, my friend.* Not giving him the chance to refuse, Wystan threw it around his shoulders and buttoned the top. *I'll have your things sent along to your master. You should have them a day or two after you arrive. Are you sure you don't want to go with them?*

Oswin smiled at his concern. *I want the few days to clear my head. It's cold, but not brutal. I'll be fine.*

You must promise to write.

At that, Oswin laughed. *I already have. Twice, in fact. But I'll make it thrice for the sake of our friendship.* He playfully ruffled Wystan's soft hair.

Wystan laughed his breathy laugh as he batted Oswin away so he could speak. *Send word when you arrive,* he said with exaggerated sternness, waggling his finger like one of his childhood tutors.

A Queer Little Fairy Book

As you say, dearest mother of mine. Oswin bowed and laughed as Wystan buffeted him with the corded end of his scarf. Then, after a moment of thought, he took the scarf off too, and wrapped it snugly around Oswin's neck.

Be safe, my friend.

Oswin's throat, despite the new warmth, tightened. He had never before been so grateful to not have to use it. *Be happy, Wystan.*

They embraced one final time and parted ways, Wystan back into the warm manse and Oswin out into the chill of the woods.

As night swiftly took over the sky, Oswin pulled the heavy coat tighter around his chest and sighed out in a gust of white, the ground hard and crunchy with frost under his boots. There wasn't an inn nearby, he knew. He groaned as he imagined a night huddled next to a campfire like a starving beggar, but he was too far now even from the dwarves' hidden cottage for it to be a worthwhile detour. Cursing himself for not setting out sooner, he continued as twilight became night, and the moon winked through the branches overhead. It had been a long time since he'd had need to travel alone. The familiar woods, usually boring at worst, were beginning to seem sinister.

He pinched the bridge of his nose and rubbed his tired eyes. Perhaps he should seek a clearing off the path in which to make camp?

Something caught his eye in the murky twilight. Quarried stone. It looked like the remnants of a low wall. Squinting into the area behind it, he could just make out the dark shapes of half-collapsed stone walls and the remains of a floor. Beyond them, it appeared some of the castle remained intact or at least enclosed.

He stood still for a moment, listening for possible bandits making their home there, but the forest was quiet. So Oswin stepped over the wall and into the ruins proper. Passing through a gaping hole in an old exterior wall, he found himself in a courtyard.

A peaceful pond, somehow unfrozen despite the chill, was the only thing with any life to it. The rest of the garden was brown weeds and winter stalks. On the other side of the courtyard was an intact part of the castle. Its shape and how detached it was from the rest made Oswin think it was a kitchen.

Light twinkled out of a window.

Oswin froze. It was too quiet to be a group of bandits. A group of a great size could never be so silent.

On the other hand, who would willingly live in such ruins besides beggars and thieves?

But as a chill wind blew through the trees, the idea of a roof and fire won out over fear. Oswin walked up to the door and knocked.

There was a long pause before anyone answered, but eventually, the door was pulled open, its ancient hinges creaking with the strain.

Oswin would never have expected who was behind it. A tall, slender man with midnight-blue skin and shockingly white eyes and hair stood in the doorway, silhouetted in firelight. His ears were long and tapered, parting the straight hair as they grew outward. Elven ears.

Oswin, bizarrely enough, knew the elf, if not well. When Wystan's angel had been struck by a curse, the dwarves had called upon this elf to help save them. His name was Calder if memory served.

Calder looked equally surprised to see Oswin. "What brings you to this place?" he asked at last, breaking the silence.

"I seek only shelter for the night," Oswin replied, his voice soft. He had trouble meeting Calder's gaze. "I had hoped to find a roof in these ruins, but instead I found you."

Calder paused, then opened the door fully and waved Oswin inside. "You are without your charge. Has he no need of his voice?"

Oswin sighed and sat at the wooden table in the middle of the small kitchen, groaning as he finally got off his feet. The air was still chilly but much warmer than outside. "I've lost my job to the angel," he explained. "Wystan has found a new voice, and this one speaks many tongues indeed." As much as he tried to keep the bitterness from his voice, it boiled up regardless.

Calder sat across from him and waved a hand at the fire in the grate, causing it to roar up. The little room grew warmer.

"I'd never seen magic before meeting you," Oswin said conversationally. "You use it so gracefully, I'm jealous."

The firelight threw Calder's face into sharp relief, highlighting the lines and raised dots on his skin. Oswin wondered if elves were born with them or if they were made with magic. They seemed too regular to be natural. "There's no need to be," Calder said. His voice was deep and measured, melodic in a way that human voices weren't. "An aptitude for magic is a weakness to magic. The same channels that allow your magic to flow allow others' magic to invade."

Oswin frowned. "I had no idea. That seems a steep price to pay."

Calder gave him a mirthless smile. "The world is full of prices that must be paid—some in spirit, some in blood."

Oswin didn't know how to respond and fell quiet. He looked at Calder's hands where they rested on the table. He had elegant fingers, almost feminine in their shape, and surprisingly pale fingernails.

The hands pulled away to the edges of the table as their owner stood. "Forgive me; I've forgotten all sense of etiquette. Would you like something to eat or drink? I've meat and turnips enough for us both and warm cider if you like."

"That sounds heavenly," Oswin said as his stomach gave an appreciative gurgle. He'd eaten some of the jerky from his pack during his journey, of course, but he'd been spoiled at his job—a body used to being filled thrice daily did not take kindly to being asked to accept only rations. "May I help in any way?"

Calder pointed at a small knife and the tub of turnips. "Peel and cut, say, three of them?" He began to fill a pot with water from a hand pump above the counter.

Oswin got to work, scrubbing the dirt off and carefully peeling away the skins. He found his gaze following Calder around the kitchen, watching as he set the pot above the fire and went to and from the pantry, gathering ingredients to rub into the skinned rabbit he'd set on the table.

He moved so gracefully, every movement well-practiced and purposeful, no extra fidgeting about. Oswin was very aware of his foot bouncing against the floor and of the way he occasionally adjusted his back and shoulders as his position grew stiff.

After he was finished with the turnips, Calder put them in the pot of water to boil and placed the meat in the coals to cook. He fetched the cider from a barrel in the larder and warmed it with a wave of his hand.

It was sweet and spicy, and Oswin was sure he would never be able to drink any other cider ever again.

"So, is the kitchen the only part of the castle still intact?" Oswin asked.

Calder shook his head. "No, but it is the only part in livable condition. I have a bed and trunk in one of the old pantries." He pointed at a door in one of the interior walls.

"So…you're the only one here?"

Calder nodded but didn't elaborate.

Oswin tapped his fingers on his cider mug. "Have you lived here long?" he tried after the silence grew too awkward to bear.

"A very long time, yes."

"How…long do your people live?"

"Between five hundred and five hundred fifty years, barring disease or injury. I am perhaps one hundred seventy-one? One hundred seventy-three? Truthfully, I've lost count."

Oswin swallowed. Nearly two hundred years… How many monarchs was that? Three? Four?

"Much of the past seventy years, however, I spent as a statue. The debt I owed to the dwarves was thanks for freeing me."

"How did that happen?"

Calder frowned. "Goblin thieves who happened to have a Medusa charm. I was simply careless." He got up, checked on the food, then spooned everything onto plates. "I am glad I was able to help the angel, though it seems my doing so robbed you of your job." He brought dinner to the table and pushed Oswin's toward him along with a knife.

"Thank you," Oswin said, taking it in hand. "And I'm glad you did as well. I would not see my friend in such despair as the angel's death would have caused, not for a job ten times as lucrative."

"You are an honorable man."

They ate in silence for some time before Calder asked, "How did you come to be a voice for the deaf? And who thought to translate speech to the hands?"

Oswin smiled. "Well, the latter is my teacher, Master Eadburga."

Calder frowned. "That is a woman's name, is it not?"

"It is indeed. But she refuses feminine title. She claims it is lesser, and I find myself agreeing. So, Master she is called. She earned it, in any case. Her son was born without his hearing, but he started being able to understand when she talked based on how she moved her hands. People speak with their hands anyway, she reasoned, so why not extend that and make it possible for those who cannot use spoken words for whatever reason to communicate on their own terms?"

Calder nodded, his expression the most animated Oswin had seen it so far. It made him want to talk more.

"She found other deaf people in the town, then in neighboring towns, collecting the signs they used to communicate, working them into something as comprehensive and consistent as she could. Then one day, she heard of a nobleman in the capital who had recently lost use of his ears, and so she and her son went there and taught him to use his hands.

"Master Eadburga worked for him for a number of years, and soon many rich folk with deaf and mute relatives were asking for her to teach them. She started taking apprentices to keep up with demand. I am one of the second group. We were taught by Master Eadburga and the first group of apprentices. Then, when I finished my apprenticeship, I began working for Lord Farnworth, Wystan's father."

Calder nodded again. "I see. Wystan's mother, where is she from? Such a dark-complexioned son does not come from the local stock."

"Amhassinia. Lord Farnworth used to travel often for his business, and the trade routes brought him there. He met Lady Dessata on one of those trips and married her."

"The world of humans grows smaller with the passing of time, it seems," Calder mused.

Oswin watched the liquid flow of Calder's hair as he pulled it over his shoulder. It was so thick and straight; Oswin had never seen hair like it before. He was filled with the urge to run his fingers through it, but he refrained. "The world feels plenty big to me," he said instead.

Calder quirked his mouth to one side. "And so, it is. Though not quite as much as it was a hundred years ago."

They were quiet again, but this time it wasn't uncomfortable. After the food was eaten, Calder cleared away the dishes and refilled their mugs with cider. Outside the windows, it had begun to snow. The tiny white flakes winked in and out of sight as the light hit them.

Oswin drank in Calder's every movement, marveling at each new detail. It was like he'd never really *looked* at anyone before that evening.

When the mugs were empty once again, Calder stood. "If you want, I can help you find a room to stay in. The ground floor is mostly intact, and there should still be some furs you can use for bedding and blanket."

"Thank you," Oswin said, getting up to follow him down a stone hallway. It smelled damp and old, much like the ruins outside.

But they found a small room that still had a working chimney and a raised stone platform, which he assumed had once held a mattress long since rotted away. It was too low and wide to be a shelf at any rate. Calder went down the hall and returned with an armful of heavy furs, which he shook out and piled on the bed platform. With a wave of his hand, the various bugs that had invaded the fibers fled, scurrying up and out of the chimney.

Oswin was a little queasy seeing it, but he was grateful all the same. Calder lit a fire in the grate and helped Oswin make himself comfortable. Between the fire and the furs, he was already getting warm and sleepy.

"Thank you again. I would have been happy to sleep beside the stove," he mumbled, no longer able to keep his eyes open.

"It's not a problem. I appreciated your company for the evening."

Oswin was asleep before the door swung shut.

He woke the next day to the late-morning sun streaming through gaps in the mortar. He yawned and sat up, shivering as he unwrapped the warm cocoon of fur. He pulled on his boots and went back down the hall to the kitchen. The fire was nothing but embers, but a small loaf of bread and a wedge of cheese sat on the table for him. There was no sign of Calder.

His bedroom door was closed, and no sound came from within, so Oswin didn't think he was inside. After finishing his breakfast, Oswin walked outside. He shrugged his coat higher against the chill and peered around the courtyard. Under the sunlight, the castle looked even more dilapidated. The black stone had probably been impressive once, stark against the blue of the sky and the green of the forest, but now, it was dirty and broken, covered in moss and lichen. Even the standing walls sagged under the weight of time, half-sunk in the earth, the once-neat lines of masonry warped and cracked. The air was still. Even the winter wind seemed stagnant and dead. No sign of Calder, but there was something big and dark in the pond.

Oswin walked closer and soon realized it was a *swan*, deep black instead of white. He froze, waiting for the aggression that usually came with invading a swan's territory, but there was none. The swan just stared at him for a moment, then returned to drifting across the surface of the water, occasionally dipping its head to pull up rushes and other plants from the bottom.

Oswin crept closer and closer, but still the swan acknowledged him without hostility until he was standing on the bank, mere feet from the impressive bird. Its coal-black eyes melded with the black of its feathers, only appearing when the light hit them. The only part that had any color was its beak, which was orange.

"Hello there, swan," Oswin said quietly. "You're a strange beast, aren't you?"

The swan stared at him.

"Don't have a mate or anything? I don't often see swans all by their lonesome." Oswin sat by the pond, the ground cold under his bottom.

The swan continued to look at him.

"I guess you're like me, huh? Sort of adrift in life. Though at least you've got that nice pond. I wonder why it's not frozen. It's plenty cold enough, I think." Oswin scooted forward and dipped his hand into the water. It was chilly, but the air was definitely colder. The swan still didn't react to the invasion of its space. "Weird," Oswin said. He wasn't sure if he meant the water or the bird. Both, probably. He pulled his hand out and wiped it on his coat, then stuffed both hands into his pockets to keep them warm.

He sighed out a cloud of white. "Well, I suppose it's just magic. Are you Calder's pet, maybe? So he keeps your pond from freezing in winter? Where is he, anyway?"

The swan, being a swan, did not answer.

"I guess I'll just wait for him to return. I want to bid him goodbye properly." Master Eadburga would be concerned if he were gone much longer, but Calder would be back soon, surely? He'd only lose a day, not enough for her to worry about him. He'd just met a friend on the road was all.

The swan tilted its head as if listening to him. It was a silly idea—swans were not particularly intelligent birds—but he'd grown used to being part of a pair. It hadn't been often he and Wystan were apart, so it felt strange to not converse.

"Okay, maybe I also want the chance to learn more about him too. He's a mysterious figure. I would like nothing more than to avoid finding a new assignment for a while. I'm just sort of frustrated, you know?"

His hands moved with his mouth as he worked through his thoughts, encouraged by the swan's presence and unwavering gaze. It should have felt threatening—animals staring was usually not a good sign—but the bird was utterly unaggressive.

"I lived with the Farnworth family for over a decade, you know?" he told the swan, exaggerating the length of a time as he rolled his hands. "It was my home. And now, here I am, adrift. I mean, I *should* go back to my master like I told her I would and then get a new job and soon. I know that. I do need to eat, after all. But I don't know if I *want* to is the issue. I don't know if I could handle being replaced so suddenly again." Oswin fell silent, staring at the swan as it stared back. "You're a very nice listener. Sorry for talking your ear off."

The swan dunked into the water and returned with a beak full of leaves, then chewed them, unbothered as it watched Oswin.

"I'm going to go wander around the grounds. Thank you for listening, swan. I'll have to ask Calder what your name is, if you have one."

Oswin got up and wandered away from the pond to the opposite end of the courtyard, across from where he'd come in. He reached the wall, still mostly intact, and followed it as it extended to behind the castle proper. There were indentations in the stone that indicated there had once been a wall there, blocking off the courtyard from this path. At the end, behind a collapsed tower, was a gate. Oswin pushed it open and walked out into a wood.

It was too regular to be a natural wood. The trees were mostly young, the thickest maybe only a handspan across, and each one had beside it a plain white stone. Each pair was about two paces apart, and the grove extended farther than Oswin could see.

Something about the place made the hair on the back of his neck stand as if he was being watched, but it was quiet with no one else in sight. One tree was somehow in bloom, despite it being early winter, small white flowers covering its branches like snow. Oswin walked up to it and ran his fingertips over the rough bark, unsure what to think of such a strange occurrence.

But nothing happened when he touched it. It was just a tree out of season like the pond.

Regardless, the grove made him uneasy, so he left only moments after his arrival...or so he thought. When he swung the gate closed behind him, he saw the sun had moved significantly across the sky. A shiver having nothing to do with the cold moved up his spine.

The swan hadn't stopped its slow drifting across the pond. Still no sign of Calder anywhere.

Oswin sat on the bank again, then sighed and looked down at the ground between his feet. "I wonder if I should just go. Maybe this is Calder politely asking me to be on my way. He seems pretty solitary. I haven't seen signs of anyone else here, after all." His stomach gave a low groan. "Would it be horrible if I used his food to cook dinner if I also cooked for him?" he asked the swan.

It tilted its head to one side.

"It would help if I knew when to expect him back. So it could be warm. Maybe I'll wait just a little while longer." He looked up at the sun, which was beginning to turn the sky orange above the tree line. "It looks like it's nearly sundown already." He considered it for a minute more. His stomach rumbled louder. "Well, if he gets angry, it'll just be an excuse to leave." He got back to his feet and returned to the kitchen.

He found some pheasant strung up in the larder and began plucking and prepping it. He was so absorbed in what he was doing he didn't even remark on the sound of the door opening and closing until Calder spoke.

"Making dinner?" he asked.

Oswin jumped, the half-naked pheasant falling to the counter. "Uh, y-yes!" he squeaked. "If that's okay."

"It's fine." Calder stretched his arms and fetched some dried herbs from the pantry. "I'm surprised to see you still here."

Oswin flushed. "Well, I wanted to say goodbye properly, but I couldn't find you, and time got rather away from me, so—" He swallowed. "—I can leave if you prefer."

"No need. It's only me here, so the company is appreciated." He took the pheasant from Oswin and shook it. In two shakes, all the remaining feathers fell off.

"Magic?" Oswin asked, raising an eyebrow.

"Magic," Calder confirmed. "For little things like this, it's quite helpful. Do you want to stuff it and roast it? It should last us for a day or two in the larder."

"That sounds delicious. Do you have any bread to use?"

Together they finished stuffing and dressing the bird, then put it in a covered pot to roast in the fire. While they waited for it to finish, they cleaned up and sat at the table. "Oh!" Oswin said after a moment. "That black swan in the courtyard, is it your pet? It's remarkably tame."

Calder looked grave. "It's no pet of mine, no. It's an unwelcome presence, to speak truly."

"Huh, strange. I didn't see it cause any mischief."

"Oh, believe you me, it has caused plenty of…mischief."

Any reply Oswin had died when he saw Calder's eyes—too, too white, the black of his pupils quivering right in the center of that emptiness. He was seeing a memory. Something fearful. Something dark. Oswin swallowed and looked away, trying not to get lost in his expression.

He scrambled for a topic change. "Th-that grove in the back. What is it exactly?"

Calder stood up. "Do not enter that grove. You do not belong there." His usual measured tone was sharp. His pupils were slitted now like a snake's.

Oswin couldn't admit to having already been inside. "I won't," he said. At least his answer was sincere.

Calder took a deep breath. "Excuse my harshness. But that grove is… It's personal."

"I'm sorry," Oswin said quietly. "It seems I'm doing nothing but poking my nose where it's unwanted."

Calder scratched at his head, frowning. "You're just asking questions. It's my fault for being so uncooperative."

Oswin wanted to ask where he'd been all day but decided against it in light of how well the last two topics had gone over. "Do you have anything to ask me, then?" he tried.

Calder sat down and ran his thumb over the raised dots underneath his eye. "How old were you when you began to work for Lord…Farnworth, was it?"

Oswin nodded. "I was eighteen or so. I don't know my exact birthday."

"Is there a story to that?"

Oswin shrugged. "Not really. My parents lived separate from the village, so I don't know how long it was before I was baptized. The standard is at a few months of age, but I may have been a bit older, maybe a year? Two? Regardless, the 'birthday' I celebrate is really my baptism day."

"Baptism," Calder said thoughtfully. "I admit I'm unfamiliar with the concept. What is it exactly?"

So while the pheasant roasted, Oswin called up foggy memories of sitting on a hard wooden bench, staring up at the single pane of stained glass behind the priest while the old man said prayers in a language he didn't know. He recalled the droning voice and the buzzing of insects in the summer months. After the prayers were finished, the priest had discussed the Lord's teachings in a comprehensible tongue. Luckily, baptism was important enough Oswin could recall it in sufficient detail.

The bird almost burned but for the quick work of Calder, who snatched it out of the oven midway through a sentence. He let it rest a bit, then sliced and served it hot. "Sorry," he said, handing Oswin his plate. "It's an odd custom, I think. Do the infants ever drown?"

"No, no," Oswin said before taking a bite. Heavens above, it was good. "It doesn't take long enough for that to happen. And besides, the priest has a lot of practice." He dug into the meal more fiercely.

"And if they do not undergo this ritual, they cannot enter heaven?"

Oswin nodded. "Infants are innocent, though, so they can't go to hell. There's a sort of middle ground between the two, where they go. If I recall, other important people are there, too, if they died before the Savior was born? Sorry, it's been some time since I gave it much thought."

"Don't apologize. I think one learns religion best from the average practitioner anyway. Is the food good?"

Oswin didn't consider himself religious. "Yes, it's excellent. Thank you so much."

"It was no trouble." They continued to make polite noises at each other as they finished, and then they cleaned up.

It was snowing again. Oswin watched it for a while until he felt a soft touch on his shoulder and turned to see Calder offering him a mug of cider. He took it gratefully. "Thank you."

Calder was thinking about something. "Does the cold much bother you, Oswin?"

"If I have a coat and a warm drink, not much at all. Why?"

A small smile grew on Calder's face, and Oswin's heart thudded unexpectedly against his breast. "Then let me show you something." He led Oswin out of the kitchen and into the snow, walking purposefully toward the main castle ruin. Oswin glanced over to the pond, but the swan was missing. Where had it gone for the night? "There is latent magic here still. It has faded with time, but there is still beauty to be found." Calder ducked under a half-collapsed archway while bringing a small light to his hand to drive away the dark shadows.

Oswin gripped his warm mug tightly and followed him through hallways held up by tree trunks and ceilings that had bowed under the weight of time. Calder stopped in front of a large archway, wide enough for doors to stand side by side, though there were no doors to be seen.

As they entered, Calder touched the wall beside him, and sconces burst into light. It appeared to be a theater, or a chapel, with long benches leading down to a central stage.

"You have seen some magic," Calder explained. "But you have not seen flashy magic, magic meant only for show. Let me share some with you before you go. I can hardly recall the last time I had an audience."

He gestured to one of the benches for Oswin to sit and walked down to the dais. As he stepped on the blue-black stone, it glowed white beneath his feet. "This normally has music," he explained, turning to face him. "But I fear I've little talent for it. I hope you still enjoy this."

With a swipe of his hand, the sconces flickered out, the hall now dark but for the light of the stage. He closed his eyes, held his arms out, and slowly swept them back to the center. The light beneath him stretched up to meet his fingertips as he did, leaving glowing trails in the air. He gathered the light, shaping it, enlarging it until Oswin realized, startled, that it was the shape of an enormous woman—an elf, judging by the ears.

Calder seemed to fade out of existence behind the glowing white figure. She turned her face upward and stretched out her arms as twinkling stars fell from her every movement. They hung around her, then drifted away. From her heart, she drew an orb and threw it above her head. It hung there, suspended, growing and shrinking—the moon, Oswin reasoned. After a beat, she looked around, then drooped in sadness.

From within the darkness, Calder's voice could be heard. "Long, long ago, when the world was young, the night was lonely. She had the moon and the stars, but they could not speak with her."

The woman gazed upward and placed a finger to her lips in thought before stretching out her hand and plucking a knife from the air.

"So, from her flesh, she fashioned herself companions."

The figure bent double in pain as she drove the knife in, then pulled outward and drew two small, blue-white figures from her body. Very small elves, just the size of her hand.

"Using the moon, her heart, she imbued her children with magic. Those touched by the full moon bore its brightness." One of the elves grew white hair that fell to their hips. The moon above waned, turning a dark blue, barely visible but for its outline. "Those touched by the new moon bore its darkness."

The second elf grew black hair, the same length as the first. Perfect twins but for the color. Gently, the night goddess bent down and placed the two elves on the ground where they embraced and melded together before splitting apart, again and again, until elves filled the stage, looking up in rapture at their mother.

The night sat among them and embraced them, the light fading.

"And so it was that my people began, the children of the night who loved them." The light faded until the hall was fully dark once again. Oswin winced at the sudden brightness when Calder relit the sconces and walked back up to where he sat. "I hope my narration was satisfactory," he said sheepishly. "I'm no orator."

"That was—" Oswin tried to find the words. "—that was amazing. Is it true?"

Calder raised one shoulder. "Who knows? I like to think so. It's comforting to think of the night as a mother."

"Why did I never see one of your people until you and I met?" Oswin asked, thinking of how many there had been on the stage, the size of the ruins, and how *close* they were to town. It was unthinkable he hadn't heard even a whisper of Calder's people until the dwarves had called him that night.

Calder's lips thinned, and he didn't answer. "I hope I have given you a pleasant memory to journey on," he said instead. He walked out of the hall. Mentally kicking himself, Oswin followed.

"Must...must I leave tomorrow?" he asked. "I will if you want, but..."

Calder paused. "Won't your Master Eadburga worry after you?"

Oswin pondered the mug in his hands. It had grown lukewarm in the cold. "Perhaps, but...but I find myself wanting to stay. If I may."

There was a long pause. Calder began walking again. His voice was soft and—Oswin could have sworn—*vulnerable*. "You are welcome to stay for as much time as you like, Oswin. I will not refuse the company."

Oswin smiled. "So, I will see you tomorrow?"

"Tomorrow evening, yes."

Oswin burned with the desire to ask why not the day, but he refrained. He'd put his foot in his mouth enough for the evening. "Then is this good night?"

Calder nodded. "I shall take you back to your quarters." And he did, leading Oswin in a circuitous route through the ruins instead of the direct one from the kitchen. Once they'd come to Oswin's room, Calder lit a fire in the fireplace and checked the furs again for invaders. When they were clear, Calder lingered in the doorway, his half-lit face hard to read. "Sleep well, Oswin. I shall see you tomorrow."

"Good night."

Calder vanished from the doorway, quick and soundless as a ghost. Oswin sat by the fire, watching it, thinking about what he'd seen. It had been beautiful. He wondered what he had done to deserve such a marvelous sight. Calder had friends, surely? He knew the dwarves, at least. Still, it was humbling, being the focus of such attention.

He got up and took off his coat, then wrapped himself in the furs, lulled by the crackling of the fire. He fell asleep thinking about what those dots and lines that marked Calder's cheeks would feel like under his fingers and whether they were limited to his face.

His dreams smelled of musk and charcoal, and a full moon hung overhead.

The next day, Oswin quickly ascertained Calder was not there, just like he'd said. Oswin sighed as he finished checking around the courtyard. He glanced toward the gate leading to the grove, but Calder's warning rang in his ears. He decided to keep his word.

The swan was there again, drifting back and forth across the small pond.

"Do you ever leave?" Oswin asked it, sitting down beside it. "It seems like a boring day-to-day even if it is a magic pond."

The swan stared at him.

"What did you do to make Calder hate you so much, huh?"

It ruffled its feathers.

Oswin laughed. "Is that a shrug?" He stopped abruptly. "I'm talking to a swan. Is this how lonely I've become?"

The swan shook itself again.

Oswin looked at it glumly. "I could leave, but I want to talk with Calder more. I keep replaying his voice in my mind, and I can't seem to banish the sight of his eyes." He groaned and covered his face with his hands. "What is wrong with me?" After a few moments, he sighed and sat up. "Well, if I've nothing to do, I should review. I haven't properly used my hands in a while. C'mere, swan, I'm going to teach you some signs."

He spent the afternoon showing the swan all the basic signs and how they fit together. Then he started coining words. Most of them were terrible—there was no use for a specific sign for "magic pond" or "mysterious black swan" or "a man born of night"—but he liked the sign he invented for Calder's name: a *C* under the eye that shifted into the sign for vanish (a quick swipe palm-down across the eye, mimicking the sensation of seeing something flash by too quickly to see). "I guess that's a bit mean," he said after practicing it for a few minutes. "I got the impression he doesn't *want* to disappear all day."

He changed the second part to a one-handed sign for "magic." He liked that one better. It sort of worked as saying his eyes were magical, which was true.

Lord in heaven, what was he even thinking about half the time?

(He made sure to note the sign in his head though.)

A few hours went by. The swan was a patient student, though it was abysmal at signing. It was good to run through the drills though. Familiar and thoughtless, they gave his mind time to wander.

The ruins were so quiet. He'd never even seen so much as a fox or even a raven. At first, he'd assumed the winter was to blame, but it really seemed to be just Calder and the swan, whom he disliked for whatever reason. A swan in a pond out of season, which never appeared to leave, and yet which had been strangely absent both the night he had arrived and the previous night when they'd walked to the main hall.

He frowned, peering at the swan in sudden suspicion. The swan looked back, the sun making its dark eyes gleam. He stood. What he was about to do was incredibly stupid—he'd seen swans defending their space before—but he couldn't let the curiosity go.

After removing his shoes and rolling up his trousers, Oswin met the swan's gaze and stepped deliberately into the pond. It didn't react. No hissing. No flapping. Just that long, unwavering stare.

He stepped closer and closer, muscles tensed to run the moment the swan got aggressive. The pond was shallow, but as he walked in deeper, the water soaked into the cloth at his knees, and then his hips. The water itself was pleasantly cool, but he'd have to get inside as soon as he could to avoid unpleasant consequences that came from wet, too-cold feet.

The swan didn't even swim away from him as he approached. Hesitantly, trembling a bit, Oswin gently stroked its head. The feathers were smooth and warm under his fingers. At his touch, the swan closed its eyes and leaned into his hand in a way that was nothing like any bird Oswin had ever met.

"Calder?" he asked breathlessly.

The swan pulled away from him, its gaze both pleased and sad.

"Am I right?" he asked tentatively.

The swan's head dipped forward.

"God's Wounds," Oswin whispered, then winced at using such a strong oath so soon after explaining baptism. He scrambled backward out of the pond, wincing at the feeling of the cold, sharp dead grass under his feet. "Oh Lord, I *was* talking your ear off. I'm so sorry."

The swan—*Calder*—swam to the water's edge and stretched out his neck to touch Oswin's calf briefly before pulling away. Oswin took the gesture to mean reassurance. "I'm...I'm going to get something to eat and hang my trousers up to dry. And I'd appreciate some beer if you have any."

Calder dipped his head again.

"In the larder?"

He nodded.

"Right. Okay. Yes. I'll be back." He picked up his shoes and went inside, removed and hung up his wet trousers by the fire, then found the beer barrel and a mug. It was mercifully full.

He might have had too much to drink because his legs were unsteady and suspiciously not cold when he returned into the kitchen proper, but it still wasn't enough for his head.

He sat at the table and tried to remember everything he'd told the swan. He groaned as he spread himself over the tabletop facedown. He'd treated the swan as a confidante. It was a swan, so who was it going to tell? *Oh wait*, the swan was actually the person he'd been talking about.

Why was the sun not down yet?

Better question, why wasn't he just bolting in the face of such embarrassment? He didn't think Calder would chase him, but it seemed rude to leave after explicitly asking to stay.

He ate some of the leftover pheasant and waited for sunset, his stomach working itself into knots the entire time.

When the sky began to blush orange, he put his trousers and shoes back on and went outside to stand anxiously by the pond. As the sun sank in the sky, so too did the swan into the water until it was completely submerged. When the last edge of the sun winked out of sight through the trees, Calder's head emerged, his white hair darkened by the water.

He stood in the pond and waded over to the shore where a box had appeared.

Oswin was transfixed by his chest. Horizontal lines like the ones across his cheeks covered his torso, and on the left side his chest, over his heart, there was a moon, drawn in a collection of tiny strokes—a long crescent filled with swirling marks of shadow. There was something profound about it, though Oswin had no idea what it meant.

Calder dressed silently after drying himself with a quick swipe of his hands. His chest, and that moon, disappeared behind his dark robes. "I assume you want to talk?" Calder asked. His voice was tired.

"If…you don't mind."

Calder ran his fingers through his hair. "Let us talk by the fire, at least."

Oswin followed him inside.

Calder stoked the fire and set the leftover meat to warm overtop it. "I know you have questions. Ask. I do not promise to answer everything, but I will do my best to give you something."

Oswin swallowed, standing awkwardly near the door, ready to bolt if things went sideways. "Right. Um. I guess the obvious one is, why do you turn into a swan during the day?"

"A curse. Please sit." Calder gestured toward the table and sat down himself then rested his chin on the backs of his hands.

Oswin did so, but he couldn't look Calder in the eye. "Um." He picked at his fingernails. "Why?"

Calder sighed. "It's a tale I'm willing to tell, but it requires a backstory. I will try to be brief." He frowned and rubbed along his jaw, perhaps trying to organize his thoughts. "When my people lived here, there were many women and few men. So, it was not uncommon for the men to be…shared."

Oswin blanched before he could stop himself. He tried to school his expression to be apologetic, or at least neutral, but he wasn't sure how well he succeeded.

"It is not a tradition I was fond of either," Calder said softly. "But whether I liked it or not, it was tradition. At that time, I was a warrior, who was quickly rising in the ranks, so after I triumphed over a warrior two ranks above me, I experienced a sudden and uncomfortable spike in popularity.

"One of the women interested was a…lieutenant, I suppose you could call her. My wife was amiable to the arrangement she proposed, but I was not."

Oswin's heart gave a sharp twinge at the word "wife," but Calder didn't seem to notice anything amiss.

He continued. "So, when I entered her room, I rejected it as politely as I could."

"Why not right away?" Oswin asked, ignoring the way he could suddenly feel his every heartbeat in his throat. "If you were against it from the beginning, why wait?"

Calder sighed. "I had hoped to spare her embarrassment. I told her I wouldn't mind if she told others that we had been together, but I wanted to remain loyal to my wife." His gaze shifted to his hands. They curled and uncurled against the table, knuckles rising and falling under the skin. "She didn't take it well. So, she cursed me to be a swan. They're famous for their monogamy." He smiled without mirth. "And of course, I couldn't explain anything to my wife. That is a part of it too, as is being bound to that pond when I'm transformed during the day, though I'm free to wander at night."

"Can you break it?"

He chuckled briefly, unhappily. "It's quite simple. I just have to fall in love with someone other than my wife."

Oswin swallowed around the lump in his throat. "T-tell me about her," he said since he was apparently a glutton for pain.

Calder shook his head. Even the bitter smile was gone from his face.

Oswin nodded. "Okay." He flailed for a topic change. "Could you explain the marks on your chest? Especially that moon?"

"Definitely not." Calder's voice was cold.

Oswin tried not to laugh nervously. "Okay! How about the ones on your face?" He was already wincing in anticipation as he finished the question.

Calder, on the other hand, relaxed. "Yes. Those are easy enough." He touched the raised dots underneath his eyes.

"These are warrior markers. You can see there are four. I was a fourth-rank warrior. There are ten in total." He paused, tensing a bit. "Were. There *were* ten in total."

Careful of your words, Oswin. "Would the next go farther up around your eye?"

Calder shook his head. "No, the next one would have started a new row." He touched between the two closest to his nose.

"And they're just mirrored? It's not like one eye means one thing while the other means something else?"

"No, it's just mirrored for the sake of symmetry."

"That's fascinating," Oswin said. "What about the lines on your cheeks?"

Calder traced them with a finger. Instead of being raised, these looked more like a strip of skin had been removed, leaving a shallow valley. "Mage's marks. They're less official than warrior's marks. Generally, your teacher gives them to you when she feels you have sufficiently grown. How many you have is more of a reflection of the teacher's esteem than your own skill, if that makes sense."

"Do you have a lot?" Oswin longed to touch them for himself.

"About the middle, I suppose. I have a talent for magic, but I had more of a passion for battle." His gaze grew faraway.

Oswin didn't miss the past tense. "Do you not anymore?"

Calder took a deep breath and held it for a moment before exhaling. "No. Not in the slightest."

Silence fell as Calder got the food out of the pot and set it on the table so they could pick off the meat that was left. He split a loaf of bread for them to eat with it.

"So, the woman who cursed you," Oswin said uncertainly. "Is she still…I mean, could you ask her to—"

"She's dead," Calder said flatly, ripping into the remnants of a thigh with unnecessary force. "But I doubt she'd lift the curse even if she were alive."

"I see."

They lapsed back into silence. This time it was Calder who broke it. "That sign you created for my name. Can you teach it to me again now that I have hands with which to make it?"

"Of course!" Oswin easily slipped into his professional role. It felt good to be using his hands with a person again.

They ended up whittling the evening away as teacher and student. The nuance and expressiveness of the signed language fascinated him. By bedtime, Oswin bid him good night silently out of habit. Calder copied the gesture, his smile almost a grin with a twinkle in his eye.

The memory of that twinkle followed Oswin into his dreams.

He slept until it was nearly afternoon. They must have stayed up later than he'd thought. He groaned as he got up. While the furs were warm and surprisingly plush, he still missed his bed at the Farnworths' manse. Well, what used to be his bed.

Pushing aside his morose contemplation, Oswin put on his shoes and walked down to the kitchen. Calder had left food for him again.

Oswin decided that was a good sign.

After eating, he went outside and watched Calder drift about the pond as usual. He sat on the bank. "So, I have an idea."

Calder looked up at him.

"Instead of talking about heavy things tonight, what if we just did some hunting?"

If a swan could look happy and relieved, Calder did.

"Okay then! I'll meet you here at sundown, and we'll go hunting. I assume there are weapons I could use somewhere inside?"

Calder nodded.

"All right then, I'll go find those. Hopefully, it won't take me too long."

Calder made a small squawk and flapped his wings toward the eastern end of the ruins, then ducked his head under the water for a second before raising it up again.

"So, the armory is in that wing and underground?" Oswin guessed.

Calder nodded again promptly, like he was happy.

Oswin smiled in return. "Thank you. I'll be back soon."

That end of the castle was in terrible disrepair. It seemed like it had once been the front, if the rotten remnants of a beautiful oaken door were any indication. Bits of gold still clung to the carved ornamentation as though the foil had been hastily chiseled off.

Oswin wondered if his initial wariness about bandits had hit closer to the mark than he'd supposed when he passed what appeared to be a makeshift firepit in the stone floor and scattered animal bones. But whoever had been there was long gone as the ruins were silent as a grave.

After a while of wandering around, looking for something that could be the stairs down to the armory, the only staircase he could find led upward to a collapsed second level, not down.

Oswin frowned and scanned the ruins again, his arms crossed in thought. Then he looked back at the floor. If it were an armory, surely the stairs wouldn't be *obvious*. He walked around the wing again, this time keeping his eyes to the ground where grass had sprung up between the dark stones.

There! Toward the back end of the wing where it connected to another part of the ruin, there were stones that were not mortared and yet had no grass between them. Working carefully, Oswin pulled out the stones to reveal a trapdoor and staircase that went down into inky blackness.

Light was going to be a problem.

He pulled a sconce from the wall and brought it to the kitchen. It burned oil, luckily, so Oswin was able to fill it with cooking oil, which would burn quickly, but he wouldn't need it for long. Just to be safe though, he filled it as much as he could and lit it before returning to the staircase.

The stone was solid under his feet as he descended, and the walls were dark and cold. The lamp's faintly nutty aroma helped dispel the creeping chill. There was another sconce at the bottom, and by some miracle, there was still oil in it. Oswin lit it carefully, unsure of how old it was, but it burned just fine.

Now that there was better light, the chamber felt less tomb-like. He looked around, noting there were many empty racks, their iron rusted nearly through from years of neglect. But there were still some weapons to be found—blunt children's swords, spearheads without poles, simple bows, and hunting knives.

Oswin picked up one of the bows and bent it a bit, testing the wood for brittleness or rot caused by age, but it almost seemed like new. He suspected magic was at play, considering the state of the metal racks. He found one that was a good length for him and strung it with one of the cords sitting nearby.

It had been a long time since he had done anything with a bow, but he was pretty sure he'd strung it correctly. He should have Calder check it before he practiced. He didn't want to break a clearly magical bow.

After finding a quiver of arrows to go with the bow and grabbing one of the hunting knives, Oswin blew out the lamps and returned upstairs, then set the stones back into place over the trapdoor.

Calder honked softly when Oswin came outside to show him the bow and arrows. "Did I string it correctly?" he asked, setting the bow on the bank so Calder could look. "It's been many years since I had to do it myself."

Calder paddled over and examined it closely, twisting his head from side to side to get every angle possible. Then he nodded.

"Thank you," Oswin said, picking it up and putting it over his back. "I'm going to go practice with it. I'm more than rusty."

Calder nodded again, and Oswin bid him goodbye, then wandered away to find a good practice tree. It didn't take long to find one with a nice broad trunk. He made a small notch in the center with the knife. Something to aim at.

He walked several paces away, took a strong stance, lifted the bow, and nocked an arrow. He took a deep breath and pulled back, trying to remember being taught many years before. This bow was nicer than any he had ever used. It drew smooth as silk.

He got the notch in his sights and let the arrow fly.

Straight past the tree.

He laughed at himself and went to go fetch the arrow. He'd certainly grown soft over the years, hadn't he?

But the lessons had not been lost entirely. By the time the shadows began to lengthen in earnest, he was hitting at least *near* his initial notch regularly. He wasn't going to be doing any trick shots, but he might get a deer if it held still long enough.

Besides, he had a feeling no matter what he did, Calder was going to be astoundingly better at it. He'd had a long time to practice and had presumably been hunting for himself for many of these past two hundred years.

Still, Oswin was confident he was not going to embarrass himself, and that was good enough.

He went back to the pond to await Calder's transformation, grateful for the short days of winter. When Calder was once again wingless and dressed, they ate a small meal, gathered a bow and arrows for Calder, and struck out into the woods.

Oswin followed behind Calder, who knew the trees best. His star-white hair glowed in the light of the moon, and Oswin wondered aloud how he would hide from the animals they hunted. Calder turned to him, bright eyes half-closed with a knowing smile. His hair appeared to ripple, though it seemed to be only a trick of the light.

Oswin squinted at it in confusion, and then he realized the ripple had been darkness running down the length of the hair until it blended in with the dark woods. Oswin reached out unthinkingly, expecting to feel paint or some sort of dye, but it was just hair, cool and thick under his fingers.

Calder twitched away before Oswin realized what he'd done.

He burned with embarrassment. "Could you do that to your skin as well?" he asked in a soft voice, looking around for signs of animals.

In answer, the same ripple went over Calder's skin making it a match to Oswin's own. It was strange to see. Who was this dark-haired, fair-skinned man in front of him? Before Oswin could ask, Calder blinked, and his irises were suddenly dark.

"That's amazing," Oswin said wonderingly.

"It's useful too," Calder said, raising an eyebrow. His skin rippled again, this time leaving it striped and splotched with a mix of browns. "You can see me easily when I stand before you, but close your eyes."

Oswin did so. Calder brushed past him, making so little sound that in a moment, Oswin had no idea where he had gone.

"Open," Calder's voice said, the whisper too faint to give more than a general direction. He turned toward it and looked around. Calder was nowhere to be seen.

Oswin continued to look, his search becoming more frantic. There was no sign of him anywhere. Had he left him alone in the wood? He wouldn't do that, surely.

There was a rustle to his right, and Calder's white eyes blinked into view. The rest of him followed and melted out of the shadows like some sort of ghost. He returned to his normal coloring but for the hair.

Oswin was in awe. "Can all of your kin do that?"

"Most," Calder affirmed. "As far as magic goes, color is simple enough to shift, especially when it's one's own. It's something you learn in early lessons, and some learn it on their own before ever working under a master. Though they probably wouldn't learn advanced camouflage like that on their own because it requires knowledge of color and light. But children take great pleasure in turning themselves fantastical colors." His expression was gentle as he explained, clearly seeing bright memories. But he soon frowned. "Well, they *did*," he finished in a soft voice.

Oswin bit his lip. "Are you…" He trailed off, recalling something Calder had said to the angel before. *It is a difficult path to walk, being the only one of your kind left alive.* "Are you alone?" he asked.

Calder sighed and answered in a near mumble. "As alone as a creature can be, to the best of my knowledge."

The silence that followed was heavy as lead.

"Come," Calder said at last. "The deer often rest in a clearing over this way."

Oswin followed, wondering what could have happened to Calder's kin. He had said he was once a warrior but now had no taste for battle, so perhaps a war? If the castle had been a stronghold, then maybe it had held those unable to fight. And if the castle had fallen…

Where would the people have gone?

Oswin's mind wandered to the grove he had not been meant to enter. How strange the atmosphere had been within it. It had felt like a graveyard.

Oswin swallowed dryly as he watched Calder duck into a crouch and raise his bow, then fire an arrow in one swift, smooth motion. A deer Oswin hadn't even noticed fell to the ground with a thump. The others bounded off into the deeper woods.

Calder gestured for Oswin to follow as they approached the body. Calder pulled the arrow from its head and stowed it back in the quiver. "Find a branch long enough for us to tie it to," he said. "It'll be better to butcher it at the castle to avoid unwanted guests."

Oswin agreed and went to scour the ground. He found a fallen bough and stripped off the smaller twigs to make a decent pole. Calder lashed the deer's feet to it, and they carried the pole over their shoulders, ferrying the reward of their very short hunt back to the kitchen.

"I'm sorry," Oswin said as they returned to the remnants of the wall. "I'd promised you a night free of heavy questions."

"It's not your fault. All roads lead there for me."

Oswin chewed on the inside of his cheek. "Well, I'm here to listen if you want to talk about it." He felt useless.

Calder glanced at him, shifting his hair back to its natural color. "I appreciate that. And your patience." He led Oswin into an unused part of the castle, shielded by a roof and three walls, and put the deer on the ground. He sat down beside it and took a knife from his belt. With a flick of his wrist, a small orb of light appeared and settled itself on the floor beside the animal, lighting it enough to see. "I imagine I'm not easy to talk to, always slamming doors on topics." He untied the deer from the pole and began the work of removing the skin.

As his hands worked and his eyes followed them, he continued. "You've likely never heard of the Fairy War. They worked hard to keep it concealed from humans, and it was over seventy years ago now." He peeled the skin and subcutaneous fat away and started cutting at the meat proper. "It boils down to this—fairies are creatures of magic. They do not *use* it as elves and some humans do, no—it is an essential part of them. And it is strengthened by the power of belief. When fairies came to this island from their home island in the west, they soon realized that if the people of this land knew magic was limited in scope and power, their magic *would* be. And they didn't like that."

Calder set the organs aside, being careful not to puncture the intestines. "So, the fairies cut off human contact with nonfairy magic. Entirely. Memory is an easy thing to change, for a fairy. It was simple enough to push living memories, turn elven guardians to fairy godmothers, turn tales of human witches to fairy enchantresses. And stories? Well, stories always change from teller to teller. Soon, humans stopped approaching us, except for those who worked with us often. And *those* humans began to vanish, one by one." Calder's expression was grave, his eyes never rising from his steady work.

"Humans are the most numerous creatures here, you see, and dwarves have never cared enough about magic to bother with how it works, so once the humans had been taken care of, the fairies had won the first offense of their war. Afterward, they tried to 'reason' with us, convince us to go north where our ancestors lived. But we had been here for countless generations and would not be moved."

The light moved as Calder worked, rolling wherever he needed it most. Oswin watched it, trying not to look at Calder's face as he spoke, for fear of somehow causing him to stop. "That's when they decided to attack us, hoping to force our departure. Or wipe us out. Whichever came first.

"They attacked our villages, those who lived outside the walls of the castle here. We sent warriors to aid them. Many never returned."

Calder's hands never stopped moving, and his eyes never left the deer. It was as if he was talking only to himself.

"I was forced to stay behind due to my curse. My wife left in one of the last regiments. I have not seen her since." He swallowed heavily as he divided the meat into sections and laid out ribs and filets neatly side by side. "I stayed with the priests and the children. And every night, I—" He took a shuddering breath and sat back. Like a child, Calder pulled his knees to his chest and wrapped his arms around them. Squeezing his eyes shut, he shook his head. "No. I can't."

Oswin tried to tell him it was okay to stop, but Calder kept shaking his head. "They came during the day," he continued, forcing his voice to strength. "Weeks after the last warriors left. I lived because of my curse. They considered me an amusement." He opened the front of his robe and touched the horizontal scars covering his chest and stomach. "Each of these," he whispered, running his fingers over them, "is a body I buried after it was over."

Oswin stared in silent horror as he took in *all* those lines. He couldn't even count how many there were. Twenty? Thirty? More? He tried to imagine Calder burying them in the dead of night with only a small ball of light, like the one before them now, to see by. It was a bleak and heart-wrenching image. And the image of him purposely cutting each one into his flesh, forcing them to scar, so he wouldn't forget.

Unthinkingly, Oswin leaned forward to touch the lines, and this time Calder didn't pull away. The patches of unmarked skin were warm and firm, a stark contrast to the scars, which were rough and almost jagged.

Calder took Oswin's hand and held it to his chest. "I have never told anyone this," he whispered. "There hasn't been anyone to tell."

Oswin took a deep breath and smiled as best he could. It was hard to find words, but Calder was expecting *something*. "Thank you for choosing to confide in me," he said.

Calder stared at Oswin's hand and squeezed it hard enough to make the tips of his fingers numb. "I had a child," he whispered. "The moon on my chest. It is for him."

Oswin couldn't breathe. He thought of that single tree in the graveyard, the one out of season. He hugged Calder as tightly as he could, not bothering to hold back his tears. "I'm so sorry," he choked out again and again. "Calder, I am so sorry."

They stayed like that for a long time, sharing the burden of grief as best they could. After the tears had run dry and personal space was regained, Calder spoke. "We should move the meat to the larder," he said quietly.

They did, and nothing else was said.

Some time later, as Calder sat at the table drinking cider, Oswin got up to go to bed.

"Wait," Calder said softly. Oswin was almost embarrassed by how quickly he stopped and turned. Calder was staring into his cup. "This is unfair of me to ask, but would you—" He swallowed, his voice dropping to barely more than a whisper. "Would you stay with me tonight? The thought of being alone in the dark..." He swallowed again. "It doesn't appeal right now."

Oswin was torn. He very much wanted to share a bed with this man but not as a comfort object. Would it be wrong of him to accept? Would it be taking advantage of a man in mourning for his wife and son?

Calder's shoulders rose as his body hunched forward. "I'm sorry. It was too much to ask. Forget I said anything. I'll just... sit outside until dawn. At least the sky is clear. Go to bed, Oswin. I'll be fine."

"I'll do it."

Calder at last looked up. "You really don't have to," he said carefully, but the relief in his eyes was clear to see.

Oswin smiled. "I want to."

Calder's room showed its roots as a pantry. The walls were full of shelves, and the light was provided by two sconces that had clearly been pulled from the front hall; they were far too large for the small room.

The bed was stuffed with goose down (or was it swan down? were they *Calder's* feathers?) and covered in furs similar to the ones Calder had given him. It was nestled against the back wall, taking up a good half of the room. There was dark-blue fabric pinned up on three sides, possibly to make the space seem homier.

"I'm sorry for the mess," Calder mumbled as he gave the furs a half-hearted tug to straighten them out.

"Don't worry about it," Oswin said. "It's not like you were expecting guests." He laughed nervously.

Calder frowned. "If this is uncomfortable for you, you are free to leave," he said uncertainly. "I'm not trying to force you." He winced. "Or guilt you."

Shaking his head, Oswin sat down on the bed. Oh Lord, it was soft. Without thinking, he lay back and sighed in contentment. "It's just been a long time since I shared a bed with anyone," he explained.

Calder lay down next to him. "You worked for a noble house and didn't have women falling over themselves trying to catch your eye? Times must have changed from what I remember."

Oswin laughed, trying to keep the bitter tone from his voice. There had been the occasional social climber, but (a) Oswin had been but a stepping-stone to the heir for them, and (b) he had no interest in women. But he was sure if Calder knew that, he would not be so comforted by his presence.

Calder rolled over, scooting up to the pillow and getting under the covers. Oswin followed. With a swipe of his hand, Calder killed the lights, settled into place, and closed his eyes. The room was suddenly pitch-black. Oswin wasn't sure whether he should face Calder or away. It was more platonic to face away, wasn't it? So, he did that.

Calder's breathing evened out and deepened as he fell asleep. Oswin was wide awake, transfixed by the knowledge that Calder was *right there*, but he couldn't touch him. Why hadn't he thought this through before he'd agreed? God in heaven, this was torture. Despairing torture. With Calder's every calm exhale, he drove home the idea he wouldn't even think to imagine Oswin as a romantic partner.

After an hour had passed and Oswin was not asleep but dozing, Calder's breathing quickened, a whimper at the edge of his voice. Oswin rolled back over and groped for Calder's hand. "Shhh," he whispered. "It's not real. It's okay. It's over."

Calder half woke, slips of white appearing in the dark as his eyes fluttered open. He curled around Oswin and tugged him close. Oswin could hear his heartbeat against his ear, could feel the ropey scars against his cheek. Calder's leg wrapped around one of his and pulled them even closer together.

A strangled cry came out of Oswin's mouth as he tried to prevent their hips from touching.

But it didn't wake Calder. He was mumbling now, garbled words, phrases always ending with the same word. *Tear? Tara?* It was surely his wife's name. Was he having a nightmare of his own?

Eventually, the dream subsided, and Calder returned to being dead weight. Oswin carefully extricated himself and lay there on his back, trying to take deep breaths and think of anything to bring the heat between his legs to rest.

The thought of his work stuck. How long had it been? Two days? Three? His things had no doubt arrived without him at this point. Master Eadburga was probably going from concerned to worried. Not to mention Wystan.

But how could he leave Calder alone now? His curse bound him to that pond, and thus, to the ruins of his old life. How was he supposed to move on from his wife if he couldn't go and meet anyone?

Oswin didn't think the curse had been intended to be that cruel, but it was, nonetheless. He tried to think of ways he could bring women here, introduce them to Calder, but jealousy roared up in his throat at the idea of playing matchmaker.

He crossed his arms over his eyes to fight back tears. He should never have stayed. He should have taken that first night's hospitality, then continued on his way, mystery and attraction be damned.

To free himself, he would need to leave Calder alone to his despair, a despair that had only deepened thanks to Oswin's incessant prying. Either he would suffer or Calder would.

And alone in the dark, he resolved to be the sacrifice. Calder had lost more than enough.

O swin dozed until dawn when Calder stirred beside him. He rose from the bed, still snoring slightly. Oswin watched as he left the room, then scrambled up to follow. His eyes burned at even the pale light of the sunrise.

Calder walked out into courtyard and dropped his clothing on the bank of the pond before stepping in. Like when he changed back at sunset, Calder sank into the water and rose as a swan, head ducked under his wing as he continued to sleep. After a moment, the robes also vanished, presumably so they could reappear in the box later.

Oswin sighed as he returned inside and went to his own space to wrap himself in the furs. Hopefully, he could sleep a bit before Calder woke.

O swin woke again a few hours later to proper daylight. It took him a moment to remember the events of the night before, which left him feeling somber and tired despite the rest. Still, he rose and went down to the kitchen. He made himself some breakfast and peered out at the pond where Calder still slept. Oswin felt a pang of sympathy. No matter how heavy his heart was, he couldn't imagine the weight of Calder's.

He glanced around the kitchen. It was intact and made homey by the crackle of the fire and the smell of the larder, but the rest of the ruins were completely barren as far as he remembered. He could hardly rebuild stone walls, but perhaps he could find something in the rubble? Some tokens of memory, perhaps? Something overlooked by brigands and thieves?

But before that—the larder. There were the remaining leftovers of the pheasant. A soup to chase away the winter's cold would never be amiss. So, he gathered some turnips, onions, and carrots, and smelled the various dried herbs that hung from a rack. He couldn't identify most of them by appearance alone, but he could match the smell to the taste, so he took some rosemary and thyme back out to the kitchen with the vegetables.

He spent the rest of the morning scrubbing and chopping, then boiling them along with the remaining pheasant bones and herbs to hopefully make a decent stew later. While he was in the larder fetching another sprig of rosemary, Oswin noticed a glass jar with a thick bread sponge, so he grabbed that too, along with some flour and salt.

Once the stew was simmering in the fire, Oswin got to work making fresh bread. He wasn't exactly *good* at cooking, but he knew his way around enough to be decent at it. He hoped Calder would appreciate the effort, at least. He smiled to himself, sure he would. He covered the bowl of bread dough with a damp cloth and set it aside to rise, then ran his hands under the water pump to rinse off the excess flour. He closed the jar with the bread sponge and put it away in the larder.

After wiping his hands dry on his trousers, he left the kitchen and walked down the hallway toward his room, but this time, he went past it, his hand on the bare, dark walls. Light streamed through cracks in mortar on one side, and there were chunks missing at regular intervals—once there had been sconces there, he assumed.

The unlit side had more rooms, though most of the doors had half rotted away. Was this the honest degradation of less than a century, or had the fairies assisted in its dilapidation? He peered into the rooms. They were much the same as his, with raised platforms for bedding and fireplaces. Perhaps they had been rooms for the kitchen staff?

The hallway ended abruptly with a huge pile of collapsed stone that appeared to have once been a staircase. Oswin peered up and squinted at distant glimmers of light, suggesting the upper floors had not fallen apart altogether, but he saw no way of getting up there or even past the pile.

He frowned. That first night, Calder had led him to his room through the ruins, so they connected somewhere, but he couldn't see where, and his memory failed him. Frowning, he doubled back to the kitchen, checked on the stew, then uncovered the dough and hummed approvingly at how much it had risen. He floured the countertop and tipped the bowl over. The dough flopped wetly down, and Oswin gave it a solid punch, pushing out the excess air.

He had forgotten how soothing it was to knead bread. As he twisted it and squeezed it and threw it about, he thought about how he was going to miss the close friendship he and Wystan had shared, how he didn't know if he could take the heartbreak of being replaced *again* in someone's life. It had been years since he'd worked under Master Eadburga, and while he liked her, he didn't want to go back to being someone's *underling* after years of being his own man.

He thought about Calder and Calder's wife and son. He thought about fairies who'd reshaped reality just to hold on to power. He thought about how Calder could never return the affections rapidly growing in his chest. He thought. He thought. He thought.

By the end of it, Oswin was breathing heavily, his arms aching. But the dough was perfect, so far as he could tell. He tucked the dough into a proper ball and covered it again to rise further, then rinsed off his hands. With his shirt, he dabbed faint sweat from his brow and stepped outside into the cold winter afternoon.

Calder had woken and was paddling slowly around the water. He turned when Oswin emerged and nodded his head.

Oswin greeted him with signed language. *How are you this morning? Did you sleep well?*

Calder tilted his head, then flapped his wings and honked softly. Oswin took that to mean *fine* and *yes*.

Oswin approached the water. "I am going to explore the castle ruins. Is there anywhere you recommend?"

Calder tilted his head again. He lifted his beak toward the main building where the performance hall was.

Oswin signed, *Understood.* "Thank you. Dinner is cooking, by the way. I doubt it will be as amazing as anything you'd make, but I figured it would be nice to have something that's been stewing all day in this cold." He kept the fresh bread a surprise.

Calder watched him for a long moment, then honked again, lowering his head as he paddled away. Oswin frowned. Had he put his foot in his mouth again?

Trying to shake off the feeling of shame, he walked over to the main ruins and ducked under the archway toward the theater hall. Instead of going through and into it, however, he walked around it and came across an intact set of stairs. Curious, he climbed them and looked around. This hallway was much wider, and the windows were larger. Between them, there were small pedestals, some still with the feet of what had once been statues. He could imagine grand tapestries adorning the walls.

The ruins were so overwhelmingly sad, especially knowing what Oswin did now. It was so hard to imagine what this place had once been like before being left to deteriorate so much. He continued down the corridor, peering into the rooms he passed. These were bigger and obviously had belonged to much more important people. They had small nooks that had once been private garderobes and larger bed platforms with plenty of room for couches or chairs to be set around the fireplace. Empty chests lay open near some of the bed platforms, clearly ransacked.

Oswin frowned, considering. These had been well-off people, and such people tended to be squirrely with their valuables. He stepped into a room with a half-rotted sofa still in front of the fireplace and climbed onto the bed platform, surveying the room and the walls. Under his hand, one of the bricks was oddly soft, like cloth. Carefully, he reached into it, his heart jumping into his throat as he watched his hand sink into what appeared to be solid stone.

Sweat broke out on his neck. He imagined some waiting snake or rat, eager to bite his vulnerable hand, and scared badly when something smooth brushed against his fingertips. But it didn't move, so he crept his fingers forward and clasped it, then pulled it out.

It was a round, silver brooch as shining as if it had just been polished. Black stone—onyx?—covered most of its front, leaving a crescent moon of silver visible. The back was engraved with stars and a mix of long and short lines that reminded Oswin of some of the designs on the gravestones of the people who'd emigrated from the snowy north. He put the brooch into his pocket and checked the strange cubbyhole for more trinkets, but it was empty.

Rubbing his hands together, Oswin jumped back to the floor and went to see if the other rooms held similar treasures.

In the end, he found quite a bit of jewelry. Chains, earrings, and some other sorts of sharp bits that looked like they belonged stuck in flesh, but Oswin couldn't fathom where. Many of the pieces had been decorated with the moon and stars, and after the folktale Calder had shown him, Oswin wasn't surprised. The moon and stars were important to Calder's people. Or had been, he supposed.

Suddenly, it felt less like reclaiming some trinkets for Calder and more like grave-robbing. These items had been hidden away, protected. Though their owners were long dead, he could suddenly imagine their angry ghosts. He considered putting them all back, but ultimately decided against it. Perhaps Calder knew who had owned them and could take them to their graves? Or to the graves of their spouses or children? If that was the case, Oswin wasn't stirring up spirits so much as putting them to rest.

He nodded to himself as he stepped into the wide corridor and looked out the window to ascertain the time. The sun was sitting over the trees, not quite setting but approaching it. He returned to the hall and tried to find the route Calder had taken back to the kitchen. Eventually, he found a narrow passage downward that took him into one of the rooms beside his own. Some sort of servant's way, he imagined, so important people could be fed quickly.

He returned once again to the kitchen. The stew had begun to make the entire room smell of cooking meat and herbs, and the bread was ready for one more knead before being tucked into the embers to bake. He kept his mind busy with thoughts of language this time, not wanting to get himself worked up again. When the dough was properly supple, Oswin sliced a nice cross into the top and got it settled in the fire. He also checked the stew properly, inching the metal lid off with his spoon to dip in the broth for a taste. A bit bland; probably not enough salt. He added two pinches and put the lid into place, his back cracking as he straightened and then sat at the kitchen table.

He wondered if Calder had any books to pass the time. He remembered his own books, sitting in his trunk that had been sent ahead to town. Master Eadburga would be worrying soon. He should at least go and come back. A change of clothes also wouldn't be a terrible idea if he was going to be staying here much longer. (How much longer was he planning on staying?)

The door opened. Calder took a deep breath. "You really did make dinner," he said softly.

"Did you doubt me?" Oswin asked. "It's the least I could do since I'm imposing myself."

Calder shook his head, resting his hand briefly on Oswin's shoulder as he walked past to sit at the table. "You're not imposing at all," he said. "If anything, I should be thanking you. Especially for last night."

Oswin's face heated. He ducked his head. "It was no trouble. You would have done the same."

"Regardless, I appreciated it." He paused, sniffed the air. "Is that fresh bread, too?"

Oswin got up to check on it. "Yes, I thought leftover stew should at least have fresh bread with it." He poked it with the spoon. Still a bit too soft. He returned to the table. "A few more minutes," he explained.

Calder was watching him again, his elbows on the table, chin resting against his joined hands, his pupils wide in his white, white eyes. Oswin swallowed and licked his lips. "Is something wrong?"

Calder blinked and shook his head, leaning back. "No, nothing; sorry. Thank you for the dinner."

Oswin chuckled. "Thank me if it turns out well."

When the bread was finished, Oswin tapped it out of the embers and set it on the table to cool. He served the stew, surreptitiously taking a quick sip of the broth to check the flavor. He breathed a sigh of relief. It was actually good, praise the Lord. He set a bowl in front of Calder, then took the seat across from him. He spread his hands. "*Bon appétit.*"

Calder smiled and spooned the stew into his mouth, closing his eyes as he tasted. "It's excellent. Thank you so much, Oswin."

Oswin was practically glowing with pride. They ate in silence for a few minutes until Calder said, "So, you know much about me. But I still know little of you. Where were you born? How did you come to work for your Master Eadburga?"

Oswin stirred his stew. "I'm from here in Saxtain, though I think I was born farther…north? I was but a child when I left my home village, so I couldn't even tell you its name." He turned a bit of meat over with his spoon. "I lived alone with my mother until I returned home one day to find her swinging from the rafters."

He regretted the casual tone as he watched Calder drop his spoon in shock. "Your mother?"

"Yes." He ate a bit of onion. "Life was hard, I suppose. If there was a story behind it, I will never hear it."

"That must have been hard on you," Calder said softly, taking Oswin's hand across the table. He squeezed it. "I cannot imagine being a child and coming home to…that."

Oswin mirrored Calder's grip, staring down at their joined hands. "Yeah," he said, surprised by how vulnerable he suddenly felt. He thought he'd long since put those feelings aside. "Yeah, it was hard. I was too young to grasp the significance of what was happening." He laughed without mirth. "I was taken in by the church, who made sure I understood my mother was being punished as a sinner for taking her own life." Calder's grip tightened briefly, and then he pulled away to pick up his spoon once again. He looked like he was searching for something to say, but after a long moment of silence, Oswin continued. "They taught me my letters and numbers well enough. However, I never had the disposition for the priesthood, if you can imagine, so when a troupe of actors passed through in need of a scribe and accountant, I leapt at the chance to travel."

Calder had returned to eating, but his gaze was unwavering. Oswin dropped his to his bowl. "We traveled together for a few years. They taught me to take care of myself and about how to live in the world when you've little to look forward to. When the troupe broke up, I found myself on the streets, begging for coin." That was a time he had no desire to revisit.

"From beggar to a voice for the voiceless?" Calder asked. "Quite a shift, from survival to selflessness."

Oswin paused. He'd never imagined it in that way. Always it had seemed to him that his giving a voice was an ultimately selfish act—a proving of necessity, of being irreplaceable. But it was probably rude to reject the compliment. "In a sense, I suppose," he demurred.

"How did you come to meet Master Eadburga?"

Oswin explained she had been teaching a client when Oswin had seen her and asked what she was doing. "When she learned I was literate and had a decent aptitude for the work, she took me on as an apprentice. I became my own master when I went to work for the Farnworth family."

"So, if you return now, will you go back to being apprenticed?"

Oswin shook his head. "No, I'd technically be her equal, but she's older and more connected than I am, and it is her home. So, I'd be indebted—more than I was previously at any rate."

"And you don't wish to owe anyone anything," Calder guessed, raising an eyebrow.

Oswin smiled wanly. "That's about the gist of it. I prefer to be relied upon rather than doing the relying."

Calder made a thoughtful noise as he gathered up the empty dishes and set to washing them. "And I suppose you wish for me to rely on you." It didn't seem to be an accusation, but it landed like one on Oswin's heart.

He crossed his arms, slouching forward onto the table. "Only if you want to," he mumbled.

The quiet slosh of water and the clink of crockery were the only sounds in the kitchen. Oswin sank forward into his arms, afraid to look at Calder. After a few minutes, something warm nudged his shoulder, and he sat up automatically to receive the mug of cider.

"Perhaps I wish to be relied upon as well," Calder said, taking his seat. "That is what a relationship is, is it not? The exchanging of reliances."

The corner of Oswin's mouth turned upwards. "I don't think that's a word. And what is our relationship, exactly?"

Calder's eyes gleamed in the firelight. "What is it, indeed? And reliances must be a perfectly good word, since you knew what I meant. Surely you relied on your Wystan as much as he relied on your voice?"

Oswin pondered this. He had considered him and Wystan friends, close ones even, and he had enjoyed Wystan's company. But had he ever relied on him for anything besides companionship? Had he ever shared his secrets or feelings? He had been privy to Wystan's, and yet he could hardly recall a moment like this one, feeling simultaneously vulnerable and *known* in a way that was as exhilarating as it was terrifying. "I…don't know if I ever did," he said hesitantly.

There was recognition in Calder's eyes and sympathy. A dark hand wrapped around Oswin's own. "When you find a person who carries you when you tire, keep them close, won't you?"

Swallowing around the sudden tightness in his throat, Oswin nodded. He suddenly remembered the jewelry.

"Oh!" He took the pieces out of his pockets and spread them on the table. "When I was exploring the ruins earlier, I found these. I thought you'd want to know they were there."

Calder's breath was shallow as he picked up the brooch and turned it over in his hands. "How? The thieves took everything."

Oswin started telling the whole story of his exploration and how he'd realized about the hidden caches in the walls, his voice growing softer and softer as he realized Calder wasn't listening. He was holding the brooch up to the firelight, the silver moon and stars glittering between his fingers.

"This was my aunt's. A wedding token," Calder whispered softly, touching the markings on the back before raising the brooch to his lips. Twin tears slid down his cheeks. "Thank you, Oswin. It is a privilege to have more than memory alone, and more than I ever expected."

Oswin didn't know how to respond at first, but he settled for hugging Calder tightly until the tears stopped. "Glad to see my years on the wrong side of the law have served you well," he said lightly, and Calder chuckled against his shoulder.

He slept in his own bed that night, though he was too long kept awake by the phantom touch of Calder against his back. However, he found the heartbreak settled better when he knew his want was impossible.

The next evening, the two of them cooked dinner together. As Calder prepared the venison, Oswin peeled the turnips and carrots. After a while of companionable silence, Oswin said, "You know, I never asked what it was you did for the angel and Wystan when the angel was cursed himself."

Calder nodded. "I linked their minds temporarily. It's a difficult modification. Typically, that particular spell is used to link the caster and one other person across short distances. Stepping 'outside' of the spell, so to speak, took a tremendous amount of power."

Oswin could believe it. "You looked exhausted afterwards. I was worried you would pass out."

Calder chuckled. "While that was the most potent spell I've attempted in decades, I was only ever in danger of falling asleep in the middle of it."

Something occurred to Oswin. "What about the fairies? Would they have noticed it? Should I be worried about them showing up to finish the job?"

Calder paused thoughtfully. "Magic does ripple, and a powerful spell like that probably rippled far, but I imagine most fairies would assume it was a fairy spell. Magic is just magic, especially at a distance, though it has a... Hm." He seemed to be searching for a metaphor. The venison lay on the counter, forgotten. "Ah, it has something like a *scent*, recognizable as belonging to a certain person, but only someone who knew my magic well would notice something like that. You'd recognize the scent of your mother but not that of a stranger, after all. So, a fairy would just assume it was the spell of another fairy they don't know personally or don't know well."

"I see... So, you're safe?"

Calder gave him a small smile. "Yes, as safe as I have been, but I appreciate your concern."

They worked quietly for a short while longer. The pile of vegetable skins in the bucket by Oswin's feet grew slowly from scattered pieces to a nice little hill.

Startling Oswin out of his concentration, Calder asked, "When do you plan to leave? It's been now a week for a journey that should have taken less than two days."

Oswin frowned and set the peeled carrot on the table, then picked up another. "I should go soon. But I find it difficult to do so."

Calder's hands, which had been rubbing salt and spices into the venison, stilled, and he gazed out the window, toward the pond. "I'm keeping you here," he said quietly.

"No!" Oswin set his work aside so he could look at Calder properly, but Calder wasn't looking back.

"You pity me, the poor wretched creature, cursed and bound to the ruins of a life that can never return. I should not have let you stay."

Oswin stood and rested a hand on Calder's back. "Calder, what's wrong? Are you asking me to go?"

Calder looked at him, his pupils wide, mouth twisted into a miserable line. "No," he said finally, turning away. "I'm not." There was a hollow silence, begging for words to fill the void.

"Do you think you'll ever break the curse?" Oswin asked.

Calder sighed heavily. "I hope so, one day. But it is difficult to fall out of love with a memory that only grows fonder with time. Perhaps had the war not happened, the curse would already be broken. Certainly, my wife and I had our struggles. We were two stubborn people who often butted heads over which was the 'right' decision when problems arose. Perhaps something would have driven a wedge between us long ago." He flipped the cut of meat over on the counter and slapped it against the wood. "But now she's dead, and the opportunity is lost."

Oswin rubbed Calder's shoulder. "Absence makes the heart grow fonder, but time heals all wounds." He smiled. "You'll get to see which cliché proves truer."

Calder chuckled at that and put the meat into the pan. "I suppose I shall. Are the vegetables ready?"

"Oops." Oswin scurried back to the table to finish, and Calder chuckled again.

After the meat was sizzling over the fire, Calder said, "When the curse is broken, I will visit you. But elves are no longer known to most, so I will come in disguise." Colors rippled over his body. "You'll need to guess which of the strangers you meet are me."

When his coloring became a mimic of Wystan's but with Calder's sharp features, Oswin laughed. "If you look like that, I'll know you a mile off."

"Well I can't have *that*, can I?" The colors shifted to mimic Oswin's, spotty skin and all.

"You know, it's not fair you can make my coloring look handsome. Then I have even less excuse for being so remarkably average."

"Oh, I don't know," Calder said, resting his head on his hands as he shifted back to his natural state. "You wear it well." The *fondness* in his voice captured Oswin's heart. He swore for a moment it had stopped beating in his chest.

If Calder noticed his shock, he said nothing.

As the smell of cooking dinner filled the kitchen with a sense of home, Calder asked, "When you do leave, do you promise to visit?"

Oswin smiled. "I promise."

Early morning the next day, Oswin woke to the sound of yelling. He frowned as he opened his eyes, then stumbled up to peer out through a rotten gap in the wall, furs still clutched around him to keep out the chill. A figure of black and dark blue caught his eye, and he was instantly awake.

He threw on shoes and ran outside as quickly as he could, not minding the cold as he sprinted around to the remains of the front gate. The elf standing there was a woman. Her skin was the same shade of night as Calder's, but her hair and eyes were coal-black, and she was dressed like a sellsword in coarse shirt and trousers with leather armor across her shoulders and around her wrists. Under her eyes, she had seven warrior's marks, but not many mage's marks on her cheeks—only three.

She looked surprised to see Oswin. "Who are you?" she asked.

"I am Oswin," he said uncertainly. "Who are *you*?"

The woman crossed her arms and shifted her hips, causing the sword at her side to sway. "I am called Tyra. I am seeking an elf. A bit shorter than me with white hair and eyes. Last I knew him, he was here."

Oswin swallowed, his stomach clenching. "By name of Calder, perhaps?"

She perked up. "Yes, do you know him?" she asked eagerly.

"He's here, though cursed."

She sighed. "Still? It's been so long, yet he still hasn't broken it?" She shook her head. "No matter. I'll go see him. Thank you, Oswin." She ran toward the courtyard, nimbly avoiding the bits of ruin in her way.

Tyra… The name echoed strangely in his head. But then he remembered: the name from Calder's sleep-talk. Surely it had been Tyra.

Oswin followed her, nauseated. When he saw her kneeling by the pond's edge, her arms wrapped around Calder's body as she wept, he knew his hunch had proven true.

"I should be happy," he mumbled to himself as he turned and walked some distance away. "I need to be *happy*." After the night in Calder's bed, Oswin had thought he'd run out of tears to shed over this doomed love, but he proved himself wrong.

After he finished crying and had waited long enough his face no longer felt hot and swollen to the touch, he returned to the kitchen where Tyra was making herself at home, sitting at the table with a plate of food. "Ah, Oswin," she said with a smile. "I had wondered where you'd gone." She frowned. "You're almost as blue as I am! How long were you out there? Please, sit by the fire."

He did as she said, sitting in one of the kitchen chairs. Tyra scooted it closer to the hearth. "So, how do you know Calder?" he asked as she sat back down. As if he didn't know.

"I'm his wife!" she answered, grinning. "I'd given him up for dead, but a month or so ago, I sensed a spark of his magic, just a distant twinkle. I was floored. When the castle fell, I never would have imagined the fairies would have let him live. He must have cast quite a spell to travel as far as it did, but when I felt it, I immediately made arrangements to come here and see if he still lived. And as I got closer, I noticed his magic more and more."

"A powerful spell?" Oswin asked. "About a month ago?"

She nodded.

"He…linked two minds," he explained. It felt like it had happened an age ago. "My friend and his lover, who was poisoned and unable to speak."

Tyra raised her eyebrows, impressed. "Ah yes, I can see how a spell like that would ripple far." Her smile was bursting with pride. "I always knew his magic was a cut above the others' even before he'd started earning his mage's marks." She sighed wistfully, tucking her chin into her palm. "I was a fool to assume him dead. I was a coward, afraid to return here in case I met death at a fairy's hand. It's been seventy-four years since I've seen him, and now that I *know* he's alive, I still have to wait until sunset to look upon his true face. It's unbearable!"

"That must be terrible," Oswin said. He hoped she couldn't hear how flat his enthusiasm felt.

"Shall we kill the time together? I could spin a tale or two, and perhaps you can as well?"

Privately, Oswin wanted nothing to do with her, but it was only petty jealousy, and he put a smile on his face regardless. "That sounds lovely."

Tyra took a bottle from her belt pouch and set it on the table. It was dark green and glimmered with a strange light when it was moved. A cork was shoved far down into the neck, and the top was filled with black wax. "What is it?"

Tyra grinned, predatory and cruel. "I managed to capture one of the fairies with the help of my more magically inclined second," she explained, giving the bottle a shake. "One of the young ones. She was stupid."

Oswin watched the movement inside, almost like it was filled with starry jelly. "Don't fairies have forms like you and I?"

"Normally, yes, but they can be squished without killing them," Tyra explained. She put the bottle away.

And that was all she had to say about the bottle.

She moved on, telling him elvish tales of spirits and magic and gods. Oswin told her adventures he'd had as Wystan's voice and of human heroes.

The moment the sun set, Calder burst through the door, interrupting Oswin in the middle of a sentence, and threw his arms around Tyra and crushed their mouths together.

Oswin wished for the ability to vanish.

"Tyra," Calder said, voice choked with emotion. "I had thought you dead! I called out for you time and again, but I never sensed your spirit. How did you survive? Where have you been that you were out of my reach?"

Tyra explained how she and some of the other survivors had decided to give up this land and travel north to the lands of their ancestors. "There are wards to prevent any incursions, fairy or otherwise," she explained. "I wish I had come back for you! When we received word the keep had fallen..." She ran her hand over Calder's face. "Well, we didn't see any hope in finding survivors." Her expression grew forlorn, her eyes dropping to her hand where it sat on Calder's chest. "Were you able to bury him properly?" she asked softly. "I was haunted by the image of ravens feasting upon him." Her voice made Oswin's heart ache, and he realized she was asking about their son.

Calder held her hands tightly, touching their foreheads together. "Yes. I buried as many as I could, but he was the first."

"May I see him?"

So, the two went to the graveyard, leaving Oswin alone with the crackle of the fire.

Calder hadn't even said hello to him. He had been all but invisible. Unneeded. That knowledge sank into Oswin's stomach like a stone. Now that Calder had his wife back, what use was Oswin?

Free now from his guilt at leaving Calder alone, Oswin found it was suddenly easy to stand, to remove his coat from the hook near the door, and walk out to the road. For a long moment, he just stood there, staring into the woods that led to the city, back to the life he was supposed to be living.

He took one step forward, then another, then another, faster, ever faster, until he was running away as quickly as his legs could carry him, the burning of his body overpowering the ache of his heart.

He arrived in the city late that night, covered in snow and soaked nearly to the bone. The gatekeeper let him in almost without question. "Need help to the inn?" he asked in a worried voice, but Oswin shook his head.

"I know the city," he croaked. "I have a place to go."

The gatekeeper still looked worried, but he let him go.

It took a few tries to find the master's house since the snow made the city strange, but he eventually did and banged heavily on the door. Leofric, Eadburga's head of household, answered, clearly in the middle of getting ready for bed. He frowned at Oswin, his blond beard twitching as he tried to figure out where he'd seen Oswin before.

He gasped when he made the connection. "Mister Oswin, it's you! Master was worried when your things arrived without you. Are you all right? Please, come in out of the snow." He stood aside and waved Oswin inside. The smell of old wood and cloth made him think of Wystan. He hoped he hadn't worried his friend as well. Oswin decided to write him as soon as he was sure his fingers would thaw. "The young Lord Farnworth has been sending messages most insistently," Leofric continued, herding him over to a sofa by the fire before kneeling down to throw on a couple extra logs. "Can I get you anything? Mulled wine, perhaps?"

Oswin groaned, angry at himself for making Wystan anxious. What sort of friend was he? "That sounds amazing, please."

Leofric was remarkably quick about it, and soon there was a hot mug in his hands, warming his aching fingers. The wine went down smooth, warming his chest and stomach as well. When it was half-gone, Oswin sighed and settled deeper into the chair, staring at the fire.

"Are...you quite all right?" Leofric asked uncertainly. "Did something happen?"

"I was just a bit waylaid, is all. Chose to do a bit of exploring. Lost myself for a while." He sipped his wine. It was rapidly cooling despite the warm room. "But I've returned now."

"I'll prepare you a bed," Leofric said as he turned to leave, but Oswin waved for him to stay.

"You should go to sleep, Leofric. I know you'll be up before the sun. I'm plenty comfortable here, though a blanket would be appreciated."

"Well, if you're sure." But he seemed relieved. Leofric fetched him a blanket and bid him good night.

Oswin finished his wine and set the mug aside, then cocooned himself in the wool. It itched. He missed his furs.

He buried himself deeper. He regretted leaving so suddenly. Calder would worry. He would visit soon, he told himself, but the thought of seeing Calder and his wife there, happy to be together again at long last, made him feel as if he were back in the snowstorm.

He covered his head. The blanket smelled vaguely of perfume and dust, but he was exhausted enough that he fell asleep before too long, the half-full mug of wine going cold as he snored.

Leofric woke him in the morning for breakfast. Master Eadburga, already dressed and working on the morning's letters, greeted him as he entered the dining room. "Oswin!" she said warmly, rising to kiss his cheek. "It's been too long. We were expecting you over a week ago; what happened?"

Oswin gave her the same vague answer he'd given Leofric and sat at the table. Someone he didn't recognize set a plate of eggs down in front of him.

Master Eadburga tucked a lock of graying brown hair behind her ear and settled back into a businesslike demeanor. "Well then," she said. "You're welcome to return to the fold as a second of mine and live here. Or would you prefer my assistance in finding another permanent position?"

Oswin waved his hand. "It depends, I suppose. I've come to like this part of the kingdom, so I'd prefer not traveling too far, if possible." If he went too far away, he'd never be able to visit Calder.

If Calder still wanted to see him after the stupid stunt he'd pulled by running away.

He suppressed a sigh.

His old master peered at him with sharp gray eyes but didn't comment on what she saw. "Very well," she said, pawing through a stack of papers. "We have a local lord who's interviewing marriage candidates for his son. The son can't speak due to a problem with his throat and is a new student of mine, so he's rough but teachable. If the son likes you, he might decide to take you on permanently. He hasn't much liked the greener apprentices."

Oswin raised an eyebrow. "Any particular reason?"

Master Eadburga snorted. "From what the apprentices have said, he's a spoiled brat. The dislike is decidedly mutual."

"Great. Looking forward to it." Oswin hoped his voice conveyed his utter lack of enthusiasm.

"That's the spirit!" Master Eadburga grinned, deepening the laugh lines around her eyes and mouth. "You'll meet him at the Red Manor at ten o'clock. Do you need someone to show you the way?"

Oswin shook his head. "No, I remember where it is. I'll get going a little early just in case though."

"Good lad." She returned to her letters. As Oswin was about to leave, she said, "And, Oswin, remember you can talk to me should you need to. You were one of my first students. I daresay I might even call you family after enough wine." She winked.

He smiled. "I know, Master. Thank you."

Oswin groaned as he returned to the manor later that afternoon, silently cursing whichever apprentice or instructor had taught the little snot vulgar signs. Oswin had been hot faced with embarrassment every time he opened his mouth to translate the young lord's hands. The elder lord had at least apologized afterward and had given him a generous tip, so that was a small blessing.

Master Eadburga didn't seem surprised to hear his report. "So, he won't be getting engaged anytime soon?" she asked wryly.

"Not unless he finds a woman who doesn't mind his letching. He's worse than an old man, my lord."

The master laughed. "What kind of old man will he make, I wonder? Either way, dinner should be almost ready. You can meet the new apprentices."

There were six of them, four women and two men. Oswin was surprised.

"Noble ladies were uncomfortable with such an intimate companion being male, which I understand," Master Eadburga explained. "So, I made sure to seek out more female candidates."

Oswin was told all their names but promptly forgot them, lost to the raucousness of a full dinner table. They had come from many walks of life: some with deaf or mute relatives, others just with a knack for the sort of learning and teaching the job required. In addition to the apprentices, there were several people like Oswin, who had finished their studies and were now no longer apprentices. All together, the group was nearly fifteen people, all chattering and laughing and drinking.

Oswin felt a bit distant from them. It had been a long time since he had been a part of such a large affair. Dining with the Farnworths had been quiet, and even among the staff, people had generally kept to themselves. He found he could no longer remember how to handle such a boisterous dinner table. He finished his food and excused himself from the dining room, grabbing Leofric to show him to his bedroom.

"It's not ready yet, unfortunately," Leofric said apologetically. "You can go rejoin the others in the dining hall if you like."

Oswin shook his head. "Please, I'll help you ready it; it's no trouble."

So, he and Leofric beat the dust from the mattress and made the bed and swept the hearth together. Despite his advancing age, Leofric was as spry as Oswin remembered. "Are you... sure you're all right, Mister Oswin?" he asked, mind as sharp as Oswin remembered as well. "You seem a bit more melancholy than I recall."

"It's just age, my friend," Oswin said with a chuckle. "I'm almost thirty now. I think."

Leofric raised his eyebrows. "Oh, to be thirty again. Such tragedy."

"Oh, be quiet, old man." But Oswin was smiling.

Leofric pretended to be offended. "Such rudeness, young man! Why, when I was a boy, no one my age would have stood such disrespect. I'll just be on my way, and if you need anything, you most certainly *shouldn't* come to me." He winked and left, closing the door behind him. Oswin shook his head, smiling fondly before frowning.

He sat in front of his trunk, clicking open the latch and running his hands over his clothes and books. It was amazing everything he owned in the world fit in this one box. It was also amazing that he hadn't missed any of it while he was with Calder.

Rather than move everything into the chest of drawers against the wall, Oswin pushed the trunk to the foot of the bed. He hopefully wouldn't be staying here long, so unpacking and repacking would just be a waste of time.

He fished an old book of astronomy out of the bottom of the trunk and curled up in the bed. There was something soothing in reading about the heavens. It made Oswin feel as if he was a part of some greater purpose, that he was a necessary piece of the intricate balance of life. He might not have been religious, but a sense of purpose was its own reward.

The next few days were much the same. Daytime work in the city, followed by dinner with the whole gaggle of people who lived in the manor, then reading before bed. He found a book about the kingdom's history at a shop and spent a while reading about the petty dramas and squabbles of distant kings.

He tried to imagine how different the kingdom had been then, before the fairies had come from the west, when people knew about the elves' existence. When Calder had lived happily with his little family. He sighed as he marked the page and set the book aside, then settled into the pillows. He wondered how Calder was doing. Probably better than he had been in decades. Oswin covered his face. He should have said goodbye.

He blew out his candle and drew the curtains around him, settling into an uneasy sleep.

Days turned to weeks. He didn't go back to visit Calder. Winter came in earnest, snow piling so high that sometimes he couldn't even open the front door for the weight of it. Meals became repetitive as they turned to the preserved food in storage. The crowd of people went from occasionally annoying to unbearable.

Oswin spent as much time as he could holed up in his room with books. He missed spending this time of year with

Wystan. He had always made time go faster. Oswin imagined Wystan was enjoying spending the time with his lover. Was he even missed?

They had been exchanging letters but finding messengers to trek through the woods in heavy snow was both difficult and expensive.

Calder remained on his mind, lingering, refusing to be forgotten. Oswin's daydreams were fond of tormenting him with imaginings of Calder in bed with Tyra, sitting with her under the stars, eating his delicious food together and watching the snow pile up around them—hand in hand, perhaps, and sometimes more.

It was like worrying a rotten tooth. It hurt every time, but by God, he just kept doing it. He almost liked the hurt because it had been a long time since he had been so sincerely in love.

He sighed at that thought and closed the book he'd been staring at blankly for the past half hour. It was still early, just past supper, but he closed his eyes and fell asleep.

He dreamed of the field surrounding his mother's house. He dreamed of it often, to the point that seeing it allowed him to realize he was dreaming. He'd heard tales of people who could take control of the dream if they realized this, but for him, it just meant he could think about the dream while it occurred.

But nothing was happening, so Oswin lay down in the grass and stared up at the wispy white clouds drifting across the sky, watching as the world moved too quickly from day to night. A world of stars now glittered overhead, a full moon throwing shadows across the ground.

A soft rustling got Oswin's attention, and he sat up and looked out over the grass. Calder was walking toward him.

He swallowed, unsure of what to say as Calder sat beside him.

"I'm glad to see you well," Calder said after a long moment of silence. "When you vanished so abruptly, I worried."

Oswin's face burned with shame. "I'm sorry. I wasn't thinking. I should've said goodbye. I'm so sorry."

"Were you really only staying because you pitied the poor, lonely elf?" Calder asked in a low voice. His face was upturned to the moon, and Oswin was reminded of the tale told in light, how the night had poured her heart into her creations. Looking at Calder now, eyes and hair shining under the full moon, he could believe it.

Oswin looked away. "That wasn't the only reason," he mumbled. He couldn't deny some of his desire to stay came from pity, but he did like to think part of it was sincerely empathy. It had mostly been love though.

Calder sighed. "I feel childish for asking this, but what do you think of me? Truly?"

Had it not been a dream, Oswin couldn't have answered in the way he did. "I love you," he said frankly.

Calder turned to stare at him. "What?"

Oswin looked into his face, wishing this was reality, wishing he could speak plainly there instead of to figments of his imagination. "I love you as you love your wife. I wanted to stay with you because I like watching you, listening to you, learning more about you." He sighed and turned away, looking back at the ground. "But you are a loyal husband, probably more loyal than most. I can't force my heart upon you, and I wouldn't want to."

Silence hung between them until suddenly Calder grabbed Oswin's hand and pulled him up. "Come with me."

Oswin stammered. "What? Where are we going?"

Calder's voice was clipped as he dragged Oswin behind him, the surroundings no longer as familiar as they had been. "Do you remember what I did for the angel?" he asked. "Linking their mind with your friend's? I'm doing that now, but for the two of us."

"Wait, you're real? This is real?!" Oswin's voice came out in a squeak, and he was sure his embarrassment was luminous. "You're actually Calder? Not a version of my own making?"

"I am actually Calder," he said, turning briefly to smile at Oswin. "I sent my spirit to walk and seek you out. That spell is complex, but simpler than the one I'm going to do now." He took a deep breath. "But I do want to show you something."

They stopped before a huge castle, its stones midnight black, its towers stretching high into the night sky. It took Oswin a long moment to realize this was what the ruins had once been.

Calder walked toward it, but when Oswin tried to follow, he met an invisible wall. Calder turned and signed, *Wait*, before disappearing into the fortress.

Oswin did, trying to focus on the small burst of pleasure in his chest from the fact Calder had remembered the sign and not on what he had just done. He covered his face and groaned. "I just shouldn't talk to anything, it seems. Swans, dreams, nothing! I end up making a fool of myself."

There was a low rumble and a sound like a bubble popping but amplified a thousand times. Oswin stretched out his hand, and the wall was gone.

Before he reached the door, Calder was there. He was glowing. "Hurry," he said, his voice thin and rough. "It is very difficult to maintain this over distance."

Oswin followed Calder quickly into his mind, tried not to stop and stare at the finery the fortress had once held. The door *had* been gilded, and there were beautiful tapestries on the walls. The colors were so rich, they looked almost real.

Echoes of sounds surrounded them. Footsteps on stone, distant voices. Out of the corner of his eye, Oswin could see the shadows of people, walking to and fro in their daily business.

Calder's hand closed on his. "Hurry," he said again.

They made their way to the kitchen where the sounds suddenly ceased. Oswin turned back, hoping to see more, but they were only ruins, once again.

Tyra was leaning against the table. Through Calder's eyes, she was bigger, fiercer, and more beautiful than in life. Oswin swallowed.

As they approached, she began to speak, but it was clearly a continuance of a conversation. Oswin thought this was a memory.

"And once we've broken your curse, you'll come back with me. The tribe of Saxtain is small, but our kin are kind and welcoming. And I think you'll like Ingfred."

An echo of Calder's voice, deeper, more sonorous, filled the room. The lips of the Calder Oswin could see didn't move. "Ingfred? Who is that?"

Tyra tilted her head. "Did I not mention him yet? He's my new husband. One of our northern kin."

Calder's voice was strained. "New husband? For how long?"

"Perhaps sixty years or so?" She was so casual about it, like it meant nothing at all. "We have two daughters, Alvilda and Signe. Oh, the girls will just adore you."

At Oswin's side, Calder balled his hands into fists. His voice from the memory rang out. "I would have mourned you for centuries! Perhaps the rest of my life! And you barely mourned a decade before taking another?" The voice cracked, becoming small, betrayed. "Tyra…"

"Our clan was dying!" she said, frowning. "And you would have me spend the rest of my life alone? Grieving for a family I thought lost to war?" She came forward, filling the room even more than she had been. Her voice turned soft. "Calder, do you think I did not miss you? That I did not mourn? How long would you have had me wait to heal my heart?"

"Not the rest of your life, but at least the length of time we were together, Tyra!"

She sighed and stepped back, crossing her arms. "What would you have me do, Calder? Leave you once again? Still carrying that blasted curse?"

"No! But—" Calder's voice stopped. "But I would want to be the only one at your side, like before."

"I cannot give you that, Calder." She leaned against the table, her head down, jaw clenching when she wasn't speaking. "Our kinsfolk take multiple spouses, rather than simply sharing as we did. They are cousins to us, so their ways are similar but not the same. It is a burden we must bear since we rely on their grace for our continued survival. I will give you the title of first husband as is your right. Ingfred will understand. But my new family is just as important as you are. Surely you understand that? Would you have me abandon my children?" She glared at him, fire in her eyes. "I will not do that again."

There was a long silence. Calder's voice was soft when it came again. "I cannot do it. I cannot watch you be another man's wife. Watch you be mother to his children. I could not bear it."

Tyra stared at him for a long moment, her chin twitching with suppressed sobs. "Is there nothing I can do to change your mind?" She got off the table, walked toward where Calder must have been standing. "Despite what you must think, I do love you still, Calder. I was overjoyed to learn you were alive. I dropped *everything* and journeyed here with little rest. The other survivors thought me mad, but I *felt* you, Calder. I had to make sure, or I wouldn't have been able to live with myself."

She was close again, and Oswin could feel the room shudder with heavy heartbeats.

"I know," he said. This time, the true Calder spoke with the memory, his mouth tight and his eyes downturned. "But I cannot do it. I'm so sorry, Tyra."

As Oswin watched, she seemed to shrink and age. Wrinkles appeared around her eyes and mouth, a bit of acne scarring spread across her chin, and her nails became brittle and bitten. She went from an implacable goddess to oddly human, mortal. Vulnerable. No longer a perfect memory.

She sighed and sniffed, rubbing her eyes. "Then should I stay with you until your curse is broken? Perhaps if we work together, we could do it." She put her hand on his arm.

"No," Calder and the memory said together. "Return to your family. They need you."

Tyra looked at him for a long time, tears spilling down her cheeks, but when he said nothing, she lowered her head. "Very well. May the moon ever guide your path, Calder. I do not think we will meet again. But should you need refuge, come to the north. Our kin are kind. You have a home if you seek it."

She vanished. The room shifted, growing taller. Oswin wondered if Calder had fallen to his knees. Soft sobs filled the kitchen. Oswin's heart broke.

After a moment, there was a strange sensation like he was being pulled by an invisible force. He scrambled for Calder's hand, but he was pulled away, farther and farther until he was once again outside the castle and back behind the invisible wall.

Before his eyes, the scenery behind the wall faded to black, and then turned into more of the field from his memories. His memories alone. Calder's presence was gone.

Trapped once again in his own mind, Oswin stood in silence, his cheeks wet and cold. His own dreams came to haunt him— sad and painful dreams of empty houses and endless rain, of a begging bowl and the sharp knives of hunger. But throughout it all, Oswin held on to that kernel of lucidity, waiting to wake.

When he finally did, he immediately got out of bed and retrieved his traveling clothes. Outside the window, snow was falling, but Oswin paid it no mind.

He didn't know what he was doing, but he couldn't leave Calder alone. If there was ever a time that he would need a friend, it would be after the events of that memory. Oswin tried not to dwell too deeply on the meaning of Calder showing it to him right after his own confession of love. The hope fluttered like a songbird against its cage, poised to break either the cage or itself.

As he left the room, the halls were empty but for Leofric wiping down the kitchen counter. It was now well past sunset but not too close to morning. He must not have slept long.

Leofric turned as Oswin entered the room. "Can I assist you with anything?"

Oswin shook his head. "Tell Master something came up, and I had to leave."

Leofric dropped what he was doing. "Are you quite sane? It's been snowing for over an hour, and it's showing no sign of stopping. What possibly could not wait until morning, at the very least?"

But Oswin was already leaving. "It would be too long to explain; I have to go." The door clicked shut behind him, covering anything more Leofric had to say.

The snow was falling steadily, not quite slowly, not quite quickly. Plenty easy to navigate in; it would just make travel a little slower. Oswin fluffed his scarf up to cover his nose and walked out into the forest.

As he walked through the eerie quiet, broken only by the crunching of his footfalls, it began to snow harder. It was imperceptible at first, but soon the wind picked up, howling over his head, shaking more snow into the air as the trees creaked around him.

And then the world went white.

The blizzard roared up in a sudden swell, ice crusting over his eyelashes as he tried desperately to burrow deeper into his coat and scarf.

This had been a bad idea. Even in good weather, he likely wouldn't have arrived before dawn, and in this? Oswin couldn't see more than three feet in front of his nose. He had no idea in what direction he was going, where the path was, or how long it had been since he was warm.

His hands, clutched tightly under his arms, were numb to the bone, and his feet were nothing more than wet lumps of cold under his legs. Every breath hurt his chest with the chill, and the wind had set his lips bleeding, fleeting warmth soon swallowed up by overwhelming cold.

The oppressing dark of the clouds blocked out any idea of time. It could have been either day or night. Oswin didn't trust himself to make the distinction anymore.

All he could think was that if he stopped, he'd die.

So he pushed onward in whatever direction his feet were facing, hoping to find something, anything to take shelter in from the storm.

His boot hit a rock hidden in the snow, and he pitched forward over it, nearly braining himself on a dark stone.

The same dark stones that marked the old wall of the elven ruins. Oswin sat up, flinching into the wind as he looked around. He said a prayer of thanks for the first time in years, surprised he still remembered the words as he frog-marched up to the interior walls and to the kitchen, twinkling through the snow.

Oswin practically threw himself inside and sighed, eyes closed in bliss, as the warmth of the fire hit him, prickling into his frozen body. He stood there for a few minutes, just thawing, before opening his eyes and deciding to sit at the table.

But sprawled across it, surrounded by a small wall of dark bottles, was Calder.

Oswin jerked forward, wincing as his body creaked in protest as he scrambled to hold a hand in front of Calder's mouth.

Still breathing. Oswin thanked heaven.

It must've still been night. Or, more likely, he had been out in the cold for almost a day. No wonder he hurt all over. His hands were now clammy, the skin raw and pink as he rubbed them together to warm them faster. He sat down across from the sleeping Calder.

As his nose drained, he noticed the stench of alcohol. It grew stronger with each passing moment, searing Oswin's stinging nose. He grabbed one of the dark-brown bottles and brought it to his face before coughing immediately from the burn.

He wiped his watering eyes and stared at Calder. Stared intently, to make sure he could still see the steady rise and fall of his chest. Willing his aching muscles to move, Oswin got up, gathered up the bottles, and dumped them into the washing tub before getting on his knees to look up into Calder's face.

"Hey," he said, gently shaking his shoulder. "I think it'd be good to move you to a bed, okay?"

Calder snorted and shifted, his eyes fluttering open for only a moment, completely unfocused. He grumbled and flopped back across the table. Oswin thought idly about how pretty his hair looked like that, curled and messy and strewn over the dark wood, before getting an arm under Calder's and hauling him up.

"Come on; your bed is only a few feet that way. Let's get you there."

It was a blessing Calder was awake enough to take maybe 30 percent of his weight since Oswin didn't think he was strong enough to carry him. They stumbled into Calder's room, and Oswin lowered him to the bed, rolling him onto his side in case of vomiting. He wondered if elves even threw up in reaction to too much drinking, but it was better to be safe than sorry.

He covered Calder with the blanket and returned to the kitchen. What time was it? The bright white of the snow made it impossible to tell. At least it would make a good base for soup. If he could bring himself to dash outside and scoop some up.

It took him nearly twenty minutes to talk himself into doing it, but soon the swiftly melting snow was in a pot in the fire and Oswin was cutting up turnips and carrots to put into it once it started to boil. Every now and again, he peeked into Calder's room to check on him, but he was still sleeping it off.

Oswin sighed. How old was the memory Calder had shown him? Had he been drinking himself into a stupor every night since? Oswin frowned. No, he couldn't have been passed out drunk when he did that spell to find him. Maybe it had been the strain of the spell itself?

Guilt twisted in his chest, and he checked on Calder again. Still alive, still breathing.

Oswin braved the cold hallway to go back to his own room, but the furs had been removed and the room was empty but for the white of his breath. He returned to the kitchen, feeling out of place and uncomfortable.

Calder knew of his feelings now. What was he going to say when he woke?

Oswin didn't want to think about it. He focused on the soup and waited for Calder to come to.

He ended up napping at the table while the soup simmered. He was woken by a hand on his shoulder and stared up into Calder's face. He was exhausted, dark bags under his eyes, his cheeks hollow. "You're really here," he said in a soft voice. "I thought I'd dreamed it." He looked to the fire. "That smells good. I'll get you a bowl."

Oswin watched him move, looking for signs of a hangover, but Calder seemed fine. He pushed a bowl and spoon toward Oswin and sat, his eyes half-lidded as he looked at Oswin's face. Oswin swallowed and asked, "What time is it? The snow makes it impossible to tell. It seems too bright to be night."

"It's day," Calder said quietly.

It took a moment for the words to sink in. "But your curse?" Oswin asked tentatively.

"It's gone." He took Oswin's hand, brushing lightly over the knuckles. "Thank you."

Oswin's heart leapt into his throat. "Then you…?"

Calder smiled. "Yes."

Oswin swallowed again. It was too good to be true. Surely this was just because of his wife. After all, who else was there? Obviously, whatever Calder felt for him had been enough to end the curse, whatever conditions it'd had, but what could he truly see in Oswin himself besides an end to his misery?

The smile faded. "I thought you—" Calder clenched his jaw. His ears bobbed. "I thought you'd be happy."

Oswin buried his head in his hands. "I don't want to be just a replacement for your wife," he whispered. "I'm sorry. I'm selfish. Your curse is gone. You can find someone better suited to you, not just someone who's available."

Calder leaned back and sighed. "I understand," he said quietly. "I wouldn't trust me either."

"I trust you! I just—" He swallowed and his voice grew softer. "I don't see what there is to love about me." He dropped his head to the table and curled his arms around it.

Calder knelt beside him and reached up to free his face. "I understand you're afraid. To be frank, I am too. It has been a long time since I had anyone to love who was *here*. I'm not quite sure I remember how." He ran his fingers through Oswin's snow-damp hair, leaving it dry where his palm touched. "But I want to try, and I want to try with you. Is that…okay?"

Oswin met his eyes, sincere and shy. "Yeah. It's been…a long time for me too. I'm okay bumbling through this together if you are."

Calder smiled and held up his hand. Oswin took it and squeezed.

"We should eat though. Especially you. Why did you drink so much?"

Calder nodded and returned to his seat. "I had an awful headache after that spell. I needed something to take the edge off, and when dawn came and I was still here and normal, I drank to celebrate." He frowned. "And then celebration turned into depression that I was celebrating alone, and the drinking just kind of continued from there."

Oswin held up his bowl. "Celebratory soup then?"

Calder laughed and mimicked him. "Celebratory soup it is."

Personally, Oswin believed Calder would have made it better, but Calder wasn't complaining, so Oswin decided he wouldn't either.

After they ate, they went to Calder's bedroom, and Oswin curled up against Calder's chest, enjoying the feeling of being held and the sound of Calder's heartbeat. Calder stroked his hair, scraping lightly against his scalp, making him shiver. Oswin got his hands into Calder's hair too, twirling it around his fingers. And when Oswin looked up into Calder's face, the kiss happened naturally, just a continuation of what they had been doing.

At even that soft contact, Oswin's lips burned—thanks to their numerous splits from the cold. Calder pulled away and dug a canine into his lower lip, drawing blood. Before Oswin could ask what he was doing, Calder was kissing him again. The blood was warm and wet, and where it touched, the pain eased.

Calder pulled away. "Blood is best for healing wounds," he explained nervously. "Saliva and tears also work, given time, but blood is the quickest and most effective." He ran his tongue over the cut.

Oswin licked his lips in response. They tasted metallic but also slightly sweet. "Thank you." He leaned forward to peck Calder on the nose. "I appreciate it."

Calder looked relieved. "You're welcome."

Oswin drew closer and straddled Calder's hips, then pressed their chests together as he eased Calder back onto the bed. "I'm happy they don't hurt anymore, because it means we can do this right." He swallowed Calder's mouth with his, proud of the soft moan he got in return.

For some time, they kissed like that, then napped, wrapped up in each other, neither one sure where the other began and ended. And when they woke in early evening, they spent a long moment just looking at each other.

"What will you do now?" Oswin asked after a while. "Is there anywhere you'd like to go?"

Calder shifted uncomfortably, curling his legs around Oswin's as they rested their foreheads together. "I don't know. For all that I've longed to be free of these ruins, I don't know where I would go." He frowned. "I won't meet my kin. I won't see her."

Oswin didn't need to ask who *she* was. He stroked Calder's neck and shoulder. "You could come back with me? We could get a house in town. I'm sure you could find work as a cook. You know, you could probably even be Master's cook. I'm sure Leofric would like a break from it. He's getting up there in years."

Calder smirked. "Well, so am I."

Oswin snorted and poked his chest. "You are different." Oh hello, depressing thoughts about how slowly Calder would age in comparison to himself. *You were easier to ignore when this relationship was impossible.*

Calder seemed to sense his shift in mood and pulled him closer. "Help me decide my human disguise then."

For all the looks Calder could imitate, in the end they decided on something that wouldn't draw attention: spotty farmer's skin and sandy-blond hair with tawny eyes that were striking without being supernatural. The scars and marks on his cheeks faded until they could barely be seen.

Looking into this stranger's face, Oswin felt a bit lonely. But his kisses were sweet, and his voice was familiar, so he knew it would just take getting used to.

They stayed in the ruins until the road through the woods was passable once again. Master Eadburga was happy to see Oswin in one piece and to meet his "friend," especially after she tasted his cooking.

It was remarkably easy to find a house in town; Master Eadburga was a solid vouch of character. It wasn't large, but it was comfortable. Oswin found he didn't miss the servants. His privacy was much preferred.

He still interpreted for the mute and deaf, working in parallel with Master Eadburga. He built himself a small collection of repeat clients and made something of a reputation for himself as support for teachers and tutors with their charges. He'd gotten plenty of practice with Wystan and his tutors, after all.

And when spring came, Calder and Oswin journeyed back to the ruins to visit the graves.

The tree over Calder's son's grave was the same as Oswin had seen before, but beneath it, waving in the warm breeze, was a thicket of daffodils. Calder knelt and ran his fingers over one of them, smiling even as tears gathered in his eyes.

Oswin crouched beside him. "Did you do this?"

Calder took his hand. "No. They are a sign a child's soul has been reborn."

They spent the afternoon there, the oppressive atmosphere from before no longer present. The sky was blue, all the trees were flowering, and the air was sweet with the scent of daffodils.

And Oswin knew, no matter what the future had to bring, whether it was angels or devils or fairies, everything was going to turn out okay.

The Fairy's Gift

Once upon a time, there was a prince born with a maiden's heart.

It is not a strange occurrence, really. It happens every day. But the tale of this maiden is long.

It begins, as many stories do, with a villain. This one was known in the kingdom of Celles as the Dark Fairy. She was known to be wicked and very, very vengeful.

So, when a blessing from heaven allowed the long-barren queen of Celles to give birth to a healthy child, it should have been known to the king that to not invite the Dark Fairy to the child's naming was to invite ruin into his home. But the king was stubborn and arrogant. And so, the baby's naming came, and the Dark Fairy did not receive an invitation.

The other local fairies did, and three of them attended. One was a senior fairy dressed in gold. The second was younger and in silver. Third was a young fairy, almost a child herself, in a plain dress, adorned only with flowers in her hair. They all had the strangeness to them that marked the fey: while beautiful by all accounts, their faces were blank as a barn owl's—beautiful, but cold.

The baby slept through most of the ceremony, waking only toward the end when it was time for the guests to present gifts to the new heir.

Most of the guests were nobles from nearby kingdoms, so their gifts were expensive and utterly useless to a child. But it was the gifts of the fey that most had come to see.

The eldest fairy stepped up to where the queen stood, her baby in her arms. The fairy touched the child's head and said, "Little prince, you will be strong in the field of battle. No blade shall long be foreign in your hand, and your feet will be quick and swift."

Light flashed and faded, and the first gift was given.

The second fairy followed, placing her hand on the infant's head. She said, "Little prince, you will have a gifted tongue and a mind for diplomacy. Your voice will bend the ear of all who can listen. But you will use this talent with honesty and integrity."

Another flash in the candlelit room, and the second gift was given.

But as the third fairy prepared to step forward, the room was suddenly thrown into darkness, all torches snuffed out in a single moment.

Some of the guests screamed. When the torches were relit by the servants, the nobles all scrambled from the center of the room like water from oil—for the Dark Fairy now stood in the room.

"I do hope I'm not late." Her voice was silky smooth, like the belly of a snake, but her tone was as sharp as its fangs. "I'm afraid I never received my invitation."

The king stepped in front of his wife and child, putting on a show of bravado that was betrayed by the trembling of the hand on his sword hilt. "You were not sent one. You are not welcome here."

She frowned, pursing lovely, deadly lips in a mockery of disappointment. "Oh, dear. I have made a terrible mistake. It's too bad, you see, for I, too, brought the child a gift."

The king made to strike her but found his feet were stuck fast to the floor. The queen tried to run, but she was also unable to move. The Dark Fairy glided up the steps, looking down at the child.

She stroked a single finger across the baby's forehead, smiling as the young maiden fussed. "Little prince, it is important you know the place into which you have been born, and for you to act in a way that is fitting for a prince. Should you touch the marks of women's work—spindle, cookpot, or wailing child—before the age of eighteen, you, too, shall become one."

And as the queen cried, light flashed through the room, burning the eyes of all in attendance. When the light faded, the Dark Fairy was gone, and the curse was laid.

When the fairy departed, so, too, did the spells keeping the king and queen in place. They held the child between them, crying as they imagined trying to keep the child away from all the things the fairy had named, lest they lose the heir to their kingdom.

The third fairy, the one unadorned, stepped forward quietly. "Your Majesties," she said. "If I may, I have yet to give my gift."

"Can you undo the curse that has been brought upon our son?" the king asked with desperation in his voice.

The fairy shook her head. "I have not the power to remove or change the spell as it has been laid. However, I could add to it."

The king spat. "And what good will that do?" he demanded. "My son will still be cursed!"

The elder fairies' eyes flashed at the treatment of the young one, and before the king could speak again, the queen laid a hand on his chest to calm him. "What can you do?" she asked politely.

"I can change its permanence," the fairy explained, and she rested a gentle hand on the child's forehead. "Little prince, should the fairy's spell come to fruition, do not despair, for the kiss of true love freely given shall restore your true form."

A flash of light and the third gift was given.

The king and queen thanked the fairy for her help and turned to the gathered guests.

"Though a dark cloud has passed overhead on this joyous day, let us not give into its darkness," the king said. "Let us welcome instead Crown Prince Wynn of Celles!"

When Wynn was five years old, her parents had her betrothed. The girl's name was Catrin, and she was a prissy snob in Wynn's opinion. When Wynn would hunt frogs in the garden or chase lizards, Catrin would whine and turn up her piggish little nose and refuse to take part in such "unladylike" activities.

Wynn only shrugged and continued her playing. She wondered why her parents let her do so if it was so unladylike. Maybe her parents were just better than Catrin's.

By the time Wynn was seven, she had realized most people looked at her and saw a boy. It was an uncomfortable realization.

Whenever she tried to correct her parents, using the polite tones they had taught her, they grew so upset and afraid that Wynn could never bring herself to yell at them properly. It didn't stop it from hurting every time they talked about "handsome" she was, how she'd one day make a "fine man and king."

Still, she filched Catrin's dresses when she could and smiled at her reflection. Her hair was unfashionably short for a young lady, but that was all right. She was a princess, so she set the trends. Soon all the women would have their hair short, and Wynn would go from princess to fashion goddess.

She giggled at the thought.

When Wynn was ten, she learned it was easy to sneak out of the palace when dressed as a servant girl. No one glanced twice at a servant girl, so long as she looked busy.

She had never been allowed to leave the palace before, so the town was overwhelming at first and scary. It was full of strange sights and sounds, but the blacksmith's son took her under his sooty wing and showed her how children had fun in such a place.

When Wynn was twelve, he was her first kiss.

At age fourteen, Wynn's voice began to change. Now, her delicate voice was gone, replaced by a deepening rasp that disturbed her when it came from her throat. She adopted a soft falsetto as best she could, but it fell like tin against her ear, and the once-loquacious Wynn fell quiet.

One rainy day, as Wynn sat in the library reading, Catrin came and settled onto the couch beside her. "Your parents asked me to see if you were all right," she said. Her voice was still melodic and sweet, and Wynn could see the beginnings of a real bosom on her frame. Her hair was long, the brown of autumn leaves, red where the candlelight struck it.

Wynn was seized by a sudden urge to cry. She realized she would never look as Catrin did. No. Her face would continue to slim down. Her jawline would harden. A beard would grow like a fungus across her lips and down her neck, and she would not be able to wear dresses anymore without being known to all. Her father was a tall man, thin and knobbly, and surely, she would be too.

"I'm fine," Wynn whispered in her cracked falsetto. "Just tired is all."

On a day not long after that realization, Wynn promised herself one last adventure. She donned servant's garb, tying the bonnet neatly over her head so people wouldn't recognize her, and brushed out the skirt of the plain brown dress. She stared at herself in the mirror, light-brown eyes wide and sad as she did so.

She could see where her chin was beginning to jut out from the shrinking baby fat of her face. Could see the looming ghosts of sideburns along her temples.

With a sigh, she covered the mirror, then ducked through the servants' door, and made her way down and out of the castle.

Shortly after they had kissed, she and the blacksmith's son had stopped seeing each other. She hadn't thought about it much in the last few years, but on this, her last day in the town as Wynn the servant girl, she was suddenly full of nostalgia.

She decided to pass the smithy. He was inside, his muscled arms slick with sweat as he pounded relentlessly on a red-hot sword blade. Wynn admired him for a moment, then moved on, seeing other children she recognized. However, they were no longer really children, but young adults, doing adult work, without any time for youthful games.

Wynn sighed and kept walking. Caught up in her thoughts, she suddenly found that she had wandered far from the main street and was weaving through unfamiliar houses and buildings. She spotted an old woman sitting on a porch, a spinning wheel before her. Wynn had only seen those in illustrated books about the history of such devices, never in person. Her tutors had always warned they were dangerous, but the old woman seemed safe as she worked, her foot tapping in a gentle rhythm to make the wheel spin.

Meaning to ask the way back to the town square, Wynn approached.

"Hello, child," the woman said in a kindly voice. "Would you like to watch me spin?"

Wynn nodded, walked closer, and stepped up onto the porch.

The old woman smiled, her wrinkles casting strange shadows on her face. "Could you fix the spindle, dear? I think it may be falling off."

Wynn nodded again and grabbed hold. But before she could move it back into place, she dropped it in shock. The wood had *burned* and was still burning, searing up her arm and across her chest and up her neck, and oh God, it *hurt, it hurt, it hurt.*

She blacked out and awoke on the ground, not even two houses from the main street. She ached all over. When she went to stand, she stumbled. Her balance was off. God, she felt so strange. She looked down to see if she was standing on a hillock of some sort and was shocked at what she saw.

Hands trembling, Wynn touched the soft mounds on her chest, wincing at their tenderness. With trepidation, she pressed against the skirt near her hips, startling when she didn't find what she had been expecting.

She ran her hands over the smooth softness of her face, feeling no hint of the sideburns she had seen just that morning, nor the rough pores that heralded the onset of her beard.

Her neck was soft and flat under her fingertips.

Surprising even herself, Wynn cried fat, happy tears that were joined by joyful laughter.

Running home as fast as her legs could carry her, Wynn dashed up to her room and opened the locked chest that held her treasure trove of dresses taken from Catrin's room. She found a pale yellow one with a pattern of roses embroidered on the bodice.

Fingers impatient, she tugged at the bodice strings, grinning as they cinched tight, hugging new curves. She took a flower from one of the indoor plants and wove it into her short brown hair, then admired her reflection.

She was *herself*. The self she had seen in dreams. The self that lived in her subconscious.

After picking imagined dust off the shoulders and putting on slippers that were slightly too small, Wynn left her room through the main door and grinned at every servant she passed on her way to the dining hall for dinner.

But her joyful mood was quickly soured by her parents' reaction upon seeing her.

The queen gasped and knocked her wineglass to the floor with a crash before throwing herself at her husband in a fit of sobbing. The king was somber, his deep-set eyes mournful and afraid. "Oh, my son," he groaned. "What has become of you?"

Wynn hesitated. "I…have become myself. I had hoped you would be happy for me."

"Happy that our kingdom has been doomed?" The king's voice was hollow and sad. "Now there is no one of the proper blood to sit upon the throne. Unless…" The king perked up. "Quickly, fetch Lady Catrin!" he yelled to one of the guards. "A kiss from her will set my son to rights again. Quickly!" The guard was already gone.

Catrin would turn her back? Had that been why they'd been betrothed so early? Had her parents been *expecting* this to happen?! Wynn yelled in shock and fear. "No! You can't make me change back, *no!*"

"Wynn!" the king yelled, but already she had dived through the servants' door and was scrambling up the narrow stairs as quickly as she could, leaving the too-small slippers behind.

Upon coming to her room, she tossed on her boots, threw some gold and the small trove of jewelry she'd nicked over the years into her hunting bag, and ran through the hidden door and followed the paths out into the garden. From there, she went through the side gate. She could hear the guards bumbling around, but they were looking for Prince Wynn, not a mousy girl in a yellow dress.

She ran and ran through the castle town and out the front gate. The guards on watch duty let her go, for they did not yet know they would be asked to stop her. Or perhaps they did not recognize her.

It was spring, and the fields were freshly planted. Peasants looked up as she ran by but paid her no real mind. *The forest*, she thought. *I'll lose them in the forest.*

The woods grew dark quickly after sunset, and if they intended to bring Catrin with them in their search, they certainly wouldn't get far without her whining and making them turn back. She was almost proud of her fiancée in that moment.

She wandered until she saw a light. Wynn tried not to think about the old stories about strange lights in dark woods, thinking of redcaps and ghosts, but the light was nothing more than a cabin. Its windows glowed with the firelight inside.

Outside hung animal skins of all shapes and sizes, so perhaps the inhabitant was a huntsman. Putting on her sweetest smile, Wynn knocked at the door.

The man who appeared was large, nearly twice the width of Wynn, with an impressive black beard. His eyes were heavy—they were eyes that had seen much of the world.

Wynn bobbed a curtsy. "Good evening, sir. I am a traveler seeking shelter for the night. Could I perhaps have a corner of your cabin? Or else permission to sleep outside it?" She tried to resist the urge to squirm with joy at how her voice didn't crack and turn suddenly deep.

"Come in, come in," the man said, opening the door wider. "You're hardly dressed for the woods. Running away from your parents, lass?"

Wynn nodded but did not elaborate. The huntsman didn't ask anything further. He pulled a heavy skin from off a chair and laid it out on the floor near the fireplace. Perhaps once it had been a bear. When she lay down on it, she was surprised at the softness of it against her skin and how much her feet ached.

"Would you like something to eat? There is plenty of stew left."

Wynn's stomach growled in answer, and she blushed.

The huntsman smiled and fetched a bowl, then spooned the thick brown liquid into it. He handed it to Wynn as she sat up. Wynn drank it quickly, gasping at the heat but too hungry to slow down.

She looked around the cottage. It was small but neatly kept. Animal pelts were stacked in one corner, and others hung from the walls. Wynn admired a particularly large wolf over the fireplace.

The huntsman followed her gaze. "I see you noticed the wolf," he said. "There's a story there, if you'd like me to tell it."

Wynn fetched herself more stew. "I'd love to hear it."

"That wolf stalked these woods not too many years ago. Had a taste for human flesh and a mind for trickery. One day, he tricked a little girl into telling him where her grandmother lived. Upon arriving there, he devoured the grandmother and took her place in the bed. When the little girl arrived, he masqueraded as the old woman long enough for the girl to approach, then, *gulp*, he swallowed her up too.

"I was nearby and heard the girl scream. I burst in and cut the wolf clean open, and the girl and her grandmother were able to escape unharmed."

Wynn was skeptical, but when she looked at the wolf pelt on the wall, it seemed more plausible than not. "You're quite the hero," Wynn said admiringly.

But the huntsman only frowned at her words. "I'm no hero, but I try to help where I can. In the past, I was... Well, let's just say there are things I'm not proud of." His tired eyes fell upon a sword leaning against the mantel, the elaborate filigree on the scabbard out of place in the simple cabin.

Wynn glanced between him and the blade. "What happened? If you don't mind the tale."

"Allow me to be brief with the detail," he said quietly. "When I was young, I lived in a country across the sea to the west. There, the kingdom was ruled by a witch-queen who was very powerful. The king was little more than her puppet, to do with as she willed.

"The queen was vain, so when she heard tell that a young woman lived in the kingdom who was more beautiful than herself, the queen bade me go and kill the girl, so that she could claim her heart. She gave me that blade as payment. Said it was fey craft. Though I doubt she spoke true, for fey cannot touch iron."

His head fell as he looked down at his feet, elbows resting on his splayed knees as his curled fingertips trembled. "I almost did it. I almost took that sweet girl's life. But at the last minute, I fled. I crossed the sea and prayed she wouldn't find me. Later, I learned the queen had been usurped and executed. And that night, I slept well for the first time in over five years."

He let out a shaky sigh. "Forgive me! I don't know why I agreed to tell you that horrible tale. Perhaps it is a sign I needed to get it out of me, and let it fade." He rubbed his eyes. "If you do not have a weapon, I suggest you take it. Let it protect you from the dangers in the world. Oh, what am I saying? You are a noble lady; surely you don't know the sword."

But Wynn was standing, holding the blade in one hand. It was perfectly balanced, an extension of her arm. The hilt was warm and secure in her grip. "I know the sword well enough," she said. "I would gladly take it and free you from the burden of its memories."

The huntsman nodded. "Then it is yours."

Wynn clicked it into the scabbard and set it down beside her bag. "Thank you. I appreciate both your gift and your hospitality."

"And I your company. But let us sleep now and talk no more of such darkness."

He gave Wynn a blanket, and she settled down on the bearskin, quickly falling asleep to the sound of the crackling fire and the gentle breathing of the huntsman.

She woke to the baying of dogs. The huntsman was squinting out the window, looking perplexed. "Those are the royal dogs, but I haven't heard anything about a hunt."

Wynn gathered up her things. "I'm sorry. Do you perhaps have a sword belt I could have? I've nowhere to keep the blade, and I really must be going."

After turning from the window, the huntsman found an old belt with a sword loop. "Will this do?" he asked.

Wynn wrapped it around her waist, cinching it as tightly as it would go. "Yes, it will suit just fine. Thank you." She slid the sword into place at her hip.

"Do you want some food before you depart?" the huntsman asked.

Wynn accepted some bread and jerky and then insisted on leaving. "I thank you much for your hospitality and generosity," she said warmly, despite the panic fluttering in her chest at every bark that echoed through the trees. "Could you point me in the direction of the nearest port?"

He pointed where she needed to go and gave her markers to look for. Pressing a plain gold ring into his hand, she thanked him once more for his kindness and then ran headlong into the trees.

The dogs were moving more slowly than usual. Wynn smiled at the image in her head of Catrin being the cause.

"What do you mean I need to dismount? Do you think I'm stepping in that muck?!"

She laughed and slowed to a jog, then a walk as the sounds grew further and further away. As the sun rose and then sank in the sky, a breeze stirred up leaves overhead and carried with it the scent of salt.

Full of excitement, Wynn started to run again, ignoring the protesting in her legs until she skidded to a stop, her body frozen in awe.

The trees had abruptly ended, revealing a tall cliff overlooking the vast sea. The night was quickly approaching, and the sky was nearly black, the line where it met the water blurry and uncertain, a world of stars twinkling both above and below.

The wind kissed her face, and the waves crashed in a steady rhythm below her. She didn't think she had ever seen a sight so beautiful. And so peaceful.

When she looked toward the south, she saw a town before the cliff. It sat near a low-lying beach, tucked away behind gray stone walls with white-sailed ships coming into dock for the night. The cliff she was on met the ground up that way, and surely one of those ships could carry her away to a place where even the most intelligent of dogs wouldn't be able to find her.

So she stretched her arms and legs, took in the view one last time, and started walking once again.

Three emerald-and-pearl bracelets got her a ride to the mainland. She was sad to see them go; white and green was one her favorite color combinations, but it was more important for her to be away than accessorized. The man was a merchant, with a thick moustache and an unsettlingly chipper attitude, but Wynn would have rather dealt with him than with her parents any day.

The port town was small, basically just a transition point for goods to go from the mainland to the cities of Celles and its southern neighbor Saxtain. But she was able to spend the night at an inn, in a proper bed, even if it was not the soft goose-down mattress she was accustomed to.

The morning came bright and early, and she, the merchant, and his crew departed.

The sea went on forever, it seemed, glittering like the most precious of gems in the sunlight. The crew largely ignored her, murmuring about it being bad luck to bring a woman on board and crossing themselves when they caught her eye. But she was almost glad for their superstition if only because it meant they really and truly saw a woman in her face. And were willing to leave her be to think about what she would do next.

The journey took only two days, and the sea was calm throughout. Still unsure of what to do upon arriving in this new land, Wynn consulted the merchant.

"I would go to the capital," he said. "Plenty of work there, especially if you know your way around a noble household."

Well, Wynn certainly did, though she suspected he meant in more of a servile way. She didn't know if such a job would suit her, but lacking any better ideas, she decided to take his advice.

"Pleasure doing business with you, miss," the merchant said with a small bow. "Don't nick your new master's possessions like the last, aye?" He laughed at his own joke and returned to overseeing the unloading of his ship.

Wynn didn't know how to feel that he'd thought her a thief, but she supposed a dirty girl in a shabby dress (for the forest had not been kind to the delicate fabrics) with a bag of gold trinkets struck others more as a thieving servant than as a runaway princess.

Trying to put the discomfort out of her mind, Wynn got directions from an innkeeper, bought some provisions at the market, and hitched a ride with a coach driver for a mere set of single-stone earrings. "I'm not going to the capital," he explained as they departed. Wynn was perched beside him on the seat, the client tucked away within. "But I am going halfway. I don't think you should go to the capital either, miss."

"Why is that?"

"Strange rumors." He looked out at the horses in front of him. "They say all the inhabitants are dead. Or perhaps turned to stone. Or even spirited away. Whatever the cause, anyone who has gone to the capital in recent weeks has not returned."

Now her curiosity was piqued. Rather than settle down at a boring job, why didn't she try to figure out the mystery? Surely if she were able to save a kingdom's largest city, she wouldn't even need a job. Perhaps she'd be knighted and given land and a manor. That would be nice to write to her parents. *After you rejected my true self, I left and became a knight. I now have a fancy house to call my own. No need to come visit.*

"I still think I shall go," she told the driver.

He shook his head. "I cannot stop you, but I do hope you change your mind soon."

Wynn bid the man goodbye and walked the cobbled road toward the capital. It soon led her into a wood. The travel was pleasant in the spring; the trees lush and green, and the sky baby blue where it winked through the foliage.

As she stopped to take some lunch, Wynn looked up at the canopy and was startled to see a tower. A single tower, unattached to any castle she could see. Figuring it would be easy enough to make it back to the road, Wynn finished her food and began walking toward it.

When she got close enough to see it truly was just a single tower alone in the forest, there was a scream and a figure fell from the top, down into the bushes below. Wynn moved to go and help whoever it was, but a black bird fell from the sky, turning into a woman-shaped creature.

She loomed over the bushes where the person had fallen, a grin evident in her voice.

"Poor prince," she said, her voice eerily familiar, though Wynn couldn't place it. "Your damsel is long gone. I meant to punish you further, but—" She laughed, the sound making the hair on the back of Wynn's neck rise. "—it looks like the thorns have done that for me. I just love it when planning works out, don't you?"

The prince groaned. "Rapunzel," he croaked.

"No Rapunzels for naughty princes who stick their noses where they don't belong," the woman said, her singsongy voice cutting through Wynn's chest like a knife. "Ta-ta, little prince. Good luck in your search; you're going to need it."

With one final echoing laugh, she vanished into thin air.

After waiting a moment to see if she would return, Wynn ran forward out of the trees, toward the thorn bushes where the prince lay. Blood oozed from his closed eyes, and his leg was definitely not supposed to be bending in that direction.

He turned at the sound of Wynn's footsteps. "Who's there?" he demanded. His voice was strained and tired. He was trying to sound intimidating, Wynn was sure.

"Just a traveler," Wynn said soothingly. She knelt next to him and took his hand. "Do you know of a place nearby I could take you?"

The prince frowned unhappily. "Yes. My horse should be tethered somewhere north of here. Can you get her?"

"Of course, Your Highness," Wynn said. She looked to the sun to find west, then set off toward the northern trees. The horse was easy to find, a fine white mare foraging through the underbrush, tied with a long rope to a low-branched tree. She was sturdy but pretty. Well-suited to a royal who did a lot of traveling.

She untied the mare and led her back to her master. The horse stood patiently while Wynn helped him up and into a sort of sidesaddle position, so he didn't have to use his leg. "The town is to the west. Follow the road," he said.

Wynn nodded, but then remembered he likely couldn't see anything through the blood that still beaded up in droplets from behind his brown lashes. "Understood, Your Highness."

She led the mare by her reins to the road and continued the journey.

Uninjured the prince would be quite handsome. His hair was short and honey blond, accented by darker brows, giving him interesting coloring. He had the freckled, sun-scarred face of someone who spent a lot of time on horseback, and the hands clutching the horse's bridle were large and square with clean fingernails.

"May I ask your name, Highness?" she asked.

"I'm Franz, son of Albrecht, Prince of Deurich. Forgive my rudeness. And your name, miss?"

"Just Wynn is fine, Your Highness."

"Wynn. An interesting name. You've come far from your island. And you've been educated, to speak this tongue so fluently." They were indeed speaking the language of nobility, necessary for any prince to know for diplomacy's sake. "I swear I've heard the name before." Franz frowned again.

"It's not an uncommon name there," Wynn said before he could draw any unnecessary conclusions. "And my education is mostly by listening." Surely it was not completely unknown for servants to learn the high speech just by hearing it spoken?

"Ah, I see," Franz said. "A servant, then, though one from a good family."

"You're a very good guesser," Wynn said, hoping her voice didn't reveal her relief. "Who is Rapunzel?"

Franz sighed heavily. "She is my princess, my love, my life. She was trapped in that tower by an evil witch, forced to use her hair as the witch's rope up into the tower, despite the evil creature being able to fly."

Franz recounted their meeting and subsequent romance, waxing poetic about Rapunzel's beautiful voice and heart. Then how the witch had tricked him with the shorn locks, throwing him from the tower into the thorn bushes below.

"I hope she's all right," Wynn said.

Franz squeezed the horse's bridle tightly, his expression determined. "I will find her. I swear it on my life. As long as I draw breath, I will seek her."

"But you don't know where to start," Wynn said. "And what if your sight does not return?"

"It doesn't matter. No matter how difficult my search may be, I will not rest until I know she is safe and free from that witch's claws."

Wynn didn't know whether that was terribly romantic or terribly stupid. She hoped he was not next in line for the throne, if he was so willing to throw his life away for the love of a woman.

Wynn frowned. She herself was in line for the throne or had been. Was she making the right choice herself?

Franz was quiet now, the color fading from his cheeks as he bled.

Wynn picked up the pace, pushing introspective thoughts aside for the time being. Franz needed a doctor—everything else could wait.

"I don't think your sight will return, Highness," the doctor said wearily, dabbing his forehead with a sigh. "Your eyes have been severely damaged, nearly shredded, really. Your leg, however, just needs time and rest. You are, of course, free to stay here in my home while it heals. Who knows, by the grace of God, your sight may recover."

Franz groaned. "How long am I to be stuck here?"

"Two months at the least, Your Highness."

"Two months? But my sweet Rapunzel needs me!" He flailed as the doctor wrapped bandages over his eyes.

Wynn reached out to steady him. "Your Highness, if she survived the witch's clutches for a lifetime, she can handle them for another few months. You'll do her no good in this state."

The doctor pinned the cloth and let Franz fall back onto the pillows. "I'm to go insane," he lamented.

Wynn patted his arm. "I have an idea," she said. "I'm currently en route to the capital. I bet I could find a friendly sorcerer who could help you track down your Rapunzel. Then, the minute you're recovered, you can go and rescue her."

Franz frowned. "There have been evil rumors about the capital as of late. I could not in good conscience send a lady there on an errand of mine."

Wynn stood up from her chair, brushing dust from her skirt. It was a hopeless cause, but it felt good to have a goal again. "Good thing I'm not a lady but a servant. Consider it not an errand, but a favor done for a friend."

Franz didn't seem happy. "Very well, but let me tell you this. One of the stories I've heard is the capital is besieged with fairy magic. Fairies are extremely powerful, and evil fairies even more so. However, this makes them arrogant. They will underestimate you. An iron blade forged with their own magic can kill them. I know not where you could find such a blade, but if there is a place where you could find one, it would be the capital. Stay safe and return alive."

"Thank you, Your Highness." Wynn gripped the sword at her hip. What luck she happened to have a sword of that nature already. Truly, it seemed *too* lucky. She bid the prince goodbye and returned outside. She tilted her head up toward the heavens and crossed herself. "If there is an angel watching over me," she said quietly, "I ask that you continue to do so until my purpose is fulfilled."

And then she put herself back on the road and continued walking.

A long the way, several days later, she was accosted by highwaymen. The three men leered at her with mouths of broken and missing teeth, demanding she hand over her bag. At first, she was terrified, but when she touched the sword hilt, a spike of courage shot through her.

She had never lost a duel to any of the pages at the castle that lay a lifetime behind her. And she had even bested some of the lesser knights. So, she drew her sword and dropped into a comfortable stance. "You want my bag?" she asked. "Well, then, you're going to have to take it."

One of them was carrying a stolen shield, the crest of whatever castle it came from chipped and peeling off, but it was a simple enough matter to attack him first and steal it for herself. Armed now with sword and shield, able to use familiar forms, she dispatched the other two easily, running them off into the woods. She sighed as she noted the bodice of her dress had torn at the seams. Well, it was a wonder it had lasted so long anyway. It was nice to be able to breathe more easily, at least.

Wynn tied the shield to her back and ran the bottom of her ragged skirt over the sword's blade, removing the blood, before sliding it into its scabbard.

She was wary the rest of her journey, but whether because those men had warned their friends or just because there were few people taking the roads, Wynn encountered no one else until she reached the outer walls of the capital.

At first, everything appeared normal. The sun was warm, and the sky was blue with puffy white clouds scattered throughout. Birds sang. Bees buzzed through a cluster of wildflowers.

But that was when she realized she was standing at the gate of a large city. Where were the voices? The shouts? Where were the rumbles of cart wheels on cobblestone?

And where were the guards supposed to be manning the gate?

Her heart in her throat, Wynn pushed on the doors, nearly falling in surprise when she found them open. She entered a silent city.

People were scattered around, collapsed where they stood when whatever happened had happened. Food vendors sprawled across their wares; carriage drivers flopped backward across their roofs; and numerous people in the marketplace curled up on the ground, some on top of one another. There was no blood or signs of a struggle to be seen.

Swallowing hard, Wynn knelt next to a woman near her feet, and held her hand near the woman's mouth. Oh, thank God, she was breathing. Just...sleeping?

Wynn tried to wake her, but the woman's only response was to grumble and roll over, snoring quietly. Where Wynn's hands touched bare skin, there was a buzzing numbness, like her hands were falling asleep. When she let go, moving to rub her hands together, it abruptly vanished.

Trying to ignore the unsettling atmosphere of the place, Wynn continued on. It didn't take long for her to notice the buzzing in her hands hadn't gone away entirely. Perhaps it was reacting to the magic in the air?

Testing her theory, she leaned over to place her hand near the face of a child sleeping in a doorway. Even though she didn't touch him, the buzzing grew stronger as she got closer and diminished as she pulled away. She thought, *I can use this to find the source of the magic.*

So, she went to the middle of the street and held out her hands in front of her like dowsing rods. She closed her eyes and turned slowly in a circle, feeling for that buzzing in the tips of her fingers. When she divined the direction it felt strongest, she opened her eyes and found herself staring at the palace looming over the houses and shops from its perch on a hill.

Wynn began making her way toward it. She wondered if she could feel the magic because her body itself had been altered by it. It was a sobering thought to remember this form was not the one she had been born in—just some sort of bizarre magical fluke. Which her parents had been expecting. She frowned, coming to wonder just *what* had happened to her, but it was hard to think in this ghost town, so she refocused and looked around.

There was some evidence of looting, especially of the jewelry shops, but not as much as she would have expected. Maybe bandits and thieves were more superstitious than she had assumed. The atmosphere of the city was oppressive and heavy, charged like the air before a thunderstorm. She could almost *smell* the way the magic hung over everything and everyone—it felt like being watched at close range, like a great ugly man breathing down her neck.

Yes, she could see why thieves had chosen to leave.

And it only got worse as she approached the palace. The buzzing was no longer confined to her fingertips: both of her hands now felt fuzzy as well as the tip of her nose and of her ears. It was uncomfortable and unsettling, making her want to give up and leave. But the very act of thinking that made her only more determined to keep going.

When she got to the castle, her whole body was thrumming with the pulse of the magic. The castle gate was locked. She walked the perimeter of the castle, looking for some servants' entrance. Instead, she found a tall hedge. Jumping to peek over top of it, she caught sight of a garden. And when she landed, she spotted the orange glint of rusting iron. Not a hedge then, but thick ivy over a fence. And surely a fence had a gate.

She walked the length of the fence, periodically pushing her hand through to feel any change, until finally she found an old gate that had been long forgotten. The metal was dull and orange and, with a well-placed kick, it fell apart, leaving Wynn free to shimmy through, sighing when her dress ripped even further. It had been such a nice dress too.

After pushing through the vines and rose bushes on the other side (*ouch ouch ouch*), Wynn walked through the overgrown garden and into the castle.

Her boots thumped heavily on the stone floors as she passed sleeping guards and servants. She found the throne room where the king and queen were leaning on each other as they snored. The magic there was strong, but it was even stronger above her. She found a servants' stairwell and made her way up, holding her hands up to keep cobwebs out of her eyes as she climbed.

As she emerged at the top of what she thought was the easternmost tower, she could feel the magic in her bones, dictating the rhythm of her heart. This was definitely where it was strongest.

There was only one room, taken up by a large bed. In it, a young man lay asleep, his expression pained as he twitched in some sort of nightmare. He was clearly the source of the magic. She could hear it now, hissing in her ears like steam.

She approached the man and looked at him more closely. He couldn't be called truly handsome—with sharp cheekbones, a narrow jaw, and a long, hooked nose—but his face was striking, even in a grimace, in a way that made it hard for Wynn to look away. His dark red-brown hair was damp with sweat, and without thinking, Wynn wiped it away from his brow.

Magic flared, and Wynn was falling.

*

When her ears stopped ringing, Wynn registered the sound of fighting. She opened her eyes, then squinted up at the back of the young man who'd been asleep in the bed only seconds before. He had a sword in his hands, using it like a club to beat away grotesque monsters pouring through the door to the room. They resembled skeletons, but they were shiny black like beetles with armor jangling loosely over the bones.

Tears had left streaks down the young man's face, and his arms trembled with the weight of the blade. It was clear he was at the end of his rope, and probably had been for some time. Wynn jumped up and grabbed for the sword at her hip and the shield at her back.

For one heart-shuddering moment, they weren't there, but after a second, the familiar grips were in her hands. When she looked down, her dress was repaired, yet infinitely more comfortable. Quickly testing a theory, she imagined the weight of her practice armor across her shoulders and chest, picturing it in bright silver, decorated with white lilies. After a second, she felt it and saw it, as pretty as she'd thought. *So, it's a dream.*

She ducked under the young man's arm, holding up the shield to block the blows coming at him. He gaped at her, panting heavily. "Who— How—" he gasped.

"I'm Wynn. I'm here to help you!" She darted her sword out from behind the shield, skewering one of the monsters like a stuck pig.

"Oh, thank God!" He looked like he was about to cry again. "I'm Benoit, and I would greatly appreciate your help."

The monsters were slow and fairly predictable, and the two of them were starting to make progress. "The first thing I would suggest is turning your sword so it can cut these creatures instead of just clubbing them," she said, grunting as she stuck her blade up under the jaw of one of the monsters. "Not that clubbing is necessarily *bad*, but it's kind of a waste of your cutting edge." Using her leverage of the creature's skull, she threw it to the ground, where it shattered to pieces.

"O-oh. That makes sense," he stammered, shifting his grip around. "I-I don't know how long I've been stuck here."

"Me neither. I just got here myself." She ducked an incoming blow and came up under the creature's guard, bashing it with her shield. "Is this it? Just fight incoming enemies forever?"

"I guess so," he panted, cleaving into a monster's rib cage.

Wynn glanced around, her gaze falling on the open door. "So, I've an idea."

"I'm listening!" He hid behind her shield as a creature grabbed for his neck.

"Why don't we push through them and figure out where they're coming from?"

"But we don't have—" His eyes fell on her shield. "Oh, right."

"Need anything from this room?"

"No, ma'am."

"Then take my hand and don't let go, got it?" She sheathed her sword one-handed, swinging the shield around to give them some breathing room.

His palm was trembling and sweaty, but his grip was tight. "Ready."

Wynn raised the shield and held it steady and close so that it was in front of both of them. "Aaaand, go!" The two of them ran, pushing the creatures aside as they went. "Swing at the ones that try to follow!" Wynn grunted, focusing on the door. Benoit swayed and shook as he did so, sending the jolt of contact through their joined hands.

As soon as they got through the door and slammed it shut, the monsters abruptly vanished. Benoit let go, his legs trembling and giving out underneath him. He looked like he was about to cry with relief. Wynn strapped the shield to her back and crouched next to him, keeping her eyes and ears sharp for whatever was coming. Because something surely was.

"Shhhh," she whispered, rubbing his shoulder. "It's not over yet, Benoit. Keep it together."

"But they're gone." He hiccupped.

"But you're not awake yet."

He frowned in confusion, and his lips pursed. "Awake? I'm asleep? This is a dream?"

"Something like it, but I think it's a cursed sleep, so the nightmare isn't over."

He whimpered before burying his face in her shoulder and choking on a dry sob. Wynn rocked him gently, keeping watch. Her heart throbbed in her ears, but her eyes worked fine, fine enough to notice the slowly encroaching darkness.

Wynn pictured her blade being made of moonlight and held it aloft, glaring into the creeping blackness. But no, it wasn't black, but rather dark green. There were vines closing in around them.

She pulled Benoit to his feet. "Come on, before we're trapped!" Holding the sword high for its light, Wynn sprinted down the hall, Benoit at her heels, the vines hissing over the floor as they tried to block the staircase. "They're trying to stop us going downstairs!" she yelled over her shoulder.

"So that's where we have to go, right?"

She grinned. "You're learning! Faster!"

They sped up, leaping over a thick clump as they reached the stairs, and jumped down them, leaping two or three at a time. The staircase opened onto a large hall with large curtains draped against the walls. Wynn shoved Benoit behind one of the curtains and joined him there as footsteps echoed closer.

Very heavy footsteps.

She peeked out, taking in the sight of a huge black dragon with an acid-green belly. She ducked back behind the curtain, looking up into Benoit's wide gray eyes. "D-d-d-d—" he stammered under his breath.

She put her hand over his mouth. "Shh. I have an idea." She slid her hand up to his eyes, shushing him as she did, then stood on tiptoe so she could whisper into his ear. "Did you ever play with lizards as a boy?"

"No, but my brother did. Why?" he hissed, angry, but he was trembling like a leaf in a windstorm.

"Humor me," she whispered back. "Think about one of them. How it looked. Hold that image in your head."

"Okay…?"

"Now, imagine that dragon out there that size. Itty-bitty. No bigger than a child's hand."

The footsteps were growing softer.

"Did you ever find the little ones that were slimy and had no teeth?"

"Salamanders? Once."

"That's the name. Think about those little guys. They're cute, right?"

Under her arm, Benoit made a face. "They're disgusting."

"That is incorrect, but oh well." She removed her hand and peeked out from the curtain again. The dragon was gone, but there was a small black salamander wriggling across the floor. She dived for it, armor clattering as it skittered across the polished marble.

The salamander hissed at her, which she was pretty sure real salamanders didn't do, but it'd been awhile. *Trespasser,* it hissed. *You are not meant to be here.*

"Well, I am," she replied cheerfully and brought it over to Benoit. "Good job, Your Highness!"

He peeked out from behind the curtain. "What did I do?"

She held out the salamander. "Turned the dragon into this. Think you can slay it now?"

He smiled weakly. "I don't know, but I can try."

She turned so the hilt of her sword was facing him. "Use mine. It's lighter and easier to aim."

"Thank you."

Wynn pinned the salamander to the floor by its tail. "Don't get me, please," she joked.

Benoit gave her a nervous little laugh. "I'll try."

He succeeded. The salamander squealed as it was sliced in half.

The dream shuddered and crumbled around them. Benoit began to scream.

Wynn gasped as she jolted awake and found she was stretched out over Benoit's chest. Benoit, who was now awake, looked at her with bright, starry eyes.

Her heart thudded, and she quickly straightened up and darted toward the door.

"Wait!" Benoit cried, scrambling up to follow, but perhaps since he'd been asleep for so long, his legs crumpled the minute he tried to use them. "Wynn!"

But the only thing she could think of was her wrecked dress and unwashed face, her unkempt hair and surely bloodshot eyes. She dodged waking guards and servants, trying to leave in the confusion. But the castle was unfamiliar, and instead of finding her way out, she found herself in a courtyard garden, boxed in on all sides.

Standing among the roses was an unearthly beautiful woman. But the longer Wynn looked, the more her face started taking on the unsettling qualities of a mask. A smile stretched across it, but didn't meet her black, black eyes.

"There you are," she said, and the summer air became very, very cold because Wynn *knew* that voice. "You are quite a troublemaker, aren't you?" It was the witch who'd hurt Franz. But she was no witch at all.

"*You* cursed Prince Benoit?"

The fairy chuckled. "I curse many royal children. They're such spoiled, pampered brats. And that means you too, little prince."

Wynn froze, all her thoughts stopping and jumbling together. "Curse?" she said numbly.

The fairy frowned, then began to *laugh*, mouth opened wide like a cat's, lips pulled back to show a mouth full of fangs. "You *like* it! I never thought I would see the day." Then she sobered. "Yes, dear, 'curse.' It will bring your kingdom to ruin. Without an heir to the throne, your family's peaceful reign will end and bring an era of chaos the like of which will not be seen again for hundreds of years." She grinned. "And I will love it."

Wynn rested her hand on the hilt of her sword, aware now of the magic that was laced through it.

"Are you going to try and kill me, little girl?" the fairy said.

Wynn froze again, feeling like a deer in the sights of a wolf.

"If I die, then you will lose your 'curse.'" The fairy crept closer. "Is that truly what you want?" she asked with mocking sweetness. "Of course, you'd save your kingdom, but you'd have to marry that obnoxious little girl, wouldn't you?" The fairy was less than a foot away now, bent so she met Wynn's gaze, eye to eye. "Can't disappoint dear mother and father, can you? It would run counter to your *princely* duty. Even if all you want is a man to call your own—a kind, handsome little thing to stick his— Urk!"

Wynn pushed the sword in harder, feeling the frantic pulse of the fairy's heart echo through the blade. "You will not curse anyone else ever again!" she screamed.

The fairy shuddered one last time, then crumbled to dust. For a moment, nothing happened, but then a burn seared through Wynn, and she cried, folding in on herself, hugging tightly, because she remembered that sensation from so long ago—the day that she had become *herself*.

But now it was reversed. Her chest was hard and flat beneath her palm, and there was pain now where her thighs were squeezed so tightly together.

She fell out of her crouch, and lay there on the garden path—an ugly, misshapen creature with a wrecked, ill-fitting dress (it gaped indecently below her neck now, lacking the shape to fill it), dirty skin, and unwashed hair.

Footsteps approached her, soft whispers on the mossy stone path, but she didn't even turn to look. It didn't matter.

She had done the right thing, she told herself. Now no one else would suffer—not her parents (their crestfallen faces when they saw her in her pilfered dress) and not innocent people (Franz's bloody eyes and his mysterious maiden). She had done the right thing.

Eventually, she would get up, put on "proper" clothing, ask the royal family for a bath and a horse, and return home where she would once again be the son and heir. She wanted to sob and rage against the world, but she was just too tired.

Slippers appeared in her vision, and they tucked themselves under legs as the person sat down. A cool hand touched her hair, stroking gently.

"I never did get the chance to thank you," Benoit said quietly. "You ran away so quickly."

Wynn wanted to run away again but found that she couldn't, not when that soft hand was holding her down. She curled up instead, hiding her chest and hips, still too numb to speak.

"I saw the last few minutes of that," he went on. "You are so dreadfully brave. It's a bit awe-inspiring, to be honest."

She didn't move. She hoped he would remember her as she had appeared in his dream, with a beautiful dress and shining armor, not like this.

"I can't imagine the adventures you must have had. I hope you'll tell me about them someday." Benoit was still stroking her dirty hair, seemingly unaware of how disgusting she was. "Please, let me thank you properly for the great service you have done."

Wynn sighed and stirred, forcing herself to sit up. She grabbed the neck of her dress with one hand, holding it up over her chest, and looked down at the path below her, not wanting to meet Benoit's gaze. She was afraid to speak, fearful of the breaking, squeaking sound that was sure to leave her throat.

With delicate fingers, Benoit tipped her chin up, his face entering her field of vision. His eyes were a soft gray, like rainclouds, ringed by dark mahogany lashes. Her heart squeezed in her chest. He wasn't handsome, not in a conventional sense, but he was entrancing, nonetheless.

He leaned forward and tilted his head just enough so their lips could touch. Wynn's eyes fluttered shut, and without thinking, she deepened the kiss, bringing their bodies closer together. She was so warm as if she were sinking into the hot bath she so desperately wanted. Benoit's hands roamed carefully over her face and down her neck, but how many hands did he *have*? They felt like they were everywhere.

When their chests brushed, Wynn gasped and pulled away, looking down. Her bosom had returned as if it had never vanished. Benoit gave her a questioning look.

"I'm myself again," she said wonderingly. "But how? The fairy is dead!"

Benoit smiled. "You were never anything other than yourself, Miss Wynn. Though I do confess to enjoying the sight of a woman's breast, if that's not too forward."

Wynn laughed. "It's not forward at all, Your Highness." She wrapped her arms around his neck and pulled him into another long kiss, this time pressing her chest firmly to his. The two of them fell to the ground, Benoit grumbling as his head bumped into the hard stone.

"Perhaps this would be better conducted on a couch," he groused.

"Or in a bath," Wynn suggested.

"Or even a bed." Benoit grinned mischievously as Wynn covered his face with her hand.

"A lady does not fornicate with men besides her husband," she said primly, imitating Catrin. "Not even princes."

Benoit draped a hand over his forehead, feigning disappointment. "Oh, no. I'll have to *marry* the most amazing woman I've ever met. My life is over."

Wynn touched her lips to his nose. "It's not so bad. Kisses are free."

Benoit sat up, Wynn still straddling his lap. "Free they may be, but cobblestone is a poor choice of venue. Shall we go inside and get cleaned up for dinner?"

A corner of Wynn's mind that wasn't screaming for kissing to recommence awoke with a cry of *Bath!* "That sounds great. Could you lead the way, Your Highness?"

Benoit got to his feet, then reached down to help Wynn to hers. "Right this way, miss. I'll have a bath drawn at once."

He had the bath prepared in his private chambers, and Wynn took the opportunity to examine her new body in full before the long mirror. It was still recognizably hers, right down to the various scars and the birthmark on her left hip. The skin was just a little plusher, smoothing the lines of bones on her sides and chest. Her breasts were small but firm and well-shaped, and her waist was better defined. She took in her every angle—the dimples on her buttocks, the softness of her thighs, and what lay beneath the hair at the apex of her legs.

She examined that more thoroughly in the bath, learning the new topography.

Wynn left the bathing room cleaner, more confident, and happier than she'd been in a long time. Two chambermaids were waiting in the dressing room when she emerged, several dresses folded over their arms.

Wynn chose the one in spring green with a square neckline decorated with small pearls. It was old-fashioned since it was an old dress of the queen's, but Wynn hoped its traditionalism made up for her unconventionally short hair.

With deft fingers, one of the maids fitted her—letting out the skirt, tightening the bodice—until it fit like it was made for her. Her first fitted dress! Wynn's smile was infectious, brightening both of the maids' faces to match.

Benoit was waiting outside the door when she emerged, dressed in midnight blue, his dark-red hair combed back out of his face. He grinned at Wynn as he took in the sight of her, his chest rising with how deeply he inhaled. "You are rapturous, my lady."

Wynn laughed. "Thank you. You are as well, Your Highness."

"Shall we go?" He held up his arm.

Wynn threaded hers through and rested her head briefly on his shoulder. "Yes, let's."

The hallways were truly grand now that Wynn was paying attention. Richly colored tapestries, beautiful portraiture…it was clear Norance was much richer than tiny little Celles. She was beginning to feel a bit intimidated.

Outside the dining hall doors, there was a very handsome man. His hair was the same rich red as Benoit's, but there the similarities ended. Benoit was average height and broad shouldered, sort of stockily built without the muscle tone that usually went with it. This man was tall and slender with lean muscles that were clear even hidden under his dark-blue coat, and his legs went on for miles.

Wynn swallowed dryly. Was she staring too obviously?

"Miss Wynn, this is the crown prince of Norance, my elder brother, Marcel," Benoit said. His expression had dimmed a bit as he watched Wynn's face, but he did his best to maintain a polite smile.

"It's an absolute pleasure to meet you, Miss Wynn." Marcel kissed both of her cheeks in greeting. She had heard the people of Norance did such a thing, but it still flustered her. "I cannot thank you enough for your assistance in ridding us of that curse."

She found herself blushing. "It was no trouble, Your Highness. I'm glad I was able to help."

Marcel opened the heavy oaken doors. "Please follow me. You're to be our guest of honor."

Wynn fell easily into step behind him. He introduced her to the king and queen. They sat at the head of the high table, the king bearing Benoit's dark-red hair, though his was curly instead of straight. He was wide and round, looking much shorter than he truly was, with a bushy beard and a friendly smile. The queen was tall with blonde hair streaked with white and Benoit's soft, gray eyes and sharp nose.

They both greeted her with kisses to both cheeks as Marcel had done, and Wynn got a place of honor at the king's side across from the queen. The formal atmosphere made her nervous since the last time she'd sat at the high table, she'd run away from her parents and left her old life behind. It was unsettling to be back under such different circumstances.

At the king's request, Wynn told the entire story, leaving out the transformation. Better they believe her a woman through and through. After all, she *was*. Her escape was now due to her not approving of her fiancé. Benoit watched her wide-eyed.

"So, you're actually a princess?" he asked. "Please forgive me for my familiarity earlier."

Wynn smiled sadly. "I'm sorry I misled you, Your Highness. And there's nothing to forgive. I've left my family, so I assume that title is no longer mine."

"Blood is blood," the king said. "Unless your father disowns you or the customs of your country are stranger than I thought, you will remain a princess of Celles."

"Thank you, Your Majesty." Wynn's reply wobbled with tears. "Oh!" she said, dabbing quickly at her eyes with a handkerchief. "I told you of Prince Franz of Deurich. He's likely still recovering in that town. Do you happen to know of any wizards who could be of assistance on his quest?"

The king nodded, setting down his glass of wine. "I do. I shall send my court wizard first thing tomorrow morning. Deurich is a great ally, and I aim to keep it as such."

"What do you plan on doing now, Princess?" the queen asked.

She tried to meet Benoit's gaze, wondering if he wanted her to announce their possible engagement, but he was looking down at his plate. Wynn's mouth quirked down, but she recovered her polite smile. "I'm not sure yet, Your Majesty. I hope I can impose upon your hospitality for a few days, at least?"

"A few days," the king scoffed. "You've done us a great service. If you no longer want the title of Princess of Celles, I would be more than happy to give you one of Norance. For now, though, I'll have a guest suite prepared for you." He gestured for one of the servants to come over.

Wynn turned toward Benoit, who was now pushing the remnants of dinner around his plate with his knife. Marcel noticed her stare and nudged his brother, murmuring something into his ear.

Benoit looked up, finally meeting Wynn's gaze. She smiled. His eyes fell back to his plate.

Wynn frowned fully now and stood up. "Excuse us just one moment," she said. She walked around the table, took Benoit's hand, and pulled him out into the hallway. Once the dining room doors swung shut, she grabbed his other hand, so he was forced to face her. "What's wrong? Are you not feeling well?"

He shrunk into her shadow though they were roughly the same height. "You're all the same, women."

She frowned. "What on earth do you mean?"

His voice was small, petulant. "Everyone prefers my brother. The minute you saw him, your eyes never left him. I know I'm not much to look upon, but I had hoped you were different."

Wynn sighed and knocked her head into his, enough to sting but not to hurt. As he flinched away, she said, "Your brother is a handsome man, that much is true. But he is like a fine painting—looking is nice, but I've no desire to own him." Her voice grew soft, and she moved her hands to his waist. "You're the one I'd like to marry one day."

He closed his eyes, resting his head on her shoulder. "We hardly know each other," he mumbled.

"That's okay. I look forward to learning more about you. Do you want to wait on the engagement?"

He nodded, his blush burning in his ears.

Wynn chuckled and folded him into a hug. "That's fine then. Believe me when I say I've no interest in pursuing your brother."

He smiled. "All right. I'm sorry for behaving like such a child."

Wynn laughed into his hair. "I'm not much better, so you're fine. Ready to go back in?"

"Yes."

They untangled and returned to dinner in high spirits.

The next few months passed like a joyful dream. It turned out Benoit was a fine musician. His instrument of choice was a small harp—old-fashioned, but singularly lovely, especially when paired with his soft vocals.

He sang hymns for the most part, praising the might of the Lord in the heavens, but sometimes he also would improvise pieces, just combining chords and notes in a way that made shivers of pleasure trip down Wynn's spine.

And those harpist's hands were dexterous and delicate, exhilarating to feel against her when she knew what magic they could pull from simple strings.

Wynn learned to dance the lady's part of the winter dances, after some hilarious practices where she spent most of the dance treading on Benoit's feet, and kept up with her swordplay with Marcel.

After spending time with Marcel, Wynn could confirm he was the sort of handsome man who was aware of how handsome he was and was insufferably, if obliviously, smug about it. By the time the winter snows came, much milder than those Wynn had grown up with, any remnants of a crush had withered away to nothing.

As preparations for the twelve-days-of-Christmas festivities began in full, Wynn became more and more convinced she and Benoit were perfect for one another. One day in the garden, as Wynn and Benoit were admiring the snow, she asked him if he was ready to announce their engagement.

He turned nearly as red as his hair as he smiled. "Are you sure?" he asked. "About me?"

"As long as you're sure about me," she replied.

He took her hand, squeezing it tightly in his. "I don't think I've ever been surer of anything." He blushed deeper and made a face. "I mangled something in that sentence."

Wynn laughed and grabbed his other hand, pulling their bodies together. "I'm clearly not marrying you for your lyricism," she teased.

"Oh yeah? Then what *are* you marrying me for?"

"Your hands, obviously. Just those, nothing else." She kissed his nose.

"So mean," he whined, but he was smiling when he finished. "When do you want to make the announcement?"

Wynn hummed as she considered it, swaying their clasped hands back and forth. "New Year's Day?" she suggested. "I don't think we should tread on the Lord's toes by announcing it on Christmas."

"Agreed. The New Year's feast would be a perfect time." Benoit nodded to himself.

"Do you have a ring for me?" Wynn asked, removing her left hand to wiggle her bare fingers at him.

He smiled and grabbed it back so he could kiss it. "Of course, my dear. Come with me and we can pick one from my collection."

They chose a gold band set with a ruby. It was simple, but it was old, carrying generations of Benoit's family history. To Wynn, who considered herself now divorced from her family, it was perfect.

She put it on a chain and wore it under her dress, the knowledge it was there buoying her up every time she remembered.

As the Christmas festivities began, she and Benoit spent most of their time together. They sat beside each other in Mass, they danced after every feast, and they spent hours talking in between since Benoit was free from tutors and responsibilities for the holiday.

Rumors abounded, and Wynn chuckled every time a hushed voice suddenly stuttered to a stop as she walked by, only to pick right back up when she'd passed.

At the New Year's feast, after the first course was served, Benoit nodded to Wynn, and they stood up. "Father," Benoit said, "before we begin, Wynn and I have an announcement to make."

The king smiled and rolled his wrist. "Continue then."

Benoit looked to Wynn. "We have decided to marry. Sometime in April, we think."

"That's wonderful, Benoit," the queen said, her smile so warm and happy it made Wynn's heart swell. "Come here, dear," she said to Wynn, holding out her arms.

Wynn practically ran into them, tears welling up in her eyes. As the queen dabbed them away with her handkerchief, the king patted Wynn on the shoulder. "I welcome you into our family, though it's yet to be official."

"Thank you so much, Your Majesties," Wynn said through her tears. "Your approval means more than you know."

The afternoon after the Twelfth Night, during a brief snowstorm, a band of messengers arrived, bearing the crest of the Kingdom of Celles. Wynn ducked into the shadow of a nearby corridor as she watched them walk by, hearing her country's native tongue for the first time in many months.

"I don't think he'll be here either," one of them grumbled. "Why would the prince come to a palace if he wants to avoid his parents? If I were to run away, I would move to a village or something, somewhere anonymous."

The second one shrugged as he shook snow off his hat. "Perhaps the king can help us. Give us a map of nearby towns, maybe?"

The third rubbed his cold-reddened face and sniffed heavily. "Why are we trusting the word of a seedy merchant that he's in Norance anyway?"

"It's a better lead than nothing," said the second, who appeared to be in charge. "I'd rather have something to report to the king even if it turns out to be dead end."

Wynn gulped as she peered around the corner to watch them enter the king's meeting room. They greeted the king warmly and made brief conversation of the strange circumstances he had recently endured. Wynn noticed that only the lead messenger seemed to speak Norench.

Even knowing it was a bad idea, she entered the room shortly after them to hear what they had to say, her back straight and her heart steeled.

The king's eyes flicked up to her as she came through the door, and he acknowledged her with a small nod. She returned it.

"So," the lead messenger continued, "the king and queen would appreciate any information you have about their missing son. Having two boys yourself, I'm sure you understand."

"I understand a parent's worry, but I also believe if a child's run off, the blame does not lie solely in the impetuousness of youth. I have information that would be of use, but I will not disclose it without the approval of that person beforehand." He met Wynn's eyes.

She smiled at him, so grateful for even his *existence* at that moment. Unfortunately, the third messenger followed that gaze, and his eyes widened. "Your Highness!" he said, running up to Wynn.

She feigned ignorance. "Excuse me?"

The messenger frowned, then switched to their native tongue. "You are the spitting image of the missing Prince Wynn."

"I don't understand," she said stubbornly.

"So," he continued, still in Cellan, "it's no matter to you the king and queen are worried sick over their child, especially since he appeared to be ill in the head when they parted ways?"

Wynn snapped. "'Ill in the head?' Is that what they think of me? That I'm some fool gibbering on a street corner?" The other messengers joined their companion, keeping a safe distance. "I've no desire to return to a family who is determined to see in me someone who does not exist. You can tell that to the king and queen. When they're ready to acknowledge me as their daughter, I will acknowledge them as my parents." She took a deep, shuddering breath and switched back to a language the king, who was watching closely in confusion, could understand. "But until that day comes, I ask you to leave. I've a wedding to prepare."

The messenger looked as if he had something else to say, but his leader grabbed his shoulder. "We will pass along your message, Your Highness. Despite it all, I'm sure they will be happy to hear you are alive. If I may ask, whose wedding is it?"

"Mine," she said, though she had a gloomy feeling in her stomach. What if the king were to retract his approval now that he knew she wasn't a natural-born woman but one made of magic?

"Congratulations, Your Highness," the messenger said and shepherded his two companions out of the hall and outside.

After they were gone, Wynn approached the throne. The king regarded her with an unreadable expression. "So, the king and queen of Celles are looking for their only child, their son," he said. "Care to explain?"

Wynn winced and hugged herself, looking at the floor. "Yes, I was born a prince," she said quietly.

"And how did you come to be a princess?" the king asked. His voice was gentler than she'd been expecting, more curious than accusatory. She peeked back up at him.

"It was a fairy curse. The same fairy who cursed your family, in fact." She heaved a great sigh. "Without an heir to the throne, Celles will be thrown into chaos after the death of the king."

The king raised his brows, surprised. "But the fairy is dead. Your curse should be broken."

"It was. But I was changed back. I consider it a miracle from the Lord and would prefer not to question it too deeply, for fear that one day I'll wake up once more as Celles's prince and not myself."

"I see." The king stroked his beard thoughtfully. "Can you have children?"

Wynn blinked. "I…I have no idea. I have yet to bleed, but when I asked the physician, he told me a too-active lifestyle can cause that and recommended I ease up on my sword practice. He had no reason to believe this was not the body into which I was born."

The king continued worrying his beard. "I see, I see." He cleared his throat. "No matter the circumstance, this city owes you a great debt, and it would be remiss of me to forget that. I must ask though, does Benoit know?"

"I've not told him in detail, but he did see a brief glimpse of my…original body."

"Tell him in detail tonight. I insist he be fully aware before I return my approval to you both." He ran his hand through his hair, taking a deep breath. At last, he smiled. "Now tell me, what exactly did you say to those messengers to send them scurrying off?"

"I told them to pass along the message to the king and queen of Celles that if they will not acknowledge me as their daughter, I will not acknowledge them as my parents."

"Those are strong words. Do you know how they'll respond?"

"Honestly, Your Majesty, I have no idea."

The king waved her over and he put a hand on her shoulder. "If they have any sense, they will. A parent who ignores the beliefs and feelings of their children doesn't deserve to have any child at all."

Wynn wiped away the tears that threatened to fall. "If they do not accept me, will you be my father, Your Majesty?"

He crushed her to his chest in a tight hug. "My dear, you're betrothed to my son. I already consider you my daughter."

That night, per the king's condition, Wynn told Benoit everything. He'd already known much, but she told him about how she used to dress up as a servant girl and roam the castle town, about her first kiss, and about Catrin. He listened, occasionally asking questions, and when she was finished, he said, "I think even if you hadn't changed back, I still would want to marry you."

And Wynn groused at him about making her cry after she'd already cried so much that day. "Between you and your father, I'm going to run out of tears!"

Benoit held her until she was finished, murmuring words of affection into her hair.

The winter was mild overall, giving up its grip to spring in late February. As April fast approached, preparations for the wedding ramped up until it seemed every day brought some new crisis that needed Wynn's immediate attention—whether it was hand-lettering the invitations going to important political guests, or meeting with the tailor about her dress, or approving various aspects of the menu being prepared.

There was no reply from Celles. They did receive an invitation, though, which called the event *The Wedding of the*

Prince Benoit, Son of King Jean V of Norance and his Bride, the Honorable Princess Wynn, Daughter of King Iago I of Celles. She'd been reluctant to put her title and lineage on there at first, but the king had insisted, telling her if her parents didn't want to acknowledge her, then the rest of the world should.

Within a week of sending an invitation to Deurich's royal family, she got an eager reply from Prince Franz, whose letter contained shock at her deceit about her family but also a lot of excited stories about his adventures in hunting down his maiden with the help of Norance's court wizard. His vision had returned with the death of the Dark Fairy, combined with the "power of Rapunzel's love," which Wynn wasn't sure how to take. She hoped it wasn't as vulgar as her imagination wanted it to be. In closing he wrote, "I am eager to see your face for the first time and tell you my tales in full. I promise I shall bring a splendid wedding present!"

By March 20, guests were arriving. Prince Franz and his Rapunzel were some of the first. Wynn greeted them both warmly.

Franz looked her up and down. "I must say," he said, "you are much prettier than I had been imagining."

"Is my voice so unattractive?" Wynn asked.

Rapunzel stopped Franz before he could answer. "No, he just has low expectations. It means he's always pleasantly surprised by what the world has to offer." She gave him a fond smile.

She was a delicate beauty, thin-boned and long-limbed with a heart-shaped face and thick golden hair. Her eyelashes were pale brown, framing light-blue eyes. She stood in distinct contrast with her prince, who was handsome but rough around the edges. She was also tall, the top of Franz's head only meeting her nose.

They looked good together, happy together, and that was all Wynn cared about.

That night at dinner, Franz regaled the table with his adventures, Rapunzel chiming in now and again to gently correct an exaggerated detail or add her own point of view during a tale of Franz's.

The "power of her love" turned out to be the tears she shed over Franz's ruined face when they had found each other, and Wynn relaxed (despite the lewd side of her imagination being a trifle disappointed).

Wynn and Rapunzel became fast friends. Wynn had known town girls when she'd gone out in disguise, but she'd never had a female friend from whom she didn't have to keep secrets. And Rapunzel, being isolated as she was, had never had a friend at all.

They learned cosmetics together, laughing as they saw the failed results in the mirror, and they gossiped about their fiancés, jokingly comparing them in any number of ways. Franz could pick Rapunzel up over his shoulder, which was thrilling, but Wynn was insistent that long, artful fingers a better lover made.

"Well, when we both know for sure, we shall have to compare," Rapunzel said, tying off the first braid she'd made in Wynn's hair and moving on to the other side. She was remarkably quick at it.

"When is your wedding?" Wynn asked.

"June," Rapunzel said with a sigh. "It's so far away, but his mother insisted our wedding not come before his elder brother's, which is at the end of April."

"Do you like his fiancée?"

Rapunzel thought about it, finishing off the second braid and tying the two together at the back of Wynn's head. "She's fine. Very polite, if a little distant. I can't see us being very close."

"That's too bad. I wonder why King Jean doesn't mind his younger son is marrying first."

"King Jean is kind. He's known for it. I think it's because he's so happy Prince Benoit found true love, you know? He's not the most handsome, especially not next to Prince Marcel, so the fact he has you is something worth celebrating."

Wynn frowned. "He's not ugly."

Rapunzel smoothed her hair and pointed her toward the mirror. "No, he's not," she agreed. "But Prince Marcel is *very* handsome."

Wynn admired the way the two perfect braids wrapped around her head. "You are amazing at doing hair, I have to say."

"Thank you," Rapunzel said with a smile. Her own hair was quite short, only hanging to her shoulders. But Wynn had noticed the little mannerisms that indicated she was used to it being much longer—the way she reached back too far to brush it away from her face or the way she grabbed it before sitting down.

"Would you like me to braid yours?" Wynn asked. "It won't be as good as when you do it yourself, but I'd like to return the favor if I could."

"Go ahead," Rapunzel said warmly.

The conversation lulled as Wynn had to concentrate on what she was doing. When she had just about finished, there was a knock on the door. "Princess, it's time for your first dress fitting," a servant said on the other side. "The tailor will be up shortly."

"Thank you," Wynn called and tied off the not-quite-finished braid. "Would you like to stay? It won't be particularly interesting, so I'd appreciate the company." She smiled sheepishly.

Rapunzel chuckled. "I'd be more than happy to. I'm sure Franz and Prince Marcel are still happily beating each other over the heads with whatever weapons they can think to try."

They both laughed. "I'd fetch Benoit, but it's bad luck for the groom to see the dress," Wynn said.

"Very true," Rapunzel said, finishing out the braid.

"Excuse me, Your Highness, Lady Rapunzel," the tailor said as she entered. "Are you ready?"

Wynn grinned. "Of course." She had never been more ready in her life. Not just for a dress fitting of course, but for, well, her life. Her *own* life, not the one decided upon by her parents and the person they had seen when they looked at her.

By God, was she ready for that.

The day of the wedding dawned bright and clear, and Wynn was up with the sun, lost in last-minute preparations and general excitement. Her dress was gorgeous, made of deep-blue silk with soft white fur trim and embroidered with silver doves.

Rapunzel, who had ended up taking the role of maid of honor, placed the veil on her head and pinned it carefully into place. "You're ready," she said.

Wynn's cheeks felt bruised from how much she was smiling. "Don't let me look until I'm married," she said quickly. "It's bad luck!"

Dutifully, Rapunzel covered the mirror.

"All right," Wynn said, and she took a deep breath. "Is he there outside?"

Rapunzel looked out the window into the courtyard. "The priest is entering the chapel now, and I see the king and queen following him. I think we should head downstairs."

Wynn eyed the stairs dubiously through the veil. "Take my hand? It's sort of hard to see."

Rapunzel laughed and did so, leading Wynn down to the chapel entrance. A servant handed her the bouquet, and Rapunzel let go of her hand so she could enter and take her place.

"I wish my parents were here," Wynn said in a small voice.

Rapunzel stopped and hugged her, removing a handkerchief from her dress to dab at Wynn's eyes. "Now, now, no tears," she said gently. "You are a fearsome warrior and a stalwart woman. You can walk yourself down the aisle just fine. Don't give them the satisfaction of making you sad on such an important day."

Wynn sniffed and straightened her shoulders. "You're right. Thank you, Rapunzel."

"That's why I'm here," she said, patting her cheek. "Now, I'm going to go inside. Wait for your cue."

Wynn nodded and squeezed her bouquet.

The distant sounds of the priest talking echoed out into the air, and then a servant was waving her inside to the swell of a choir. The world became soft around the edges, and though she was walking alone, Benoit was waiting for her at the end of the path, the smile on his face the same as the one in her heart.

He held out his hand for her as she mounted the steps and didn't let go as the priest read the vows.

"Do you take this woman to be your wife?" the priest asked.

"I do," Benoit said.

"Do you take this man to be your husband?" he asked.

"I do," Wynn said.

Benoit took the ring from his pocket and slid it onto her finger, tears glimmering in his eyes.

"By the power vested in me by the Lord, I pronounce you man and wife." The priest shut his book, and Benoit lifted away the veil, tucking it over her head so he could kiss her.

The crowd cheered, and rice was thrown as the two exited the chapel, hand in hand, smiling the blissful beaming of fools and children.

The ball that night was grand, the grandest event Wynn could ever remember. Wine flowed like so many rivers, and everything, just everything, was perfect. She and Benoit danced until their feet rebelled, and then they sat in each other's arms and watched the festivities die down.

As the night drew to a close and most of the guests had returned to their rooms, Wynn and Benoit were approached by a masked woman. Wynn had seen her throughout the night, drawn to her by some familiarity. But there had been too much joy in her head for thoughts of suspicion.

The woman, whose hair was the brown of autumn leaves, removed the jeweled mask from the top of her small nose, revealing a face Wynn would've happily never seen again.

"Catrin," Wynn whispered.

Benoit took her hand and squeezed it tightly, taking in the sight of his wife's former fiancée.

Catrin curtsied to them both politely. "Your Highnesses," she said. "I was sent by the king and queen of Celles to see how Prince...ss Wynn was doing."

Wynn narrowed her eyes. "I'm the best I've ever been. They could've seen for themselves if they'd wished."

Catrin seemed to bite back her first response, then tried to think of a better one. "The king is…he's very busy, and the queen did not want to come alone."

"That's unfortunate," Wynn said coldly. "Do you have anything else to tell me before you scurry home like the world's worst spy?"

Catrin stuck up her nose and sniffed. "Rude," she said. "In truth, I only wanted to congratulate you." Her face softened into something almost likeable. "I've known you a long time, Wynn. And I have never seen you as happy as I did today. And that's what I'm going to tell your parents." She shuffled her feet, a blush coloring her face. "In truth, I'm a bit relieved we didn't marry. We're different people. *Very* different."

Wynn's heart melted. She got up onto her swollen feet and opened her arms for Catrin to enter. They hugged for only a moment—years of thinly veiled resentment didn't fall away so easily—but it was enough.

Catrin smiled at her and her husband. "I'm holding you responsible if I don't find someone decent to marry. A lifetime of betrothal to someone else is something of a black mark."

"I can vouch only that you are a proper lady who refuses out of hand to do anything remotely resembling work."

Catrin pouted and playfully swatted her hip. "So rude! I'll have you know in the whole journey here, I complained only once, and it was because it was raining and muddy, and I ruined my favorite shoes."

Wynn grinned. "I'm sure it was the happiest day in their inanimate lives, being free from your feet."

Catrin crossed her arms, lip jutting out like a child. "Hopeless! I hope you know what you've gotten yourself into, Your Highness!"

Benoit laughed and tugged on Wynn's dress to pull her back toward the chaise longue he was sitting on. "Come on, dear. She did come a long way to give us her congratulations."

Wynn sat down again and leaned against Benoit's chest. "Thank you, Catrin. If I hear of any desperate nobleman, I'll point them in your direction."

Catrin threw her hands up in the air. "I suppose I'll take what I can get. Enjoy your evening, Your Highnesses." She curtsied again and left the hall.

The two of them looked around the room, watching the servants rouse sleeping guests and remove them, watching others cleaning up the empty dishes. "Shall we go?" Benoit held out his hand.

"To your bedroom?" Wynn asked.

Benoit's smile turned mischievous. "If you'd like to consummate this marriage properly, certainly. I, personally, am not averse to consummating it right here, though the servants might be."

Wynn made a show of thinking about it. "We do have to be able to look them in the eye later. Might be best to do it in your bed." She held out her arms. "Carry me?"

Benoit snorted. "You think highly of my nonexistent strength."

"I'll carry you, then," she said and got to her feet, then pulled Benoit up over her shoulders. He squealed most indignantly. She tried to walk, but between Benoit weighing basically what she did and her sore feet, she put him almost immediately back down. "New plan," she said. "We walk arm in arm." She offered her elbow.

"An excellent plan," he replied, sliding his arm into hers. "Let us depart."

And so, they did.

The next day, when Rapunzel asked how it went, the only reply she got was a fox-like smile and a wiggle of Wynn's fingers.

Several months went by. Wynn and Benoit attended the wedding of Franz and Rapunzel. Despite her fretting about the date, Rapunzel was resplendent in a sky-blue gown that made her golden hair look like the sunrise. Franz began to cry halfway through their vows, and Rapunzel laughed as she wiped them away, teasing it was his turn to save her with his tears.

Afterward, Wynn and Benoit went on trips around the kingdom. He was eager to show her the breadth of his homeland, from the fertile farmlands to the glittering southern sea. In between trips, they spent a lot of time in Benoit's bed.

Then one day, Wynn got a letter. It was sealed with the Celles royal crest. Benoit sat beside her when she slit the wax and removed the paper.

It was a very long letter, the handwriting the small and loopy cursive of her mother. It asked her to come home so they could talk as a family. And so they could discuss Celles's future. It explained the whole story, how the Dark Fairy had been snubbed by her father, how she had been gifted and cursed by fairy hands, why they had betrothed her to Catrin so young.

In closing, her mother had written, "Now you're married to someone we've never even met, and it is due our own negligence. Please come home, Wynn, my child. My daughter."

Wynn looked to Benoit. "Should I go?"

"I can't make that decision for you," he said.

"Would you go? If it were you?"

Benoit nodded. "At least to hear what they had to say."

Wynn sighed and placed the letter down on the bed, staring at those final two words. *My daughter.* She lay down and put her head in Benoit's lap. "Will you come with me?"

He lifted her hand to his lips. "You only needed to ask."

*

Celles was much the same as Wynn remembered. It was hard to imagine it had been barely more than a year since she'd left. It felt like a lifetime ago.

When they entered the castle, Wynn and Benoit were ushered into a small sitting room in the king's private quarters. Wynn's parents were summoned.

Her father could barely look at her, choosing instead to stare at his hands or the stack of books on the table before him. But her mother held her close and congratulated her on her marriage, chattering to fill the empty silence that threatened to close in on the little group.

"So," Wynn said when her mother ran out of things to say, "you wrote you wanted to discuss the kingdom's future. So let's discuss."

The king cleared his throat, then spoke for the first time. "We are currently without an heir. But you are our child and now have married. Therefore, we could make Prince Benoit the heir to the throne, and thus preserve the line as such."

Benoit swallowed dryly. "I've no desire to rule a kingdom, Your Majesty. Especially not one about which my knowledge is so limited."

But Wynn put a hand on his arm. "You wouldn't have to make any important decisions. We just need you to be a pretty face to put on the money." She smiled and tweaked his nose. "You could leave the actual politicking to me."

The king nodded. "It would be unorthodox, but, well, so is everything about this situation." He tugged nervously at his beard, gaze still fixed on the table.

Wynn sighed inwardly, disappointed he couldn't look at her, though not surprised. She looked at Benoit, who was nervously scraping at his fingernails. "Give us the evening to talk it over," she said. "We'll have an answer for you in the morning."

The king and queen agreed, and Benoit and Wynn left the room. Wynn steered her husband to her old chambers, which had been left practically untouched. She grabbed the portrait of herself as a young child from the wall, but not quickly enough Benoit didn't see it.

He gazed at the child there, red-faced and mischievous, still in the ungendered play clothes all children wore. Wynn waited with bated breath for his reaction.

"You were cute as a kid," he said. Then he took it from her hands and leaned it against the wall, picture side hidden.

Wynn laughed away her anxiety and lay down on her old bed. It seemed small now. Benoit lay down beside her. "Are you so opposed to being king?" she asked him.

"It's just unexpected. I had the basic lessons, but we've always known Marcel would be king. I never expected a kingdom to just…fall into my lap like this."

"I'd take good care of you," Wynn teased, rolling over so she was straddling his legs, her hands on his chest. "It's up to you. Honestly, I would hate to see the kingdom fall into ruin, but my own father can't even look me in the eye, so maybe it just should go to hell." She sighed and stroked the wool of his jacket. "But that wouldn't be fair to the common folk. I wouldn't want them to suffer for my selfishness."

Benoit sighed, convinced. "You're right. I trust you." He cradled her face. "Let's do it, Your Majesty."

She grinned. "I'm not anyone's majesty. My father's not in the ground yet."

"You're the most majestic woman I've ever known," he continued. "And you're wearing far too many clothes."

Wynn's grinned turned feral at the edges. She opened his jacket and undid his shirt before running her hands over his soft chest. "I was afraid you'd never ask."

And so, it was that King Benoit I was crowned in Celles. He was known for being a patron of the arts and for sitting at the knee of his wife, the true heart of the monarchy. Some foreign nobles attempted to fault him for it until they met the infamous queen. She was skilled at winning hearts and minds.

The people of the capital put up a statue in her honor. Older folks would tell their children and grandchildren about how the queen used to play with them, disguised as a servant girl, and the children in turn were always respectful to strange children, lest they turn out to be royals too.

Wynn and Benoit had three children who lived to adulthood, and their line would run strong for many generations thereafter.

History quickly forgot the prince who became a princess, but it never forgot the queen she became. And that is exactly how she would have wanted it.

About H.R. Harrison

H.R. Harrison is the penname of an unfortunate soul whose ancestors opted to Americanize pronunciation…but not spelling.

She has worn a lot of hats in her day jobs, but always spends a lot of time thinking about communication, language, and how words… word.

She has a love for fantasy, mythos, and genre subversion, and that is what drew her toward writing LGBTQ fantasy. She also tends to fall into research pits while trying to write and therefore knows a lot of random trivia about a lot of random topics.

Email
hrharrison.author@gmail.com

Facebook
www.facebook.com/hrharrisonwrites

Twitter
@mythstakes

Website
www.hrharrison.com

Also from NineStar Press

A Little Fairy Dust by Mell Eight

Nine tales of magic, love, and a little fairy dust: A military posting at the Rapunzel Tower to avoid war in *The Tower*; a Brownie that just wants to do something right in *Cleanly Wrong*; a dream of love unfulfilled in *A Heart's Dream*; saving the victims of an evil witch in *The Red Apple Witch*; a boy who just wants to go to the ball in *Cinder-Elle*; a cursed kingdom and search for lost love in *The Curse*; a thief and his fairy godparent with different ideas about love in *Happily Ever After*; a lightning strike, a lost egg, an ancient battle, and love at first spark in *Thunderbird*; and a prince trapped, knowing his true love will never save him in *The Beast*.

The Q by Rick R. Reed

Step out for a Saturday night at The Q—the small town gay bar in Appalachia where the locals congregate. Whose secret love is revealed? What long-term relationship comes to a crossroad? What revelations come to light? The DJ mixes a soundtrack to inspire dancing, drinking, singing, and falling in (or out) of love.

This pivotal Saturday night at The Q is one its regulars will never forget. Lives irrevocably change. Laugh, shed a tear, and root for folks you'll come to love and remember long after the last page.

The Door by Dmetri Kakmi

Living paintings, spectral children, cannibal serial killers, lost souls, haunted houses, and ancient evil proliferate *The Door and Other Uncanny Tales*. Everywhere reality and fantasy collapse to create a new unstable world, even the body is not what it seems. Combined with Dmetri Kakmi's gothic imagination and mordant humor, the result is fiction that is as memorable as it is unsettling.

Connect with NineStar Press

Website: NineStarPress.com

Facebook: NineStarPress

Facebook Reader Group: NineStar Niche

Twitter: @ninestarpress

Instagram: NineStarPress

www.ingramcontent.com/pod-product-compliance
Lightning Source LLC
Chambersburg PA
CBHW050610110726
47899CB00001B/48

* 9 7 8 1 6 4 8 8 9 0 2 1 7 8 *